THE VEILED TRUTHS TRILOGY

BOOK TWO

UGLY TRUTHS

Running bought her time, but the truth is done waiting.

BRIANA SULLIVAN

Published by Briana Sullivan
Cover design by Dami Shawn

To find out more about Briana and what she is working on, please visit authorbrianasullivan.com

ISBN: PB: 979-8-9924658-2-2 eBook: 979-8-9924658-3-9
Print locations vary by retailer and fulfillment partner.

For my family,

No matter how many times I warned you all about the sex scenes in the first novel, you supported me and read the book anyway. I do think that reflects more on you than it does on me, but I digress.

I don't know what I did to deserve the type of love you all give me, but I hope you know I love you just as hard right back.

From the bottom of my heart, thank you.

Also for my dumb bitches,

Is it rude to refer to you guys by this name in a dedication? Probably. But, I know you'd be offended if I didn't.

You are some of my biggest cheerleaders and closest friends. Thank you for sharing your love of smut and popcorn books with me.

I love you all so big.

CHAPTER 1
ONE MONTH AFTER THE EXPLOSION

Silas

The afternoon summer sun shines through the windows of my office, its heat casting patterns on the carpeted floor. I sit behind my desk, staring at my phone, where Natalie's text glares back at me. For four days, I've left it there, unanswered.

> **Natalie:** Silas, where are you? I just want to see you and make sure you're still breathing. Leslie won't even let me into your office. Call me. Please.

I tap my fingers against the desk. *What do I even say to her?*

She wants to talk about Scarlett. We haven't told my sister what little we *do* know about that little snake or the only security footage retrieved from that night at the warehouses; Scarlett surrounded by men with guns, her face almost defiant as she wields a metal rod, smashing open the valve of a hazardous waste truck. Liquid gushes out, and with almost no hesitation, she lights it on fire.

Natalie doesn't understand that Scarlett is never coming back—at least, on her own terms. And the woman I thought she was? She doesn't exist.

She never did.

My phone slips from my hand and clatters onto the desk. The rage that permanently lives under my skin simmers, waiting for the smallest excuse to explode. So I force it down, just as I've been doing for the past

1

month. If it's not the seething hatred I have for her, it's the mounting frustration with my father and his endless delays.

Every day, there's some new revelation or crucial piece of information leading up to our executive transition that he's been "meaning to tell me" or "was going to explain later." The excuses are never-fucking-ending, and I'm at my limit.

I roll my neck and force myself to focus on my laptop, pulling up the financial forecasts and production schedules for the meeting I have to attend in forty-five minutes. The numbers blur together at first, my mind still circling back to that damn footage. Eventually, the metrics and timelines begin to steal my attention, and the endless well of anger starts to ease. Just enough to take a full breath without feeling like my ribs might crack under the weight of it.

The relief isn't nearly long enough when a knock at the door cuts through my thoughts. I've been utilizing the privacy feature on the glass wall that separates my office from the rest of the executive floor more often than not recently, the now-frosted glass making it impossible to see who's on the other side.

Before I can respond, Davey enters.

"What is it?" I ask, my voice unnecessarily sharp.

Davey doesn't react to the hostility as he crosses the room, laptop tucked under one arm. "We have an update on *her*," he answers.

The emphasis on the last word letting me know exactly who he's referring to.

I motion for him to sit across from me. He doesn't. Instead, he walks around to me and places his laptop next to mine before opening it, fingers flying across the keyboard. My hands curl tighter, the violence I've been suppressing trying to claw its way to the surface.

"The hair samples from the guest bathroom," he starts, either oblivious to or ignoring my annoyance. "Our labs extracted enough DNA from the follicles to send to some commercial ancestry testing sites using a fake name. The results came in, and we have matches."

I don't say anything. I'm not sure I can.

We'd assumed that Scarlett was an alias since finding her backpack and its contents at the warehouses, which is the reason we brought in experts to search for DNA samples in the guest room. The specialists had said there was a high probability they wouldn't be able to use them, but I didn't give a shit what they thought. I was willing to turn over every stone, no matter the price.

All I can manage is a nod for Davey to continue.

"Most are distant relatives–third or fourth cousins. But we did find a match for a maternal aunt. Diane Fetton, originally from Arizona."

A woman's face appears on the screen from the ancestry website; her eye and facial shape are unmistakably similar to Scarlett's.

"Diane has one sister, Lydia Fetton," Davey continues. "She married a man named Darren Cross when she was eighteen. They had a child a few months later. A daughter."

His fingers tap a few more keys before the next image comes up. My pulse stutters as I stare at a yearbook photo in front of a standard water-colored dark blue background. *Her* yearbook photo. The caramel wavy hair, the light brown eyes. She looks younger than her years and a little too slender. Innocent.

"Her name is Elena Cross," he says quietly.

Elena Cross.

The name doesn't fit–like it belongs to someone else entirely, but it should feel that way. Scarlett was a lie; a carefully constructed facade meant to lure me. And now that I'm staring at the truth, it still does nothing to smother my anger.

Davey clears his throat almost hesitantly. "Grew up in Kingman, Arizona. Poor town. No siblings. Had average grades but high SAT scores. Went to Arizona State University and graduated with a degree in computer science and a 3.8 GPA."

My eyes narrow. "And?"

"The trail goes cold, except for this." He clicks on a link before a news article fills the screen.

25-Year-Old Woman Found Murdered in Chandler Apartment in Apparent Robbery Gone Wrong

I skim the article. Drew Bennet was stabbed twenty-six times with one of her kitchen knives while her roommate, Elena Cross, was grocery shopping. The building didn't have cameras, and there was no forced entry. No leads or suspects outside of Elena, who was cleared by surveillance footage showing her at the grocery store at the time of the attack. Less than one thousand dollars' worth of items were stolen.

There's a photo of the woman with a big smile and bright green eyes, which are amplified by the camera flash. She's clearly in a bar, leaning close to a person cropped out of the image. She appears happy and so damn young.

It takes me a moment to process the connection he's making. "You think she did this?" I ask.

Davey doesn't answer right away. He's frowning at the screen, fingers tapping against the laptop's edge. "It's possible she planned it, at least. It'd help explain why she went underground."

I stare at the screen. Twenty-six stab wounds. That's not a random act of violence. It's calculated, personal, and not the woman I thought I knew. But then again, what did I actually know about her?

"What else?" I demand, leaning back in my seat.

"Her parents divorced and moved to different states after she graduated from high school. Cill's trying to figure out if she has any contact with them, but it doesn't seem likely. We also found a bank account and a safety deposit box connected to her name at a local bank in Arizona."

Something hot thrums in my chest. "They'll notify us if there's any activity?"

Davey nods. "Already in the works."

"And these details?" I gesture towards his laptop.

"In your personal inbox."

I tap my trackpad and pull up the email from Davey, skimming through it again while he waits.

"Good," I finally respond, stopping at the yearbook photo. My stomach churns even looking at her again. "She'll need money eventually."

Davey straightens, closing his laptop as he says, "I'll keep digging." He only manages to take a few steps toward the door before pausing to look over his shoulder at me. "Silas, are you sure this is what you want?"

I release a long breath.

This isn't the first time he's tried to check in on this... fixation. He's been concerned about it since I met her. He was worried that I was moving too fast, especially since I had never acted that way with a woman before. Davey has always had a good read on people, and I trust his judgment without hesitation almost always, but something in me didn't want to listen this time.

She was just different, and that was the point, wasn't it? Never gave me the time of day, which I wasn't used to. Strong-willed, strong physically. Always had a smart-ass remark. I hadn't realized how much I liked that in a woman until the first time we spoke and she insulted me almost instantly. No hesitation or second-guessing. Just cut straight through me like she already decided I wasn't worth impressing.

It had been a long time since someone looked at me like that, and even longer since I found myself caring, but that was the thing about her. Scarlett didn't try to charm me or win me over. If anything, she was daring me to prove I was worth her time. And damn it, if that wasn't the quickest way to get under my skin.

It doesn't help that she was so goddamn *beautiful*. The kind that didn't just turn heads, it messed with them. That face, with its sharp cheekbones and full, knowing lips. Always poised like she was in on some secret the rest of us weren't clever enough to figure out. But it was her eyes that hooked me. Light brown and in the right light, they turned gold like whiskey. Or honey.

Since she left, Davey has tried to pull me back from the edge, especially after we combed through local and regional hospitals looking for any woman admitted with injuries consistent with an explosion. Not a single patient fit the description.

Then, there was the official police report that stated an unidentified female body was found during the clean-up. My team was there from start to finish thanks to our law enforcement connections, and there wasn't any sign of said-body.

And yet, every time I've questioned where this supposed body was, not a single person could give me a real answer. Just a constant loop of half-assed explanations and conflicting stories. Enough to make it clear that no one actually knows who reported the finding, but they're all too cowardly to correct it on the off-chance it is true.

Somehow, she managed to get into the police reports and alter the files. She thought she could fake her own death right under my nose and expect me to believe it. She underestimated me, just as I did her. The difference is, there's nowhere she can run where I won't eventually find her.

Stupid girl.

Davey thinks we should wait and see if anything surfaces on its own, but that's not good enough for me. It never will be. Not until I look her in the eyes and demand all the answers she's denied me.

I hold up my hand to him. "Just get me her location."

My brother-in-law holds my gaze for another moment before conceding. With a curt nod, he turns back to leave but pauses at the door, his hand on the handle.

"Call Natalie." His voice is quieter now, but firm. "I know you don't want to talk about what happened, but don't shut her out. All she knows is you won't answer her calls, and it's killing her."

The guilt hits instantly, a sharp twist in my gut as the door clicks shut behind him. I drag a hand down my face, cursing.

He's right. It's not fair to Nat. I need to grit my teeth and bear it, no matter how much I'd rather gouge my ears than ever talk about that traitorous bitch ever again.

Even as the guilt eventually settles, something else lingers. The gnawing, relentless irritation that a month has passed and we still don't have a single damn lead on the men at the warehouse that night.

They vanished like smoke. It's infuriating and the kind of thing that makes me want to rip through my own team and demand to know what the hell they've actually been doing. I handpicked men and women who are trained beyond measure. They extracted the backpack without the cops ever realizing it was there. Scrubbed the one clip of surveillance that showed Scar–*Elena*–and what she did.

But these ghosts? There are still no connections, no trace of where they came from or where they went. They clearly weren't working with Elena with how they drew their guns on her, but were they after the same thing? And if that's the case, we need to figure out exactly what they wanted before we find out the hard way.

In the silence of my office, my gaze returns to the over-decade-old photo of her on my screen. Elena Cross. Scarlett Page. Two names for the same woman—a woman I don't know at all.

But none of that matters anymore. Regardless of who she's pretending to be now, I'll find her.

Chapter 2

Two Months After the Explosion

Elena

In all the different lives I've been forced to live over the years, I'd never imagined spending a summer in the Colorado mountains. Even as I step out of the old Toyota Tacoma Luis lent me a month ago, the mid-afternoon August heat feels like a light kiss against my skin, not the oppressive blaze I've known of other summers.

Luis's secluded home sits on an upward slope nestled in a cluster of hills. Off the opposite edge of the gravel driveway, the hill drops off to a small river that offers a comforting, consistent hum of rushing water. On the elevated porch, the view is even better.

I stretch my arms over my head, feeling the pull in my shoulders and lower back. The thirty-minute drive to and from Breckenridge always leaves me stiff, especially after hours on my feet, but it's hard to complain when I get to look at this.

I climb the incline to the porch with my shoulder bag in one hand, the wooden planks creaking faintly under the weight. The key turns easily, and the cabin greets me with comforting silence. To my left, the open living room is empty, and to my right, the door to Luis's office is shut tight. I tread lightly up the stairs directly in front of me to the second story, where two bedrooms and a shared bathroom sit.

The guest room is to the left, where I drop my bag onto the bed, turning to rummage for a clean pair of clothes in the dresser. The smell of Bluebird Brunch Co. clings to me like a second skin. No matter how good the food tastes, it always makes me nauseous after a shift.

When Luis brought me here, I barely lasted a week before asking him if he could help me find work. The weight of doing nothing was unbearable, as was the idea of trying to do anything like I used to. By the next day, he lined up a job for me at his friend Sarah's popular breakfast and lunch spot in Breckenridge. He told me to "dust off my apron" and handed me the keys to his old truck that he rarely used. I cried and hugged him when Sarah said she was willing to keep me off the books.

It was the lifeline I didn't know I was so desperate for after the few months I'd barely made it out of.

Clothes in hand, I head for the bathroom. Once the door is locked behind me, I turn on the shower faucet, letting the water heat up as I start to strip. My jeans come off first, then the staff t-shirt, which sticks awkwardly to my hair clip as I pull it over my head. The motion makes me stumble, and when I regain my balance as it comes off my neck, I'm partially facing the mirror that hangs from the back of the door.

The scars on the edges of my hips and thighs are visible from this angle, disappearing around my backside. I look away just as quickly, but the cruel reminder makes the memories churn, dragging me back to that night.

"Elena, move! You have to move!"

A sharp gasp rips from my throat as I jolt back into consciousness, vision swimming. For a moment, everything is disjointed–flashes of fire, the acidic bite of melting metal coats my lungs, the ringing in my ears still present but dull enough for Luis's voice to slice through the haze. By some miracle, the earbud remains lodged in my ear.

"Head for the fence behind you! There's a gap–get up!"

The fire roars. Every movement sends a sharp, electric pain through my lower back and sides. As if the flames have seeped into my muscles and bones and now burn there instead.

I don't even know if I can move, but Luis's voice pulls back.

"Elena! Get up, damn it!" he screams, and this time, my body obeys.

I push myself to my knees. My palms scrape against the gravel, but it's nothing compared to the pain searing through the rest of me. Stumbling forward, I try to catch myself and groan, trying to answer Luis, but whatever I say is barely coherent. Still, he lets out a shaky exhale when I respond.

"The gap is fifty feet behind you, past the stacked barrels," he continues. My head pounds against the sides of my skull, making it even harder to see through the towering smoke. "Stay low. Don't stop."

Each step feels like it might be my last. My lungs burn. There's only a little relief the further I move from the fire, and the smoke thins enough to no longer choke me.

The gap Luis mentioned is located at the base of the metal links, and barely wide enough for a person to squeeze through. I unceremoniously drop to my knees, pressing myself against the ground, and wiggle through the opening. The jagged edges of the metal catch on my arms, scraping against my already angry skin, but I grit my teeth and push forward.

When I'm nearly through, there's a sharp tug somewhere in the middle of my body. I turn my head just enough to see the backpack snagging on the fence, the fabric wrapped tightly around a piece of twisted metal.

Panic flares in my chest, and I try to rip it free by continuing my crawl. Once, twice, but it doesn't budge.

I must say something out loud because Luis tells me to leave it. The metal ends bite against my fingertips when I try to reach around my back to work it loose, making it almost impossible to focus.

"Elena!" Luis's voice is a sharp command. "Leave it. Move! Now!"

Tears sting my eyes, but I know he's right. The equipment can't be traced. Trembling, I work my arms free of the straps and finish pushing myself through the gap, refusing to look back at the bag.

"Keep going," Luis urges, his typing becoming more audible the longer I'm awake. "I have Ben keeping tabs on Peter. He's gone, but I don't know if he'll circle back." There's a pause while I sway on my feet. "I'm tracking your phone now and cutting the cameras like we planned. Go straight and then right at the end of the first warehouse."

I don't know how long I'm moving. Minutes? Hours? Time feels warped, stretched thin by the pulsing of my tight skin against the summer air and my singed clothes. The fire eventually fades into the distance and the streets become more residential.

With each step, my legs shake. Every inch of me screams in protest. It only worsens when I stop to wait in a dark corner for Luis's next instruction or potential witnesses to pass. At one point, I hold myself against a brick wall and silently cry while a slew of fire trucks cruise by.

"Left," Luis breathes. "Keep going straight after that."

There's no room for thought. My skin feels like it's seconds from peeling away from the rest of me. The only other thing I'm aware of is the slow, steady melting of night into dawn, the sky turning the softest shades of blue, then purple, and then pink.

"There," Luis exhales, his voice quieter after sending me through a series of turns. "You're almost there. The house is coming up on your right. Two hundred feet."

A small South Side craftsman comes into view. The porch light is a faint glow in the early morning light.

A beacon calling me home.

It takes every ounce of my remaining strength not to release the most pathetic sob at the sight.

My feet drag against the cement stairs to the front porch. My hand slaps once against the door in a knock. It sounds so weak and hollow against the wood. The door swings open almost instantly, as if he'd been waiting for my arrival.

Jeff's broad frame fills the doorway. He takes me in–my destroyed clothes, my blistering skin, the dried blood that seeped out of the shallow cuts on my arms–before taking a step forward, arms outstretched.

"Scarlett," he rasps, horror painted across every inch of his stern face.

I don't even have the strength to respond. My knees buckle, the world tilting as I collapse into him. The last thing I feel is the searing sting of his steady grip as he pulls me inside. He murmurs something I can't quite make out.

11

And then everything goes dark.

Jeff once told me that when it was the end of the line, he'd help me in any way he could. I just never imagined I'd actually take him up on that offer. It feels surreal now, thinking about the last time I saw him at the gym. I'd been desperate when I arrived with the duffle bag I bought online, stuffed with my personal laptop, IDs, and whatever clothes I could fit. I passed it off as a gym bag, hoping it wouldn't draw Cillian's attention. He was more concerned with keeping guard over me and not the details of what I was doing, anyway.

Between drills, I quietly asked Jeff if he could take the bag home and hold onto it for me until early Saturday morning when I'd come to retrieve it. His brows furrowed and, in true Jeff fashion, the only question he asked is if I knew his address.

Even with our scheming, neither of us anticipated I'd show up at his door looking like *that*.

I stayed with Jeff and his wife, Lauren, for three weeks. They kept the televisions off and didn't address the fires they could see the smoke from—the ones that happened the same night I stumbled into their home looking like a burnt mess.

Lauren, sweet but sharp-tongued, is a nurse. She works in cardiology, but has extensive experience in emergency care. She took one look at my injuries and declared it was a miracle I wasn't dead or more badly burned, though she never expanded on why she believed that to be true when I refused to tell them where they came from.

The backpack I wore that night absorbed most of the blast's heat, shielding me from far worse damage, but many areas it didn't cover hadn't been spared, especially my lower half. Second-degree burns, Lauren told me, while carefully cleaning and dressing each wound across my ass, thighs, and the curves of my hips. I was lucky to have ducked my head and tucked my arms in time to prevent damage there, but the ends of my hair and the back of my neck were a different story.

It took a few days for me to be conscious enough for Lauren to show me the seared strands, melted and jagged. We watched enough videos to correct it with a pair of kitchen scissors. All things considered, it's a nice shoulder-length cut now, though I do miss the length.

The burns took time, however. Some healed completely, the skin smoothing over. Others haven't, pale and puckered, though I still see improvements with the ointments and lotions Lauren suggested I use.

I can't look at them. Every line and mark reminds me of the pain and my failure. Nights spent shivering in the throes of a fever, Lauren or Jeff petting my hair while I cried, both for how I felt inside and out.

Peter got away, and worse than that, I left behind two people who now think I'm dead, a liar, or both.

Blinking, I shake my head. Thinking about what I left behind won't change anything. It never does. As hard as it is, I try to focus on what came after.

While I was healing, Luis orchestrated a network of friends to transport me by car across multiple states when I was well enough to travel. Each ride brought me closer to Colorado, the handoffs strategically conducted in secluded areas in the darkness of night. When I finally arrived three hours outside of Alma, Luis was waiting for me.

I'll never forget the relief in his eyes when he saw me get out of that final car. I was barely out of the backseat, half delirious from the nap I'd been in the middle of, when he wrapped me in his arms, trying his best to avoid the injuries I'd told him about countless times on the phone.

Our reunion was cut short as he ushered me into his car. Luis was the only one who knew his home's exact location and was extra cautious in the final stretch, taking routes that doubled back and looped to ensure we weren't followed. Even then, I don't think I breathed fully for those first few nights in the guest room.

I have so much to be thankful for. People like Jeff, who didn't even argue when I told him I couldn't tell him where I was going or give him a way to contact me. People like Luis, who gave me a place to get back on my feet. But gratitude doesn't stop those other voices in my head.

They still scream.

I release a shaky breath and strip off the last of my clothes. The bathroom fills with steam. I don't bother testing the water with my hand before stepping in. It scalds away the grime from my shift and the weight of my thoughts. The sting is welcome against my scars. Even if it's only for a few minutes, it seems to drown out almost everything besides the ache in my chest I didn't think was possible to still feel so deeply.

I probably stay in the shower too long, selfishly wasting Luis's hot water. By the time I've gotten dressed, deposited my dirty clothes in the hamper, and brushed out my hair, my stomach is growling loud enough to echo in the quiet bedroom.

I head back into the hallway and descend the stairs, counting each step out of habit. Fourteen to the bottom.

Getting used to Luis's home has been an adjustment, to say the least. It wasn't until I started working and contributing to groceries that I began to feel more settled. At first, he vehemently refused my money, but I wore him down quickly by hiding cash under his leftovers, tucking it beneath his car keys, or slipping it into his wallet when he wasn't looking.

Eventually, he realized that the faster he gave in, the smoother things would go between us. We've found a routine now, even though we're on almost opposite schedules most of the time.

The cabin has all the charm you'd expect without being overly kitschy or drowning in wood paneling. The walls are a mix of warm, neutral tones and subtle stonework, and the living area has high ceilings with large windows that flood the space with natural light. Luis has kept the decor simple–just a comfortable couch, a couple of well-worn armchairs, some bookshelves, and a coffee table that looks like it's seen more than its fair share of late-night drinks. It's not fancy by any means, but it's comfortable. Normal.

Before I even reach the kitchen, the rich, warm smell of coffee drifts toward me. I smile.

Luis has come out of his cave.

UGLY TRUTHS

Rounding the corner, I find him with his back turned, pouring coffee into a ceramic mug. The sight is still a little surreal to me. Though we met in person on a contract, most of our friendship has been him on the other end of a phone call or text thread.

Luis is a couple of inches taller, with the kind of face that immediately puts people at ease. Handsome, sure, but not intimidating. His hair is shorter now than it was a few years ago, but the wild curls are starting to push through again with a few streaks of gray at his temples. His tan skin is a shade of warm brown that reminds me of Arizona summers.

"You're alive," I tease, heading straight for the refrigerator.

Luis glances over his shoulder at me, the corners of his brown eyes crinkling. His smile is his best feature: big, warm, and entirely genuine.

"Barely," he replies, voice thick from hours of silence.

As I poke through the fridge, he reaches around me for the half-gallon of milk, his bicep brushing against my shoulder as he pulls it out. I grab the container of pasta salad I made earlier in the week and close the door with my hip.

"How was your shift?"

I shrug, fishing a fork from the drying rack. "Fine."

Luis turns, cradling his mug in both hands. I can feel his eyes on me as I stab a bite of pasta. Finally, I look up, leaning against the counter with the Tupperware balanced in one hand and the fork in the other.

"Do you like it there?" he asks, tilting his head slightly.

"It's good."

The truth is, the work is tolerable. Long hours and customer service aren't exactly my calling, but it's better than what I used to do. It's safe, and that isn't something I've felt when it comes to work in a long time.

Luis studies my face; he does this often, trying to read me like a book I didn't agree to open. It's only when his eyes land on the side of my neck, where the edge of a burn scar creeps out from under my shirt, that I realize where he's trying to direct this conversation, as he has several times in the past few weeks.

"Don't," I say almost too fast.

Luis exhales, his shoulders sagging. "I know I've said this before," he begins carefully, "but Colorado's a popular place for veterans to settle down after they leave the military. There are therapists here who specialize in PTSD. It might be time to start thinking about talking to someone."

The words land like a detonating bomb, and all I can think to do is turn around to set the pasta down on the counter, creating space between us as I struggle to keep the panic from spilling over into anger.

"I'm not ready," I snap, gripping the edge of the stone counter.

The silence that follows is suffocating, but what else is there for him to say? He doesn't understand this, not that I've been able to find the words to explain it to him.

Luis's voice is gentle when he speaks again. "It's never going to feel like the right time," he pauses, "I know it's hard. Scary. But it's the path forward."

He's right, of course, but just because it's true doesn't make it easy to do. There is a decade's worth of unforgivable actions I've taken and selfish choices I've made. Nightmares that I've been pushing down into that well inside of me that once felt infinite but now threatens to spill over at any slight movement.

Confronting it will only make it overflow and drown me.

"Maybe one day," I concede, the lie coming easily, "but not now."

There's another long pause while I stare at the countertop.

"Okay."

His quiet acceptance feels both a relief and a disappointment. I've spent so long fighting against people who pushed me—Peter, Silas, even myself—that I don't know what to do with someone who lets me set the pace.

There's a sudden pressure on the edges of my shoulders before his arms wrap around the top of mine from behind.

Luis rests his chin lightly on my shoulder. His warmth is comforting, and for a moment, I let myself lean back into it, closing my eyes and exhaling shakily.

"I just want you to feel better," he murmurs.

"I know," I whisper, reaching up to awkwardly pat his forearm. "I appreciate it. When I'm ready, I'll tell you. I promise."

He holds me for another long moment before stepping back, hands lingering briefly on my shoulders before dropping away. "I know."

Ceramic slides against granite as Luis picks up his coffee mug and heads back to his office, giving me the space I didn't ask for, but he knows I need. And for a while, I stand there, staring at my uneaten food, wondering if there will be a day when I feel like I can face all of the damage I've done.

CHAPTER 3

Silas

The gym doesn't look like much from the outside; just one of many brick-front businesses in a long strip on a main road in South Side. The only discernible difference between the other businesses that surround it, apart from the faded Ironworks Training Center sign above the door, is that it occupies significantly more street-front real estate.

For a moment, I wonder if I'm wasting my time and if this is just another dead end.

I step inside anyway.

The gym door swings shut behind me with a faint *clang*, the sound swallowed by the low hum of activity. By some miracle, no one looks in my direction.

I've spent years cultivating a certain level of anonymity, but even so, I'm not exactly invisible, especially in this city. If someone recognizes me before I can get a read on things, this whole idea could blow up before it even starts.

The air carries that unmistakable mix of sweat and disinfectant. Matted, open floors stretch before me, only broken up by black grappling mats, scuffed and worn but meticulously clean. Heavy bags dangle from chains bolted to exposed beams, kettlebells and dumbbells are scattered along the edges, and a row of dented lockers lines the far wall next to a rack holding gloves and headgear.

It feels familiar in a way that reminds me of Scarlett. Or, I guess, Elena. She always spoke highly of this place and how much she learned here. We spent hours discussing her training after the alley attack and all the ways it had paid off, even with a bruised eye and a split forehead.

She was so convincing.

I wonder how smug she felt when I stepped into the role of protector without hesitation. She didn't even have to try; that's how far gone I already was. Still, credit where it's due. She figured me out fast and used the soft spot for my sister like a goddamn weapon.

My jaw tightens, like it always does when I think about her. I push the thought aside and step farther into the room.

There are a few people training. A guy works the heavy bag, his punches landing in a steady rhythm. A woman curls free weights in front of a mirror, her movements slow and controlled. Two others grapple on the mats, their bodies locked in a quiet struggle. No one lingers or chats idly.

"Hey, man. Can I help you?"

A deep voice cuts through the music playing through the speakers, pulling my attention to a man walking toward me.

Jeff.

I've seen him in photos. Cillian mentioned him two days ago, almost in passing, while talking about Elena. He'd brought up the last time she trained here, saying he wished he hadn't brushed off her odd behavior that day. She was acting skittish and distant the whole prior week—not just with him, but with everyone—so he thought little of it.

The conversation made me realize she visited this gym the morning before she left. Something compelled me to look at the surveillance footage of my home from her last day here. She went to her training session with an unassuming black duffle bag and didn't return with it several hours later.

It could've been nothing, but it felt like *something*.

Now I'm here, clinging to the theory that she trusted this man enough to ask him to help her disappear. Until she accesses that goddamn bank account, he might be the only lead I have.

Jeff's shorter than I expected, maybe just a couple of inches taller than Elena, but solid. His arms are covered in tattoos—a snake curling up one forearm, constellations sprawling across the other—and his shaved head glows faintly under the fluorescent lights.

"I'm here for a kickboxing one-on-one. John," I say the fake name with ease as I point to myself. "Heard you're the guy to see."

His sharp blue eyes take me in. My pulse kicks up, but there's no flicker of recognition in his gaze.

"You train before?" he asks.

"I've taken a few classes," I reply, adjusting the strap of the duffle bag hanging from my arm. "Wanted to give this place a try."

A grin tugs at the corner of his mouth. "Alright, let's see what you've got. We'll start with an assessment. You fill out the forms online?"

"Yup."

Without another word, he turns on his heel and strides toward a small plastic bin with several pieces of equipment. The faint hum of the gym's lights buzzes in my ears. I drop my bag just as Jeff is reaching for a jump rope. He tosses it to me, chin jutting toward the rubber flooring next to the mat.

"Warm up," he says simply.

For the next fifteen minutes, he puts me through a series of stretches, activations, and cardio drills. Sweat beads at my hairline, but he seems pleased enough with what I'm doing before strapping on some focus mitts and moving us onto the mat.

He raises his hands before speaking. "We'll assess where you are and then create a schedule if you want to keep coming back. Sound good?"

As I dip my head in acknowledgment, Jeff taps the mitts together once before holding them steady. "Jab, cross," he says.

I step in, keeping my stance loose, and fire off the two punches—snapping the jab out clean before driving a sharp cross into the pad. Jeff doesn't react much, but there's a small shift in his stance.

"Hook, cross."

Rolling my shoulders, I throw the hook, smooth and controlled, before following with a crisp right cross.

"Not bad," he mutters.

I exhale slowly, flexing my fingers.

Throwing another jab, I keep my movements fluid. "I had a friend who used to train here," I say casually. "She only ever had good things to say."

Jeff raises an eyebrow but doesn't lower the mitts. "That so?"

He absorbs my next jab smoothly. "Said you were tough, no-nonsense. She was impressive, honestly," I continue, my tone conversational. "I had to see for myself if the trainer she talked about was as good as she made him sound."

Jeff shifts his weight, keeping his hands up. "Who exactly are we talking about?" he asks with a sharpness that wasn't there before.

"Scarlett Page."

There's something in his eyes that he buries as quickly as it surfaces. He lowers the mitts slightly. "Ah," he responds with a shrug. "I trained her for a while."

I nod once. "She took off a few months ago." I hold his gaze. "Something about her seemed... off. Any idea where she went?"

Jeff doesn't flinch.

"No."

Liar.

Though I'm poised to call him out, I don't. People hate silence and rush to fill it.

Jeff's eyes narrow, just slightly. "I don't get into personal stuff with the people I train."

I throw another combination, harder this time. Jeff adjusts, catching the impact without effort. For a moment, the only sound is the dull *thud* of my gloves against the mitts.

"She left without saying anything," I explain between combinations, my breath hitching with each point of contact. "None of her friends have heard from her. We're all worried."

The mitts snap back under my force, and Jeff moves with me, shifting defensively as he keeps up with my increased pace, absorbing my next punch and blocking the next instead of letting me land it. He looks between me and my glove with an expression unreadable before his eyes flick up to hold mine.

"You ever stop to think," he starts, "that maybe sometimes people don't say goodbye because they don't want to be followed?"

My jaw clenches, and the next hit lands harder than necessary. Jeff doesn't call me out for it.

"I want to know if she's okay." The lie doesn't come out as concerned as I want it to. "If you helped her, that's fine. I just need to know."

Jeff drops his hands, stepping back slightly. "Look, if you came here to interrogate me about something I don't know, you're out of luck. If she needed to start over somewhere, I'm happy she was able to do that, but that's all I've got for you."

My restraint frays. The fury I've been forcing down, the frustration of chasing ghosts, of running in circles with half-truths and dead ends, threatens to rip free.

Was he part of her plan, or just more collateral damage? Used and discarded like the rest of us?

I inhale slowly, recognizing the line I'm about to cross. I'm not sure if the jaws of life will be able to retract my arm from his neck if I give myself the opportunity.

"I think we're done here," I say, voice devoid of all emotion.

After a moment, Jeff nods and slips off the mitts, though he doesn't take his eyes off of me. "Good luck finding whatever you're looking for."

The words I want to say won't help me any, so I don't respond. Turning on my heel, I rip my bag off the floor and head for the exit.

I'll find another way to get the answers I need.

I *have* to.

CHAPTER 4

Elena

The air in the cell clings to my lungs. My vision blurs with tears, but all I can see is Natalie. Her lifeless body sprawled across the cold concrete floor, blood pooling beneath her. It creeps closer and closer to my feet, the rich crimson soaking into the rough surface. Her dark hair fans out like a halo, and though I can't see her face, I don't need to. The glint of her wedding bands under the flickering fluorescent light confirms what I already know.

Dead. Just like Drew.

"Do you see what you always make me do, Elena?" Peter's voice cuts through the air as he twirls a knife between his fingers. My stomach churns, but I can't look at him for long. My eyes are drawn to the other figure in the room.

Silas is on the floor, trying to push himself up onto his hands and knees. Blood stains his shirt, spreading from somewhere in his torso, and his breaths come in ragged gasps.

I lunge, restraints biting into my wrists, the ropes cutting deeper with every frantic tug. "Silas!" I cry, my voice cracking. "Get up!"

Peter watches him struggle, tilting his head as though he's studying a particularly pathetic animal.

With a speed I didn't know he was capable of, Peter closes the distance between them and grabs Silas by his hair, yanking him into a kneeling position. Silas grunts in pain, his glasses askew and cracked, blood dripping

24

from the corner of his mouth. The hatred in his eyes when they meet mine steals the breath from my lungs.

"Please," I whimper, turning my attention to Peter. "Please. He didn't do anything—it's my fault."

Peter raises an eyebrow, lips curling up. "Oh, I know it's your fault," he drawls, dragging the tip of the knife along Silas's jawline. "But it's so much more fun to make you watch." His smirk widens, a flash of teeth that makes my skin crawl. "Now, what do you think, Silas? Should I kill you or her?"

Silas doesn't answer right away. His head hangs for a moment before he forces himself to look at me again. The man staring back at me is a stranger.

"I'd rather die," he spits, hoarse but venomous, "than be saved by this bitch."

I flinch, the tears streaming down my face blurring my vision even more. "Silas," I whisper. "Please."

Peter laughs.

"You heard the man," Peter bellows happily, just as he drags the blade across Silas's throat.

Even as I scream, Silas's dark eyes remain on mine until they lose focus, blood spilling out of his jugular and splattering onto the floor. The life drains from his glare, body slumping forward to join Natalie's in the growing pile of crimson.

My sobs echo as Peter's laughter rings in my ears, louder than anything else.

The sheets cling to me like a second skin, damp with sweat and tangled around my legs as if the ropes in my nightmare have followed me into the waking world. I shove them away, gasping for air as I press my hands to my chest.

The early morning light filters through the thin curtains, casting muted purples and grays over the room. The aftershocks hum through my body. No matter how many times I try to count my breaths, my lungs refuse to fill enough for relief.

I hug my knees to my chest, curling into myself as the tremors in my hands subside.

These nightmares are a plague I can't escape. I deserve them as a punishment for everything I've done, but that knowledge doesn't make them any easier to endure.

Natalie's lifeless body flashes in my mind again, her rings catching the fluorescent light. I press my forehead to my knees, trying to block it out. Nausea climbs in my throat.

Peter managed to escape the warehouse district alive. That much was evident when he began his relentless hunt for Luis.

Luis expected it. He was already careful to keep his personal life hidden from Peter before all of this. He led Peter on a wild goose chase across the country, leaving only dead ends and fake trails.

Not only did Luis cover his own tracks, but he also covered mine.

Somewhere along the way, he pulled the right strings and altered the official police report to include an unidentified female body found in the ashes. The body didn't exist, of course, but Peter didn't know that, and through his network, Luis all but confirmed that Peter believed I was dead.

So while he looked for Luis, Peter believed the explosion had erased me from the equation entirely. Eventually, Peter called his dogs off the chase. At least for now.

As for Silas and Natalie, I suppose they think I'm dead, too. Or a coward.

If they had tried to call me since then, I wouldn't know. I cut off my old phone provider the night I left and ditched it on the street just a few blocks from Silas's home. If Silas's team managed to salvage even a fragment of the footage Luis scrubbed, then they saw me trying to destroy something of theirs and killing myself in the fallout. Either way, they won't mourn me, and rightfully so.

My hand trembles as I reach for my phone on the nightstand. The screen lights up, its glow harsh against the darkness. My fingers hover over the search bar of a new browser, hesitating before typing his name.

It's a ritual I despise, but one I'm powerless to break. Those dreams always leave me needing to make sure they're still alive and breathing.

The first result is an article about a charity golf tournament.

My heart tightens as I tap the link, waiting for the page to load. It's a glowing piece about the event Natalie and Leslie planned before I left. The photos are polished and bright. Players holding trophies, group shots of attendees, including Natalie and Davey.

And him.

He looks the same with his sharp features and confident posture. His hair is a little shorter, and he's wearing a tailored polo and fitted golf pants that sit too perfectly on him. He looks... God. He looks incredible.

My stomach twists as I scroll to the next photo. He's in the center of a group, arm draped easily around the waist of a striking redhead with sharp cheekbones and a smile that practically leaps off the screen. I've seen her before in recent headlines.

In the next image, she's leaning toward him and laughing. Silas is looking down at her, his expression warm and open. The ache in my chest deepens. I swipe to another photo, this one of the two of them standing closer together on the green.

The captions discuss the established rumors that Silas has taken an interest in this Alice woman, but I don't even have to read it to know. I can see it. He looks happy, and she's beautiful.

"This is what you wanted," I whisper to myself.

The words feel like ash on my tongue. It's true, isn't it? I didn't want him dragged down by me. I wanted him free. But now that I'm seeing it, watching him *be* free of me...

My hand moves almost unconsciously, exiting the article and pulling up the hidden folder on my phone. There are only a handful of photos of us in it, all saved from local gossip sites.

I never dared to take any myself. It always felt like holding onto a dream I didn't deserve to have. But now, I'm desperate to remember that it wasn't all in my head.

I open my favorite photo. The candid shot of us on the dance floor of the one gala we attended together. Silas is holding my face in his hands, his lips pressed to mine in a kiss that made the headlines for days. I remember that moment so vividly, the way he struggled to find the words to say that he didn't believe a word his father said about me. How he saw me. Wanted me. Despite everything.

A tear slips down my cheek, followed by another, until I can't stop them. The pulsing throb in my heart spreads to every inch of me.

I'd nearly convinced myself when I left Chicago that distance would help, and I'd see things more clearly. Separate myself from the little bubble I created with him. Maybe I'd even realize it was something I built in my head because it all happened so fast. There was no slow unraveling. No warning. I was drowning in whatever it was we had before I even had the chance to take a final breath.

The pain hasn't dulled the way I thought it might. Its edges aren't as sharp, but the ache is worse. Deeper. And it flares up in the quiet moments, in the nights I can't sleep. As if some part of me refuses to let go of it.

I drop the phone onto the bed, curling back under the damp covers. The cold air from the open window brushes against my skin. I squeeze my eyes shut, willing myself to fall asleep and escape the memories clawing at my mind.

But all I see is Silas. His face. His hatred. All that's left is the unbearable weight of knowing that whatever he thought of me, whatever we had, has ceased to exist.

I collect the plates off the small two-top, tucking the black check folder under my arm. "Thanks for coming in, you two. See you next week," I say to the pair of women in their early twenties who have quickly become my Saturday morning regulars.

Maria, the blonde, returns the gesture as she stands. "See you then, Elena," she replies, scooping her bag off the back of her chair. Her friend, Quinn, with soft brown hair, waves as they link elbows and head toward the glass doors just a few feet away, already lost in laughter over whatever conversation I interrupted.

I watch them go, my chest aching at the sight.

Though summer is Bluebird Brunch Co.'s slow season, there's still a steady stream of locals who come into town to dine. Saturdays are usually bustling, but today is quieter than usual. Probably because the kids are about to head back to school.

"El, was that your only table?" Sarah calls from behind the order counter. She's been manning it all morning since Justin, a flaky twenty-year-old, called out again. I nod. "Want to come help me clean? Might as well take advantage of the downtime."

"Sure thing," I say, stifling a yawn. The early wake-up call from that nightmare has me dragging. "Let me buss this table and then I'll be right over."

The restaurant owner grins back before turning towards one of the espresso machines with a rag. "Thanks."

I collect the last few dishes and wipe down the surface, glancing around the room at the few diners that McKenna is handling. Sunlight streams through the floor-to-ceiling windows, casting long streaks across sleek marble tabletops, caramel-colored leather banquettes, and matte black metal chairs.

After disposing of the dishes in the back and tucking the check folder into my apron pocket, I head towards Sarah with a rag in hand. At the front of the café, the order counter serves as the heart of the morning rush, though right now, it's uncharacteristically calm.

The glass pastry case, located just below the counter, displays cinnamon rolls drizzled with icing, lemon scones dusted with powdered sugar, and thick slices of banana bread. A handwritten chalkboard menu mounted on the wall lists the café's signature drinks.

"The insides of the cases have seen better days," Sarah says, giving me a grimace of a smile. "Can you wipe them down?"

"You got it."

We fall into an easy rhythm. Sarah works on the espresso machines up top, wiping down the steamer wands, and handling the occasional to-go customer, while I focus on the display cases.

Though I never wanted to see another black apron again after quitting my diner job in college, working here isn't the same. A lot of that has to do with Sarah.

Since the moment I walked through the doors in July, she's been nothing but kind. Sarah is the type of boss who doesn't just bark orders but jumps in when things get hectic. She remembers how people take their coffee and notices when someone needs an extra five minutes to pull themselves together.

She's pretty in that effortless, girl-next-door kind of way, with long, dirty blonde hair she keeps tied back in a ponytail. Even on the shorter side, she moves with easy confidence. Always flashing an easygoing smile even during the busiest shifts. She carries herself like someone who's used to being relied on.

Early on, she'd asked what had brought me to this part of Colorado. I kept my answer vague, something about needing a fresh start, about Luis being a great friend for helping me get settled. She hadn't pressed for more, and I'd been grateful for it.

I replace the last of the cleaned pastry trays, aligning the fresh croissants. Sarah finishes wiping down the counters and steps back with a satisfied sigh.

"Almost too quiet today, huh?" she muses, glancing at the mostly empty dining room. I nod but don't say anything.

Quiet is good. It means no surprises.

Sarah rubs her hands with a towel as her gaze drifts toward the dining room. She watches McKenna for a moment before turning back to me, a thoughtful crease forming between her brows.

"I was talking with Luis the other day," she says like she's feeling out the words before committing to them. "About something unrelated, but you came up in conversation."

My hands still on the tray I'm rearranging, careful to keep my expression neutral as I glance up at her. "Oh?"

She hesitates, then exhales softly, lowering her voice just enough that no one else could overhear. "The way he spoke sounded like you came here to get away from someone, like an ex."

The words slam into me with a force I'm not prepared for.

"It's me reading into it more than anything he said," she continues quickly to reassure me. "I just want you to know, if that's the case, I get it. I've been in a bad place like that before, too."

What the hell did he say? Why were they talking about me in that way?

I grip the edge of the case, fighting to keep my breathing even. He might have been speaking of Peter, but all I can think of is Silas. My chest tightens painfully.

Silas isn't the problem. I'm the problem.

The urge to correct her nearly burns its way out of my throat. I want to tell her she's wrong, that whatever she thinks she knows, she doesn't. But it would only invite more questions I don't have the luxury of answering.

Sarah gives me a small, tentative smile. "I just wanted to say, if you ever need to talk, I'm here. No judgment."

I force a small, tight smile in return, tucking the tray back into place. "Thanks, Sarah. That means a lot."

She pats my shoulder gently before stepping away, moving toward the counter as another customer walks in. I keep my hands busy, but my mind is spinning, my pulse hammering in my ears.

She thinks I ran to escape someone, but I'm the one people like Silas need to escape from. Not the other way around.

CHAPTER 5

Elena

"Elena!"

Luis's voice carries through the closed guest room door, just seconds before it swings open. His curls bounce with the momentum of his movements, chest rising and falling like he's climbed several dozen flights of stairs.

I'm still not used to him calling me Elena.

He hasn't called me Marilyn since the warehouse debacle. I'm not entirely sure what made him decide to drop it, but I've never really had the courage to ask.

Silently, I'm relieved.

I've spent years slipping into names that weren't mine, bending myself into whatever shape Peter demanded to get the job done. I never thought I cared much about shedding them until I had the option to do so.

With an arched eyebrow, I closed the mystery novel I've been reading and set it next to my legs. "Luis?" I mimic his tone with a sugary smile.

My friend gestures wildly towards his room at the other end of the hall. "Where the hell did *that* come from?"

He found the money I left tucked under his bedside lamp, but that doesn't mean I'm going to make it easy for him.

Shrugging, I straighten my back against the wooden headboard. "Maybe the tooth fairy is a little late delivering?"

The laugh I'm hoping for never surfaces. Instead, Luis's jaw flexes as he exhales hard through his nose. "Don't be cute with me."

Tilting my head, I take in his frustration. "Lu, this feels a bit dramatic."

When I arrived in Alma, Luis had added the contacts of Corey and Ben, his friends who had helped us decrypt parts of the Wells cloud files, to my new phone. "Just in case," he'd said. At the time, I didn't know what I'd need them for, but I've reached out since.

The day I found Drew lying in a pool of her own blood in our Chandler apartment was just days after I saw my last payment from Peter. Once he knew he could control me with blackmail alone, compensation stopped. He did, however, still give me credit cards tied to my false identities. It was always under the guise of blending in while on a job, but it didn't take a genius to also realize it allowed Peter to keep tabs on my day-to-day life and hold me financially hostage.

So, instead of fighting it, I used it to my advantage. I lived off the cards while he housed me, spending within reasonable limits to avoid retaliation, and keeping my head down more often than not.

Meanwhile, the money I saved before my life turned to shit sat untouched in a high-yield savings account, quietly growing. I'm not sure why Peter never attempted to take that money from me, but I wasn't going to ask questions or draw attention to it. Though it's not enough to live on for more than a few months, it gives me some options.

And the first way I wanted to use it was to start paying back the person who has been housing and feeding me for a month.

Though Peter more than likely thinks I'm dead, I can't be too careful. I knew that if there were any people out there who could help me set up a new bank account and show me the best ways to transfer the money without drawing attention, it'd be Corey and Ben. Unsurprisingly, they'd done something like this before and felt confident in their process.

Once we had everything set up, I began making small transfers, just enough to avoid raising any suspicion. In a month or two, I'll have everything cleared out. Eventually, I'll go back to Arizona to retrieve the items in my safety deposit box—the only other piece of my old life I left behind—but for now, going to one of the big branch locations in Breckenridge and working with a teller instead of the machines will do.

Luis steps fully into the room now, the door closing slowly on its own behind him. "I already told you, I don't want your money. I have more than enough of it."

"And *I* already told *you* that I owe you. So take it."

"You don't owe me a damn thing," he snaps, though the words sound tired. "I don't know what it's going to take to get that through your head."

I sigh, rubbing the bridge of my nose. "Luis," I say softly, "I'm never going to stop. Just like with the groceries, it'll be easier if you let me help where I can."

His frustration gives way to something softer. "You do know that friendships aren't supposed to be transactional, right? I didn't help so you would owe me something. I helped you because I care about you."

The tender words crash into me in an almost violent wave. Luis *is* my friend, but I've always tacked on other descriptors too—colleague, ally, strategist. We've never had the chance to only be friends, because friendships without strings or expiration dates aren't something I know how to do anymore. Not really. The idea of being that and nothing else makes my skin heat uncomfortably.

I fold my arms across my chest. "It doesn't change the fact that I want to show you my appreciation," I mutter.

Luis's expression is unreadable as he steps closer to the bed. He sits on the edge, the mattress dipping as he pulls one of my arms loose to hold my hand in his.

"El." His thumb brushes against the back of my knuckles. "When I invited you here, I meant it. What Peter did to you," he pauses, jaw clenching briefly before he continues, "I just want you to feel like yourself again and figure out what you want to do next. None of this comes with strings attached."

His sincerity chips away at tiny pieces of the walls I've been carefully reconstructing since June. I smile faintly, squeezing his hand in return. "I know. You have no idea how much that means to me. Really."

My answer gives way to a moment of silence, and Luis nods. I start to relax, assuming that he's receptive to my answer. The feeling fizzles out when his lips turn up on the corner.

He huffs out a laugh. "I can't even pretend like I'm agreeing with you. I'm still not taking your money," he admits.

I roll my eyes, tugging my hand from his to cross my arms again. "Over my dead body."

Luis grins, leaning back on one hand over the top of my legs. "Now *that* feels dramatic."

"Says the man who just made a speech about friendships not being transactional," I shoot back, blinking incredulously. Still, my own smile widens at his amusement.

He lets out a low chuckle, tongue scraping against his top teeth. The hand he isn't leaning on moves—quick and precise, to latch onto the top of my knee and squeeze just enough to make me jerk.

I yelp, fingers curling around his wrist instantly. "Luis!"

His smirk grows, full of unrepentant delight. "Oh, so you *do* have some nerves left under all that ice."

My fingers tense around his wrist in return and glare at him, even as a reluctant laugh bubbles up in my throat. His grip loosens. "That was uncalled for."

Luis lifts a shoulder in a half-shrug. "So is trying to bribe me."

There's no stopping the long exhale I release while I search for the words to tell him it isn't a bribe, but they on my tongue when I look back up.

Luis is close enough that I can catch the faint scent of his spiced cologne and the subtle flex of his jaw, but he isn't looking at me. He's looking between us, where his hand still rests on my bare knee, my fingers encircling part of his wrist.

He lifts his gaze to mine. His eyes have shifted from teasing into something almost nervous. They track every feature of my face, studying it, as if seeing something for the first time and trying to decide if I see it, too.

My breath catches, and suddenly, I'm not in Alma anymore.

I can feel the air rearrange itself. Luis's curls darken, taming themselves into something neater, more intentional. His soft brown eyes deepen into pools of ink, framed by glasses and sharper features I know far too well. I can almost hear Silas's reassuring voice, low and smoky, as he tells me he wants me. Us.

I blink once, then again, harder this time. Silas's face melts back into Luis's, but the expression remains. Restraint of wanting to say something but holding it back.

The weight of Luis's touch feels too warm. Too intimate.

Wrong.

"I—I think I'm going to start on dinner," I blurt, pulling away from him. He flinches. "It's my turn tonight, remember?" I add, though the words sound hollow.

Before he can respond, I'm crawling off the opposite side of the bed and across the room, putting as much distance between us as I can. My heart is pounding so hard that my body vibrates. I fumble with the handle. "I'll, uh, let you know when it's ready."

And just like that, I'm gone. My feet move on instinct, carrying me down the hall and toward the stairs, but the distance doesn't help. The pulse hammering in my ears is loud enough to drown out everything else.

Have I read this all wrong?

My thoughts scramble, desperate to land on something solid—any moment, any memory that hinted at more than friendship between us. Even back when we were stuck together for nearly a week in that apartment in California years ago, there was nothing but mutual respect. We left on good terms and an unspoken promise to have each other's backs. It wasn't until this spring that our conversations started to feel deeper. But even then, it felt safe. Steady.

Did I miss something? Or did something change?

No—maybe I'm reading too much into this. Maybe this has nothing to do with Luis at all, and I'm so wrecked from Silas that even the smallest gesture of affection feels like a betrayal. Like accepting kindness from someone else means letting go of a man who probably doesn't even care if I'm alive anymore.

My stomach knots as I step into the kitchen, the bright afternoon light pooling in through the windows. I take a shaky breath, willing my hands to stop trembling.

Get it together.

No matter how many times I say it, the pressure in my chest doesn't budge.

Chapter 6

Silas

The hot coffee that burns down the back of my throat does little to distract from the way my frustration has been building with every passing minute.

Across the conference table, Davey scrolls through his tablet, the glow from the screen reflecting off his reading glasses. Neither of us says a word. I set my mug down with a bit too much force before running a hand through my hair.

My father is late. Again.

We're heading into Q4, and there's still so much to finalize before the executive transition in the new year. Since the board signed off on the paperwork with a definitive date, William treats these meetings like they're optional. I've been doing my best to manage my temper around him lately, but it's a Herculean effort.

With a deep breath, I lean back in my chair. The irony isn't lost on me that despite everything, I owe him more than ever. I'm thankful that he saw what I couldn't. That Scarl—*Elena*—was using me. He might not know that she is the reason those warehouses went up in flames, but he knows she left town only a couple of weeks after he cast her out of our "family" dinner.

But it's almost impossible to be grateful when William seems intent on testing me at every turn, with those goddamn servers being at the top of the list.

They've been a thorn in my side since June. William oversaw their relocation and security. At first, I was too murderous about Elena to care much at all, but now, I don't know what to think. Even Davey hasn't been able to get much information from him. The fact that I've been shut out only fuels my need to find whatever Elena thought he was hiding in them.

The door swings open, yanking me from my thoughts. My father strides in with his advisor, Brenden, trailing behind like a shadow.

"Apologies for the delay," William says, though there's nothing apologetic about his tone. He sets his leather portfolio on the table and unbuttons his jacket.

There's an unshakable certainty that the world will snap in half to accommodate my father. I used to try to emulate the charisma he wields like a sword and can turn on in the drop of a hat, but forcing myself into a skin that didn't fit never worked. For him, he doesn't need to even think about it. It just *is*.

Although I mostly resemble my mother in appearance, there's no denying the similarities between my father and me. Especially our eyes—dark brown, sharp, unrelenting. His, because he expects the world to fall in line voluntarily. Mine, because I know I'll have to bend it to my will.

"It's fine," I respond, my voice tight. "Let's get started. We need to finalize the plans for Q4 and iron out some of the transition details."

William waves a hand dismissively as he finally takes his seat. "We have time for that. I'll still be here after the end of the year to assist with the transition. There's no need to rush."

I grit my teeth. "I'd prefer to have as much squared away beforehand as possible, especially because we're about to announce it to the public at the end of the week. Our team needs continuity and stability."

He leans back. "Stability doesn't happen overnight, Silas. It's a process that I'll oversee when the time comes."

I exhale sharply. "I'd also like an update on the servers. It's been months, and I still don't know where things stand."

A flicker of annoyance crosses his face. "The servers are secure," he says, giving nothing else.

"They're an essential step to ensure transparency during the transition," Davey cuts in before I can respond. I glance at him, surprised. William raises a brow, the faintest lift, but Davey doesn't back down.

"Silas can't do his job properly without complete infrastructure access," my brother-in-law continues, setting his tablet down. "And from a procedural standpoint, I also need that access for the audits. If we're expected to conduct a proper review, we can't do that with blind spots."

Brenden shifts in his seat, eyes darting to William. My father has been pushing to skip the audits for weeks now, arguing that my current level of involvement is sufficient. I've refused every time.

Skipping a standard procedure during a leadership transition would send the wrong message to our teams, and too much has surfaced recently to justify overlooking anything.

It's been small but significant things. The first was a quiet restructuring of the R&D division, and then a last-minute renegotiation with one of our largest raw material suppliers. Both are technically within my father's authority based on our bylaws, but the way he dismissed my concerns about the entire board being left in the dark didn't sit well with me.

Apparently, he and Brenden have been holding out hope I'd change my mind.

William adjusts the cuff of his shirt. "I won't lie," he says finally, voice smooth as glass. "The tone here catches me off guard. I didn't expect this level of urgency or mistrust. Especially from you," he adds, his eyes narrowing ever so slightly on my Davey. "When I offered you your current role, I assumed we were aligned on preserving stability; not manufacturing alarm where none exists."

My blood heats at the insinuation, but Davey only nods, unbothered.

"I agree. Stability should be the priority," he replies, "and the best way to ensure it is by following the standard procedures every company in our position would take during an executive transition."

William's jaw tightens. Davey pays it no mind as he continues.

"As the future CSO—" he begins, then glances at me. I give a single nod. The board vote is a formality. He'll have the title by the end of Q1 of next year. "As the future CSO, we both need to be fully briefed on all critical infrastructure. If I'm going to be accountable for our security posture, I need full visibility."

William's expression hardens for just a breath before he hides it behind a polished, controlled smile. "Well," he replies, "that's quite the response. Spoken like a true leader."

My father's gaze flicks between Davey and me. I can see the calculation behind it—he's searching for a way to pivot, but there isn't one. Not without making this harder on himself in the long run.

He exhales quietly, the faintest concession. "Brenden will send over the details. I expect you to keep this information confidential, just as we did with the warehouse."

"Thank you," Davey answers with the slightest hint of relief in his voice. "We'll review the information as soon as it's sent."

William nods, already standing even though he just arrived. "I'll leave you to your Q4 planning, then."

Brenden rises wordlessly, following William out of the room. The door clicks shut behind them, followed by a short silence.

"That was telling," Davey says cautiously.

I push back my chair, leaning as far back as it allows while my mind churns. "Agreed."

Before June, I might have thought my father was being his usual, paranoid self. Now, I have Elena's letter screaming in the recesses of my mind, reminding me of what she was trying to do that night. Was she onto something, or was it another elaborate ruse to divide my family further?

Either way, I don't like it.

CHAPTER 7

Elena

I t's a cloudy afternoon when I get back from Breckenridge. I've been sitting in the truck, staring at the porch of my temporary home for at least ten minutes. The engine is off, but I can't bring myself to move.

Things between Luis and me have been awkward. Most of it's my fault. He's been giving me space. No jokes that could be misread, no lingering glances or unnecessary touches. Just quiet kindness and a little small talk. It hasn't exactly made it easier to figure out what—if any-thing—he's feeling toward me. Maybe I've just built a narrative in my head that doesn't exist.

Still, the distance has helped a little. Enough for me to breathe and try to understand why my reaction was so visceral in the first place.

I love Luis, I really do. The kind that comes from showing up without being asked, from listening without judgment, from making space for silence without trying to fill it.

Luis has been that for me. Constant in a way that's unbalanced and completely undeserved. He's become one of the most important people in my life, but even with all the closeness we've built, there's no current under my skin when he's near. No part of me that reaches for him without thinking. No pull. No ache.

With Silas, everything was sharp, consuming, and overwhelming in a way that felt impossible to outrun. It wasn't always good, and God knows it wasn't always healthy, but it was undeniable. The kind of connection that sank its teeth in and didn't let go.

Some days, I wonder if that was my one big, messy, all-consuming love. The one that burned too hot, too fast, too beautifully, and the only thing left to do was let it die. Maybe I'm broken now. Or I've just changed.

I release an exhale.

We need to talk about it. I owe him that.

If he truly feels something more, we need to determine if there's a way to salvage the friendship we do have without further damaging it. Luis deserves more than confusion, and far more than whatever mixed signals I might have given without meaning to.

I grab my bag and sling it over my shoulder before sliding out of the front seat and shutting the door behind me. My boots crunch against the gravel as I clasp my hands behind my lower back and push out to stretch my chest.

The clouds hang low today, cloaking the valley in a thick mist. There's something hauntingly beautiful about it, even when the view is obscured. I smile and inhale deeply. The air smells heavy and clean.

Lost in thought and the quiet rhythm of my footsteps as I approach the edge of the driveway to look out at the view, I don't hear the second pair of boots behind me until it's too late.

A hand clamps down around my still-clasped wrists, locking them in place. Pain shoots through my shoulders as I'm yanked backward, nearly losing my footing. My bag slips from my shoulder and catches at my elbow, throwing me further off balance. I twist, struggling to break free.

"Relax," a voice hisses in my ear, low and calm. "If you don't, this is going to hurt."

Every muscle in my body locks up.

That voice.

Before I can place it or even move, a sharp sting pierces the side of my neck. I gasp as the pain flares hot and fast beneath my skin. My vision is already starting to flicker. I try to turn my head just enough to see dirty blonde hair and a flash of bright, hateful eyes.

The world tilts. Sound warps. My arms go limp.

His name surfaces just as my knees buckle.

I sink to the ground, and he lets me fall. The impact is distant and muted. Whatever was in that needle is already taking hold, pulling me under enough that I barely feel the sting of hitting the ground.

The last thing I register before everything goes dark is the quiet *zip* of my bag being opened and the low, distant rumble of thunder echoing across the trees.

The first time I come to, I'm laying down. My neck throbs from the angle my head is hanging. Vibrations hum against my cheek, rhythmic and low, but my body feels miles away. Even peeling my eyes open feels like a monumental effort.

Shapes melt together in streaks of shadow and light, the edges of the world refusing to stay still.

"...don't know why you didn't just take her out," a voice mutters somewhere nearby. Male. Gruff. It sounds like it's coming through a wall of cotton.

"Orders are orders," someone else replies, calm and detached. It's the person who whispered in my ear.

"Yeah, but—"

"Shut up. She's waking up."

I try to speak, to form anything that might sound like a question or a threat or a plea, but my tongue won't cooperate. The only sound I manage is a faint, garbled moan.

Something causes me to jolt, sending a wave of nausea through me as my body shifts deeper into whatever seat I'm in.

The air smells faintly of leather and something sharp and chemical—too sharp. My eyes flutter once, twice, and the blur starts to spin.

Then everything fades again.

The next time I wake, the engine is louder. A low, constant roar that buzzes through my skull and rattles in my teeth.

Through half-lidded eyes, I catch glimpses of my surroundings. Metal walls. Narrow aisle. Oval windows with pale light bleeding in through clouds.

A plane?

"She's really fighting those sedatives," a familiar voice says somewhere nearby. There's a faint note of amusement threaded through it.

"She should enjoy them while they last," a female voice replies. "I can't imagine what they're going to do with her once we get back."

A cold wave moves through me, but my body doesn't respond. I try to lift a hand, shift my head, but it's like being pinned beneath my own weight.

My mind screams at me to stay awake, to memorize their voices, to find an exit, but the pull of unconsciousness drags harder.

My eyes flicker shut before I can stop them, swallowed by the dark once again.

When I wake for the final time, the first thing I notice is the silence, because the ringing in my ears is almost deafening.

My head throbs with a slow, pulsing ache radiating from the base of my skull. Nausea surges up fast, curling through my gut. I turn my head just in time to retch bile onto the floor, the acid burning the back of my throat and nose. Thin bands of pressure cinch against my wrists, chest, and calves, digging into skin already rubbed raw.

My vision swims as I blink and force my gaze downward. I'm tied to a chair. Coarse rope winds around my limbs, pinning me to the arms, legs, and back of it. The wood creaks beneath me as I shift, but the bindings don't budge.

It takes several minutes for my mind to stop spinning long enough to absorb the rest of it. The room is bare with concrete walls. No windows or furniture aside from the chair I'm in. A single fluorescent light flickers above, casting harsh shadows and an unsettling hum that buzzes under my skin.

My chest tightens.

I pull at my arms again, but the ropes only dig deeper, cutting off circulation and leaving more angry, red marks in their wake. Terror rushes in to fill the space, flooding my veins like fire. My fingers go numb. My toes, too.

I force myself to count my breaths.

One. Two. Three.

I can't lose it. Not now.

Before I can steady myself, there's a sound outside the door. A low rumble, then the sharp screech of metal scraping metal.

"Well, well, well."

My lungs seize. The breath I've just managed to take vanishes as my body locks up on instinct. I don't need to see his face to know who it is.

My gaze drops to the floor before the door even fully opens, like some part of me remembers exactly how to protect itself.

"Look who's back from the dead," he announces, voice laced with both amusement and pure venom.

I don't have to look up to feel it—his fury, thick and oppressive, trickling into the room ahead of him like smoke before a fire. His shadow stretches across the floor. It crawls over the concrete, swallowing the light until it touches me.

Not skin, not breath, not voice. Just the weight of him. The presence. The promise. It wraps around me and chokes.

Silent and inescapable.

CHAPTER 8

Elena

My eyes are fixed on the raw marks forming around my wrists, on my jeans stained from my shift at Bluebird's, on the cement directly in front of me. Anywhere but him.

Even with all our careful planning, he still found me.

Why did I expect anything less?

Footsteps echo, each one a fraying thread in a rope of a guillotine. My body refuses to move, even when the tips of his polished shoes enter my line of sight.

The rage rolls off of him in waves, pummeling me.

"Don't be a coward, *Elena.*"

A hand clamps around my jaw, thumb and middle fingers pressing into the hinge, an ache already settling deep in the muscle and forcing my mouth open. With a quick jerk, my gaze is forced upward. His eyes—hell's own inferno—burn into mine.

"Look at me when I'm speaking to you."

For a split second, I hoped my many nightmares would dull this pain, but Silas's hatred cuts through me as sharp and effective as any torture.

Just as I part my mouth further to speak, his grip digs into my skin to keep me still. Pain laces through the joint and I gasp.

"Don't say a fucking word until I tell you to," he seethes, face only inches from mine.

Tears well behind my eyes, and I blink them away furiously. There has to be something so deeply wrong with me because, despite everything, feeling his calloused fingers against my skin—to have him standing directly in front of me—feels like taking my first real breath in months.

And almost instantly, it's replaced with a weight so heavy that I could swear I'm drowning.

"Already starting with the theatrics?" He bares his teeth, lips curling into something that's almost a smile.

Cillian. Cillian was the one who grabbed me.

"How did you find me?" I whisper, forcing my mouth to move against his hold.

His laugh is low and mirthless, twisting the sharp pain already embedded deep in my chest. "Your bank account in Arizona." My stomach plummets. *How could I be so stupid?* "You held out longer than I expected." His eyes narrow, poison lacing his words. "Did your little boyfriend run out of money?"

Holy fuck. Luis.

Whatever they drugged me with must melt brain cells because it hadn't even crossed my mind that they'd take him, too.

"Where's Luis?" My voice somehow remains even, despite my hammering pulse.

Silas's grip intensifies before he shoves me back, releasing my face like a filthy rodent. He recovers quickly as he turns, shifting to lean against the wall a few feet away, composed once more.

"Is that his name?" His voice is almost bored. "He's been... uncooperative."

I squeeze my eyes shut, trying to push past the roaring static in my mind. God only knows how long I've been out and how long they've been trying to get answers out of Luis. Of course, he's still holding out to protect me.

Damnit, Luis. You stupid, stubborn asshole.

"Silas," my voice teeters on desperate despite my best efforts, "all he did was help me leave Chicago. This is all on me."

"How noble of him," Silas sneers, tilting his head. "If he involved himself in your mess, *Elena*, then he's as guilty as you are."

He says my name like a curse, and I wince. The slight reaction fuels him; his lips curling until a diabolical smile settles onto his perfect face.

"You hate it, don't you?" His voice dips. "That I figured out who you really are. I know more about you than you ever thought possible, Ms. Cross."

A bitter laugh bubbles up before I can stop it. I can practically see Davey at his computer, Cillian hovering nearby, the others not far behind. Each of them pulling apart the pieces of my life like they're solving some puzzle. Every police report from a neighbor calling about my parents screaming through the walls. Every address tied to a building that should've been condemned. The few ER visits that only happened because the school nurse threatened to call someone if they didn't. The media coverage of Drew's death.

My eyes burn as I drop my gaze, my head hanging under the crushing weight of shame.

"You're the most capable person I've ever known," I murmur barely above a whisper. "I have no doubt you figured it all out."

Silence settles while I stare at my lap, and I start to wonder what he's thinking about before he breaks it.

"Why?"

I turn my head toward him, my voice worn and heavy. "Why what?"

"Don't play dumb with me," he snaps, pushing off the wall and stepping in front of me again. "You owe me more than that."

I swallow hard, the words sticking to the back of my throat. I want to explain—to give him something, anything—but I can't. Not when Luis's life hangs in the balance.

I force myself to meet his stare. "I had a contract I needed to fulfill."

He closes the remaining distance between us with predatory precision. "And what did this contract entail?" he presses, towering over me. "Who do you work for?"

Typical Silas—bulldozing his way through a negotiation. Why wouldn't he? He holds almost all the cards, but not the few I have left. If he's asking, that means there are still missing pieces. Whether he likes it or not, he needs me to fill in those gaps.

The only questions are how much they know and what I can do to leverage it to get Luis out of here.

"Why am I still alive?" I ask. "Why not just kill me when you found me?"

His jaw tightens, the muscle twitching as if he's holding back the full brunt of his rage. Then, his hand shoots out, gripping my chin with bruising force. His face is so close that I can feel the heat of his breath and smell the faint scent of his aftershave beneath the bitterness clinging to him.

"I don't think you're exactly in the position to be asking questions," he growls.

He wants to hurt me. I can see it in his eyes, feel it in the way his fingers dig into my jaw like he's trying to keep himself from doing something worse. The fear is instant, but there's something else clawing its way to the surface. Maybe it's stupidity or survival. Or it's just the last shred of my dignity refusing to let him see me cower.

Whatever it is, it wins.

"When has that ever stopped me before?" I whisper.

My answer catches him off guard, forcefully reminding that I never backed down from his challenges before. Then, he leans back, running his tongue across his teeth.

"I wouldn't have gone through the trouble of keeping you alive if I didn't have a use for you," he replies finally, shrugging. "Now quit wasting my time."

"I don't work for anyone anymore."

His grip tightens. "Who gave you the fucking contract?" he demands through gritted teeth.

Silas will never relent on this; I know that much. His determination for and loyalty to his family—two things I once loved most about him—won't allow him to let this go.

"I have people to protect." My answer is quiet. "The same way you do."

For a split second, frustration gives way to confusion, but it's quickly lost under another wave of violence. "So, you're protecting the person who gave you the job?"

"That's not what I said."

"Then what are you saying?" he snaps.

"I won't tell you anything unless we make a deal," I say, my heart threatening to explode out of my chest.

Silas's hand drops. For a long moment, he watches me. Searching for an answer or a weakness, but he won't find one. It doesn't take long for his expression to shift, a bitter smile creeping onto his lips.

"I think you will."

Finality laces every syllable. I don't have to guess what he's thinking. I can practically see the twisted, methodical ways he's already planning to break me. He'll drag it out for as long as he can, savoring every second, inflicting as much pain as it takes until something gives—my body or my mind, whichever goes first.

It's the pleasure he takes in the thought, barely masked beneath the fury, that undoes me.

I don't know this man.

The quiet, careful one I watched movies with in his attic. The one I challenged without fear. The one I chipped away at, piece by piece. He's buried alive beneath whatever *this* is. The force of all of it is a bullet that ricochets through me.

The tears I've been holding back spill over, quick but silent, streaking down my face as I meet his gaze head-on. "Then I guess we're done here."

His eyes blaze with something I can't quite place, but I know he understands me. If he doesn't want to meet me halfway, we won't be meeting anywhere at all. I'll take it to the grave, or the bottom of Lake

Michigan, or on the floor of this room. It doesn't matter where it happens. I'll leave this earth with every secret he wants to pry out of me.

Whatever emotion flickered in his expression vanishes as quickly as it came before his mouth curls into something cruel. "I'll decide when we're done. And when I do, I'll make sure it's finished properly this time."

Something inside me fractures. The pain wraps around my ribs, seizes my organs, and squeezes so tight I swear they'll spill out of my pores. Still, I refuse to look away from him.

"Did you find what was on the servers?" My voice cracks on the last word.

Silas's frustration flares like a match struck too close. "I know everything on those servers. What I'm still trying to figure out is what *you* were looking for."

If it's possible for the vice already squeezing the life out of me to tighten, it does.

That can't be true.

"You've seen what your father is burying?"

His face darkens, a shadow falling over his features. "I'm about to run this company, Elena. I know everything."

My vision blurs as the words slam into me, but they don't make sense. They can't.

The Silas I knew would never be capable of standing by and letting it happen. He was fighting for his employees. For his sister. Hell, for a woman he barely knew because she was in trouble. He cared about people.

But maybe I never knew the real Silas.

Maybe the person in front of me, coiled with hatred and something darker, is who he always was, but I just never experienced it. Maybe I misread him all along, and I risked my life just to give another terrible man the chance to bury his sins.

Even as my thoughts spiral, my mouth betrays me. "I don't believe you." I think it's more for myself than for him.

White-hot pressure flares in my neck as Silas grabs me, cutting off my air. Pain radiates down into my chest. I instinctively yank against the restraints to grab his wrist, only for the coarse rope to dig deeper into my skin, slicing into flesh already rubbed raw. The chair jerks and creaks.

"Don't you dare speak like you know me."

My lungs burn as black blotches bloom at the edges of my vision. Pressure builds behind my eyes.

"I do know you, Silas," I rasp, even though I'm not sure that's true anymore.

His armor cracks, and the agony crawls its way to the surface, carving itself on every feature. And for a second, I see him—my Silas. He's right there, just within reach.

The fingers around my throat loosen just enough to make the dark edges of my vision sharpen once again. "I thought I knew *you*," he breathes out like he's trying to exhale the pain before it consumes him. "Why did you do this?"

Fresh tears slide down my cheeks and onto his hand. The warmth of them seeps into the creases of his skin. I feel it. So does he.

"I didn't have a choice," I whimper.

"You did," he hisses. "Me. You could have chosen *me*."

The venom of his words wraps around me like a noose. It tightens with every second, pulling me deeper into the infinite depths of his hatred.

This is what happens with everything I touch.

My voice wobbles through quiet sobs. "I wanted to. So badly."

He hesitates. Like there's something lingering on the tip of his tongue, right before icing over.

"Bullshit."

The assertion severs any traces of doubt I thought I might have just seen, but I can't let it go. Even if it changes nothing. Especially if it changes nothing. I barely recognize the man standing in front of me, but the one I knew deserves to hear the truth, regardless of whether he wants to or not.

My throat bobs against his palm as I swallow, the edges of his face watery from unshed tears. "I gain nothing by lying to you," I whisper.

His jaw tightens. In that silence, I feel the inevitability of the end drawing closer and it clicks into place. It's etched into every hard line of his face, the sharp set of his mouth, the cold finality in his dark brown eyes. This has consumed him, and there's no space left in him for doubt.

Or mercy.

He steps back. "I'll be back in a few hours." His frigid eyes cast a final glance over me. "Hopefully, you'll have smartened up by then and have a name to give me. We won't be making any deals."

The certainty in his voice shatters the final images I've held onto for months, and I have no one but myself to blame.

As he reaches the door, something desperate rises within me, clawing its way up my throat. "When the time comes to..." My words trail off, unable to say them, "let someone else do it. You shouldn't have to."

He freezes.

Time stretches, suspending us both in the weight of my words. It presses on him, trailing down his spine and outward, like a heat I could almost reach out and touch.

Then, he opens the door and slams it shut behind him, leaving me with nothing.

Just like I deserve.

Chapter 9

Silas

I slam the three steel bolts into place, each one thudding into its reinforced socket with a *snap* that echoes down the hallway. Above them, a panel beside the door blinks to life. I swipe my keycard, waiting for the faint beep and the reassuring green light. An electromagnetic seal hums quietly as it activates.

My chest heaves when I finally lean my back against the cold metal, trying to find my breath. She's in there, tied to that chair, and I hate it.

It shouldn't matter. It *can't* matter, but it does.

And that pisses me off even more.

Every thought I had in that room was a contradiction. Do I want to punish her or protect her? Hurt her or kiss her? Kill her or untie and fuck her? I was teetering on the edge when she looked me in the eye and told me with her whole chest that she wanted to choose me.

It sounded so convincing.

By the time I reach the elevator, my hands are shaking. I punch in the code and press my thumb to the scanner. The door slides open. This private elevator is a fortress, just like the rest of this building. It's designed to keep people like Elena out. And yet, here she is. In my world. Living under my skin. Again.

Though I'm the one who dragged her back here, it already feels like I've lost control. I hadn't expected her to threaten to die with the information I need.

All to protect precious fucking Luis.

Cillian came back from Colorado with Cora and the two runaways, but Paul and Lloyd stayed behind. They're tearing through every inch of that asshole's life—his home, his records, every breadcrumb he's ever left behind. Anything to figure out who the hell he is and how he got Elena out of *my* city without leaving a trace.

There aren't many institutions I haven't been able to influence, and that locally owned bank in Arizona was no exception. One well-placed bribe, and the owner agreed to notify us the second there was activity on the account. A week ago, that call came through about small transfers trickling into a new account at a national bank. More challenging to trace, sure, but not impossible. She made finding the routing trail easier by taking out cash. I didn't bother asking about the details or how Davey did it. All I cared about was dealing with her as quickly as possible.

Cillian and Cora were enroute to her within a day. Still, they had to wait a few more to make sure all our safeguards were in place, including access to their smart devices so we could intercept and answer any messages if questions started coming in.

The elevator shifts gears, rising smoothly. In less than a minute, the doors are opening onto the executive floor, opposite the public elevator.

After offering Leslie a curt greeting, I'm pushing my office door open. Davey is at my desk, the glow of my laptop illuminating his face. He looks up as I step inside, a slight furrow on his brow.

"That didn't go how I expected." His voice is quiet, almost tentative.

I round my desk, loosening my tie just enough to take the pressure off of the lump it's pressing against. "What do you mean?"

Davey scratches the back of his neck, glancing at the screen as he stands. "I don't know." His confusion is evident. "I thought she'd have more to say. Try harder to negotiate with you, something. But she's just sitting there."

I follow his gaze to the screen and sink into the seat he just vacated. The video feed from the basement shows Elena exactly as I left her, head bowed to hide her face. The trembling in her shoulders tells me she's crying, though she makes no sound.

"She hasn't tried to talk her way out of it?" I ask, my voice tight, knowing she saw the security camera in the corner of the room. She wouldn't miss something like that.

Davey shakes his head. "Not a word. It's strange. This isn't the woman I remember from before." His eyes meet mine, searching for some explanation I don't have.

My fists clench. "She'll talk."

There's a beat of silence. "Maybe," he responds.

I want to dismiss his words, but the way she sits there gnaws at me. Scarlett would still be fighting tooth and nail, spitting fire and venom at me or whoever would listen until her throat was raw.

Was that all just a part of her facade, too?

"What about Luis?" I ask.

Davey stands up straighter, visibly relieved to move on. "He's starting to bend. Says he knows Elena through work, helped her get out of a bad contract, and let her stay with him for a while. Cillian pressed him about their relationship, but he insists they're just friends."

I scoff. "You believe him?"

Davey hesitates. "I don't know," he admits. "It feels too clean, but he hasn't changed his story, even after some of Cill's... convincing."

I sink my teeth into the inside of my cheek to keep my thoughts to myself. We'd agreed it was best if I wasn't the one to question Luis. Davey figured I wouldn't know when to stop, and he's probably right. There's not a single punishment I'd give that wouldn't have him screaming loud enough for Elena to hear through the walls, and I don't want either of them to realize they're only three holding rooms apart.

The basement of this building hasn't always existed in its current form. Almost a decade ago, my father offloaded some of his assets as he began to consider retirement. It made sense for him to sell the building to me, given the trajectory of my career. I hadn't even considered what

I'd do with the space until the world stopped seeing me as just William Wells's oldest son and started seeing me as the heir.

That's when the threats really started.

First, they were subtle: hushed whispers, veiled warnings. Then they became louder, more violent. A kidnapping attempt at a charity gala. A bullet through the front door of my old penthouse. My father kept telling me that I just needed to increase my security as he had, as if another guard or another system would be enough.

When the threats got too close and I found myself waiting for someone else to handle it, something in me snapped. Not from fear, but from rage. A deep, soul-splitting fury that hollowed me out and made space for one truth: I'd never feel that powerless again.

So I stopped waiting.

That's when the training started. Combat, firearms, strategy—anything that would make me a weapon instead of a target. I built my own team, piece by piece. People I handpicked to protect me and everyone I gave a damn about. I never made a show of what I was doing, but people close to me saw the change.

I stopped going to events unless I had to. Changed my routines. Cut access to anyone who didn't have a reason to be close. The more I learned, the tighter I drew the lines around my life. Privacy stopped being a preference and became a necessity.

My father noticed the change too, though he never acknowledged it directly. In typical Wells fashion, he offered criticisms wrapped in concern.

"Trying to be a one-man army now?"
"Most people outgrow that kind of paranoia."

I told him it was my business to worry about, and that was the end of the conversation.

He still makes comments now and then about Cillian and the rest of my team, but I choose not to respond. His judgment is the reason I never disclosed the holding rooms and other utility spaces I built in the basement, or what my team uses them for. To his knowledge, I employ a bunch of overqualified bodyguards. He's never asked in earnest about any of it and, if I'm being honest, I didn't want to hear what he'd have to say.

And in some small, sick way, I enjoy having a piece of something that he has no part in. Something I made and run on my own. Damn well, too.

"How's Colorado going?" I ask to redirect my thoughts.

Davey's quick to tell me what Paul and Lloyd have been able to find out about Luis so far, which is oddly reminiscent of the life Elena led. They're in the process of locking up his home to avoid suspicion.

When Cillian was on his way back to Chicago, he contacted Elena's boss at the restaurant from her phone to say she had a family emergency in Arizona, Luis joined her for support, and she wouldn't know when she'd return. The woman didn't even question it, and we haven't run into any other issues yet.

My brother-in-law clears his throat. "We also got an update on the servers." He nods towards my laptop. "Brenden sent the location. It's an office building close by. Basement level. We'll head over this afternoon, but I need to see what we're working with before I can give you any timelines."

Then, he hesitates, glancing at me with uncertainty. "Jeremy was looking for you earlier," he says. "He said he wants to have lunch with you and talk."

I let out a frustrated sigh, dragging a hand down my face.

Of course he does.

Jeremy has been more adamant than ever about becoming more involved at Wells, and I've had to take several meetings to discuss his "ideas."

"What does he want now?" I mutter, more to myself than anything.

Davey shrugs. "Not sure. He's been, I don't know, weird lately. I'd tread lightly." He pauses, then adds, "I'll round up the IT team. Let me know if you decide to come with us."

As he leaves, my focus returns to my laptop. Elena hasn't moved an inch. She looks thinner than when she left, her hair now chopped off to her shoulders. There's a heaviness pressing on her that I only remember seeing her the last week she stayed with me.

Before I allow myself to fixate on her any longer, I slam the laptop shut and lean over to my landline to dial Leslie's extension.

If I can't figure Elena out, I'll deal with Jeremy instead.

Chapter 10

Elena

I have no idea how much time has passed. The fluorescent light above me doesn't change, the room doesn't have a clock, and no one else has come in.

At first, I cried silent tears. I didn't want to give anyone watching through the cameras the satisfaction of seeing me sob, but I couldn't stop. The tears fell for what felt like an eternity, soaking into the collar of my Bluebird's work shirt as I stared down at my lap.

Eventually, the well ran dry. I started counting the seconds in my head through two hours before my mind betrayed me and forced me to start over.

Now, the aches in my body are impossible to ignore. My ass has gone completely numb, but the rest of me is alive with pain—every muscle stiff, every joint locked. The ropes dig into my skin, cutting off circulation so thoroughly that even the smallest shift sent a rush of pins and needles screaming through my limbs.

The chair offers no relief. Any attempt to readjust amplifies everything. That's what starts the tears again. The kind that don't even feel worth wiping away. Not that I could if I wanted to.

I'm going to die here.

Despite the tears and the endless aches, the thought doesn't scare me as much anymore.

More than likely, Silas isn't coming back, and I don't think I'd want to see him again, either. The only thing I care about now is Luis. Maybe I can persuade whoever comes in next to hear me out. I'll tell them everything if they'll let him go. And when they're done with me, I'll welcome whatever comes after.

Weirdly enough, it's peaceful. A sense of finality I've never let myself consider before because I've spent so many years running from it. Still, there's this nagging voice in the back of my head, whispering its disappointment.

After everything we've fought for? After years of clawing our way through every obstacle, every failure? Is this how it ends?

I've been fighting for as long as I can remember. For my parents' attention as a child. Against their anger when I was a teenager. To get into college, and then to stay there when things got hard. To survive Peter for over a decade, Chicago, and what came after. I've fought so hard, for so long. And yet, here I am.

The sound of the door being unlocked pulls me from my thoughts. My entire body tenses, cause the ropes to embed themselves deeper in my raw skin. I blink up at the figure stepping into the room.

Davey.

I stiffen. He doesn't look in my direction as he drags in a chair and sets it a foot or so in front of me. Without a word, he unbuttons the front of his suit jacket and sits down, holding a water bottle with a straw in his free hand.

For a long moment, we sit in silence as he studies me with that calculating gaze of his.

Davey hates me. He never trusted my intentions, and his suspicions only worsened after I was attacked in that alley, though he was less obvious about it. I can't blame him.

He leans forward and I brace myself, waiting for him to demand answers and drag me into a worse nightmare to make good on his promise to hurt me if I ever hurt Natalie, but he only holds the straw of the water bottle to my lips.

I blink at him "What's in it?" I croak, my voice dry and cracked.

The look he gives me can only be described as one of exasperation. "Water," he answers flatly before pressing the straw into the seam of my lips.

Though every instinct tells me to refuse, I don't. If it's drugged or poisoned, it doesn't matter. I never planned on giving them any information if they didn't make a deal with me, and I'm so damn thirsty.

My lips close around the plastic before cool liquid rushes down my throat in instant relief.

Christ, that feels good.

I finish the entire bottle before I can stop myself. When it's gone, I lean back against the chair, the water already sloshing uncomfortably in my empty stomach.

"Thank you," I whisper.

Davey doesn't respond as he places the bottle on the ground at his feet, crossing his arms over his chest. Not much has changed since the last time I saw him. I bite the inside of my cheek, watching him watch me.

The seconds turn into minutes, and I wonder briefly if this is supposed to be some intimidation tactic to get me talking. Still, he continues to sit and stare, eyes darting across my features, brows drawn together.

Eventually, I break our unofficial contest. "Are you going to do something, or are you just drawing out the suspense?"

He sits up straighter, and the corner of his mouth twitches, almost imperceptibly.

"I guess there *is* still a little fire left in you."

That response surprises me, and I tilt my head. His posture shifts slightly as he leans his elbows on his knees, looking me straight in the eye.

"What were you looking for?" he asks.

Of course. Silas sent him down here to try the good-cop-bad-cop routine. I wonder how badly he wished he could've been the bad cop in this situation.

I sigh, my shoulders sagging. "I already told Silas. I *will* talk, but there are conditions."

Davey's lips press into a tight line. There's no flicker of recognition or knowing glance. Just stillness. The kind that settles in when someone hasn't found what they were hoping for or doesn't even know exactly what they were looking for in the first place.

Relief trickles in, easing some of the tension in my chest. Silas lied. He doesn't know everything on those servers. If he did, Davey wouldn't be here. Silas wouldn't keep something like that from him. He values Davey too much to keep him in the dark.

Davey surprises me with a curt nod. "What kind of conditions?"

I swallow hard, the words heavy in my throat. "I'll tell you everything, but only after you ensure Luis's safety. You'll get him out of Chicago discreetly, take him home, and leave him alone. Forever. That's the deal."

Davey's eyes narrow. "Why does Luis's safety mean so much to you?"

The pointed question hangs in the air. They all suspect something, and I can understand why. Not long ago, I was staying in the guest room of Silas's home, and we were anything but friends.

I hesitate. If I lie and say we're dating, will they use him to make me talk? Or do I say we're just friends and risk him being killed because he's not strong enough leverage?

There's no correct answer.

I draw in a slow, unsteady breath. "Luis was there for me when I was in trouble," I admit. "My old employer... they're not the kind of people you can walk away from."

His expression sharpens, but I keep going.

"Luis helped me leave before my handler could hunt me down. He came up with a plan to get me out of Chicago to maybe start over, away from all of this." I shake my head slightly at the memories. "I owe him, and he shouldn't die because of my choices."

Davey studies me for a long moment as the words sink in, probably trying to figure out how much of what I just said is true. Whatever the case, he doesn't press me further. Instead, he asks, "And what happens to *you* after you talk?"

I meet his gaze, shrugging. "I don't care. I just want to make sure Luis is safe, and that what's on those servers is dealt with by people who can fix it."

His eyebrows lift, not quite knowing what to do with an answer like that coming from me. After everything, I'd be shocked to learn I'm not always motivated by selfishness, too.

Now it's just about Luis and whatever the hell William is hiding. Nothing more.

Davey studies me for a beat longer, the surprise slowly melting into something steadier. "I'll talk to Silas."

I blink as he stands and buttons his jacket, casually collecting the water bottle and chair. My brain doesn't register his words right away.

Did Davey just agree?

A spark of something jolts in my chest, and with it, a flicker of boldness I didn't know I had left.

He's almost to the door by the time I collect myself enough to call out, my voice trembling. "There's one more thing." My heart pounds. I have one opportunity to do this right. "I need to talk to Natalie."

Davey's expression flickers—annoyance, maybe, or curiosity—but I press on before he can respond. "If I'm going to trust that you'll keep your word about Luis, I want her to know about it. She will hold everyone accountable."

"And I need to apologize," I add quietly. "She deserves the truth. And if she wants to hear my reasons for doing it, I'll tell her those, too."

My body tenses, bracing for the sharp reminder that I've already done enough damage. That I don't get to ask for things like this. Not with Natalie, not ever.

But it doesn't come.

Davey studies me. Really studies me. Then tips his head in acknowledgment.

"I'll see what I can do."

And then he's gone.

Chapter 11

Silas

The slam of my office door reverberates through the room. Through the glass, I catch a parting glance of Jeremy storming down the hallway, a takeout box clenched in hand. Leslie glances up from her computer as he passes, her eyes flicking to mine for the briefest second before returning to the screen. I stay seated, eyes returning to the remains of my lunch, appetite gone.

The conversation had started the way so many do: with Jeremy eager to pitch ideas he hasn't thoroughly researched. Today's gem was a project management software he clearly didn't understand, but I gave him the courtesy of listening. I always do, though my constructive feedback rarely makes it through that thick layer of pride and hostility he always wears.

What I didn't expect was the pivot to something even more absurd: our open Chief Operating Officer role.

William has floated the idea several times this summer, dropping it into conversations as if it weren't completely insane. I remember the first time he suggested it, and I nearly choked on my coffee when I realized he was serious.

Jeremy. Hot-headed. Impulsive. Chronically underqualified Jeremy.

It would have almost been funny if my father hadn't doubled down on me nominating him in the new year.

I explained to Jeremy the reasons we've kept the position open and what it would take even to consider him for the role. At first, he seemed to be shocked by the standards I gave, but it wasn't the arrogance that got to me. It was the final shot he threw over his shoulder before slamming the door.

"What a fucking surprise. The golden boy doesn't want anyone else to succeed besides his best friend. So much for family, huh?"

Jeremy's outburst wasn't the real issue. It was what he revealed about my father. While I've been painstakingly navigating the transition to CEO, William's been making promises I wasn't even aware of, let alone agreed to. And to make matters worse, he also told Jeremy that Davey is earmarked for Chief Security Officer.

I exhale slowly, but the anger simmers and threatens to boil over.

Davey *is* my choice for CSO. That decision has been made for months, and my father has been fully supportive of it. But Jeremy tried to spin it as if it were some family handout; as if Davey hadn't spent years working his ass off to prove he was the best person for the job.

I can't figure out what my father's angle is. I already told him no. So, why keep pushing? Does he actually believe Jeremy's qualified? Or does he see this role the same way Jeremy does—as something owed to him because of who he is? And if that's the case, why not nominate Jeremy himself?

Unless that's the whole point. Maybe he told Jeremy *I* would do it so he wouldn't have to be the one to say no. So he could continue playing the part of the supportive father to the one person he has coddled most in this world. Or maybe he's just finally lost his goddamn mind.

I lean back in my chair, dragging a hand down my face. The way my father has been acting recently has only made my life harder, and he just made it worse by recruiting Jeremy to start "advocating" for himself in this way. As if our relationship hasn't been on a downward trajectory since his addiction spiraled out of control.

We've never been close, and the gap only widened after all of the horrific things he did in high school to be expelled and started using.

I won't pretend I handled it the right way. I didn't. Instead of compassion, I met him with anger and disappointment. Jeremy had the world at his fingertips, and he threw it all away for coke and prescription pills.

We bailed him out more times than I can count. After the first overdose in Aspen. After he crashed one of my father's cars into a storefront in Scottsdale. After he passed out at a company holiday party and had to be carried out the back door so it wouldn't make headlines. But that was only the start.

Not only did William pay off the family of the freshman in high school he nearly beat to death hazing for football, but he did it a second time when Jeremy nearly broke a woman's jaw in a bar fight. It was excuse after excuse with that one.

"She just wanted our money, anyway."
"Jeremy didn't know what he was doing."
"It'll only make things worse if it went public."

All of it was my father's way of preserving the family image, allowing Jeremy to skirt the consequences of his actions, and I resented my brother for it. I still do. Sobriety doesn't erase what came before it. It doesn't guarantee growth or accountability; it just means he stopped using. And the way he carries himself now? Entitled. Delusional. As if the world should still be handed to him on a silver platter because it always has been, and why would that change now?

Despite all of this, part of me can't shake the feeling that this wasn't even Jeremy's idea.

Throughout our entire conversation, he just kept parroting the same lines I've heard from my father, which only makes this more confusing because William didn't *hand* me my position.

Yes, I started as the Strategic Initiatives Manager. My father is the CEO, and there's no pretending I didn't benefit from that. I've always known exactly how privileged I am, but it never meant instant job protection. It was made clear that if I wasn't cut out for the position, William would give it to someone else.

He was ruthless. Held me to a standard so impossibly high it often felt like failure was the only way forward. He broke me down, built me back up, then did it all over again. I spent years clawing my way toward *his* version of readiness, not my own. Every promotion felt like a calculated risk he was barely willing to take.

And now he's offering my unqualified younger brother the second-highest executive position we've been hesitant to fill with barely a second thought.

Making Shaw resign as COO after catching him with his hand up Natalie's dress at that summer party wasn't enough, but it was the only justice she was comfortable with at the time. Since then, I've been deliberate—to a fault—about who I bring into the executive team. Bethany, the Director of Operations we eventually hired, has been a godsend. She's intelligent, capable, and above all, trustworthy. When I decide to nominate a COO, she'll be my first choice, but even that decision is a year or two down the road.

I glance at the clock, realizing I've been stewing for far too long.

The reprieve doesn't last. I've barely settled into the quiet of my office to finish the last of my lunch when my phone buzzes on the desk. Davey's name lights up the screen.

I pick up, pressing the phone to my ear as I stab a piece of chicken with my fork. "What now?"

"The servers." Davey skips the pleasantries.

I release the fork back into the takeout container. "What about them?"

"The team's been digging through them for a few hours," he begins. "Half the files are locked behind layered encryptions using different methods and structures. None of it is mine."

I flex my fingers and he continues, "There are also safeguards built in. If we don't decrypt the files the right way, in the right order, it triggers silent internal activity logs to be sent to the primary administrator's account."

I ask the question I already know the answer to. "Do we know who that is?"

Davey clears his throat. "I'd assume your father."

My skin prickles with heat. "So you're saying—?"

"I need specialists," he admits with a sigh. "Cryptographers, specifically. Our team isn't equipped for this, and we don't have the bandwidth to figure it out while juggling the rest of the audit, especially not if we're trying to do this subtly."

The pressure behind my eyes builds fast—tight, hot. I squeeze them shut, and the first image I see is Elena, tied up in the basement. I'd bet every cent I have that whatever she was looking for is in those files.

What the hell is my dad hiding?

"How long do you think it'll take to find someone?"

"I'm hoping a week, maybe less," Davey replies.

"Good." I remove my glasses to pinch the bridge, warding away the growing ache. Christ, I need a good workout to relieve some of this tension. "I want updates daily."

"Already planned on it."

For a moment, silence hangs between us. I glance at the clock, the nagging thought in the back of my mind surfacing. "When are you coming back to the office?"

Davey hesitates, which immediately puts me on edge. "I'm still here," he says.

I frown, sitting up straighter in my chair. "What do you mean by 'still'?"

"I haven't left. I was handling something else."

"What?"

"Elena."

I stiffen, my grip tightening on the phone. "You were with Elena?"

"Yes." He replies, tone calm. "She wants to make a deal."

"We already knew that. I said no."

"She'll talk." Davey blatantly ignores my response. "She wants Luis safe and to speak to Natalie."

Every muscle in my body coils. "Are you insane? She's going to try to use Natalie against us—to guilt her into—"

"I'm not saying we trust her blindly," Davey interrupts. "She's desperate for us to let Luis go, and whether we like it or not, she knows more than we do. If we play this right, we can get what we need from both of them."

"Or we could force it out of her," I counter through my teeth.

Davey lets out an audible breath. "Why make things messier than they need to be? She's going to cooperate, and we can avoid getting our hands dirty."

I rake my fingers through my hair, frustration swirling in my chest. "And you just decided to handle this without telling me?"

"I wanted to see what her angle was before bringing you back into it." His words are almost clinical. "You're too close to this to see her clearly."

The words sting, but he's right. My judgment has been clouded ever since she introduced herself to me at that art exhibit. Still, the idea of Davey playing mediator between us grates against every nerve.

"What did she say about Luis?" I ask, forcing my voice to stay steady.

"She wants to get him home," Davey answers. "And honestly? He's more useful to us alive. If we can leverage his cooperation, he could help decrypt the servers. They were already trying to access them before, so it's not a stretch."

I exhale sharply, a sudden weight pressing down on me. "Fine. But Nat needs to know what happened, bare minimum."

"Agreed." Davey's voice takes on a new edge that only exists for my sister. "She's still hurt that Elena never even called her. It'll be the closure she needs to move on."

"And what do we do about Elena now?" I ask, fingers rubbing the muscles in my jaw so hard that the joint cracks.

"She's been tied to a chair half a day," Davey replies bluntly. "Hungry, thirsty, probably in pain. Natalie won't take kindly to seeing her like that.

I told Cillian to move her to a long-term room, give her a meal, and let her shower. Cora is helping."

His calm, practical tone only fuels my irritation. "You're advocating for her now?"

"I'm advocating for what's effective," Davey shoots back. "This isn't about her or you. It's about the bigger picture. You know that."

Any retort I have is lost on my tongue, leaving a bitter aftertaste.

"Fine," I say finally. "But I want to talk to Natalie before she sees her."

"Of course," Davey promises. "I'm sending the IT team back to the office and will head home early to talk to her. We'll bring her down when she feels ready to. Just try to keep your head on straight until then. We can't afford for emotions to get in the way right now."

The line goes dead, and I drop the phone onto my desk with a sigh.

For months, Davey was her biggest critic, the first to warn me, the one who insisted something about her felt off, even when he couldn't explain why. And now that we finally know the truth and he was right, he's the one going soft?

What the hell did she say to manipulate the one person I thought was impenetrable to her lies? Is it because Natalie misses her? Maybe he'll smarten up if Natalie is as pissed as I am once she knows everything.

Or maybe this is exactly what Elena wants. Natalie will want to see the best in her, and that will put Davey in a position he hates: choosing between his wife and me. He'll choose her, as he should, but fuck. Just this once, I wish he wouldn't.

CHAPTER 12

Elena

Based on the meals I've been served, I've been in this room for two days and left with nothing but my own thoughts.

I don't know if that's the point—if they're waiting for me to break from the lack of human contact, if Silas rejected my deal and they're trying to figure out what to do with me, or maybe Natalie decided she didn't want to see me after all. Which is, honestly, more than fair.

Cillian and Cora are the only ones I've seen. Cora is a new face, but I recognize her voice from the day I was taken from Alma. She was there when Cillian first moved me, untying my wrists while he mocked my discomfort. Then, they blindfolded me, led me through what felt like a maze of hallways, and brought me to a communal bathroom where I was told to shower. Cora stood watch the entire time.

After that, they moved me blindfolded again. Either to another room or the same one. I couldn't tell. Both look identical in my eyes. The only change was that the chair had been replaced by a thin mattress on the ground with scratchy sheets, a wool blanket, and a pillow barely thick enough to be useful. A step up from being tied and just enough to make me wonder what they wanted in return.

Cora brings most of my meals, always watching me like she's waiting for me to do something. What, I don't know. So far, she's barely spoken a word to me, but she doesn't need to. Everything about her presence tells me she's not one to be messed with.

The visits are brief, just long enough to drop off something bland but nutritious, which should be reassuring. If they were going to kill me, they wouldn't bother keeping me in good shape, but in good shape for what?

I'm still sore, though they let me shower again an hour ago and handed me another set of sweats. My sleeves are bunched up on my forearms, exposing the scabbing raw marks on my wrists. One still looks particularly angry, but it's not worth mentioning.

Instead, I sit on the mattress with my back against the wall and think. I need something else to offer. I could help with the servers if they trust me enough to allow it. I could offer the money sitting in my account, though none of them need it. I could—

Metal scrapes against metal.

Lunch. That's my first thought, only because the last meal was breakfast food. But when the door finally opens, it's not Cillian or Cora.

It's Natalie.

She's *actually* here, and she's not alone.

Davey is just a step behind Natalie, whose hazel eyes blaze with betrayal and fury. I expected them to tell her everything before bringing her to see me. They wouldn't let her walk in here unprepared, and though I wouldn't lie to her now, I don't blame them for thinking I would.

Once they clear the doorway, Silas steps into view. His broad shoulders almost fill the frame. Our eyes meet, and I swear the temperature in the room plummets.

Even under their poisonous gazes, her presence means they're taking me up on my deal. I'm going to be able to get Luis home safely.

The realization sinks in slowly, and when it finally hits, the relief is almost painful.

I shift my gaze to Davey.

"Thank you," I say quietly.

Davey nods once. "We're staying in the room while you talk. We'll do our best not to interrupt, but we'll be here."

I nod. Nothing I'll say to Natalie will change my fate, but it doesn't stop the small, flickering ember of hope in my chest that, for once, I can follow through on something good. Maybe I can fix one piece of the damage I've caused before I go.

Cillian steps inside behind Silas, carrying three foldable chairs. He moves silently, unfolding and placing them near the trio before disappearing back out the door.

I look at Natalie before whispering, "It's good to see you."

Her expression tightens, lips pressed into a thin line. And though I wait for her to speak, I don't expect her to. The silence between us is so foreign that it makes my skin itch. And just like her brother, being the subject of her hate rips at something in the center of my soul.

My fingers twist together in my lap. "I know they've told you what I was trying to do—"

"Oh, you *know*, Elena?" Somehow, her voice grows louder and sharper with just those four words as she steps closer. "How dare you. How dare you do this to us?"

Davey follows behind his wife, one arm outstretched to catch her by the elbow if necessary. Shame floods me, clogging my throat and making it impossible to answer.

"I trusted you." Her voice wavers. "I thought we were friends. And then you left without a single word or phone call. I wondered what I did wrong and why just because things didn't work out with Silas, you had to throw me away, too."

She shakes her head like she can't believe she's even standing here. Like the sight of me makes her sick.

Davey's hand drops, but he doesn't move away.

"But that's not even the worst part, is it?" She continues, her voice dropping lower. "You didn't leave because you were scared. It's because you were using us."

The chill from my still-damp hair evaporates as heat explodes over every surface of my body. I open my mouth, trying to summon the courage to respond, but nothing comes.

"We took you in, showed you kindness." She lets out a humorless laugh. "And then that whole show in the alley. Well done. You figured out the exact way for us to let our guards down. I bet it was worth letting someone kick the shit out of you, wasn't it?"

Her words slip into my veins, burning me from the inside out.

"What else did you lie about?" She demands, tilting her head in the same predatory way Silas did when we spoke days ago. My body remembers how he grabbed my face, and I press myself further into the wall. "Your hobbies? Your stories? Did you fake every laugh at my jokes? Compliment me just to get me to trust you? Snoop through my things when I wasn't looking?"

I want to tell her no, but I can't.

Natalie watches me, waiting for some kind of defense, but when I say nothing, she starts up again. "What do you have to say for yourself?" she demands, her hands clenched into fists at her sides, body vibrating.

The quiet between us is so loud that my ears ring. As much as I want to look away from her wrath, I don't deserve to. She needs to show me her pain, and I need to see all of it.

My fingers curl around the sheets at my sides. "I did all of those things. There's no excuse or justification. I won't insult you by trying to offer one." I take a shaky breath. "But I am sorry. For everything I put you through, for every lie and choice that hurt you. If I could undo it, I would."

My words mean nothing, and I know it. I wish she would believe me, if only to save herself from any more heartache than necessary.

God knows I'm not worth any of it.

"I'll answer all of those questions and any others you still want to ask." My throat tightens, but I push through it. "And hopefully, you'll help ensure my friend's safety. He was dragged into my mess when he shouldn't have been, and all I want is for him to go home."

Natalie's jaw works as she processes my words, arms now folded so tightly over herself, I can see the indents her fingers are making on the opposite biceps. After several long moments, she blinks, huffing out a defeated breath.

"I don't even know what to do with this." She gestures with her perfectly manicured hand towards me. "With you." As if she's trying to clear her thoughts, she shakes her head. "Now I get to sit here and listen to you tell me that I was just, what? A means to an end?"

"You don't have to do anything," I admit, curling my knees into my chest and wrapping my arms around them. The pressure feels good—like it's keeping my insides from spilling out onto the floor. "As long as Luis can leave safely, you can ask me anything you want or nothing at all."

Biting the inside of my cheek, I force myself to meet her eyes again. "I'm not asking for understanding or forgiveness. I just need you to believe this was all my own doing. Luis only got involved to help me hide from my handler." I shift slightly, my shoulders pressing harder against the cold wall behind me. "You're a good and fair person. I know you'll keep your word."

Her eyes flick over my face like she's searching for something, but whatever she's looking for, she doesn't find it. "I don't even know if I want to hear what you have to say," she admits. "Because it's not going to change the fact that none of it was real, is it?"

Still, she reaches behind her for one of the chairs, sliding it closer to the mattress and sitting. Davey, taking her cue, drags the two remaining chairs towards Silas and mimics her actions. I don't even bother looking at Silas—his sister's glare is more than enough hatred for me to handle right now.

"But I'm here," she says flatly. "So talk."

Chapter 13

Silas

I've lasted in this room longer than I expected. Seeing Elena cleaned up had eased some of the lingering guilt, but it did nothing to cool the fury burning through me since my visit to Luis's holding room.

Cillian really did a number on him. Luis was still tied to a chair—silly me for forgetting to instruct the team to make him more comfortable. It must have slipped my mind.

His face was a mess of deep purple bruises, his arms marked with nicks and gashes. There was even a raw indentation around his pinky and thumb where Cillian had threatened to sever them with an industrial-grade crimper. Still, the bastard hadn't lost all hope. There was fight left in his eyes when I walked in.

His first mistake was demanding to know where Elena was. As if he had a right. As if anyone but *me* had a right.

The way he cares for her was written all over his stupid, battered face, and he still had the nerve to deny any relationship between them. I only started to believe it when I asked if it was unrequited love. His glare told me everything.

The twisted satisfaction I felt from that was something I wasn't ready to unpack.

I only visited to inform him of the deal Elena struck with Davey and that I'd return after she and Natalie spoke to discuss the conditions of his release. The entire interaction was forgettable. Except for his parting words.

"You're a sick fuck, you know that?" Luis spat, lunging forward as far as the ropes allowed, dried blood splitting on his skin. "If you're in here pressing me, you haven't even asked her. She tore herself to pieces trying to protect you and your sister."

With a bitter laugh, he looked me dead in the eyes. "You don't deserve El. You never have. I hope to God she sees that now that you've done this to her."

I blink, forcing Luis's words from my mind, but they linger like a splinter beneath the skin.

El.

The way he said the nickname grates on me. It was so casual. Intimate.

I should've told Cillian to slit his throat and be done with it. I still could, but there's more work to be done, and whether I like it or not, I need him. So he'll be fed, given medical attention, and kept in one piece. No matter how much I want to feel the life drain from his body.

I inhale slowly through my nose, relaxing my jaw.

Natalie is leaning back in her chair now, arms folded across her chest as she probes Elena with questions. She's keeping them about their friendship, which is what Davey and I expected. Still, I underestimated my sister. She's handling this better than I anticipated.

I should give her more credit. Nat's always been the most resilient out of all of us.

The few answers Elena gave about her childhood align with the information my team has found. It should be reassuring, but she's smart enough to know there's no hiding those details. What a convenient way to try to lull us into a false sense of security.

Without warning, Natalie's questions shift. "Why did you come to Chicago?" Her words are sharp, and I expect hesitation, but Elena doesn't flinch. "What were you looking for?"

The questions I was close to choking out of my ex just two days ago sit heavy between them, but Elena steadies her back against the wall, straightening her legs out in front of her.

Without thinking, I lean forward, elbows on my thighs. Beside me, Davey straightens up, crossing one ankle over the opposite knee. Our slight movement has Elena's eyes flicking toward us for only a second before landing back on my sister.

The way Elena speaks is as if she's rehearsed this story a hundred times in her head before saying it aloud. Maybe she has. She tells Natalie how she found her handler, Peter Lynch, when she was desperate in college. The jobs seemed harmless at first, and the money kept her afloat; however, before she knew it, she was trapped and blackmailed into compliance with no way out.

There's something she isn't saying. She pushes past certain details too quickly, fidgeting with her hands as if she's trying to prevent herself from spilling another truth. Before I can demand an explanation, she moves on.

"This past winter, I was told to breach your cloud," she says. "Your contract was vaguer than any other I'd been given. Peter gave me a list of terms and phrases to run searches with, but it never amounted to anything. Any file that might have had value was encrypted beyond my capabilities. When I exhausted all my resources, he sent me here."

Davey and I exchange a glance. She was already inside, digging, before I even knew her name. I exhale slowly, frustration settling deep in my chest.

How the hell did I not see this sooner?

Elena shakes her head with a pitiful chuckle. "I don't know why Peter didn't just bring someone else in when I couldn't get anywhere. He usually didn't waste time when something wasn't working, but he also loved to punish me. Sending me out on jobs was something he knew I struggled with, and sometimes he did it because he could."

"I knew who you were the moment we met," she continues, casting her eyes down at her lap. "That night when you saved me from that banker who wouldn't stop flirting with me... I saw an opportunity, and I took it."

The words settle like a stone in my stomach. I already assumed this; I just never really thought about what it would be like to hear her admit it.

"I sought you out after that to see what you knew." She runs her fingers through her caramel hair, drawing attention to the irritated skin at her wrists from the bindings. "But it got harder the more time I spent with you."

Elena doesn't let the quiet linger for long before clearing her throat. "I told myself it was just part of the job, but you made me feel normal, and the more time I spent with you, the harder it became to separate the two."

Her body language is open, but I know better than anyone how easily she can mold the truth into whatever shape suits her best.

And yet...

I shake the idiotic thought from my head.

"I started to question everything." Her voice takes on a hardened edge. "Then, I was sent to the Gilded Sear. I didn't even know why I was there other than to help Harrison with a job. It wasn't until the end of the date that I realized Peter staged it as a way to upset Silas. He seemed to realize we were attracted to one another."

I've already made peace with the fact that what I saw that night was staged. What doesn't settle well is how she describes it.

Attracted to one another. As if it were that simple.

I suppose for her, it was. She's the one who orchestrated it, after all. Played God with my life to make every chance meeting feel like fate. Like something bigger than us kept pulling her back into my path.

And Elena played the part to perfection. Gave me what I didn't realize I wanted until I was drowning in it. She pulled me in so fast and deep, I couldn't imagine a version of my life where she wasn't orbiting somewhere inside it. Two planets destined to collide.

She wanted me to feel that way. She *designed* it.

"I threatened to kill Harrison and Peter for the way they used me," she admits. "I knew I'd be punished for it eventually, and that's why I was mugged. Everything I told you about what happened in that alley was true. I have no idea who that man was, but he was sent there to hurt me and put me in my place."

Elena shakes her head in frustration. "At first, I thought they wanted to use you to punish me, but I learned later that was only part of it. Peter hoped I'd turn to you all for help and force us even closer. If I looked like someone who needed it, you would step in. And I... I accidentally played right into it."

Davey stiffens at this news just as I do.

The past two months, we've assumed that Elena's "attack" was staged. But if she's telling the truth, Peter might still be watching Natalie. Waiting.

Elena keeps going. "After that and all that you did for me, I realized I needed to find whatever was on those servers to have leverage against him. I wasn't convinced he would leave you alone with how angry he was at me."

Before I can even look at him, Davey is on his phone, shooting off what I assume is a message to Cillian and the rest of the team.

"I didn't think anyone would believe me if I told the truth." Elena almost shrugs in defeat. "I understand why, but I had to do *something*. That's when Luis started to help me."

My teeth grind so hard, I'm surprised a molar doesn't crack.

She looks up at Natalie, guilt weighing on every inch of her expression. "And then, I was trying to find any excuse to stay longer. I lied to myself more than once about it, but that dinner with your father is when I knew it was time to go. Before I caused more damage than I already had."

I inhale sharply.

Elena turns toward the sound. Her brown eyes glisten, full lips trembling as the tip of her nose reddens the way it does when she's upset. Despite everything, the instinct to reach for her still crawls its way to the surface.

I beat it down.

It doesn't matter if my ribcage feels like it's caving inward, crushing my lungs, my esophagus, my heart.

It doesn't matter.

"Leaving was the hardest decision I've ever made." She speaks with such conviction and longing that it almost pulls me under. Then, as if she can't stand the reminder of what happened, she drops her gaze to break the spell. "But I knew that in order to keep Natalie safe, I had to."

The tears she just barely held back while looking at me finally fall, darkening the fabric of her sweatshirt, one by one.

"All I wanted was to disappear so you could all move on with your lives. After everything I've done..." Her voice cracks. "I deserve everything that happened to me. How I felt after and still feel. And you all deserve to be free of me."

Free of her.

Like I haven't been trapped in this purgatory for two months—chasing shadows, unable to last ten fucking minutes without a thought that contradicted the last. Missing her. Loathing her. Clinging to the memories I also wanted to let die. Wishing we'd never met. Mourning her. Wanting to burn her at the fucking stake.

And now she's here, talking about choices and handlers and reasons that don't change the facts. She chose to betray us and leave.

Something sharp lodges itself in my chest and twists. It leaks under my skin, and the pressure builds with it. Tightening up through my shoulders and down my spine. I stare at the woman who caused it, trying to keep my breathing steady, but it's slipping.

Her tears don't help. And the ones Natalie starts to shed don't either.

All I can see is her face that night, crumpling when I pleaded for her to stay. Her voice, trembling as she promised me she wouldn't leave, even though I *knew* she was lying. I just thought I had more time to convince her and fix it.

Begging her wasn't enough. Confessing my stupid fucking love to her never even stood a chance. She was always going to do this. No matter what I said or did or offered, it was never going to change a damn thing.

My chair scrapes loudly against the floor as I stand, cutting off whatever Natalie was about to say. Elena's wide, tear-streaked eyes snap to mine. For a split second, she looks exactly like she did that night—lost, fragile, breaking.

It's almost enough to make me stop.

My feet carry me towards the door and I shove it open, rushing into the hallway. The sound of it slamming shut behind me barely registers over the roar in my ears.

CHAPTER 14

Davey

Whatever restraint Silas was clinging to snapped long before he actually stormed out the holding room. This bomb has been waiting to detonate. I just don't know if this is the peak or the lead-up to something worse.

Unsurprisingly, Silas has always been the one to hold his cards close to his chest. When I was getting to know him at work, I couldn't tell if he hated or respected the people around us, or even me. He takes his time assessing everyone around him. It's what makes him great at his job, but impossible to read. The closest I've seen him to losing control of his emotions have all involved Natalie.

The first time I saw what Silas was capable of was about a year into my relationship with her. An older man had been stalking her. He'd show up near her apartment and follow her after events. He even left semen-covered underwear at her door once. The police were dragging their feet, which floored me given who she is, and Natalie didn't want to "bother" Silas with it. But I was fed up, so I told him, hoping at the very least he had some connections at her local precinct to actually *do* something about it.

I'll never forget the way he stilled. The energy emanating from him was a complete juxtaposition to his quiet response. The silent rage matched what I felt in my own chest, beat for beat. We didn't have to ask each other any questions. There wasn't a single doubt about what needed to happen.

That's when I learned about the extent of his team and how he handles threats to his family. Since then, I've been part of that process. We've dealt with more incidents than I care to count. Some still keep me up at night. It's something I've done with a mix of emotions. Mostly pride, because it's always been about keeping Natalie safe.

However, the person I've just gotten out of my seat to follow now isn't that same man. He's been unraveling piece by piece since June, and now there's nowhere left for him to tuck those emotions away into.

Cillian is leaning against the wall directly next to me when I open the door, his eyes tracking Silas further down the hallway. "What's going—"

With barely a glance at Cillian, I nod toward the holding room. Without hesitation, he listens, slipping through the door and shutting it behind himself, leaving me and my best friend alone. I jog to catch up with him before he reaches the elevator panel.

"Silas."

He ignores me. So I grab his arm and pull. Hard.

As he whirls around, there's more than just hatred swimming in his eyes. His chest heaves.

"Breathe," I say, my grip tightening slightly. "You hear me? Breathe through it."

His glare sharpens in an instant. "Don't tell me to fucking *breathe*, Davey."

I don't flinch. "Losing your shit right now doesn't help anyone. Least of all you."

The words hit their mark. He yanks his arm out of my grasp and starts pacing. His shoes echo against the floor, each step heavier than the last.

"What the fuck am I supposed to do?" His voice is raw. "Pretend I didn't just sit in that room and hear her justify ripping my goddamn heart out?"

I exhale, crossing my arms over my chest. "I don't think she was justifying it," I say, choosing my words carefully. "She was explaining why she did it."

Silas stares at me like I've just sprouted an additional head. His lips part slightly before the frustration ignites.

"You spent months telling me not to trust her," he seethes. "Now you're trying to see her side of things?"

The irony isn't lost on me. I knew Elena was going to be a problem from the first time she and Silas shook hands. It took him a few weeks, but once his obsession took hold, it was fast and intense. So much so that it surprised me. I'd barely seen Silas show interest in a woman for more than a handful of dates, let alone chase one who wanted nothing to do with him. And yet, she was always conveniently around.

It set off every warning bell in my head.

For months, it put me on edge every time she was in the room. I watched her closer than anyone else, thinking it was about power or money, but now I know it wasn't. At least, not for her personally. It was about survival. That doesn't erase what she did or excuse the wreckage she left behind, but it makes me more willing to listen.

"I'm not in the business of torturing or killing anyone so trapped that making enemies of *us* felt like their best option." I pause, letting my words settle. "I'm not saying she doesn't deserve consequences, but I'm not making any rash decisions, and neither should you. Give me more time to sort this out."

I expect him to bite back with something vicious, but he only exhales, slow and harsh, tension still rippling under his skin. Then, he turns and moves toward the elevator at the end of the hall, his fingers already reaching for the panel. Over his shoulder, he snipes, "Keep asking her questions."

"Where are you going?" I demand.

He doesn't look back. "Anywhere but this fucking dungeon."

Pressing his thumb against the biometric scanner, he waits for the soft beep to confirm the match before the screen prompts him for his code. He enters it without hesitation, and the doors slide open with a muted hiss. He steps inside before pressing the button for his office floor. Another biometric scan. Another beep. Then the doors close, and he's gone.

That went about as well as expected.

Turning on my heel, I heed his instructions and head back to the holding room door, pausing for only a moment to let out a long, deep breath before opening it.

Cillian is leaning against the wall directly to the left of the threshold, arms crossed, listening. He barely acknowledges me, eyes focused on Elena and Natalie as he teases out something in his mind that I clearly missed.

My body tenses as I take in my wife's expression.

She's more upset now than when I left. Her eyes are glossy with fresh tears. Their tracks stain her high cheekbones and gather beneath her chin. The physical ache that envelops me seeing her like this is so violent and fast that it steals my breath, but I shove the fear aside.

Silas is already acting irrationally enough for both of us.

Natalie clears her throat and looks back at Elena, nodding toward me. "Tell Davey what you just told me," she says. Her voice is stronger than I expected. "About Drew."

The girl who was murdered.

Elena shifts, adjusting her posture against the wall, her expression unreadable. Then, finally, she speaks, "Drew was my best friend. I met her in my freshman year of college. She was the type of person who would drop everything to help someone." She pauses, staring at the floor like she's stuck in some memory. "She even moved into my shitty studio apartment just so I could afford rent and stay in school. She didn't have to. She just... did."

She exhales before forcing out the next words. "I know you've seen the news articles, and you're smart enough to know she wasn't killed in an attempted robbery. Peter killed her."

The muscles in my jaw tighten.

"She found out about the work I was doing and confronted me. Said she had to report me because it was the right thing to do." Her voice wavers slightly. "I tried to talk to her out of it, but she made up her mind."

Elena chews the inside of her cheek so hard that it creates a visible indent. "I panicked and told Peter. I thought maybe they'd bribe her to stay quiet." Her bottom lip quivers. "They killed her as punishment for my carelessness. And Peter made sure I knew that I'd be next if I ever stepped out of line again."

Every emotion that passes across her face is raw and fast.

"I tried to leave after that," she confesses. "But he wouldn't let me, and I was too much of a coward to fight back. Instead of doing the right thing and turning myself in, I let Peter blackmail me."

Though she attempts to swallow it, a gut-wrenching sob breaks free from her throat. Elena covers her face with her hands, curling into herself on the thin mattress.

Natalie doesn't even think twice. She moves from her chair to sit beside Elena, wrapping an arm around her shoulders and tucking Elena's head under her chin.

I want to protest and remind her that this woman is still a liar and a threat, but when my wife looks up at me, I know there's no fighting her on this.

She believes Elena, and though I don't want to admit it, I understand why she does.

There have been times in Natalie's life when she's felt like she didn't have a choice. When she's had to deal with the hand she was given, no matter how unfair it was. It's why she's always been so soft toward people and given them more grace than they deserve.

I don't know if I believe Elena yet, but there's no denying whatever Natalie wants. And right now, she wants me to figure out who the hell Peter Lynch is.

Cillian, reading the room, murmurs, "I'm on it," before opening the door and closing it behind himself without another word.

I stand there, watching my beautiful wife comfort the woman who, just months ago, set fire to multiple warehouses and tried to break into our company servers.

Every instinct in my body is screaming to turn away from this.

Against all better judgment, I step forward, lower myself into Natalie's abandoned chair, and wait as Elena's sobs quiet and her shoulders stop shaking beneath Natalie's embrace. Finally, she composes herself enough to lift her head and meet my eyes.

I motion to the camera in the corner of the ceiling. "You need to tell me every detail. Clearly. So the recording can hear it, and we can get to work."

Elena doesn't hesitate; she nods once, wipes at her face, and begins.

CHAPTER 15

Elena

It's been a week since waking up in that first holding room, and I have no illusions about leaving unless it's in a body bag. I've accepted that.

In those first few days, I told Davey and Cillian everything I could remember—every detail, every past job that might help them find Peter, even though he's notoriously impossible to track down. When I reached the end of my story, I was a shell of myself and had nothing left to offer.

So, why am I still alive?

The uncertainty is starting to make me feel a little insane.

Natalie is the only person who visits me consistently. She's come every day, usually with food from a restaurant we tried together last spring, and we have a meal on the mattress. It's a quiet reminder of the friendship I destroyed.

She also brings things to read. Usually, she stays for a few hours, just talking. It's surprisingly easy to fall back into conversation. We discuss the plots of the books she brings, the fundraisers she's been working on, the Pilates class she still attends. She still has plenty of questions about me and my life. I tell her everything because what's the point in keeping secrets anymore?

Throughout our conversations, it's hard not to notice that she speaks with more confidence now. There's a steadiness to her that wasn't always there before. It makes sense; she has the power here, but I don't mind.

I never thought I'd have the chance to speak to Natalie again, and I like that she doesn't hold back anymore.

Someone always accompanies her. More often than not, it's Davey, sitting off to the side in an uncomfortable folding chair, tapping away at his laptop. Sometimes he listens, cutting in with a sharp question about something I've confessed. Cillian does the same when it's his turn. And then there's Cora, who just sits in the corner, silent and unreadable. I haven't even seen any of the other men I saw slinking through Silas's home when I lived there. It has me wondering how many people actually know I'm here. Wherever *here* is.

Silas hasn't been back, but that doesn't surprise me. I was fighting a losing battle the moment I looked him in the eye and told him that leaving Chicago was the hardest decision I've ever made. There's too much anger and distrust for him to take anything I say at face value. Still, I wanted him to because he's stubborn enough to convince himself that everything between us was a lie, and he was a fool for ever feeling anything at all.

Maybe it's egotistical to think I meant enough to leave a scar like that, but he's the kind of man who would let anger do that to him. He'd let it build a wall so thick that he'd mistake it for strength.

The door locks turn. I glance up from my spot on the mattress, a romance novel propped against my bent knees. Within seconds, Natalie pops her head around the corner, two paper bags in hand, wearing a small smile.

I scoot closer to an edge, making room for her, and she falls into the routine we've settled into since this started. One bag—filled with magazines and books—goes next to the growing stack on the concrete. The other, she unceremoniously plops onto her lap after lowering herself to the mattress, ripping open the staples at the top to pull out whatever food she's brought today. I smell it before I see it. Rich, spiced, and steaming through the clear plastic lids. Indian.

In the background, Davey enters, but this time, Cillian follows behind, silently carrying a folding chair to the corner and a laptop tucked under one arm. Davey has a cardboard box in his grip.

Without a word, Davey walks toward me and sets the box directly next to my leg before standing straight. Eyebrows furrowed, I peek over the edge and see a laptop and a phone. My heartbeat picks up.

"What's this?"

Davey crosses his arms. "There are going to be stipulations on Luis's release."

I swallow. *Of course, there are.*

"Okay," I answer, bowing my head in a small nod. "What are they?"

He juts his chin toward the box. "You and Luis are going to help decrypt the files on our servers."

I knew this might be coming. Days ago, I was prepared to offer it myself when I thought my original proposition wouldn't hold. It doesn't stop the shame from curling low in my stomach.

Davey runs a hand through his auburn hair, letting out a tired breath. "Most of the encryptions aren't my work, and they're too complex for me to handle alone," he admits, his gaze meeting mine. "I've already started the process of finding contractors because my team is busy elsewhere, and it'll draw attention."

That small admission tells me more than I've heard in days. I already knew they hadn't decrypted the servers yet. Davey said as much when he first visited me, but now I know why. William has no idea that Davey and Silas are doing this.

Does he even know I'm here at all? Does he know what I did?

The questions swirl in my head, but there are more pressing matters to attend to. I don't want Luis here a second longer than he has to be, and we struggled enough on our own with their cloud files the last time. But we also know people who didn't.

I take a breath. "I might know two people who can help," I say.

Davey raises an eyebrow. "Who?"

For some reason, this feels like a death sentence, but Corey and Ben are Luis's friends. They'd help him just to ensure he gets out of here safely.

"The two men who helped us with your cloud," I admit, grateful I didn't omit that detail to Davey when he asked about the vulnerabilities I exploited. "They're skilled cryptographers. If I can explain the situation to them, they might help."

Davey tilts his head slightly, eyes narrowing. "You think they'll say yes?"

I shrug. "I think if they know it'll get Luis out of here, they will." I press my lips together for a brief second before exhaling slowly. "If you guys still have the phone that was in my bag when Cillian grabbed me, their numbers are in there."

Davey studies me for a moment longer, then nods. "Cill?" he calls out without turning.

"It's in the office at Silas's," Cillian answers instantly, his eyes still trained on his laptop screen.

Natalie has already peeled the lids off the food she brought, the smell filling the room. My stomach growls, and Davey takes that as his cue to leave, kissing his wife goodbye and telling me he'll be back in a few hours with the phone.

Before he reaches the door, the one question I've wanted to ask for days finally slips out. "Does this mean I can see Luis?"

Davey stops mid-stride, glancing over his shoulder at me. Even Natalie pauses, looking between us.

He mulls over my question for a moment before admitting, "I don't feel comfortable being the one to make that decision."

The appetite I thought I had is consumed by a cold weight settling in my stomach and my eyes drop to the mattress.

Because it's not his decision to make. It's Silas's.

"He's being treated the same as you," Natalie says quietly beside me. "I've been over to check on him. He's okay."

Gratitude surges in my chest. There's relief in knowing that if nothing else, she'll be the moral compass that ensures Luis gets back to Colorado.

I manage a nod and a smile. "Okay. Thank you."

Davey excuses himself, leaving the room. As soon as the door clicks shut, Natalie hands me a container of tikka masala. The rich spices curl around me like a memory.

After murmuring another thanks, I pick up my fork and force myself to take a bite. It's hard to enjoy it when my stomach is still in knots.

I hesitate for a moment before setting my fork down. "How's Silas?" The words are so quiet that they're almost nonexistent.

Natalie sighs. "I wish I knew," she admits, poking at her food. "I haven't seen much of him since June. He's been avoiding me."

Guilt settles in. I know I'm the reason he avoids her; every conversation circles back to me.

The quiet lingers between us before, softly, Natalie asks, "Did you have real feelings for him?" She looks at me then, eyes searching.

I could lie to make this easier, but it would be unfair to what I want Silas to know.

"I couldn't fake what I felt for him." My voice trembles just slightly at the admission. "I tried to keep my distance, especially when I realized how much I liked having you as a friend. Deep down, I think I knew that if I let myself do it, there'd truly be no going back."

The lump in my throat bobs as I swallow down the pain. "He wasn't supposed to keep showing up like that. I figured I was just a passing infatuation, but he kept trying. Then, after the alley, I gave in because I wanted to, even though I knew it'd hurt like hell at the end."

Natalie nods, absorbing my words without argument. She doesn't offer me sympathy. Doesn't offer me anything, really. And I knew she wouldn't.

I clear my throat, shifting the conversation. "Were you aware of how extensive Silas and Davey's extracurricular activities are?"

She snorts but still takes my question to heart, nodding her head side to side. "I always knew there was more happening, but I didn't ask questions," she says finally. "I didn't really want to know, but had to learn after you asked for me."

Shame claws at me again. I drop my gaze. "I'm sorry," I whisper.

Natalie surprises me by patting my arm. "I'm actually relieved." She smiles. "At least now I understand. This all makes more sense to me, and that made it worth it."

The unexpected kindness tugs at something deep in my ribs, but I push past it, taking another bite of food.

For a while, we eat in silence before Natalie speaks again. "Tell me about Luis."

I glance up at her, chewing slowly. "What do you want to know?"

"How did you meet?"

I tell her the basics—us working together, helping each other out when we could on other jobs, and becoming friends over time. She scans my face for any indication of the unasked question I know she wants an answer to.

"We've never been more than friends," I clarify, anyway. "Though there was one time in Colorado I thought maybe he'd try to cross that line," I pause, pushing my food around the take-out container with my fork, "but I ran from it."

"Why?"

"Because it felt wrong. And I was still mourning my life here."

Natalie studies me as she takes a bite of her lunch, weighing my words. "Do you think you'll ever want that with him?"

"No."

The answer comes out fast, instinctual. Even if I were allowed to leave here, a new relationship is the furthest thing from my mind.

Natalie nods, and I'm grateful she doesn't push to understand why. There's no point in dissecting the what-ifs or the maybes. Those are long gone, and that's okay.

Maybe that's the beauty in all of this. The worrying is over. For the first time ever, I know how this ends, and it's almost comforting that there's nothing left to run from. Only acceptance and whatever comes after.

CHAPTER 16

Silas

The warm Chicago air clings to my skin. Alice leans into my side, her frame light and soft against me. She's scrolling through her messages, her auburn hair catching the glow of the restaurant sign, and I force myself to focus on the curve of her smile, the faint scent of some type of flower.

She really is beautiful.

I tell myself that over and over, trying to make it stick.

Alice was one of the few distractions I let myself have when I was trying to fuck Elena out of my system. It didn't work, but Alice stuck around the longest. She's nice, easy to be around. We attended a few events together, and I let people think whatever they wanted, especially from that golf tournament. It didn't go anywhere, but when she called the other day, I found myself agreeing to dinner.

The city hums around us. Distant sirens, laughter from a nearby group, the shuffle of cars pulling out of the valet. I planned every detail of tonight. Dinner at my usual table. The car I sent for her. All of it has worked. I felt it in the way she touched my hand, let me rest my palm on her thigh, and leaned in when I spoke into her ear. It's all gone exactly how I wanted it to.

Meanwhile, at the edges of my mind, Elena lingers. Like she always does.

Alice glances up at me, her blue eyes sparkling. She's having a good time. More than that, really. She's been sweet and accommodating. It should be enough.

It *is* enough.

I shift my weight slightly, my hand tightening just a little at her waist.

This is what I need. Someone uncomplicated, pretty, has a great career, and looks at me the way Alice does with that big, genuine smile. Like, I could be her whole world if I wanted to be.

I just have to want it back.

Leaning down, I speak into her ear, voice low. "You ready to get out of here?"

Her grin widens, and for a second, I feel the faintest flicker of guilt because even though it makes my blood heat, it doesn't last for more than a moment before cooling again.

"Absolutely," Alice says, slipping her phone into her bag. She presses into me a little more, and I nod, signaling for the valet.

They pull up with my car, the headlights washing over us as I open the passenger door for Alice. She smiles as she slips into the seat like she belongs there. After getting her in the seat, I pull my phone out of my pocket while walking around to the driver's side.

The string of texts from Davey is exactly what I don't need. My eyes scan the messages, my pulse kicking up with each line.

Davey: They both agreed to decrypt the servers. Elena gave me the names of two others willing to help for Luis's sake, and they're in.

Davey: Natalie's refusing to leave the holding room without her. We've been at a stalemate for almost an hour.

Davey: She's demanding we bring Elena home, or she isn't leaving. I'm not leaving my wife in a fucking basement.

The last one comes twenty minutes after the third text.

Davey: We're taking her out through the private elevator. I'll cut the cameras and get her into the garage without anyone seeing. She'll stay at the townhome under constant supervision.

My grip on the phone tightens. I told him it was a bad idea to let her down there every day. This was inevitable for my sister, who is always so easy to forgive—but *Davey*? He was supposed to be the one person who saw this mess objectively.

I haven't been able to bring myself to go back into that room and listen to her lies. Instead, I've had Davey or Cillian debrief me at the end of each day with any new information they receive. I've been tempted to watch through the camera feed, but haven't been able to stomach it.

Maybe he really believes the bullshit she's been feeding them. Or maybe he's so whipped by Natalie that he let himself be convinced this is a good idea. Either way, it's a mistake.

I shove the phone back into my pocket. Every muscle in my body tenses as I round the front of the car, trying to shove Elena from my thoughts, but it's no use, because I won't be able to think of anything else until I handle this.

With a tight smile, I try to keep my tone light as I slide into my seat. "I'm so sorry, Alice. I need to make a quick stop at my sister's place. It won't take long, I promise."

She tilts her head slightly. "Oh, no problem. Is everything okay?"

"Yeah." The word comes out too fast. I inhale deeply and soften my tone. "Just something I need to speak with my brother-in-law about in person. It'll only take a few minutes."

Alice nods, but I barely register it. I throw the car into gear and pull away from the curb, my mind already miles away.

The entire drive is a haze. Alice makes small talk, her voice light and melodic, but every ounce of my attention is consumed by the fire raging in my chest. I keep replaying the texts in my head, each word stoking the flames.

Of course, Natalie would fall for it, but for Davey to give in and allow her to *move* Elena into their home?

My grip tightens on the wheel, knuckles white as I navigate city streets. The pulse in my ears drowns Alice out. I offer the occasional robotic hum of acknowledgment.

Elena was supposed to be out of sight and out of mind. Tucked away in that basement, where she couldn't keep poisoning everything. She's only been back here a week, and she's already undoing every carefully laid plan I've made.

I glance at Alice briefly at a red light. She's looking out the window, oblivious to the storm brewing next to her.

She deserves better than this—better than me right now.

Eventually, the car rolls to a stop in front of the townhome, and I put it in park, glancing over at Alice. She's been nothing but patient. I force myself to match her unbothered expression, leaning over to give her a soft kiss.

"I'll just be a few minutes," I murmur against her mouth. She nods before I step out of the car.

The iron gate groans faintly as I push it open and stride up the steps. I don't hesitate to pound on the door. It swings open almost too quickly, and Davey's standing there.

"Silas," he says cautiously. I push past him without waiting for an invitation.

"You and I will talk later," I bite out over my shoulder before turning toward their living room, where Natalie and Elena sit side by side on one of the light blue velvet couches. Natalie's expression is a mix of surprise and irritation, but it's Elena who holds my attention.

Her head jerks up the second I walk in, posture tightening like a coil. The mug in her hand stills. Those whiskey eyes that once used to meet mine with challenge now flit downward after barely holding my gaze for a heartbeat. It throws me for a second before the anger flares up again, drowning whatever the emotion was out.

Of course, she's afraid. She knows exactly what she's doing.

"What the hell is this?" I snap, the words slicing through the silence as I turn to Natalie. "You brought her here? Are you out of your mind?"

"Silas—" Natalie starts, standing halfway from the couch, but I cut her off.

"No," I growl, my gaze snapping back to the woman who keeps ruining everything.

Elena's eyes dart to Natalie's profile for a fraction of a second before returning to her lap, and that small, silent plea only makes my blood boil hotter.

"*You*," I seethe as I step toward her. She flinches. It tightens something in my chest, but the next words still come out. "How does it feel to still be manipulating everyone around you? Is it satisfying to be sitting here when you should still be tied to a goddamn chair?"

Her chest rises and falls with each quick breath. She doesn't even lift her head.

"Scar–*Elena*," I bark, stumbling over her name as I step closer. She stiffens and her lips part like she might finally say something, but nothing comes out.

The woman who used to throw my words back in my face with twice the force is nowhere to be found. Whoever this person is just sits there, small and still, bracing herself for a storm she can't stop.

"What, you've got nothing to say? No excuses? No smart-ass remarks?" I demand, my words growing even sharper.

Her silence is a wall, and I can't decide if she's hiding behind it or if she's just given up.

"Silas, stop." Natalie's voice cuts through my thoughts. She's standing fully now, moving between us to shield Elena.

I turn on her, the rage desperate for a new target. "She's lying to you, just like before. You're falling for it, Natalie—you know better!"

"No," Natalie snaps back. "She didn't ask for this. She told me it was a bad idea and you'd be livid. She hasn't stopped saying it since we left."

I look past her. Elena hasn't moved an inch.

"She didn't want to come here," Natalie continues, regaining my attention. "This was my decision. Mine. Not hers."

"She's playing you, Natalie." My voice is lower, but no less hard.

"Don't talk to me like I'm a child," Natalie fires back. "I've spent days in that basement talking to her about everything that happened. She's been honest, and when she could, she provided proof that Davey was able to confirm."

My sister takes half a step forward, pointing a finger at me. "You haven't even taken the time to do that. So don't tell me I've been manipulated when you haven't even done the bare minimum."

Elena still won't look at me. One part of me is glad after the destruction she's left in her wake, and the other part of me I hate can barely stand to watch her like this.

I start to turn back to Natalie, my mouth opening.

"Silas?"

I whip around to see Alice standing just outside the slightly ajar door, her expression a mix of concern and confusion. She crossed the threshold, her heels soft against the hardwood, passing Davey with a polite nod.

She moves to me without hesitation, her fingers slipping into mine as if it's the most natural thing in the world. "I could hear you shouting from the car," she says softly. "I wanted to make sure everything was okay."

I glance down at our joined hands. Her thumb is already tracing slow, soothing circles against my skin.

My gaze moves instinctively to Natalie—her arms crossed, expression unreadable—then past her, to the couch behind where Elena is still seated.

The usual color in her cheeks is gone, leaving her pale beneath the soft light. Her eyes are glassy and bright, though her lashes flutter to blink the sheen away. She looks at Alice's hand in mine, then Alice's face, and finally her lap again. My chest burns.

Elena stands so carefully that there's no sound. With hunched shoulders, she rounds the couch, slips through the cased opening, and takes all of the air in the room with her.

I swear I can feel the gravity shifting under my feet.

Alice waits a beat before speaking, her voice gentle and close. I hear her, but the words don't register. I can't look away from where Elena just was.

Natalie releases a long and tired exhale. "Silas, you need to go."

I nod. Or maybe I don't. My body is stuck, caught in the stillness Elena left behind.

CHAPTER 17

Elena

The intake vents on my laptop hum against the bare skin of my legs as I scroll through the shared notes Ben sent over. My new phone sits nearby on speaker, filling the silence with Corey and Ben's voices. We've been on this call for the better part of an hour, discussing logistics and how I can support them in the upcoming weeks.

Natalie's guest room is peaceful, with muted mauve walls and light streaming through the sheer curtains on the windows. It's late morning now, and though I'd like the feel of the late summer humidity on my skin, I don't want to waste the central air that my too-gracious host has running.

It's crazy enough that I'm being allowed to stay in this room at all. I'm still shocked that Silas didn't drag me out of her living room by my sweatshirt collar when Natalie brought me back here four nights ago.

I squeeze my eyes shut hard enough to see stars behind them, trying to wipe the memory of his disgust. I'm still not sure if it hurt more to experience his unfiltered hatred when I wasn't expecting it or to have to witness the woman I saw in the tabloids claim him and his anger so effortlessly.

With a small head shake, I refocus on Corey's words. "—and based on what we pulled from their cloud last time, I think it's worth revisiting the program we used. With some modifications, it could work." He pauses, likely scanning over notes on his screen. "From what Davey was able to send over, I'm seeing a lot of the same encryption patterns. They're just more layered and aggressive."

There's a beat before he adds, "On the bright side, even if Elena was able to get into that warehouse in June, I doubt she would've pulled anything meaningful in the small window she had. This is going to take some time to figure out."

I almost want to snort at his attempt at a silver lining, but manage to hold my bitterness and tongue. At this point, I'm just grateful that Corey and Ben are even on this call with us.

Davey did eventually return to the holding room with my phone, and neither man was particularly pleased to hear from me when I called. Even after learning that their supposedly "difficult-to-trace" bank account had failed, they weren't up for chatting until I explained the predicament Luis and I were in.

Corey stayed quiet before finally agreeing, muttering something about how Luis needs to be more picky about the company he keeps. Ben was more vocal about his frustrations and made it crystal clear that he'd help for Luis's sake and not mine, naturally.

Since then, Luis and I have been given laptops and phones, all loaded with every monitoring system imaginable, so Davey can track our activity every second of the day. Under any other circumstances, I'd probably get a kick out of imagining someone listening in on these calls or watching me run my mouse across the screen for hours on end.

"I'll be sure to bring that with me in case Davey decides to be stingy." I have no idea what Ben's talking about, but I hum in agreement anyway.

Luis has barely spoken. That's normal for him, especially on strategy calls like this. Still, I wish I could see his face, even for a second, to see what he might be thinking.

According to Natalie, he has been moved to an apartment that he'll share with Corey and Ben when they arrive tomorrow. Silas's team will be put on a rotation to monitor them around the clock. The three men will work on the server under the guise of being IT temps brought in to assist with the server audits. With Davey's team already being spread thin, it was surprisingly easy to get the "hires" approved.

"Alright, I have some packing to finish," Corey admits with a sigh. Ben is quick to mutter his agreement, and they both sign off quickly. I'm about to hang up when I realize Luis still hasn't.

The static hums on the line, and eventually, Luis breaks it, his voice soft and steady.

"Elena."

I close my eyes and exhale a breath I didn't realize I was holding. "Hi, Lu."

In just those few words, I can feel the distance between us. It's strange, considering how much we've been through together. When I couldn't handle Peter on my own, Luis just opened his door and let me in. I barely even put up a fight when he offered it; I convinced myself he wanted to help. And maybe that's true, but any decent person would have considered the consequences for him. I was so damn desperate that I threw any morals out the window for survival. Again. Just like I did by allowing Peter to control me after Drew.

I'm still the same piece of shit I've always been; just in a different font.

My eyes burn while I stare at his contact on the screen. "I didn't think you'd still be on." My voice is so brittle that the strain makes me wince.

"I figured you might stay," he replies simply. There's no anger or venom. And somehow, that makes it worse.

He's given me so much without receiving anything in return.

"I'm so sorry."

His forgiveness comes instantly, effortlessly. "You know better than to apologize to me. I always knew something like this was a possibility."

The guilt digs in deeper between my ribs and twists.

I push the laptop aside and curl my knees to my chest, wrapping my arms around them. There's so much I want to say, but none of it feels like enough. So instead, I just sit there, looking down at the phone in silence.

Luis releases a quiet breath. "How are you? Are you safe?"

My skin tingles with shame as I glance around the pristine guest room and its tasteful decor. The most beautiful space for the person who least deserves it.

"I'm fine." The words feel like a lie, even though they are technically true. "What about you?"

"Better than before," Luis replies, his tone lighter now. "I even have real food. So, thanks for that, though you really shouldn't have done it."

I huff out an incredulous laugh. "It was the bare minimum, and you know it."

He chuckles, the sound warm and familiar. "That's all I'm getting of your usual sass? You've gone soft, El."

My lip twitches in a hint of a smile before disappearing. "I think these past few months have taken all of it out of me."

Luis doesn't respond right away. The silence stretches just long enough to feel uncomfortable before he clears his throat. "So, does this all mean you and Silas have hashed things out?"

A bitter laugh escapes me before I can stop it, and I tilt my head back to blink away the fresh onslaught of tears.

"There's nothing to hash out," I say, my voice trembling. "He hates me, and his new girlfriend..." My lips press together as I try to steady my shaking. "She seems really lovely."

Luis's voice softens, sympathy woven into every syllable. "I'm sorry. That's—"

"Don't be sorry." The words are sharp but empty. "There's nothing to be sorry for. I did this to myself. And he deserves someone like that."

"Someone like what?" Frustration edges into his question. I shake my head, even though he can't see me.

"Someone good," I whisper. "But that doesn't matter, anyway. If the only thing I can do is love him from a distance and hope he's happy, then that's what I'll do."

I swallow hard, forcing the emotion down, but it's bubbling so deep inside me that if I stay here any longer, it'll all spill over. The last thing Luis needs is to coddle the person who put him in this position.

"I should let you go," I say on a breath, trying to end the call before the lump in my throat chokes me.

"Wait," Luis says, his tone soft but insistent. "Listen to me. You've made mistakes, but I know you. You're not the person he or even you think you are. Silas is a moron if he won't take his head out of his own ass and hear you out."

A watery laugh escapes me. "I don't agree," I say, voice cracking just slightly. "But thanks for saying that."

"Anytime," he says. "And for the record, you're wrong, but we'll come back to that later."

I take a slow breath, though the ache in my chest doesn't loosen, not really. There was never going to be a world where I ended up with everything I wanted. I sure as hell don't deserve it, either. Silas wants me dead, and I'll have to make peace with the fact that I'm never going to be able to fix what I've broken.

But I can do something.

I can help figure out what William's been hiding. If it's as bad as I think it is, I can make sure it never hurts anyone else. And if Peter really is still circling, then Silas and Davey won't let that stand with Natalie involved. They'll hunt him down, and they'll end it.

Maybe, if we're lucky, I'll finally get Drew the justice she's always deserved. If nothing else, I can hold onto that.

I clear my throat, forcing a hint of lightness into my voice even as everything inside me still feels splintered.

"You ready to end this shit with Peter once and for all?"

Luis doesn't hesitate. "Let's do it."

And for the first time in months, I feel the faintest flicker of hope.

CHAPTER 18

Silas

I smash my fingers against my phone and throw it across the desk, as far out of reach as possible. The recording I had been listening to cuts out mid-sentence, but I don't need to hear any more. The words are still echoing off every corner of my mind.

It must be late afternoon now, though I'm not sure how many hours have passed. The curtains in my study are drawn and the only light illuminating the room is my desk lamp, which casts long shadows across the walls. I don't remember the last time I looked away from my laptop other than to use the bathroom or make coffee.

I had only meant to listen to their phone call before eating dinner last night. I needed to hear for myself whether Elena and Luis were telling the truth about their relationship. It was their first conversation since being separated, and I wasn't stupid. If there was anything between them, it would come out after Ben and Corey hung up.

And then Luis so perfectly posed the question to her about us, as if there was anything left. Instantly, my jaw set, convinced that somehow they planned this exact dialogue, knowing I'd be listening in.

"If the only thing I can do is love him from a distance and hope he's happy, then that's what I'll do."

Her words have dug into me like a splinter I can't pull free, and all I need is some goddamn relief.

After listening to their phone call the whole way through, I found myself pulling up the security footage from her week in the basement and started from the beginning.

Elena began with her parents and childhood, and how college was her way to escape them. I'd heard snippets of those memories in the spring, but I never realized just how bad it had been. It might be the one story that wasn't a lie. She talked about getting into college, trying to survive, and her friend who was murdered for wanting to do the right thing when she found out how much Elena had lost her way.

I hadn't intended to watch the almost twenty hours of footage, but hearing the story from her instead of the broad strokes Davey and Cillian provided me made everything worse, because I could feel all that she lost before she ever had the chance to really hold onto it.

Though my bloodshot eyes would say otherwise, the time felt like it passed in seconds. Before I knew it, I was watching her on her last day in the holding room with Natalie, as she admitted that she tried to keep her distance from me, but my persistence had worn her down.

My skin still tingles at the memory of that high—those moments when she'd try to mask her surprise at whatever crass thing I said. The way her gaze would flick to my mouth before her cheeks flushed pink. How I'd prepare for five different reactions, just to stay one step ahead of her and keep some semblance of control between us.

Every narrowed look, every sarcastic jab, every involuntary shiver. I caught them all and I reveled in them, because they told me that she felt it too.

The pretty lie I told myself over and over was that if I had her once, I'd get her out of my system like all the others. This only felt different because she was trying to prove a point, and the chase was as maddening as it was addictive.

But Elena's denial only hardened the closer I got to breaking her. She used her friendship with Natalie as an excuse and insisted she didn't want to be just another woman I brought home. I figured she'd read the worst of the tabloids, which got louder after I started keeping parts of my life off-limits. She knew that I might lose interest the second she gave in. Everything she'd orchestrated could fall apart the moment I was done.

Maybe she knew how deep she'd buried her talons into me and how unlikely it was that I'd let her go.

My grip on the armrests of my chair is so tight that my joints ache. Despite everything she did, it's more obvious than ever that Elena whole-heartedly believed she had no other options. And for the first time in months, I don't know where to put all of this anger.

I've never known that kind of fear. Some decisions I made for myself, some I allowed to be made for me—whether out of loyalty or convenience—but they were still choices. I had resources and people who cared, whether I wanted them to or not.

What if she really did believe there was no way out and everything that happened was collateral damage in her trying to survive?

What if I was wrong?

The thought lodges in my chest, and my mind clings to the remnants of hatred that have been crumbling like drying sand since Alice took my hand in Natalie's living room. All I could see was the same misery in her eyes that I saw the night she left in June.

I saw Scarlett. The woman I had to grieve in pieces.

Mourning the living is its own version of hell, but mourning someone who didn't even exist at all? It's like slipping into a slow psychosis. Sometimes, it felt like I had made the entire thing up.

But in that holding room, buried beneath the cracks in her voice and the weight in her eyes, I caught glimpses of someone I recognized. A tilt of her head. A clipped breath before a sharp remark she instantly wanted to take back. The same strange mix of calculation and conviction I'd become so addicted to.

But this person was messier. Less sure of herself. She looked like someone who had been running on fear for so long that she didn't know how to stand still. Maybe that's why I feel so goddamn wrecked.

Because suddenly, it doesn't feel like Scarlett is completely gone.

The pressure in my chest pushes against my ribs so violently that I can only manage small, shallow breaths.

Before I even realize what I'm doing, I'm out of my chair, grabbing my keys, and heading to the garage. My phone vibrates in my pocket—likely Cillian asking where I've run off to in such a hurry from where he watches in the basement office, but I leave it be as I back out of the garage and through the already parting metal gate.

I don't think about where I'm going. My hands grip the wheel so tightly that it feels like my knuckles might split. The city streets blur around me, and my thoughts race faster than the car.

I shouldn't be doing this. I don't even know *why* I'm doing this.

The drive is too quick. I cut the engine, step out of the car, and head through their courtyard to the steps, barely noticing the late summer air pressing against my skin.

I knock once, twice, and after too many minutes, Natalie opens the door, glaring at me through the crack.

"Silas," she says, her tone cautious. "What are you doing here?"

I open my mouth, but the words get caught in my throat. My brain is too scrambled to give her more than the most basic words.

"I need to see her," I manage, almost desperate. "I'm not here to fight. I just... need to."

My sister studies me for a moment. Something in my expression must convince her because her shoulders slowly relax, and she steps aside, opening the door wider.

"She's in the guest bedroom," she says softly, gesturing toward the staircase.

I nod, brush past her to take the stairs two at a time, and storm down the hallway. My nerves vibrate between dread and hunger. I don't know what I'm going to say, or even what I want from her. It's not rational. None of this is.

Without thought, I push open the door and step into the room.

Elena is near the bed, tugging a shirt down over her torso. She's fresh from the shower with damp hair falling to her shoulders in waves, the smell of her coconut body wash wafts in my direction, reminding me of so many things, but mostly how it feels to press my lips to the hollow of her throat where the scent tends to linger the longest.

Her movements falter at my noisy arrival. In an instant, she braces for an attack; eyes hardening, hands crossed tightly over her chest. Even her knees are slightly bent, as if she might run toward the bathroom or maybe out of town, if given the chance.

The room is silent except for the faint hum of the central air. For the first time since she's been here, I allow myself to take her in.

Her oval face, the way her cheeks still flush under my scrutiny. She's strong, but leaner than when she left. It seems like she isn't working out as often or at all.

When the quiet becomes too much to bear, Elena clears her throat. "If you're looking for my morning updates, I sent them to Davey." Her tone reminds me of the time she gave me and one of my senior IT analysts an impromptu demonstration of several email security tools, though it's missing the same confidence. "I'll send over more by the end of the day."

I shake my head. "I'm not here for that."

Her brow furrows. "Okay," she says slowly. Tilting her head, she studies me, and for a second, I wonder what she sees. I don't have to wonder long because her gaze narrows. "If you're here to make me go back to that basement, at least tell Natalie first. No need to drag me out of here when I'll go willingly."

Heat spikes in my blood at that small taste of attitude.

There it is.

My mouth kicks up, and I take another step into the room, shutting the door quietly behind me before locking it.

"What are you doing?"

I don't bother to answer her question as I turn back around. Her eyes sharpen, and the ember I thought had been snuffed out glows faintly behind her cautious demeanor.

That spark is my undoing.

My feet carry me toward her without permission, and she retreats at equal speed until her back meets the wall. There's no missing the clench of her fists or the way her chest stutters when she realizes there's nowhere to run or hide.

There's barely time to process her gasp as I haul her to me by her waist. She steadies herself on my bicep; her still calloused fingers against my skin feel like a live wire.

I lean into her until my nose is buried in her hair, inhaling that warm, sweet-scented shampoo she still uses, just as one hand curls to the damp strands. It wraps around me like a velvet tether, squeezing until it burns.

Using my hold, I tilt her head toward me as I pull back. The hair framing her face is more copper than I remember, but maybe it's the way the afternoon light hits it.

The tips of her impossibly white teeth are visible in her open-mouthed shock, cheeks growing more crimson by the second. I drink in her weary eyes, streaked with golden hues that look like sunbursts.

Fuck. She's so beautiful.

And alive.

My thumb brushes the delicate skin of her neck, landing on the hammering pulse point just under her ear. A frantic rhythm that makes me want to hold harder just to remind myself that she's right here.

Elena swallows, her full lips closing and opening again as she searches for words, but nothing comes. Her stare is nothing short of terrified as she scans my face from top to bottom, looking for some clue or sign, but my thoughts are moving so quickly that I can't pin one down. She's overwhelmed every one of my senses except for taste.

My mouth waters at the thought.

I should stop; God knows I should. But only one thought cuts through the chaos still tearing through my head.

"I'm so fucking mad at you," I rasp, and then crash my mouth into hers.

CHAPTER 19

Silas

My insides detonate, the ache ripping through me before settling into a low hum that anchors itself in the center of my chest. Because *nothing* has ever felt so fucking right.

And it shouldn't.

Elena freezes beneath me. For a moment, there's nothing but the press of my mouth against hers and the rush of blood in my ears. I sink into the heat of her lips and the softness I've tried so hard to forget.

A breath shudders out of me—rough and unsteady—and that's what breaks her stupor. Her fingers curl to the front of my shirt as she fuses our chests together.

Her tongue slides across my bottom lip in a hot, slow swipe, and I'm done for. I fall headfirst into the feeling I've been hating myself for needing ever since she left.

I shift to press my weight into her, pinning Elena against the wall and giving myself better leverage. The perfect height for me to devour, and strong enough to take it. But her body goes rigid again. The hand that was just pulling me forward is suddenly flat against my chest, feebly pushing me back.

The sting of her sudden rejection barely registers. I cinch my arms tighter, mapping out the space below her ear with my mouth when hers stops responding, teeth scraping lower against her neck.

Every inch of her tastes the same; the lingering mint toothpaste in her mouth to her clean, salty skin. I should hate her for it, because it shouldn't be possible for something to hurt so deeply while still being the only thing that feels like home.

"Silas, we can't," Elena breathes, voice shaking. "We can't do this. You have a girlfriend."

My lips still against the curve of her throat, her coconut scent leaving me disoriented.

Girlfriend—right. Alice.

A bitter chuckle escapes me. I should let her believe it and use it as a shield to keep the remaining hatred sharp, but all my fight is gone.

My words are half surrender, half confession. "There's no one else, Elena."

The hand against my chest twitches. "That's not what it looked like the other day," she says.

When I'm sure she won't push me away, my lips return to their exploration, skating across her jaw until I'm looking down at her again.

"Alice is sweet," I admit, hands roaming upward, tracing the familiar lines along her ribs, up the curve of her breast. The way she arches into me, even as she fights it, makes something vicious twist in my gut. "Intelligent. Beautiful. And she hasn't tried to ruin my entire life."

Shame flickers across her face, followed by doubt as she starts to shrink into herself. She thinks this is a game or a punishment. Maybe it should be. I could walk away before I let myself feel anything beyond this.

Even though those words scream in my head, my hand curls to the nape of her neck to keep her in place and the truth bubbles up like acid in the back of my throat.

"But she isn't you."

Elena's eyes widen just a fraction. There's no missing the pain in my admission, and her mouth pulls downward at the corners.

It takes several moments for her hand to relax. Her fingertips trace the fabric of my shirt in a tender gesture that contrasts with the sudden tears she attempts to blink away.

Her throat bobs. "I want to say yes," she whispers, though she doesn't pull back, "but this is a bad idea."

The second the words leave her mouth, something caves in my chest. My lungs won't fill.

Then heat pours out of that hollow space. It drenches me—surges through every open inch of me—flooding my veins with a rage so blinding I can barely see straight.

A bad idea.

She must feel the way my body tenses, but her hands keep moving, soft and careful over my pec like she's trying to soothe a wound she didn't cause.

Her voice is so brittle that it breaks on the edges. "Nothing good will come of it," she murmurs. "We're both still hurting. I can't speak for you, but I—" her eyes cast down to my chest. "I can't go through this again. Not a second time."

Not

A

Second

Time?

My fingers twist further into her hair, yanking down to angle her face up. She grunts at the pressure, swallowing the rest of her cry as I lean in, towering over her. The tears in her eyes are thicker now, clinging to her lashes, but she doesn't look away.

Good. I want her to see this. To feel it.

Because how fucking dare she.

"*You* can't go through this a second time?" I seethe through gritted teeth. "Because of the things *you* did—the decisions *you* made—without letting me have a say?"

Did she mourn me the way I mourned her? Was she haunted by nightmares of me so vivid they bled into the morning? Did she learn to love me and hate me in the same breath? To wake up burning for someone she swore she'd never touch again?

My punishing hold tightens.

There's no coward's way out this time. If I'm suffering, she'll be shackled right alongside me.

"I'm going to fuck you exactly how I want," I growl, dark and final, "and you're going to take it—" I lean in to make sure she sees me, hears me, feels *everything* I'm saying, "because you deserve whatever I'm willing to give you."

A tremble ripples through her as the tears fall freely.

Time suspends between us.

I wait.

Her chest rises and falls in shallow bursts. Those honey eyes search my face. Maybe for a hint of softness or a way out. I don't offer either.

And still, I wait.

The fear in her eyes doesn't disappear so much as it bleeds from her in a slow leak. It's as if all the fight in her is being sucked out from the bottom of her feet. By the time her shoulders slump, her gaze locks onto mine, wide and glassy and unblinking, before nodding just once.

It's all I need.

Our mouths collide. There's a sharp bite of pain where her nails dig into my chest, and my whole body ignites once again.

We only part long enough to tear off our shirts, returning to each other like magnets before the fabric even hits the floor. I nearly groan at the way her bra drags against me, her nipples stiff beneath the thin lace. One practiced flick of my hand and the clasp gives, the bra slipping down her front and catching between us for a second before it's gone.

My hands clamp around her hips as I pivot, forcing her back toward the bed. Elena stumbles, knees hitting the edge before she falls onto the mattress.

She's breathing unevenly, eyes dragging down my body with the same hunger I feel clawing at my insides. My gaze rakes over the curves scorched into my memory and breasts that fit perfectly in my hands.

Why do I still have to feel this way looking at her?

My descent starts at her mouth when I finally close in, and she gives in greedily—tongue stroking mine with new desperation. I take and take and take, hands roaming up her stomach until I circle one of her nipples, already tight and ready between my fingers as I pinch.

She moans into the kiss, thrusting her chest into my touch. The response sends a wave of satisfaction tearing through me, vibrating through both of us as I pull harder, coaxing another gasp from her lips.

My hand drifts lower until it brushes the button of her jeans, and I break the kiss to follow my own movements like a starving dog. Suddenly, her fingers curl around mine with hesitation.

Frustration flares as I glance up at her, but the panic in her eyes stops me dead in my tracks.

Her grip loosens a little, but she doesn't let go. "There are scars," she whispers, small and unsure. "From the explosion. On my backside, mostly below my waist."

She said in the recordings that she'd spent weeks recovering at Jeff's place, but I was too angry to think much about what that could mean.

As if any of that could matter to me after everything else.

Without breaking eye contact, I continue my reach, slower this time, giving her a chance to pull away. She doesn't.

The button pops open with ease, and I lean forward to press a lingering kiss to her sternum. I take my time, mouthing down the front of her body, pausing at each breast, lavishing both with my tongue and soft sucks until her breath hitches and her fingers tangle in my hair to tug at the root. Her skin is silk under my lips, and I can't seem to pull away long enough to suck in a breath.

When I finally reach the waistband of her jeans, I drag the zipper down and peel the denim from her hips, tugging her panties down with them in one smooth pull. Only when they're both discarded on the floor do I see one scar that starts at her left hip. The uneven lines continue down and disappear where her backside meets the mattress.

With too much force, I'm flipping Elena over and tossing her further onto the bed. She lets out a startled yelp from her as she bounces into place, and I can see everything.

Most scars are faint now, healed with time, but some stretch across the curve of her ass and down the backs of her thighs. My jaw tightens as I picture Jeff's wife treating her in their home. Her body fevered, unable to move. Alone. Sick. In pain.

And I wasn't there.

It rips through me almost as viscerally as everything else.

My index finger traces every ridge, every curve, marred and perfect. Goosebumps rise under my touch, and Elena shivers.

Over the fullness of her ass, I palm her, watching the skin indent around my hand, and that's when I realize how hard I am. Aching, straining, fucking desperate. My other hand moves without thought, unfastening my jeans, freeing myself with a hissed breath as I stroke once just to keep from losing control too fast.

Elena lifts her hips slightly, pressing into my touch in a silent permission that nearly obliterates me.

I yank her up by the hips, dragging her into place. Knees wide, elbows down, ass high. And fuck me, the view steals the breath from my lungs.

I can barely see the scars anymore, not with the way lust clouds everything as she opens for me, exposing the pussy I've been dreaming of but haven't allowed myself to think about outside of the darkness of my bedroom. Pink, glistening, and so fucking perfect.

Why does she have to be so perfect?

I grip her thighs and fit my face between them. She's already trembling when I lean in and give her one, slow sweep of my tongue, from the base of her slit all the way to the top.

She exhales a shaky, wrecked whimper—her whole body shuddering like she wasn't ready for it. I groan.

I thought I'd built this up in my head. The grief and confusion gave me a warped sense of reality, but it's exactly how I remembered it.

And it's fucking delicious.

Without thought, I go in for another taste, working her with my tongue. Her thighs quiver around my shoulders, muscles taut like she's trying to hold herself together.

Every twitch, every choked little moan she lets slip just makes me harder. Her raspy mewls fuel me, especially when she tries not to rock against my face but fails, over and over again. She pushes just enough to bear herself down on my tongue and feed me more.

All summer I'd been chasing this high, convinced that I'd romanticized it, turned her into some perfect illusion, and that her body never responded to mine like this.

Now, there's no denying it. Not with the way she soaks my beard, how her body seizes every time I circle her clit just right. It's in the quiet, breathless way she whispers for me not to stop.

Goddamn it.

It was always this good.

Elena starts to unravel. Her voice turns into broken little begs as she pushes harder into my mouth. Just when I feel her about to tip over the edge, I pull back.

She groans, hips twitching to follow the friction. My chest hums.

I rise to full height, watching the way her back arches, a sheen of sweat highlighting every curve, every muscle coiled with need. I bow over her body, pressing the hard length of my cock into the dip of her spine, and she whimpers at the contact.

My hand slips between her thighs again, cupping her as she grinds into my drenched palm without shame, chasing anything I'll give her.

I lean down, lips grazing the shell of her ear, breath hot as I whisper, "Don't worry, Lena." I nip at the lobe. She gasps. "I'll give you exactly what you need."

The nickname slips out before I can stop it. She might be El to the rest of the world—to that fuckhead Luis—but Lena is *mine*.

I pull back just enough to move between her thighs, sliding my cock into the slick warmth between them, not entering but instead nestling in the delicious heat. My hand follows the swell of her ass until it finds one of the larger scars across her left cheek. I trace the edges with my fingertips, slow and reverent, even as something dark flares in me.

How the hell did I end up here?

I don't know what I'm doing. Not with her. Not with any of this. She's had me in a chokehold since the beginning, and I don't know how to get free.

I haven't moved in seconds. Maybe longer. That's when she turns her head, still propped on her elbows, one flushed cheek pressed into the sheet and the other visible to me. She glances back like she's about to say something, but my frustration bubbles over before she can.

I rear back and bring my hand down.

The sound cracks through the room. Her body jolts from the force of it, and a broken moan rips from her throat before the noise fades completely. Every vertebrae bows, pushing into my touch, chasing the sting. My body blazes at her reaction.

"Fuck," I rasp, smoothing my hand over the reddening flesh like I might soothe it and show mercy. Then I do it again.

Harder.

Elena buries her face in the mattress to muffle the sound, but I can still feel her hips jerk and thighs shake. I keep going, watching the bounce of her ass after each hit. My handprint becomes more defined as her skin starts to turn a subtle purple.

Between the strikes, she speaks—barely above a whisper. "Keep going," she breathes. "I can take it."

Goddamn her.

Each time my palm lands, I can feel her dripping down the length of my cock. It's obscene. Addictive. Infuriating. She's supposed to hate this. I'm not supposed to want to bury myself inside her right now.

She's taking it like it's a gift. Giving me softness when all I want is something to wrap my fury around. To break. To burn.

It shouldn't be like this.

Another wave of heat rolls straight through her and then me. She shudders, fingers twisting in the sheets. "Silas—"

I don't let her finish. My hand moves to the back of her neck, forcing down her upper body until she's pinned against the mattress. The sheer control of holding her exactly where I want her sends a violent shiver down my spine.

I lean over her. "You love this, don't you?" My lips run along her shoulder blade before I bite down, leaving indentations on her creamy skin. "I should make you beg for this," I hiss as I straighten, grab her hips, and push into her in one unrelenting stroke.

My mind blanks.

She's tight. *So* fucking tight. Wet, hot, and pulling me deeper. Welcoming me home.

It's salvation and ruin.

My pace starts slow, each thrust sending heat racing up my spine as I watch the way she takes me, swallowing me down like her body never forgot.

I can't look away.

She fits around me so fucking perfectly, and I don't understand it. Don't understand why she has to feel this good.

Why it has to be her.

It only takes a handful of pumps before she's pushing back into me, her ass meeting my hips with a small *smack*, matching me stroke for stroke. Each one sends a jolt straight to my balls—tightening, pulsing—and suddenly I'm hunting it down, needing to feel it again and again.

My hands tighten on her hips, fingers digging into muscle as I drive into her. Broken thoughts spilling out in gasps and growls. It doesn't matter. She doesn't hear me anyway. She's too far gone and so am I. All I can focus on is the way I press her into the mattress like I can fuse her to me as the pleasure coiling inside me becomes unbearable.

"Yes, yes, yes," she pants, voice muffled against the bed. "I'm... I'm so close."

I press my chest to her back to reach around her waist and between her legs. My fingers find her clit instantly, tracing the circles her body craves. The reaction is immediate. A sharp inhale, her muscles locking up like a bowstring pulled impossibly tight, and then she shatters.

Her back bends, body clenching so hard around me that my vision whites out. I ram into her, chasing the edge until I slam straight past it. Searing pleasure crashes over me. My hand fists in her hair, holding her as I ride it out, each stroke wringing more from me, making it last.

Only when my rocking subsides do I give her more of my weight, and she sinks down flat onto the bed, my sweat-slicked skin pressed fully against her back.

For a long moment, our ragged breaths are the only sound in the room. I'm not sure how long I stay like that, but eventually, when I can no longer feel her heart racing, I shift to slide out of her, smoothing a hand over the curve of her ass where the skin is slightly raised. And somehow, this one touch breaks the spell as the reality of what I just did crashes into me in violent waves.

I let myself touch her. Taste her. Take her. I let myself forget.

And I shouldn't have.

CHAPTER 20

Davey

I lean against Leslie's desk, watching Silas through the glass wall of his office. He's in the middle of a meeting with Jeremy, and it's not going well.

No surprise there.

Silas's assistant barely glances at me. She knows how these things go better than almost anyone. Amy, our Chief Human Resources Officer, walks by with a cup of coffee, raising it to me in a silent greeting as she trudges back toward her office.

"How long have they been in there?" I ask once Amy is out of earshot.

Leslie sighs and checks the time on her phone. "At least an hour."

Silas doesn't drag things out unless there's a problem. Judging by the way he leans back in his chair with his fingers steepled and eyebrows drawn, there is. Jeremy, on the other hand, has no subtlety whatsoever, throwing his hands around like a cartoon villain.

This all started the second he and William's advisor, Brenden, showed up at the satellite office, claiming William sent them to "help." Help with what? No idea. Jeremy isn't trained in any technical field. Brenden is just as useless. They've done nothing except get in the way.

Ben, Corey, Luis, and I have been working around the clock on the servers, but we have to drop everything we're doing when they stop by unannounced. Although I am confident they can't discern that what we're working on is far more extensive than a standard audit, it's putting the guys on edge. Between the hovering and endless questions, I had to ask Silas to step in and handle him.

By the looks of it, Silas seems closer to throwing his little brother out the window than coming to an understanding.

I cross my arms, shifting my weight to the edge of Leslie's desk so I'm not in her way any more than I need to be.

Despite Jeremy and Brenden's constant disruptions, we've made progress. Ben and Corey's skills are miles ahead of anyone I have in-house. If they're this good under these circumstances, what could they do long-term? I haven't asked about their livelihoods outside of this, but I'll admit I'm tempted. They could work remotely to keep dissecting our vulnerabilities.

I make a mental note to think about it later.

Luis, though—not a chance. Even if I wanted to make the offer, Silas would kill me in my sleep if I even suggested it.

"How the hell am I supposed to prove myself if you don't even give me a chance?" Jeremy bellows at Silas.

I wince.

Silas hasn't budged on his decision not to nominate Jeremy for COO, and honestly? That impresses me. I've always had to walk a fine line with William—he's my boss, my father-in-law, and a ruthless son of a bitch. Silas has always been quick to follow his lead, but he's really started pushing back in the last year or two.

Perhaps it's the security of having the board's written approval of the executive transition. Or he's finally sick of his father dictating his every decision. Whatever it is, it makes me happy to see him starting to carve his own path.

Still, I don't get William's sudden obsession with the position. For years, there was an unspoken agreement that there was no rush to replace Shaw.

Just the thought of that asshole makes my jaw clench, the pressure so sharp it pulses behind my eyes. Shaw should be rotting in a goddamn cell. Or a landfill. If it were up to me, he would be.

I take a breath and then another, tucking the rage into the neat little box I have to file it into within the corner of my mind to keep it under control.

William had decided to take his time to fill any vacant executive positions after Shaw left. He framed it as an opportunity to see our internal team step up to the challenge and allow current directors to grow into the roles before an eventual nomination.

So, why the sudden change of heart for a position that Jeremy would fail in, especially when we already have a Director of Operations who is the logical next choice?

"Looks like things are wrapping up," Leslie notes, which means Jeremy is about to storm out of Silas's office like a child who just got told no.

On cue, Jeremy yanks the glass door open and stomps down the hallway, muttering under his breath as he ignores both of us. Leslie doesn't even blink. She just shakes her head slightly before refocusing on her screen.

Silas remains seated at his desk, pinching the bridge of his nose beneath his glasses, chest rising and falling deeply while he tries to put his remaining patience back into place.

I give him a moment to collect himself before pushing myself off the desk and stepping inside. Silas doesn't even look up as I shut the door.

"Update?" he barks.

My fingers are unbuttoning the front of my suit jacket as I lower myself into Jeremy's still-warm, abandoned seat. "On Peter or the servers?"

His eyes narrow at the question. "Start with Peter."

Testier than usual.

"Nothing good." I lean back into the chair. "From what we understand, he started a legitimate business in the early 2000s as a PI. The details in the middle aren't clear, but it's slowly transformed into whatever it is now. Cillian is having a hard time getting anyone to talk."

Silas's jaw tightens. "Why?"

"Why do you think?" I ask, scoffing. "No one wants to be associated with what he does. He's hired for very specific and *illegal* purposes.

Most of the information we're hearing is second-hand through personal assistants or in-home help. He's been hired for almost everything you can imagine, and his network is vast."

"A fixer," Silas concludes, though his frustration doesn't wane.

I shrug. "To put it simply, sure."

"I'm assuming his clientele..."

"Our peers and people similar," I finish his thought. He nods.

"Do we know where he is?"

"We're working on that," I answer, and Silas releases a long, irritated breath.

"Okay. The servers," he says with a wave of his hand.

"The sandbox environment is holding," I start. "We've been running tests all week, mirroring the encryption structures we're seeing on the servers."

Silas waits for the part that actually matters.

"We haven't triggered any security alerts that would notify William yet. The obfuscation layers are holding, and as long as we keep operations isolated in the sandbox, we don't anticipate any immediate red flags. Ben and Corey think we'll be able to deploy soon and start working on decryption."

Silas nods again. "Do you have any idea how long it'll take once you deploy?"

"Depends on how deep it goes," I admit, biting the inside of my cheek. "If the encryption is static, a week or two. If there are adaptive layers—and I'm assuming there are—it could be a while."

Another deep, exhausted sigh escapes the man sitting across from me. He leans back in his desk chair, pressing into the side of his temple with several fingers. "Fantastic," he mutters.

He looks like shit. Not in a disheveled, I've-had-a-long-meeting way. More of a something-is-eating-me-alive way. His skin is paler than usual, exhaustion etched into his face. His usual perfectly trimmed beard is overgrown, and his suit is slightly wrinkled.

Silas Wells doesn't do unkempt.

I tip my head slightly. "You want to talk about it?"

"No."

I raise an eyebrow. "It's not normal for him to get under your skin like this."

He says nothing, shows nothing.

I shrug. "You two bicker all the time, and the COO demands aren't anything new." I watch him closely. "What's different this time?"

Silas levels me with a glare. "Fuck off, Davey."

"Sure," I say with a smirk. Silence settles over us before I can't stop myself from adding, "Natalie mentioned you stopped by the house the other day."

His jaw clenches. "Drop it."

I hum, dragging out the pause. "She said you spent a lot of time in the guest room."

The hand lying on the armrest flexes once. "I'm telling you." His voice is low, controlled. A warning. "Don't push it."

Of course, I already know why he showed up at my house. As if I needed Natalie to tell me after getting the security notification for movement at our front door. I followed him on our cameras as he went up the stairs, down the hallway, and through the door to the guest room without knocking. He stayed much longer than was necessary for a friendly conversation before leaving, wide-eyed, and not so much as a goodbye to my wife.

There's no chance in hell he'd tell me what happened, so I've been biding my time, but he's already unbearable. The shame and anger have been radiating off him in waves for two days straight, and there's no sign of it letting up.

"You could just let it go," I suggest. Silas's gaze snaps up, but his incredulous look doesn't deter me. "See how things unfold. Let nature take its course. Whatever the saying is."

My best friend blinks at me. "You can't be serious," he mutters.

I shrug.

It pains me to admit it, but Silas was happier in the spring. Subtly so. Carrying himself a little lighter, not spending every waking second in this damn building. Whether I wanted to acknowledge it then or not, it started when he began dating Elena.

As for Elena, knowing her story makes her choices easier to process and, if I'm being honest, I like her better for it. She was trying to survive. It doesn't make anything she did right, but it's preferable to some of the alternatives I was assuming when Scarlett's background check came back too clean.

Silas, though, is still wading through it. I barely tolerated Elena when she was Scarlett, so there was no love lost for me, but I'd have to be blind not to see how it crushed him.

My gut says he'd be better off if he let himself *have* this, even if only for now. Cillian and I agree: without Peter, Elena's main risk is her technical skills, and right now, she's being monitored like a prisoner on work release.

My instincts rarely steer me wrong, so I push.

"Holding onto all of that anger isn't doing you any favors," I respond, stretching my arm to check the time. "It just keeps you miserable by your own design."

A spark flares behind his eyes before he barks out a laugh.

"You've actually lost your mind," he says, disbelief dripping from every word. "If I didn't know any better, I'd say you were conspiring with her."

His accusation is filled with such disgust that I should probably take offense, but it's hard to when you've known someone for so long. Silas is many things: a great leader, a good brother, and a loyal friend. He'll absorb someone else's emotions and turn them into action, walk you through hell with logic and understanding. When it comes to himself, he's never been able to do the same.

"You think I stayed in that basement for two days interrogating her for my own health?" I ask. "Sure, it was for Wells, but it was also for *you*. I needed to know everything I could because if you were going to keep destroying yourself over this woman, I had to at least see if she was worth it."

Silas doesn't say anything, but I can see the tension roll through him.

"I understand her now," I go on. "Maybe too much, to be honest. She told me things I didn't even ask for that make a hell of a lot more sense now that I've had time to think about them. That's why I let Natalie move her in."

The muscle in his jaw flutters at the mention of the sore subject.

"I didn't like it at first either, but Nat was probably onto something. Elena's done everything right; answered every question without hesitation or attitude, kept her head down, shown remorse, and hasn't stepped a toe out of line yet."

I push off the desk, standing slowly. "I'm not saying I trust her, but I'm leaning toward believing her."

Silas looks at me like I've just punched a hole through his chest.

I could leave with just that. Maybe I should. But he always does better when I give him one last shove off the proverbial cliff and force him to figure out how the hell he's going to land.

My movements to button my suit jacket are intentionally slow. "There's no reason you can't let yourself be happy. For whatever reason, she makes you happy, so why torture yourself when you just have it? She'd let you."

I'm already turning toward the door. "It's okay to change your mind," I say over my shoulder and let him sit with it. Silas never lets something go once it gets under his skin.

And I just gave him *plenty* to think about.

CHAPTER 21

Elena

It's been five days since Silas stormed into the guest room and took me on the bed like it was the only thing keeping him alive. He didn't linger, and as much as I wanted to beg him to stay, I didn't have that right. So when he messily dressed and walked out with barely a goodbye, I had to just let him go.

Every minute since he closed that door feels like tearing open an old wound, exposing something raw and vulnerable. It almost hurts more than the first time.

But I suppose I got the best of what he could offer me, didn't I? Just one more chance to feel him, even if most of it was buried under all that rage.

The look on his face when he admitted that he still wanted me makes my teeth ache. So, I gave him what he demanded; partially for myself, but mostly because he was right. He deserved to take what he wanted, and he delivered.

I absorbed as much of his anger as I could, even if it broke something in me. Now I'm left to exist in the aftermath, doing everything I can to push it from my mind.

Most of my days have been consumed troubleshooting program issues with Ben, Corey, Luis, and Davey over the phone. The logic bombs have made the entire process delicate, but they're close to making it work.

Soon, we might finally have answers, though I'm not sure I'm ready for them.

In the spaces between, I've tried to fill them with distractions. I spend time with Natalie when she isn't charity event planning or committed to other obligations. She's been kind enough not to ask questions about the day Silas showed up and left without a word.

Hell, I've even been trying to get to know Cora, who must've drawn the short straw because she's stuck keeping an eye on me. She mostly stays in the kitchen, perched on one of the barstools, scrolling through her phone while ignoring me. She's here before I wake up and only leaves when Davey gets home at the end of the day and locks up the house like Fort Knox.

When I slip in for coffee, I talk her ear off. Anything to keep my mind from spiraling. Her responses are clipped, but sometimes, I catch the smallest hint of amusement when I ramble on about something. Entering the kitchen today is no different. Before I even see her, I'm picking up where I left off yesterday.

"Also, it drives me nuts when someone accuses you of 'spoiling' the plot of a movie that came out twenty years ago. If you have watched it yet—"

I expect Cora to be rolling her eyes at me, phone in one hand and coffee in the other. Instead, Silas is leaning against the counter near the coffee maker, arms and ankles crossed in that effortless way he always manages to carry himself.

His head jerks toward me, a dark curl slipping over the frames of his glasses, and my entire body locks up under his stare.

"Oh."

The word escapes before I can catch it, and my cheeks heat. Folding into the nearest corner feels preferable to this, but I force my hands behind my back, gripping them together so hard it hurts.

He's dressed for the office—dark blue suit, black tie, polished black shoes, and his signature subtle accessories. Immaculate and self-assured.

Those deep brown eyes sweep over me in a slow drag from my face to my toes and back again. The way he takes his time makes my skin prickle. His expression is blank. No appreciation. No disdain. Nothing.

There's the faintest lift of his brow in a silent invitation to speak again, but my thoughts scatter, leaving me standing there like an idiot, hyper-aware of every nerve ending.

"Is everything okay?" The words are the only ones I can manage.

"Yes." His gaze lingers on me for a beat too long before he continues, "I got an update on Peter during a lunch meeting nearby and figured it was a conversation worth having face-to-face."

Disappointment churns in my chest just beneath the apprehension. *Of course.*

Davey mentioned they started putting out feelers for Peter. They may not have known who he was before, but their networks are capable of unearthing information I never could.

Peter still occupies too much space in my mind, haunting my dreams, ensuring I rarely sleep soundly. The terror of his catching up to me has been my constant companion for months.

"Should I start a drumroll?" I attempt, the joke falling as flat as my voice.

A flicker of something curves the corner of Silas's mouth. It's brief, but it's there, and it sends my heart skittering.

"According to Davey's sources, Peter's in Southern California," he starts. "Apparently, he's been bragging that he killed one of his preferred contractors for stepping out of line." His gaze pins me in place. "Unless he's developed a habit of that, we're under the impression he's talking about you."

Though I've spent months living under the assumption that Peter thinks I'm dead, it doesn't stop the flood of relief from crashing over me to hear it confirmed. For the first time in over a decade, the ever-present fear eases just a fraction.

"He's not above killing anyone," I murmur, untangling my hands from behind my back. "But Luis would've heard if someone else went missing when we were in Alma."

Silas doesn't respond right away. His arms cross over his chest, studying my reaction. "That's good," he says finally, pushing off the counter. When he straightens to his full height, his sheer presence fills the room.

I take a step toward the refrigerator and open it. The idea of fumbling with the coffee maker under his scrutiny is unbearable, so I grab the iced tea off the top shelf. The pitcher hits the butcher block counter with a small *thud*.

Avoiding his eyes, I reach for a glass in the cabinet above me. "Yeah," I pour the tea with forced focus. "It buys us time for the servers, at least."

"True." Silas's reply is measured, but it feels like his thoughts are elsewhere.

My fingers tighten around the glass, the etched design pressing sharply into my skin. Looking at him will unravel the fragile composure I've managed to piece together.

"Do you need me to do anything?" I ask before taking a long sip of tea, if only to shut myself up.

"No," he answers. After a pause, he adds, "But I've been thinking, it might mean you could actually start over for real at the end of all of this."

The words stop me cold, and the glass finds its way back to the counter as I process the weight of his suggestion.

"Start over?" My eyes are fixed on the dark liquid instead of him.

"Yes," he continues, his voice steady. "No more running or hiding. A clean slate."

His gaze burns against my profile, like he's searching for the response I can't seem to form. Suddenly, this whole interaction makes complete sense. He's already created a plan. It's written all over his carefully neutral expression and the easy cadence of his voice.

This is how he sets me adrift so I'm no longer his burden.

There was never going to be another outcome. I should just be grateful he's thinking about letting me walk away, but it doesn't stop my organs from feeling like they are turning themselves inside out, twisting and knotting until I can't tell where the pain begins or ends.

My grip on the butcher block tightens, knuckles turning white. "Yeah," I agree in a whisper, "I guess you're right."

Just as I start to think the conversation is over, Silas's voice cuts through the air—sharp, almost angry.

"Is that all you have to say?"

The words hit me with such force that my back straightens. When I turn to face him, his indifferent expression hasn't changed.

For a second, I wonder if I imagined it.

"What?" The question comes out quieter than I intended.

Pain surges forward in his eyes. When he speaks again, it's a frustrated growl. "Do you even care?"

I swear I can feel the second the blood freezes in my veins.

He's a blur of motion, closing the distance between us in three quick strides. The force of his presence pushes the air from my lungs.

I instinctively step back, but there's nowhere to go. My spine hits the counter, the edge biting into my skin. Before I can blink, his hand is just under my jaw, firm enough to make my pulse jump.

"Do you even care?" he repeats. His pupils are blown wide, swallowing the brown of his irises.

My mind reels. I search his face for answers, for something—anything—that will help me make sense of his words, but I'm just as lost as when this conversation started.

"I..." My voice shakes, throat bobbing against his hold. "Of course I care."

His fingers don't tighten or loosen. They simply stay, as if daring me to give him something more. Hesitantly, I reach for him, brushing a hand under his jacket and against his abdomen through the fabric of his shirt in a featherlight touch.

A test. A question.

An attempt to understand.

Though I'm still not sure what he's looking for, I decide to be honest. "I'll do anything you want me to, Silas." The words spill out in a soft yet certain whisper. "You just need to tell me."

The emotion that flickers across his face shifts too fast for me to pin down and know which one might be the most prominent.

He doesn't know what he wants from me, either.

My free hand moves to his wrist, fingers brushing his skin before I gently pull his hand away from my throat. Without much resistance, he lets it fall to his side.

"What do you need?" I ask. "For me to come to you?"

A faint wash of pink suddenly appears on his cheeks, and I dip my head to maintain eye contact. His abdomen expands under my touch in a long, shaky breath before lifting his focus to me again. All of the same conflicting thoughts he hissed at me in the guest bedroom swirl through his eyes and press on me like a physical weight.

And suddenly, it clicks.

He wants me to choose him.

My vision spins.

How is that even possible?

I blink. There's no world where this makes any sense, but I can see it as clear as day. He's asking because some part of him wants to let me try one more time.

What made him change his mind? Was it something I did? Something someone said to him?

My heart pounds so furiously against my ribcage that my body shakes.

I could turn away right now and lick my wounds until they eventually heal or at least scab over enough for the pain to be tolerable. In a few weeks or months, I could be halfway across the world, starting over and figuring out who I am. It's the life I'd been fantasizing about since I was twenty-five. No one to answer to. No fear.

Or I could try to dissect Silas's emotions and stay with him, however long that might be. I'd spend my time trying to convince him of my feelings and show him how much of what we experienced before was real.

We'd argue. He wouldn't trust me. And I'd have to take every second of it. There would be no more pretty lies or careful wordplay. Only fractured, imperfect, ugly truths.

And at the end of all of it, he might decide that he still doesn't want me.

"Si," I breathe, the nickname soft and intimate in a way I never thought I'd be able to say again. His expression flickers, the faintest crack in the armor he's so carefully built to protect himself from me.

My hands glide up his chest. His skin is warm, but he stays rigid.

"It never even crossed my mind to try to win you back after everything," I murmur. My fingers keep moving, brushing lightly along his stubble, wishing my touch would ease some of the tension radiating from him the way it used to. "I don't deserve it. Or you."

The faint, familiar scent of cedar from his cologne fills my senses, wrapping around me, anchoring me in the only comfort I've known in years. He exhales sharply, shoulders loosening just a fraction beneath my touch.

Still, he doesn't speak. "If you'll let me, I'll choose you first this time." Our faces are mere inches apart as I continue, "You can decide if you want me back."

His hands twitch at his sides, caught between what he wants and the part of him that insists he shouldn't.

"I love you," I admit as I rise onto my toes. My hands slide into his nape, fingers threading through the soft curls as I say the words he once had the courage to tell me in the spring. "I'm here for as long as you'll have me."

My mouth presses to his in a promise and a plea. Every ounce of longing, every regret, every broken piece of me that still belongs to him is laid bare. Hesitancy coats every inch of his body. Still, I press closer, pulse hammering while I search for a response.

Only when my tongue swipes the seam of his lips do the floodgates open.

Hands find my sides in a snap, dragging my softness along the hard planes of his chest. His bruising grip on my hips, the scratch of his beard, and the small bump of his glasses pressing into my nose are almost painful in their familiarity.

Silas is the one person to quiet the static that hums beneath my skin. He is my opposite and equal, a force that both challenges and complements me. And now, with the weight of his body pressing into mine, I feel the balance returning. Like a gravity that was once off-kilter has been corrected.

When we break apart, our breaths mingle in the narrow space between us, heavy and uneven. My body still thrums with uncertainty, but for the first time since he dragged me back to Chicago, the hatred in Silas's eyes has dimmed to a faint flicker.

"And if you decide you don't want me..." My fingers trail lightly along the space where his neck meets his shoulder, the teasing edge in my voice tempered by the truth behind my words. "Killing me is still on the table."

For a moment, his expression softens. And then it happens.

He gives me that breathtaking, soul-shattering smile that he guards so carefully. The one I've only seen directed at Natalie, Davey, and Scarlett.

But now, it's directed at *me*.

"Let's go home." His voice is a low rumble as he leans his forehead against mine, our noses skimming gently. "Please."

Home.

My heart swells so tight it's hard to breathe, but I still manage to nod and softly echo his words. "Let's go home."

CHAPTER 22

Silas

E lena moves around Nat's guest room quietly, folding clothes, gathering the few belongings she's accumulated in the short time she's been here.

I lean against the doorframe, watching as she tucks a shirt into her bag. There's stiffness in her shoulders, and the way her hands move just a little too fast tells me she might be as unsure about this as I am.

Pulling out my phone, I type a quick text to my sister. At the very least, she deserves an update after I demanded she and Cora leave the house only five minutes before I showed up on her front step.

Me: I'm taking Elena with me.

The reply comes almost immediately.

Natalie: You don't say?

A second later, another message.

Natalie: I'm happy for you.

I don't answer. Mostly because I still don't know what the hell I'm doing.

When we make it outside, Elena is wearing a baseball cap and sunglasses, her head tilted down to keep her face hidden. It's probably unnecessary, but neither of us wants to take chances.

Only once we pull onto the road and are protected behind my tinted windows does the tension seem to ease. Being in the car with her relaxes me in a way I didn't expect.

My hand finds her thigh, right where it used to rest, simply because she's next to me in a way I never let myself consider again.

Her fingers tracing the outlines of the veins on the back of my hand with delicate, deliberate strokes. Each time the tip of her nail becomes the only point of contact, my grip tightens reflexively, pressing into the soft flesh.

For the first time in too long, my mind is finally—*finally*—quiet.

When we pull into the garage, I kill the engine. The only reprieve I feel for my sanity is that Cillian agreed with Davey's assessment of the threat Elena poses, but it doesn't stop the paranoia from creeping in.

What if I'm inviting a fox back into the henhouse?

I move efficiently to grab her two bags from the back seat before opening her door. She looks up at me, searching my face like she's trying to gauge what I'm thinking, but I just nod, a silent cue to follow me inside.

Walking her back into this house through the side entrance feels like stepping through some distorted version of reality, like no time and a century have passed all at once.

The hallway grows darker as I shut and lock the door, blocking out the garage's motion lights. I quietly disarm and rearm my security system on the panel. The routine has always been second nature, but now, the air around me crackles.

Just as I turn, I'm being pressed backward. The bags slip from my hands, landing on the hardwood as presses me into the wall. One hand slides over my shoulder while the other fists into the already-wrinkled fabric of my shirt through my unbuttoned suit jacket. Then, she stands on her toes and presses her lips to mine.

She's more tentative at first, her tongue moving achingly slow, teasing and retreating. It makes my blood burn and pulse pound against my ribs.

If nothing else exists between us, this still feels real. Tangible. The one last shred of hope I've been holding onto because there's just no way she can fake this. The goosebumps on her arms aren't self-made; her panting is too uneven for it to be forced.

Right?

Her hand roams my chest, stroking the sensitive spots along my sides, each movement against me growing more confident. Even through my shirt, I feel everything. The light drag of her fingertips, the way she's touching me with purpose. Elena pulls back just enough to expose the flush of her cheeks and the lust brimming in her eyes when she opens them, half-hooded and relaxed.

This is different. It has to be.

Gripping her firmly at the waist, I start walking her backward, guiding us toward the kitchen doorway. She allows me to move her, and that's when I cup her face between my hands, tilting her head to give myself better access to that beautiful, swollen mouth.

"I'm taking you in the kitchen," I murmur the demand.

I'm going to fuck her on that counter. Not just because I need to be inside her again—though God knows I do—but because I need to erase what happened the last time we stood in that space. I won't let her goodbye be the memory that lingers in that room, even if this is all a colossal mistake.

Her eyes gloss over, and she nods in understanding. Her hands move between us, fingers curling around the leather of my belt, tugging just slightly, voice barely above a whisper.

"Please."

My mouth is on hers again as we step through the threshold, keeping her where I want her. She moves with me, and for a second, it feels like nothing exists outside of this.

But all too quickly, a prickle of awareness creeps up my spine. The smell of hazelnut, a slight *clink* of ceramic, the muted movements of someone trying to be invisible.

My body tenses as I pull back, eyes landing on Kendall standing at the island, who just finished serving coffee from the glass pot, but not just to anyone.

To my father.

William sits on a stool, poised as ever, his mug halfway to his lips, eyebrows raised in that way that makes it impossible to tell if he's amused or irritated. Kendall's eyes, meanwhile, dart from the back of Elena's head to me and back again, like she's regretting every life choice that led her to this moment.

My hands still on Elena's face, just as panic flickers across her expression. She swivels her head enough to see both of them, and the second they all recognize one another, their expressions change.

Kendall's features soften as she presses a hand over her heart. "Scarlett. It's so good to see you."

I feel Elena slip seamlessly back into that persona, her posture adjusting, as she offers Kendall an embarrassed smile, cheeks stained a dark shade of pink. "Hi, Kendall. It's good to see you, too."

My hands drop just as my palms begin to sweat. Hers also fall.

I shift my gaze to my father, taking him in fully now. At first glance, he's composed—his expression carefully arranged. But I know him. It's in the sharpness of his jaw, the way his fingers flex subtly around the handle of his mug.

He's furious.

Letting out a slow breath through his nose, William lifts his mug slightly in a silent toast, his smile thin. "Scarlett," he says, voice laced with false warmth. "What a lovely surprise."

Elena nods and greets him with a simple, "William." Her tone is polite but curt as they take one another in. "I'm in town for a few weeks," she offers, giving him nothing more than necessary.

I don't miss the way his fingers flex around his mug and how his eyes jump to me briefly.

Kendall grins, giving Elena another approving look. "Well, I hope I'll be seeing more of you then."

Elena responds with a strained, closed-mouth smile. Thank God her bags are still in the hallway, tucked out of sight.

William hums, lifting his coffee in that effortlessly dismissive way of his. "Wonderful." Then, just as smoothly, he turns his attention to me. "Alice should meet Scarlett," he muses. "You two have been spending quite a bit of time together, have you not?"

Elena tenses before her hesitant smile transforms into something sharper, all teeth.

"We've met," she responds, the half-truth slipping out a little too easily. "She was lovely."

My father bristles, and I level him with a look. "Whatever you came here to discuss, we can talk in the den." Somehow, my voice stays even. "Or my study."

William doesn't respond right away, but eventually waves me off with a flick of his wrist, taking his coffee cup as he stands and turning for the door. He doesn't say another word or wait for me to follow.

Kendall exhales quietly and moves to the sink, rinsing out a dish like she hadn't just been standing in the middle of a silent war. Elena is still against me, and I know, without looking at her, that her mind is already working.

I lift her chin, holding her there for just a second. Though she softens under my touch, the corners of her eyes and mouth are pulled down. I take her lips against mine, but the moment has been doused.

When I pull back, I run my fingers along her jaw, trying to draw out the remaining apprehension in her stare. Without looking away from her, I say, "Kendall, could you make us something small to eat?"

The chef nods easily. "Of course." Then, she looks to Elena. "Anything in particular?"

Elena doesn't miss a beat. "Whatever's easiest."

Kendall gives her a smile before moving toward the fridge.

I press my mouth to Elena's forehead. "I'll be back in a few minutes," I say against her skin before pulling back.

With one last drag of my fingers along her side, I force myself to step back, then turn and head toward the den. As I walk down the hallway, my mind starts reeling.

I should have known he was in my house, uninvited, but there was no one here to tell me. Lloyd is in California. Paul and Steven are focused on the server audits. Cora will continue to stay at Natalie's now that we know Peter might be keeping tabs on her. Cillian has been handling some other tasks I need to straighten out ahead of the executive transition. Everyone has a role, and for once, no one is stationed at the house.

Then, there's the more pressing issue: my father has security access to my home.

I gave it to him a long time ago and didn't think much of it. That means the system wouldn't have flagged his entry as a breach. Just a log that someone let themselves in with a code. Cillian probably saw the entry and assumed it was me or Kendall.

I hadn't thought about it in years, but as I enter the den to find William sitting in *my* chair, I realize that needs to change.

With barely a glance in his direction, I walk to the window and pull back the sheer curtain just enough to see the street.

My father's black SUV idles in the pull-off at the front of my house, the tinted windows reflecting the afternoon sun. We came through the back street and straight into the garage, avoiding the front entrance entirely.

I had no intention of William finding out Elena was here. The fewer people who know, the better. I don't trust that Peter doesn't still have someone hanging around Chicago, and if the wrong person hears Scarlett Page is back in town, it won't take long for him to come sniffing.

I let the curtain drop and turn my attention back to my most immediate problem.

William sighs, setting his coffee mug down on the side table. "I came here to talk to you about your meeting with Jeremy yesterday," he says, his gaze sharpening. "But now, I see there are more pressing matters."

I drag a hand over my jaw. "I'm not discussing my dating life with you," I say flatly, leaning back against the window frame and crossing my arms. "But I'm happy to talk about how Jeremy and Brenden are disrupting the audits. Let's start there."

William doesn't so much as blink at the change in subject. "You're a fool to fall for this woman's schemes a second time." His voice is clipped.

The words don't hit like he thinks they should. I roll my shoulders, forcing the irritation down.

"Jeremy is still insisting on the nomination," I say instead. "Even though I've told him multiple times that it's not on the table." I tilt my head, watching him. "What's the point of making him promises you know I won't keep?"

Annoyance passes over William's face, but he doesn't take the bait. "You *do* seem to have a type, don't you?" He almost sounds amused. "Women who know how to get the kind of attention they want. You can't possibly think you're the only person she's played like this."

He leans forward slightly. "She was on a date with another man, kissing him in the middle of that restaurant, right before she landed in your bed. Then she ran off the second I questioned her motives." The way he shakes his head drips with disapproval. "You can dress it up however you want, but at the end of the day, a woman like that only has one goal."

This isn't the first time he's brought up that date. He tried to use it against her back in the spring after hearing about it from several acquaintances, slipping it into conversation when he wanted to convince me she was a gold digger.

Back when I thought I witnessed a real date between Elena and that asshole Harrison, I was furious. When I found out it was staged and I assumed she was a willing participant, I was murderous. But now, knowing someone forced themselves on her?

I exhale through my nose to tamp down the rage.

Straightening off the window frame, I uncross my arms. "Jeremy will not be allowed in the satellite office until the audit is complete." My tone is calm, final. "He has no authority to be there, is delaying Davey, and makes the temp workers uncomfortable. If he has any questions or concerns, he can come to me and I will facilitate them."

The moment I say it, the shift is immediate. My father, who had been playing his part well enough up until now, goes rigid.

I hit a nerve. *Good.*

The silence settles, and I watch him try to reconcile what I just said with how he can change it, but he can't. If any other board members catches wind of a non-employee trying to involve themselves in the company's operational authority, the consequences would be dire.

Almost as quickly as the realization sets in, he recalibrates. The fury in his expression fades, replaced by something that's somehow even more insidious—pity.

"So, this is how it's going to be?" he asks. Then, with a breath like the words pain him, "Your mother would be so disappointed in you about all of this."

My skin heats just as my blood turns to ice.

Caroline Wells was compassionate, endlessly so. Even when she had every excuse not to be. She could have handed my siblings and me off to nannies like so many women in her position do, but she raised us herself. She believed in kindness, in fairness, in taking care of the people you love.

She instilled that in all of us, but Natalie is the only one who carries it the way she always hoped we would. Me? I work for it. Relentlessly. I never wanted her to see me as anything less than a son she could be proud of. I still think about what she would want, what her advice would be—admittedly more than I've thought about my father's in recent years.

He knows that and highly I regard her, even in death.

The anger I've been holding back ignites, clawing at my throat, demanding to be unleashed. But I don't let it. Because if I do, I'll say things

148

I don't mean. Or worse, I'll say things I do. I'll admit truths I have no intention of giving him.

So I force it down and squeeze it into submission until it's nothing more than an irritating ember somewhere deep inside me, if only for a few minutes.

"You can leave." My voice is devoid of any emotion. "This conversation is over."

William studies me, his gaze measured, searching for a crack. After a long pause, he adjusts his cuffs like this was just another business meeting.

"Suit yourself."

Then he stands and leaves. I count the seconds until he's outside, his back visible through the window as he walks towards the SUV where his driver is already standing with the back door open. Only then do I let out an uneven exhale to cleanse myself of his words.

However, the anger and resentment stay.

CHAPTER 23

Elena

When it's finally time for bed, I hesitate, my fingers grazing the zipper of one bag I left beside the long dresser near the door.

I didn't ask Silas if I could stay in his room. It might be the only thing today I didn't get his permission for, but I couldn't go back to the guest room. Not after two months regretting every second I was away from him. If he wanted me elsewhere, he'd say so. I'd be crushed, but I'd listen.

Earlier in the afternoon, when Silas left me in the kitchen with Kendall to speak with his father, I excused myself, promising I'd be back downstairs shortly. Truthfully, I just needed a moment after seeing William so unexpectedly.

The encounter reminded me why I left in the spring. I was going to regardless, but William's loathing made it easier—a final, brutal confirmation I'd never be good enough. Like I didn't know that already.

Though William Wells's opinion means little to me, it still burns. When I allowed myself to dream of a future after Peter, I hoped to have a good relationship with my partner's parents, as I'd never had that with my own.

Not that Silas and I are a couple or have any idea what we're doing. All I know is that he asked me to come home with him, and there was no way I'd say no if he wanted me here.

That thought was running through my head when I stepped into his bedroom. The muted tones, crisp scent of his cologne, and the bed I'd slept in more times than I should have hit me all at once.

I hesitated before sitting on the edge of his side, letting my gaze drift over the room, taking it all in. It felt like I'd stepped into a memory, only for the details to shift under closer inspection. My fingers brushed over the soft bedding, and that's when I noticed a small slip of paper wedged between two books on the bedside table.

Curiosity got the better of me. I reached for it, pulling it free, only to feel my chest tighten the second I recognized the handwriting.

My note. The one I left behind the night I walked away.

I remember how quickly I wrote it up before I got on my final phone call with Luis in the bathroom, just wanting to get the pain over with. It's evident in the messy tails and smudges where my thoughts were moving faster than my hand.

My fingers traced along its worn edges, lost in thought, when I caught movement next to the open door. An apology was already forming, but the words died on my tongue when I looked up and saw that Silas wasn't looking at me or the note I was holding. He was looking at the bags I had brought upstairs with me and placed inside the door.

I braced myself, waiting for him to tell me whether or not I was welcome here. But he didn't. He just stood there, eyes darkening in a way that sent heat curling low in my stomach, silently confirming I made the right decision.

Even with all that intensity, Silas seemed distracted for the rest of the afternoon. I wondered if William got in his head the same way he once got in mine after that family dinner we left before it even began.

The only relief I have is in the moments I've been able to pull him back to reality, and his stare softens. That, at the very least, tells me that whatever William said to him might not be about me at all. Still, I don't feel like I have the right to ask.

With Silas getting dressed in the closet, uncertainty creeps in like a slow, unwelcome tide. This thing between us is fragile, and I feel like I'm one misstep away from shattering it.

As if sensing the spiral of my thoughts, Silas returns in a soft t-shirt and sweatpants, the fabric clinging to the lean, defined lines of his body. His coffee eyes find mine like he already knows what I'm thinking.

"Come on," he says, nodding toward the bathroom door. By the time I get the courage to follow him, he's already pulling open the solid-wood drawers of the vanity.

"Get changed, and I'll grab you some toiletries," he murmurs, glancing over his shoulder at me.

Swallowing the dryness in my throat, I nod. As I change, he unpacks a brand-new toothbrush and hairbrush, face wash, and lotion. My stomach twists as a quiet, intrusive question creeps in before I can stop it.

Who were these items meant for?

I press my lips together, forcing the thought away.

It's no one's fault but mine if someone else was here while I was gone.

The dull ache lingers as I pull my sleep shirt over my head and my shorts over my legs. By the time I finish, he's already brushing his teeth, standing beside the sink like this is something we've done together a hundred times before, but we haven't.

I used to get ready for bed across the hall, careful to never leave my things in this space. Making myself at home in a place I knew I couldn't stay felt like planting roots in sand. It would've given me a false sense of hope I couldn't afford to hold on to. Sharing space like this was too intimate. This is where you see each other at your most human, and I couldn't risk letting him see more than he already had.

Silas braces a hand on the marble countertop, his tired eyes meeting mine in the mirror. We both still, and then Silas smiles around his toothbrush, foam catching on the corner of his mouth. Heat creeps up my neck, and I avert my gaze.

I busy myself with the hairbrush he set out for me, running it through my hair even though it doesn't need it. He doesn't say anything about it, just keeps brushing his teeth, that knowing smile still lingering.

Once we're both finished, Silas moves through the bathroom and then bedroom, shutting off the lights one by one until only his bedside lamp remains. It casts everything in a soft, golden glow. I hesitate at the edge of the bed as the memory of my last night here hits me, instant and visceral.

My tears soaked into the pillow I'm about to rest my head on. Silas beside me, his arm draped over my waist, as if, even in sleep, he could keep me from slipping away. I watched him for hours, memorizing the contours of his face in the darkness, waiting for his grip to loosen so that I could leave.

I barely breathed as I grabbed my bag and vanished into the night.

"You okay?"

My head snaps up as Silas moves to his side of the bed, slipping off his glasses and folding them carefully before setting them on the nightstand. Something in the way he watches tells me he knows exactly where my mind just went.

Instead of answering, I follow his lead, slipping beneath the covers as he flicks off the lamp and plunges us into darkness. The crisp scent of freshly laundered sheets surrounds me and the familiar weight of the duvet settles over my body.

Still, I can't relax.

I stare at the ceiling, listening to his breathing. My body aches to move closer. All I do is curl my fingers into the sheets.

We never used to fall asleep wrapped up in each other. The most contact we'd have was Silas gently holding my forearm while I desperately tried to keep him at arm's length—literally and figuratively. It was futile, though. In the middle of the night, I'd often wake to find us tangled together, as if our bodies knew better.

Swallowing my anxiety, I roll onto my side to look at him. He's on his back, eyes closed, the arm closest to me tucked behind his head, exposing the strong curve where his shoulder meets his chest. His lips are slightly parted, his breathing even but not quite deep enough to be asleep.

Quit being a baby and just do it.

My movements are jerky, nerves getting the best of me as I close the space between us. The mattress dips under my weight, Silas stiffens, and I freeze. Doubt creeps in, whispering that I've overstepped, that I shouldn't have assumed I could just *be* here like this. For a split second, I consider retreating, but the louder voice in my mind tells me to forge ahead.

I settle my head against the curve of his shoulder and tilt my chin down so he can't see my embarrassment. Only when I press my palm flat against his chest does he finally exhale a long, slow breath that sounds like it reaches his bones.

A beat passes, then another. Slowly, his head dips, nose brushing through my hair. The warmth of his lips follows, lingering there. Fingers shift over mine, his palm covering the back of my hand, pressing it more firmly against his chest. The steady thrum beneath my touch makes my own heart hum in response, hot and relieved.

I shift, hooking my top leg over his hip, closing any space between us. His body adjusts to mine, molding me into the contours of his frame.

For a long time, I let myself feel the rise and fall of his chest and the scent of cedarwood, strong by his collarbone. The relentless tingling under my skin lessens, and the usual rush of blood through my veins slows to a calm flow.

This must be what home feels like.

The darkness, the quiet, and his not pulling away embolden me to break the silence. "Do you have questions?" I whisper on a breath.

Silas doesn't ask what I mean. I know Davey filled him in on most of it, but there are things I didn't tell him or Natalie that had nothing to do with contracts or Peter. I'm referring to things that would only matter to Silas. To *us.*

His fingers shift against mine, sliding between the spaces and curling the pads into my palm. A quiet pause.

"Yes and no."

That's more than a fair answer, and I have no right to expect anything more, but I'm not above begging if that's what it takes to drag every last truth into the light, so he can see exactly who I am.

My eyes adjust to the dim light filtering through the sheer curtains drawn over the windows. Soft shadows cast faint lines over the sharp cut of his jaw and the tension there.

Carefully, I squeeze his hand. "Ask me anything," I murmur. "Please."

Silas casts a glance down at me, but his chin stays tipped toward the ceiling. He looks back up and takes his time finding the words.

"Did you sleep with me to manipulate me?"

The ache in his words settles deep in my chest, but I don't look away.

Instead, I extract my hand from his, reaching toward his jaw. Slowly, hesitantly, I run my fingers along its stubbled edge, coaxing him to look at me. It takes three passes before he concedes, allowing my fingertips to guide his face lower, our mouths only an inch or so apart. A dark curl slips loose, falling over his forehead from the shift in angle.

I drink him—memorizing every sharp line and soft edge, the high cut of his cheekbones, his freckles, the small lines that linger at the corners of his mouth. Even as exhaustion weighs on him, he's so painfully beautiful.

"I never intended to sleep with you." The words come easily because they're the truth. "I had a hard line to never sleep with the subject of my contracts. It was the one thing Peter couldn't convince me to do."

His jaw flexes under my fingers, eyes dragging over my face and lingering on my mouth. "But *someone* chipped away at my defenses," I continue before pressing the lightest of kisses to the corner of his lips. "I slept with you only because I wanted to."

He breathes out through his nose, the sound uneven. "Did you sleep with anyone else during that time?"

The question sends a jolt through me. "No." The speed of my answer causes Silas's eyes to narrow. "There were opportunities, sure, but I didn't take any of them. They didn't interest me. Especially after we met."

Almost as the words are out of my mouth, it strikes me that Silas might not be ready for monogamy. We didn't discuss it today, though we definitely should have. Why would I ever think we'd just fall back into what we had before? How could I expect that of him when he's taking this gamble on me now?

I swallow hard. "I... when I'm with someone, I'm with them completely." I search for the right words. "If you're not on the same page, I'll figure out how to be okay with that."

The force of his stare is so tangible, it's as if his hands are on me, holding me still.

"I don't share, Elena." Each word is a final stroke on an unwavering stance. "It goes both ways."

I nod, the assertion reverberating through me like a series of rolling waves, each one escalating the relief that spreads across my skin.

There's a brief pause before his next question. "Did you feel guilty at all?"

"At first, not really." I don't sugarcoat it. "I was doing that type of work for Peter for over five years. It was almost second nature to me."

His expression doesn't change, but I feel the way his breath hitches. I press closer, our noses skimming.

"But it only took a few weeks before I started looking for different ways to get what he wanted." My voice is softer now. "It was gradual at first. But after the alley..." I trail off, exhaling shakily. "I don't know if I'll ever stop hating myself for all of it."

My hand slides to his neck, fingers curling at his nape as I pull back just enough to see his face. His expression is strained as he speaks, "Why didn't you just tell me you were in trouble?"

I gnaw on the inside of my cheek.

"I was terrified. Of Peter, mostly. But also of you." The admission is quiet. "I couldn't imagine telling you everything I'd done and you not killing me for it." A humorless laugh escapes before I can stop it. "Forget forgiving me. I never even considered that a possibility."

After waking up partially drugged in an undisclosed basement a few weeks ago, I had official confirmation that he wouldn't have taken the confession well. Though that doesn't make what I did forgivable, at least I wasn't wrong for fearing it.

"And the more you showed me how much you cared, the worse it got, because I didn't want to hurt you." My thumb traces lightly against his skin. "I was selfish and scared and wanted to hold onto you as long as I could."

Silas's eyes flare as I hand over every terrible piece of me without excuse or justification. He studies my expression before something in him shifts. It's subtle, but it's there.

The hand he left resting on his chest moves to my face, fingers sliding into the side of my hair, angling me toward him as if he needs to see all of me.

"Okay," he concedes. "That's enough for tonight." Those endlessly dark eyes trace over my features. "Now I just want to look at you."

I frown slightly, but before I can ask, he speaks so softly, it's as if the words are something he's only just found the strength to say.

"There were two days when I thought you were dead and I'd never be able to look at you again." The confession slices through me, claws deep, and settles in places I don't know how to reach. "I hated you." A thumb sweeps over my cheekbone. "But I also loved you so much that knowing you were gone almost destroyed what was left of me."

His gaze is distant even while looking at me, and my heart splinters. "Until I saw you in that holding room with my own two eyes, I don't think I'd taken a real breath since June."

Silas repeats the first thought I had when I laid eyes on him again. He felt that, too, despite everything I did.

Tears blur my vision, the edges of the dark room turning soft and watery. "I was supposed to get in and out quietly. I didn't want anyone–"

Silas hushes me, his fingers warm against my face. "I know."

His thumb sweeps over my cheek again, catching a tear before it can fall. Then, slowly, he leans in, pressing a lingering kiss to my hairline.

"You haunted every goddamn minute of my day," he murmurs against my skin, his breath rustling the loose strands. "Awake or asleep. I couldn't escape you."

He moves lower, his mouth finding my damp cheekbone, lips soft but unyielding. "I hated you for making me feel like that." Another kiss, this time on the other cheek, slower, deeper. "For making me love you so quickly that losing you felt like it would actually kill me."

His lips brush the tip of my nose. My hand moves to his chest, fingers curling into the fabric of his t-shirt.

"I swore if I found you, I'd make you pay for it." He tilts my chin up slightly, his mouth ghosting over the edge of my jaw, whispering the threat that never quite made it to reality. "But now that you're here, all I want to do is lock you away so you can't run from me."

His lips skim the corner of mine. "So you can never disappear like that again. Or drive me out of my fucking mind hunting you down."

The ringing in my ears is deafening, but still not loud enough to miss his quiet vow as he moves to speak against my mouth. "*Never* again."

Never.

My soft, shuddering breath is swallowed by Silas as he finally kisses me. I tilt my head, lips parting beneath his. Those words snake around my spine, squeezing so deliciously that it aches.

His fingers knot in my hair, the grip almost punishing as he yanks me closer, pulling me deeper into him like he doesn't care if he breaks me.

And I'd let him.

He shifts, dragging my body up and over his until I'm straddling him, my knees bracketing his torso. His hands roam greedily—palming my hips, skimming my spine, pressing possessively at my ass. It's like he doesn't know where he wants to touch me most.

I manage to tug up the hem of his shirt, my fingers seeking the heat of his skin, feeling him the way I did in the hallway earlier today. Hard muscle flexes beneath my touch. Molten heat spreads, burning in my veins until it's the only thing I can feel.

"I missed you so much," I breathe, the words trembling against his mouth.

A low groan rumbles from deep in his chest, vibrating through my palms where they press against him. His fingers tighten at my waist, and then he presses me down, my core sliding over the thick, hard length of him. The contact is enough to punch a small, broken whimper from my throat.

I kiss him harder, more desperate now, nails digging into his ribs like I need to hold onto something. "No one—" I gasp as he thrusts up again, my forehead falling to his. "No one has ever made me feel like this."

His eyes snap to mine and flash with a brightness that seems to illuminate the room.

"Show me," he rasps.

For the first time all day, I don't hesitate.

Sitting up, I hook my thumbs under the waistband of my sleep shorts and push them down, pulling them off one leg at a time until they're lost somewhere on the bed.

It's only been a few hours since he decided to try to stop hating me. I need to earn back his trust slowly. Prove myself with time, consistency, and patience. It's the only way this will ever work. But his being under me like this stirs something dark and deep inside me to demand that he believe it. Right now.

I press my palms over his abs, trailing lower, silently instructing him to lift his hips. He obeys, and I slide his sweatpants and briefs down just enough for his aching cock to spring free. The sight of him like this makes my breath hitch.

How is he even real?

All lean muscle and olive skin, hard lines softened by the low light. Even in the dark, I can see the flush creeping up his neck and onto his cheeks.

I lick my palm slowly, and when I wrap it around his length, his breath shudders like I've stolen it from his lungs. I take my time, savoring the way he twitches under my strokes, hips raising off the bed for more friction. There's a slight sheen to his forehead as he holds back every instinct to take over.

With my free hand, I reach over to the bedside table, fingers grazing the familiar weight of his glasses. I bring them to my mouth, opening the arms with my lips before sliding them onto his face.

For a split second, Silas just stares, but when his vision adjusts, the reaction is instant. His pupils expand, and his tongue flicks impatiently across the inside of his cheek as I slide further up his chest to position him at my entrance, the tip settling just where it's supposed to be.

Then I sink down.

A sharp gasp tears from my lips as he stretches me open, inch by inch. Silas curses low and filthy, hands snapping back to my waist with a grip that borders on bruising. The fullness makes my head spin. I don't stop until there's no space left between us and I'm full of him.

Even in the best moments with Silas in the spring, a part of me detached when we were like this. Probably to preserve whatever shreds of my heart remained.

But I can feel everything now. The slide of his buttery skin on mine, the faint trail of hair that leads down under his naval, the erratic pulse under my fingers. I stay like that for a moment, letting the burn settle into something deeper.

Then I reach for the hem of my sleep shirt and tug it over my head, tossing it aside without a second thought. His eyes track every movement, dark and wild and completely wrecked.

My lips curl into a slow, devious smile as I roll my hips once, testing the drag of him inside me. His head tips back against the pillow, a sound somewhere between a groan and a prayer escaping him.

He told me to take what I want.

Until he tells me to stop, I will.

CHAPTER 24

Silas

A s much as I want to stay buried in Elena for the next week, reality has other plans and we still have work to do.

While having breakfast together at the kitchen island the next morning, I tell her that I need to spend some time in virtual meetings. A part of me braces for her reaction, half expecting her to fall into old habits and retreat to that damn guest room I still want to demolish, but she doesn't.

Quietly, almost shyly, she asks, "Can I work in your study? On the couch, I mean. You won't even know I'm there."

Each word is carefully chosen, and I can feel something start to weld itself back together inside of me, white-hot and burning. It's the same sensation I felt yesterday when I found her in my bedroom, claiming the space she wouldn't even leave clothes in four months ago.

All I can manage is a nod. Anything else would have resulted in me taking her on the counter, as I had promised I would, Kendall prepping for dinner next to us be damned.

That's when it really hit me how insane this is.

I should be disgusted with myself. Hell-bent on making her suffer for what she did to me. I'm not the kind of man who forgives, and I definitely don't let people back in once they've betrayed me. And yet, here we are, just three weeks after bringing her back to Chicago, and she's already in my house again. In my study. In my bed. I swore I wouldn't allow this, but I just don't give a damn about the potential consequences right now.

Elena is the most potent addiction I've ever known, a drug that laced itself into my bloodstream from the moment I first touched her. No matter how much I tell myself I need to keep my distance, it's already too late. There was never any staying away. I proved that the second I hunted her down and dragged her back here.

I still don't trust her. I can't pretend the past never happened, but I have to know if she's telling the truth. If there's even the smallest chance, I can't walk away yet.

Davey was right.

The bastard.

I need to let this run its course because if this is real, then I have to see it for myself. And if it's not, then at least I'll know when it ends.

We both work quietly in between my meetings. She hasn't overheard anything too sensitive, always donning a pair of headphones without being asked. Still, before each one begins, she tilts her head slightly, voice soft as she murmurs, "Should I leave?" Ready and willing to do whatever I ask.

It's a heady feeling, holding that kind of control over the woman who once slipped through my fingers and is now looking to me for direction. On one hand, I want to tell her to stop acting like someone she isn't. It feels like a mask she's wearing for my sake. But on the other hand, it feeds something primal that thrives on the responsibility of it.

"Can I ask you a question?" Elena asks, her voice cutting through the silence and my thoughts like a whip.

My head snaps up from the financial summary I'm supposed to be reviewing. She's lounging on the couch, laptop now resting on the floor beside her. She's pressed into the armrest, her long legs stretched out and crossed at the ankle at the opposite end.

Forcing my glasses back up my nose, I arch an eyebrow.

"Lena," I begin, the nickname slipping from my mouth with such ease it feels as though I've been saying it my entire life. "Though I'm thoroughly enjoying this new submissive attitude," I pause, my eyes raking over her slowly, deliberately. Her cheeks flush the most delicious shade of pink. "I want you to speak freely, like you always have. That smart mouth is still my favorite trait of yours."

"Even if it makes you violent?" she asks, her sinfully raspy voice dipping lower as she echoes the words I said to her the first time I claimed her months ago.

"*Especially* because it makes me violent," I reply, my tongue running over my bottom lip.

Is this how it's always going to be? I had her this morning, and I'm already calculating the next time I'll have her again.

She looks at me like she knows exactly what I'm thinking, her lips curving ever so slightly. "How long has your dad been pushing for Jeremy to be COO?" She redirects me without missing a beat.

I lean back in my chair, running a hand through my hair as I think. "A few months," I reply, tilting my head side to side as I sift through my memories. "He's always been trying to find a place for Jeremy, but nothing has ever really fit. You've met Jeremy a few times. He's... my brother, and I care about him, but he doesn't have the right temperament for what that role needs."

She absorbs the information, already working through what it might mean. It reminds me of why I told her about it at breakfast.

Even if I don't fully trust her, I *wanted* to tell her. To hear her perspective the way I used to. When she lived here before, I confided in her, talking about my work more than hers for reasons that are clearer now, but it wasn't just about having someone to vent to.

As Scarlett, she *got* it. Sharp, practical, and when it came to business, we saw things the same way. That compatibility was one of the first things that made it possible to fall in love with her so quickly. How easily we aligned when talking strategy, how she took an interest in my plans for Wells.

For all the ways she's betrayed me, I need to know if that part of our relationship—the way we *thought* together—was real. Was she interested in my work because she cared for me and the company, or was it only to gain insight to use against me? The way she reacted this morning felt like it was the former, but time will tell.

It also gives me the opportunity to see what she does with this smaller bit of information. If she can prove herself by keeping this secret, I'll figure out if I can trust her with anything else somewhere down the line.

Elena nods, her brows knitting. "Interesting," she says slowly. "Your father doesn't seem like the type of man to make a decision like this based on emotion. Is there a reason he's so set on operations?"

I weigh her words for a moment. "Likely to offer him something similar to what was offered to me."

"That's what I'm struggling with," she answers, drumming her fingers against her bicep. "William has always been concerned about how your work and actions reflect on him, and that doesn't seem to matter with Jeremy. Why is the risk worth it now? Does he gain something by having Jeremy in that position that he doesn't already have with you?"

I straighten in my seat.

Since deciding a few years ago to leave the COO position vacant, William and I have been splitting the responsibilities that landed outside of our current director, Bethany's, scope. If he ever cared to be a part of the conversations I've wanted to have about the the transition, he'd know that I had a multi-step plan in place to start off-loading some of his tasks onto Bethany and, hopefully in the next couple of years, she'd be prepared to step into the position and take the responsibilities I hold currently, as well.

But maybe this demand isn't about trying to make things "fair" between Jeremy and me as much as it's about what he loses by giving up those responsibilities. Considering how often we're at odds over the direction of Wells nowadays, maybe it's about keeping his hands on the wheel, because if he can't do it through me, he thinks he can do it through Jeremy.

My skin pulses with the realization.

"Probably because Jeremy would follow his instructions or advice to the letter, no questions asked," I say finally through a clenched jaw.

My chest constricts. No wonder. This isn't about Jeremy's career, and it's definitely not about guilt. My father doesn't give a damn about what's best for his son or for the company, for that matter. He's doing this because it benefits *him*.

Elena watches me process this idea, swinging her feet to the floor. "From what I learned in the cloud, there's a good chance that whatever Peter is after is operations-related. If it's something only your father is currently aware of, could that be the kind of information he'd pass on to Jeremy if he were to step into the role?" She pauses. Then, with a slight tilt of her head, she adds, her voice lower now, "Or could he be planning to use him as a scapegoat?"

It's a horrifying thought, but one that fits far too neatly into the way my father functions. The answer churns uneasily in my gut.

Resting my elbows on my desk, I steeple my hands in front of my face as I try to untangle the mess her question just dropped in my lap.

"He could," I admit, the words heavy on my tongue as she stands. "Both feel possible."

Elena crosses the room to lean against the edge of my desk, right by my side. "I'm not trying to put ideas in your head," she says, her voice tinged with worry. "There's always the possibility I'm reading too much into this. But as an outsider, it just feels too coincidental to me."

She says "outsider" like it's a simple fact, and I guess I have my father to thank for that. He cast her out the moment he decided she was using me. While he wasn't wrong about her intentions, the reasons he believed were entirely off the mark. Those reasons make all the difference in the world because they're why she's standing here in my home right now and not still tied to a chair.

"No, you're right," I admit. A restless energy pushes through me. I push back from my chair to stand, lifting my glasses to rub my eyes. "We've been disagreeing a lot. I wouldn't put it past him to turn to Jeremy to regain some leverage there."

Elena watches me as I readjust my glasses, and I can practically see the gears turning in her head. Her honeyed gaze flickers as she plays out scenarios, piecing together possibilities she hasn't voiced yet. I can feel she wants to say something, but she's holding back.

It frustrates me more than it should.

I take a step toward her, and her eyes widen a fraction as I catch her chin between my fingers, gripping it a little harder than necessary.

"What did I just say about speaking freely?" I mutter, thumb brushing over her bottom lip in a deliberate stroke. Her breath catches, but I don't let up. My gaze narrows as I wait for her to give me what I want.

"I have a kind of deceptive idea," she finally admits, her face flushing with shame as she looks down. Something in me recoils that her first instinct is still to manipulate, but I force it down. Instead, I dip my head, silently urging her to continue.

She exhales, her voice quieter now. "I think you need to know if Jeremy has any idea what's going. Maybe if you try to spend some time with him, he'll open up about what he knows. It could make a big difference in how you decide to handle him."

For some reason, her words surprise me, and I find myself smiling at her despite the weight of the conversation.

"A little deceptive," I concede, leaning down to brush my lips against hers. Her hands reach for my sides, and that new instinct of hers, the one that leans into me rather than pulling away, is something I could definitely get used to.

"But I agree," I murmur against her mouth, pulling back just enough to meet her eyes. "It doesn't hurt to try and clear the air between us, anyway. I'll text him and see about getting dinner. Maybe I'll bring Davey as a buffer. You know how he has a knack for keeping things light."

Her expression softens. There's a flicker of something in her gaze—pride, maybe? Or relief. Either way, it's enough to ease some of the tension inside me, but plenty of it still lingers. I can't ignore the resentment for my brother's blind loyalty, or how easily he might let himself be used as a pawn. Worse, he might know exactly what's going on and is willingly complicit in whatever mess my father has created.

Right now, I honestly can't decide which would be harder to accept.

CHAPTER 25

Elena

"We've identified metadata references connected to Sierra Blanca, Texas," Ben announces through the speaker. My head snaps up from my laptop and toward Davey's phone on the coffee table, interest piqued.

For about two weeks, Davey has made it a part of his routine to stop by Silas's mansion in the late afternoon. His mornings are spent working on-site with Luis, Ben, and Corey until he leaves them under Paul's supervision—along with a rotating set of Silas's security team—so he can focus on his regular workload. Then, without fail, he comes here, settling in for the daily debrief.

Usually, Davey finds me in the music room, either on the lounge chair or by the window, laptop open, trying to keep myself busy while Silas sticks to his usual office schedule. His presence has been a welcome change of pace, considering how confusing things have been between me and Silas.

Some days, it feels like we're making real progress. Silas asks the hard questions, and I answer every one of them. On those days, we have endless communication and understanding. There's nothing I can or want to hide, and the approval radiates from him. By the time we're done talking, he's reaching for me or I'm reaching for him, trying to soothe the jagged cuts of whatever difficult conversation we had to claw our way through. And for those fleeting moments, I think we're healing.

But those good days are inevitably followed by colder ones, and the distance feels like an impassable chasm. I can see the way his mind tries to reconcile the person I am now with the one who broke his trust. Those moments have branded me with a shame I don't think I'll ever get used to, but I follow his lead.

It's the least I owe him.

In a way, Silas's going back to the office has helped. There's something almost easier about having a clear structure to our days. It's given us space to breathe and adjust to this strange, new state of existence together.

"Davey told me this morning," Silas responds, voice coming through the phone. "Have you figured out what the connection is yet?"

Ben clears his throat. "No. The location markers weren't explicitly labeled, but we found them embedded in metadata strings across several archived files. When we cross-referenced them with older logs, Sierra Blanca kept coming up. Someone intentionally embedded the location, like they wanted it hidden but still traceable if you knew what to look for."

I frown at the phone. "But everything on the cloud was pointing to New Mexico."

"We've been discussing why that might be," Luis says, "but we hadn't thought of anything that felt reasonable yet."

In the holding room, I told Davey and Cillian about the Wells cloud referencing coordinates in New Mexico. They were quick to assume it was connected to a research and manufacturing facility the company operates in Deming. On paper, the place is spotless. Fully regulated, every protocol followed to the letter.

The only red flag was that all of the facility's most sensitive data is stored locally, so there's no legitimate reason for any encrypted file on the cloud to point there in the first place. Davey took a closer look himself, but couldn't get past most of the encryption. He told me it was a miracle Ben and Corey even managed to extract the warehouse location when they did.

What little he could see looked painfully ordinary—standard reports, outdated forms, facility logs. The kind of baseline paperwork he'd expect to be floating around in internal archives, which only made the cloud references to Deming even weirder.

Corey finally breaks the silence, impatience edging his words. "Does Sierra Blanca mean anything to you?"

Silas answers immediately. "No. I've barely heard of it." For a moment, there's only silence. Then, Silas exhales sharply, controlled but clearly irritated. "Is there anything else useful you've gathered?"

Another pause.

"No," Luis mutters.

Another long breath is audible through the line. "Alright. Let's wrap up for today, but keep your focus on Sierra Blanca." With a slight shift in his tone, Silas adds, "Lena, will you stay on the line?"

I nod even though he can't see me. "Sure."

Ben, Corey, and Luis mumble their goodbyes before dropping off. Davey makes no move to leave, sinking back into the couch as his hands flick across his keyboard in sure strokes.

Snagging his phone off the table as I place my laptop down, I take it off speaker and press it to my ear.

"What's up?" I ask, moving to stand from my spot on the floor. My muscles strain after sitting on the carpet next to the coffee table for so long. I stretch my free hand over the top of my head.

"Natalie is on her way over right now. She should be there in a few minutes. You're going to want to get changed into something you can work out in."

"Work out in?" I repeat, eyebrows knitting together. "Why?"

"Jeff will be there in half an hour to work out with you," Silas says simply.

Every muscle in my body tenses, and I swear I can feel my system short-circuit. Even as a strange heat blooms in my chest, I'm half-convinced I misheard him.

"Silas," I finally say, my voice slow with disbelief, "you hired Jeff?"

"He was reluctant at first," Silas says, sounding slightly amused. "But I told him who it was for and he suddenly changed his tune."

For months, I'd told myself I'd never see Jeff again. It was better that way. He and Lauren had done more than enough. They let me fall apart in private and gave me the space to exist between survival and recovery. Even now, I never let myself consider it, no matter how much I missed them.

Silas didn't have to give me this; he doesn't owe me anything, especially not an olive branch, but he's offering me one anyway.

I open my mouth, close it, and then try again. "And *Natalie* agreed to this?"

"Unhappily," he admits, though his tone betrays no actual concern.

I let out a breath, pinching my nose to keep emotions back. "You're unbelievable," I mutter, voice cracking.

Silas chuckles. "Am I now?" I can hear the smile in his words. "You miss him and need the outlet."

I swallow hard. Davey isn't looking directly at me, but the smirk curling his lips tells me he's silently enjoying my reaction. The knot in my throat tightens.

"Thank you," I whisper, then laugh. "He's going to kick my ass."

"I have no doubt you'll bounce back just fine."

"Elena? Dave?" Natalie calls out somewhere in the mansion.

Davey stands without a word, closing his laptop and placing it on the coffee table before striding toward the door to find his wife.

"I'll see you when I get home," Silas promises.

"Okay," I respond. Three additional words threaten to spill out, but I refrain. I'd said them that one time in Natalie's kitchen weeks ago, but I never want him to feel obligated to say it back. He deserves to decide if he does without pressure from me. "Thank you again."

When Silas speaks, his voice is low, almost reverent. "Anything for you, Lena. You know that."

The line clicks off before I can respond, and I stare down at the phone, my fingers curling around it as something warm and unsteady presses against my ribs.

I push out a slow breath and follow Natalie's voice down the hallway.

Cillian snorts from the desk chair he dragged out from the basement office. It echoes through the room just as Jeff flips me over his back and slams me onto the mat. The impact steals all of my oxygen.

"You really are rusty," Jeff grunts as he looms over me, hands on his hips, exposing his mouthguard with a smirk. "C'mon. Get up."

I glare up at him, the sting of humiliation bubbling in my gut. Silas, in his ever-meticulous way, rearranged part of the gym to fit a full section of grappling mats. Of course, he couldn't just leave me alone to be rusty in peace—he had to set the stage for my failure in high definition.

"I've gotta say," Cillian begins, still grinning. "I've missed watching you do this."

"I'm going to kick your ass next," I snap, ignoring the burning in my lungs as I roll onto my knees and push myself to my feet. My body aches already, but I refuse to let them see how much this is taking out of me.

"That's the spirit," Jeff replies, bouncing lightly on the balls of his feet. He's already circling me, eyes darting from my toes back to my face.

I square my shoulders and meet his gaze head-on. My pride won't let me back down now, not with Cillian watching, as if this is the best show he's seen all week.

"You got it, El," Natalie huffs out from the treadmill Jeff stuck her on, breathless but encouraging. Sweat drips from her brow as she struggles to keep pace. After Jeff's quick assessment of her fitness level, he decided endurance was her first priority, and she's been pounding away on the treadmill for the last forty-five minutes.

"Don't give her too much credit," Jeff quips, sparing Natalie a quick glance as he circles me again. "You're lucky I'm not flipping you onto this mat, too."

Natalie rolls her eyes, though her focus doesn't falter from the treadmill's unrelenting rhythm. "Please. I could take you down in five seconds if I wanted to." She flashes a playful smirk, but the effort in her voice betrays just how hard she's pushing herself.

"Let's stick to jogging for now, champ," Jeff fires back, returning his attention to me. "Alright, kid. Ready?"

"Bring it, old man," I grit out, planting my feet firmly on the mat. The ache in my ribs is a reminder of just how out of shape I've become.

Jeff snorts, the corner of his mouth quirking into a grin. "Trash talk like that will only make me work you harder."

"Good," I retort, wiping my forehead and dropping into a defensive stance. "Maybe you'll actually break a sweat this time."

He steps closer, the teasing light in his eyes giving way to a flicker of seriousness. "Alright then," he mutters, his voice dropping an octave as his weight shifts forward. "Show me what you've got."

Before I can blink, he's coming at me again. I lunge to meet him and gain ground by hooking his leg and shifting my weight to drive into him. His grip falters and I slip into position, my heart pounding as I move to trap his arm.

My lips curl into a smile just as Jeff's low chuckle reverberates in my ear. His hand snaps to my wrist mid-movement, twisting just enough to throw me off balance.

"Close," he murmurs, his tone half-praising, half-mocking, "but not close enough."

In one smooth motion, he sweeps my legs out and redirects my momentum, slamming me onto my back again. The mat slaps against my shoulder blades, and the ceiling suddenly spins.

I groan. "You're such a show-off."

Jeff only gives me a moment of reprieve before he's extending a helping hand. "You're the one who called me old. What'd you expect?"

He hauls me to my feet. My legs are shaky, but a grin tugs at my lips despite it. I spit out my mouthguard into my hand, and Jeff mimics my action just as his eyes land on the scar peeking out from under my rash guard.

"Those are still fading pretty well," he comments, nodding toward the burn.

I run my fingers over the raised skin. "They are," I say simply, before shifting the focus. "How's Lauren?" I ask, moving for the water bottle I left on the edge of the mat.

He follows me away from Cillian and Nat instead of demanding we continue. Usually, Jeff is relentless. Though he'd never admit it, he definitely has an even softer spot for me now after seeing what my body went through a few months ago.

"Working like a dog, but what else is new," he jokes, grabbing his own water bottle and squirting a stream into his mouth.

I lean against the wall, the coolness of it seeping through my overheated skin. "Does she still like the hospital she transferred to?" I ask. We spent a lot of time talking over those few weeks, with Lauren handling my care and taking far too much of her newly instated PTO to do so.

"Yeah," he says, capping his bottle and sitting down on the mat in front of me. "They're impressed with how she's managing the department. Barely has time to breathe, but she's happy."

"That's great," I grin. "She deserves it."

Jeff smiles back, leaning back on his hands. "She told me to make sure you don't push yourself too hard." His eyes narrow teasingly. "So don't go pulling any more hero stunts."

I laugh, rolling my eyes as I take a sip of water. "I've learned my lesson. No more hero stunts."

He raises a brow, unconvinced. "Uh-huh."

Jeff's eyes linger on me for a moment, his expression shifting, though it's hard to read. "So," he starts, his voice low, careful. "How's it been? You doing okay?"

I consider brushing it off with a generic response, but this is Jeff. He's one of the few people I trust, and I know he won't let it go until I give him something.

My eyes skirt across the room to a distracted Natalie and Cillian. "I'm good," I say finally, fiddling with the cap of my water bottle. "We're still getting some stuff sorted so I can go out and be normal again, but that'll take some time."

"Good," he says with a nod before wrapping his arms around the tops of his knees. "You know, I wasn't so sure about him," he admits. "Silas, I mean. After that day he came looking for you at the gym."

My brows knit together in confusion. "What are you talking about?"

Jeff's brows shoot up. "Maybe a couple of months ago, he showed up for an assessment under a fake name, asking questions about you. Wanted to know where you were." He lets out a low whistle. "Honestly, I thought he was bad news. The kind of guy who might burn the world down just to prove a point."

Silas planning a calculated visit to Jeff's gym, demanding answers, doesn't surprise me. If anything, it feels like exactly something he'd do. Still, hearing it out loud is... something else.

"I didn't know he came looking for me," I admit quietly.

Jeff shrugs, his lips quirking into a wry smile. "Didn't stick around long, but the way he was—" he pauses, searching for the right words. "I was worried. You'd been through enough. The last thing you needed was someone dragging you into more chaos."

The inside of my cheek stings as I bite into it. "He had a right to be angry with me."

Jeff watches me closely, his gaze sharp but not unkind. "And now?"

I exhale slowly. "Things are better. He's not the guy you saw that day. I'm safe with him."

"Safe is good," he says after a beat. "I can live with safe. But if that ever changes..." His voice trails off.

I smile, shaking my head. "You'd be the first person I'd call."

"Damn right," he nods, but there's a softness to his tone now. "Still, keep your eyes open. Safe's a good start, but don't settle."

A quiet warmth creeps in as Jeff holds my gaze, his emotions clear as day. My happiness matters to him. It always has.

"I won't," I promise, meaning it.

For a moment, neither of us speaks. The sounds of Cillian and Natalie's quiet conversation are lost beneath the noise of the treadmill and the playlist she put on in the background.

As if suddenly aware of where we are, Jeff clears his throat and stands. "Alright, enough heart-to-hearts. Ready to get your ass kicked again, or do you need more time?"

I laugh, the tension easing as I push off the wall. "Bring it, old man."

He grins. "That's more like it."

Chapter 26

Silas

The boardroom next to my father's office is meticulously designed. Floor-to-ceiling windows stretch along one side, offering a clear view of the skyline, as if Wells Corporation itself is staring down at the city, reminding everyone who built it.

The black conference table is long enough to seat the entire board with space to spare, and the tan leather chairs, which are usually neatly arranged, are slightly off-kilter and settled into by our twelve board members, myself included.

Along the walls, framed articles showcase Wells's achievements. Expansion milestones. Regulatory victories. Pharmaceutical breakthroughs.

Proof of dominance.

My father is perched at the head of the table, flipping through his papers as if he has all the time in the world. There's a power in forcing people to wait for you. On you. It makes every decision seem like it's his and his alone. I've seen him do it a thousand times before.

We'd been steadily making our way down the quarterly agenda, with most of it being centered around the executive transition. My eyes move to the next item on my tablet, and I frown slightly at the item that wasn't listed when I reviewed it several days ago.

Strategic Operational Growth Proposal – Discussion

The verbiage makes the hairs on my neck stand up.

Across the table, our CFO, Everett, is the picture of neutrality, other than his fingers tapping idly against his tablet. Next to me, Natalie is scrolling through the agenda too, her mouth pressing into a tight line when she stops on the same item.

"I'd like to open the floor for an important discussion about the future of Wells Corporation," William starts, leaning back. "Jeremy has been working on an exciting operational initiative. I'd like him to introduce it to the board."

To my father's left, Jeremy straightens his posture along with the front of his lavender tie. Even from my seat at the near opposite end of the room, I can see the way his body vibrates with excitement.

Natalie pokes my leg under the table, but I don't allow my eyes to even flicker her way. I reach for my coffee cup, positioning it at my lips to conceal my grimace as Jeremy smacks his hands down against the table, jolting everyone to attention.

"Right now, Wells is standing at a crossroads," he begins in a conspiratorial voice. "One way leads to innovation, the other to irrelevance."

The confident grin he flashes reminds me of the many pharmaceutical presentations I've attended over the years. At the very least, he fits the part. "Automation is the future of pharmaceutical manufacturing, and we're behind. If we don't integrate AI-driven processes and rethink our global footprint, we're going to lose our competitive edge."

I blink, setting my mug back down.

There's a small beat when I expect a slide deck to flash on any of the three wall-mounted televisions, or for my brother to reach under the table to pull out board briefing packets with supporting documents and research. Instead, Jeremy leans back in his seat, his voice taking on that particular brand of enthusiasm that comes when someone has never second-guessed themselves a day in their life.

His chair squeaks. "Our current facilities are outdated and expensive to maintain. If we fully integrate AI-driven automation into our manufacturing plants, we could reduce labor costs and increase production efficiency by nearly forty percent. And, if we shift certain key facilities overseas, we can cut expenses and improve global distribution."

He gestures broadly, like this is a no-brainer. "Think about it. Leaner operations, faster output, lower costs. If we're serious about long-term market positioning, this is how we get ahead."

Silence settles, and I wait for something else. Jeremy folds his fingers together over his abdomen as he scans our reactions and smiles with such conviction it's like he's expecting us to give him a standing ovation.

Natalie's foot finds my calf under the table, kicking me with the point of her heel. Though it burns, my brain is churning too quickly through the past few minutes to have a reaction.

This is insane.

Not just because AI-driven automation is still in its infancy in pharmaceuticals, but also that Wells doesn't have the necessary infrastructure or regulatory framework in place for any of this.

Next to my brother, William offers him a small nod and shifts his chair just slightly. His arms stay loose on the armrests, but I've seen this move too many times not to know what he's doing.

It's in the slight lean, the relaxed shoulders, the faint crease in the corner of his eyes like he's genuinely considering something. The cues are subtle enough that most people won't even clock them, but they'll feel it. The nod. The openness. The implied agreement. He's pulling out all the stops to show his approval without saying it.

I slide a glance past Natalie and to Elias, a prominent business leader in the city I'd brought onto the board several years ago, who is watching the room. Mark, the board's representative for outside capital, lets out an unimpressed breath.

The silence seems to gain weight with each passing moment.

Everett blinks furiously, as if he's trying to figure out what fresh hell he's fallen into. "Have you run the numbers?" His voice is clipped as he leans his elbows on the table. "The financial risk alone would be substantial, if not disastrous."

Jeremy shrugs, flashing that same lazy grin. "We'll figure out the financials as we go. The cost savings on labor alone will balance it out over time."

There's barely time to register Everett's open-mouthed shock before Dr. Miriam Alden, our medical research expert, says, "What about compliance? If we shift production overseas, how do you expect to maintain regulatory approvals in every market?"

Jeremy waves off her concern with the flick of his wrist. "Regulations always catch up to innovation. We'll be ahead of the curve."

Amy, our CHRO, bristles. "Have you considered the implications of mass layoffs? The lawsuits? The PR fallout?" Her voice takes on an edge I so rarely hear from the soft-spoken woman.

These words seem to land harder than the others so far, making Jeremy sit up in his seat, but he recovers quickly. "It's about efficiency. We'll restructure and reallocate resources. There's always a way."

Elias shakes his head. "What's the actual roadmap, or are we just throwing out buzzwords?"

Jeremy hesitates just a second too long.

William leans forward, commanding everyone's attention with the slight raise of his hand. "These are all details we can work through as we move forward into the planning process."

It takes a moment for me to realize those words just came out of my father's mouth.

Someone who built his entire empire on meticulous planning and absolute control is suddenly advocating for *winging it*? The same man who used to demand five-year projections and contingency plans for the smallest operational changes, is now brushing off critical logistics like an afterthought?

In the midst of the chaos circling in my head, something cold settles in my chest as what I'm witnessing dawns on me.

Just weeks after I reminded him that Jeremy's COO nomination is still off the table, my brother suddenly has a large-scale operations pitch for today. A Hail Mary, though I'm not sure I can call the trainwreck we just witnessed that.

These two conniving...

Though I'd love nothing more than to wipe that smug smile off of Jeremy's mouth for having the audacity to embarrass us with that pathetic excuse of a presentation, the anger brewing under my skin isn't directed at him.

It's toward the man who just put his son in front of the board, giving him the confidence and permission to think that this would make Jeremy look like a viable COO candidate. And worse, that we'd all just readily go along with some half-baked idea without any materials or projections.

Either William has lost his ever-loving mind, or he's so desperate to paint Jeremy in a good light that he is willing to risk everything on one of the most reckless and ill-prepared ideas ever brought forward in the over ten years I've been a board member.

"They aren't *just* details. They're the foundation of the entire plan," I respond.

Both Jeremy and my father zero in on me, one pair of brown eyes narrowed with unfiltered emotion, the other delivering a glare so precise it stings like the slice of a scalpel.

My brother lets out an exasperated breath, clearly not having the patience to keep the same composure with me as he did with the others. "Every great innovation carries risk. If we're always waiting for the perfect conditions, we'll never be ahead of the competition. Leading companies don't sit around debating logistics while the market moves forward without them."

I inhale sharply through my nose, shaking my head. "It's not about risk. It's about *calculated* risk. And the difference between the two is preparation. These AI-driven systems aren't proven to be reliable at the scale you're talking about. We'd be restructuring everything based on technology that hasn't been fully stress-tested in a regulated environment like ours. What happens if the automated systems fail? If production bottlenecks because an algorithm miscalculates a batch of a medication? Do you know what the financial hit would look like if we had to recall an entire line of product due to a single unnoticed AI error?"

Jeremy opens his mouth, then shuts it just as fast.

I gesture toward the rest of the table, sweeping my gaze over the board members. "The people in this room are experts in their fields. You came in here today with no presentation, no projections, and no real solutions to their very legitimate concerns. And yet you're telling us all to just take a leap of faith?"

Jeremy's jaw tightens, the color in his face darkening with frustration. I can feel his fury from across the table, but I'm not here to stroke his ego. I'm here to make sure we don't burn Wells to the ground.

Still, I ease back just a little.

"If you want us to truly consider this idea, show us how you'd address these pain points and focus on putting together a proposal for a pilot program at one of our smaller facilities. If you can come back with something tangible, then we can have a real discussion."

Jeremy's throat works as he tries to think of something else to say, but nothing comes. My father does nothing to rescue him. To his right, Randall, our former CLO, who is as loyal to William as a hound is to its owner, remains motionless with his hands folded neatly in front of him. His eyes are fixed on the table with such concentration, I'm surprised the wood doesn't crack.

Venessa Hawke doesn't immediately rush to William's defense like usual, either. Her perfectly manicured nails tap against the table to Everett's side, the only outward sign of her thoughts, but she stays quiet.

Jeremy's hands ball into fits that he quickly moves to his lap.

William looks around the room, likely noticing the same thing the rest of us have, and finally exhales. "Well," he says too smoothly, closing the folder in front of him with deliberate slowness. "I suppose we'll need more discussion before we move forward."

The conversation quickly shifts back to normal territory—updates on existing projects, supply chain logistics, and upcoming regulatory audits. Business as usual.

Jeremy spends the rest of the meeting staring into the side of my temple, his shoulders tight, arms crossed.

In his head, I did this to him. Not because he came in here with none of the credentials or information to make a good case, but because I didn't immediately give in the way he and my father assumed I would.

Jeremy doesn't even see the way William gave him a stage, let him talk himself into a corner, then abandoned the entire thing the second it became clear it wouldn't work. He set Jeremy up to fail.

And for what? To prove a point to me? That he can put Jeremy in front of the board whenever he damn well pleases, just to see if he can make something stick?

I need to talk to my brother. I told Elena I'd do it; I just wasn't sure when. But now, seeing him sit there, seething with misplaced rage, I can't wait any longer—because William isn't going to stop.

Whether Jeremy wants to believe that or not, he deserves better than to be humiliated by our father for his own gain.

Chapter 27

Elena

Before I even realize I'm awake, I'm seated upright. My pulse pounds as the duvet falls to my waist, letting cold air rush over my sweat-slicked chest and neck.

It takes a moment to realize where I am—the massive bedroom, the ornate curtains, the eight-foot windows. Silas's side of the bed is empty, an imprint on the pillow still visible in the darkness. The bathroom light is off.

My fingers curl into the sheets, rubbing the buttery-soft fabric between my fingers as a reminder of what is real and what is not.

It was just a nightmare.

Or something like it. I don't even remember what I saw before I ended up here again. It's just a blur of fragmented images, but I know something terrible was happening. I was fighting for my life in my own head.

I used to have a lot of these dreams after Drew. I rarely remembered the specifics, but I woke up screaming her name more times than I can count. Sometimes I wondered if she was doing it to punish me from some afterlife.

Those type of dreams came back after the warehouse explosion, but they hadn't been as frequent since I moved back in with Silas. I thought maybe things were starting to settle because I was beginning to feel more like myself. I don't know. I'm not sure why I expected anything different.

The sky outside is still blanketed in darkness as I slide back down onto the mattress and onto my side. The small analog clock near my head says it's just after five in the morning. I curse.

There's no world where I fall asleep after that.

With a sigh, I roll onto my back. Davey and the guys made solid progress on the servers yesterday, and Corey managed to extract coordinates for a general area in Sierra Blanca, which feels promising, but there's nothing I can do about it right now.

I find myself putting on a pair of biker shorts and a t-shirt. I never work out this early, but getting rid of the electricity that's zipping through my veins feels like the only productive thing I can do.

By the time I brush my teeth and make it down to the basement, the space is already thick with body heat and sweat. "Basket Case" plays over the speakers, loud enough to muffle the impact of Silas's gloved fists against the heavy bag in the corner.

He throws perfectly controlled strikes into the leather, footwork light. His shirt is discarded on the floor nearby, and his glasses have been replaced with contacts. Sweat glistens along the ridges of his back, sliding down to the waistband of his shorts, and catching on the deep cut of his muscles. Heat curls low in my stomach.

Am I about to become a morning person?

Silas doesn't break his rhythm or even glance in my direction through the mirrors on the surrounding walls. He lands several hard hits against the bag before finally speaking.

"Did you come down here just to ogle me?"

My cheeks flush. "It wasn't my plan," I admit, crossing my arms with a smirk, "but it's a big perk."

That gets his attention. He drops his hands and turns to me, fighting a smile. My body relaxes almost instantly at the way his eyes linger on me without a guarded edge. No measured silences, no distance.

Today is a good day.

I cross the room, placing a palm against his glistening chest, meaning to just press a quick kiss to his jaw. But before I can move away, Silas pins my hand against his skin with one of his gloves.

He tilts his head in question. "Why are you awake?"

I shrug. "Couldn't sleep." Then, with a smile, I free my hand and back away. "Don't let me interrupt. Jeff isn't coming today, so I was just going to lift and do some cardio."

Silas watches me for a beat as he strips off his gloves to reveal the tape wrapped around his fingers. Then, he reaches for his water bottle, tipping it to his lips as he speaks against the opening. "Or we could run some drills together."

I arch an eyebrow at him, intrigued. "Oh?"

The idea of circling each other—searching for weaknesses, trying to best one another—sends a spark of adrenaline straight to my bloodstream.

Silas's grin darkens, his shoulders lifting casually. "I have to see if all this money I'm paying Jeff is actually worth it."

A sharp, incredulous laugh escapes me. "You're an ass."

The corners of his lips curl even further. "So I've been told." His gaze stays on me, daring me to say no.

I pretend to contemplate my options as I sink to the ground, stretching my legs out in front of me. "I guess I have some time to teach you a thing or two," I muse, swaying my head side to side. "Give me a few minutes to warm up."

Silas snorts, shaking his head. "How generous of you."

A smug grin forms on my lips as I reach forward to touch my toes.

While I stretch and cycle through a few quick cardio drills, Silas adjusts the tape on his hands and moves to one of the cabinets in the back corner. He rummages through the shelves until he pulls out the pair of mitts Jeff uses for striking drills and gloves that are my size.

By the time I'm finished warming up, he's already wearing them, standing at the edge of the grappling mat, waiting. I roll out my shoulders and shake out my limbs. "You know how to run these?" I ask.

He smirks, flexing his fingers in the mitts. "I think I can handle it."

I put on the gloves and we start slow.

Silas gives me the first few sets, calling out strikes. He's taller than Jeff, has a more rigid stance, and his reach is longer, but I adjust quickly.

Soon, we fall into a dance between his instruction and my execution.

Jab. Jab. Cross. Reset.

Lead hook. Rear hook. Step back. Again.

Silas keeps his tone even, his cues sharp, but I barely hear him. My mind is the kind of quiet I used to only find when I was in Jeff's gym.

"I'm kicking myself for never watching you train before," he admits with sparkling eyes, tracking my movements with the precision of an apex predator.

I huff out a laugh, stumbling through my next step before catching myself. "I was thinking the same thing," I respond.

I'm rewarded with the most devious smile, but I don't give him a chance to respond more than that before I step back into position, reset, and we begin again.

He's good at calling out my strikes and keeping me on pace, but he's not pushing me the way Jeff does. It's endearing, really, but also kind of annoying.

I don't need to be handled.

So when I see the opening to land a clean shot, I shift my body into the movement and my glove connects solidly against the mitt with more force than before. Then another. A little faster. A little sharper.

Silas's nostrils flare, and something dark and thrillingly familiar flashes through his gaze.

I smile, refocusing on the mitts. "What's on your schedule today?"

Silas shakes his head slightly. "Mostly meetings. Checking in with Everett on next quarter's financial projections. A research and development update on the latest trial phases for an arthritis medication. And a call with the legal team about the executive transition."

I nod, bouncing on the balls of my feet. "Anything else?"

His expression flickers for a moment before he adds, "I need to call Jeremy."

My movements slow. He told me about what had happened after he got home yesterday, still seething from the board meeting. I sat on the couch as he paced the den. I hadn't interrupted while he tried to make sense of how his own father could do something like this.

What makes it so cruel is that Jeremy wasn't aware of William's real motives. He thought his father was giving him a real shot to prove himself.

The first night I met Jeremy, I knew something was off. Not in a shy way, but in a way that felt studied. As if he were taking cues from the people around him, mirroring their reactions instead of forming his own. It unsettled me then, and it still does now. But even I can see that the poor guy is lost and his father is doing nothing to help him find his footing.

"Maybe you'll be able to find some common ground," I say, trying for optimism. "Work some stuff out."

Silas nods, but he's only humoring me. I don't press him on it. Instead, I refocus, falling back into the rhythm we've built between us.

Jab. Cross. Reset.

We move together in the same way river water passes over rock. His voice is gruff, precise—a tether pulling me forward. The satisfying weight of every hit lets me lose myself, until my gaze flickers past him and lands on the digital clock above the door.

6:32.

Silas notices it in the mirror's reflection, too. The hard lines around his mouth reappear as he exhales. "I need to get ready."

I wipe the sweat from my forehead, offering him a small, knowing smile. "Duty calls."

He peels the mitts off his hands and tosses them onto the mat. I barely have time to blink before he's in front of me, the heat rolling off him. I jolt at the sudden proximity. The tape on his hands is rough against my face before he kisses me so slow and deep that it stokes every ember in my body white-hot.

"I might need to drag you out of bed for drills more often," he murmurs against me. "Never seen anything sexier."

A laugh bubbles up, and I press a still-gloved hand against his chest, pushing back just enough to breathe. "Try waking me up before I'm ready and see what happens," I joke.

Something dark and pleased rolls through his eyes as he threads his fingers through the end of my ponytail. "Maybe I will."

His grip tightens, arching my body against him. His mouth descends on my throat, all teeth and lips, biting before immediately soothing with soft sweeps of his tongue against my already damp skin.

For a second, I forget how to work my own limbs. The electricity from earlier has turned into something more pleasure than pain. Then, too quickly, he pulls back.

"Shower," he demands, his coffee eyes unflinching.

The words linger between us for only a second before he pulls off my gloves and starts moving, but not before curling his fingers around my wrist to go with him.

CHAPTER 28

Silas

L eaning back into the plush leather of the booth, I drum my fingers idly on the side of the lowball glass in front of me. My phone buzzes in the opposite hand, and I glance down to see Elena's reply to the text I'd sent just as we sat down.

Me: I'm going to be later than I thought. Jeremy's dragged us to one of his favorite clubs.
Elena: The horror. Anything but that!

I smirk despite myself, my fingers moving quickly over the keyboard as I type back a response.

Me: Watch the sass.
Elena: Should I wait up for you, or will you be too busy dancing to bad club remixes?

I can practically hear the teasing lilt in her voice, and it stokes the heady fire that always seems to lick at my veins whenever she is involved.

Me: Keep the bed warm. I'll deal with you later.
Elena: (;

My tongue skims over the front of my teeth to suppress the smile tugging at my lips before locking my phone screen. The whiskey Jeremy insisted on getting me sits mostly untouched, condensation pooling around the bottom. The bass of the music makes the glass shake slightly, and strobes of light reflect off the melting ice cubes.

Across from me, my brother is entirely in his element, teeth shining in the darkness as he grins at the waitress lingering at the edge of our circular booth. The staff greeted him when we walked in and escorted us to his "usual table" within seconds.

I'd stepped back from Jeremy's opioid recovery a long time ago. Between shielding him from the press, running Wells, trying to get him professional help, and fending off my father, who often fueled the problem, I'd burned out completely. I had nothing left to give either of them. After some convincing from Natalie, I decided to wash my hands of it the day Jeremy checked into that last rehab facility in California and was officially in their care.

After that, I made it clear that I could no longer have an active role in his recovery. A lot of angry words were exchanged during that conversation, but by the end of it, he got the message.

He's remained sober of those substances as far as I know, but the royal treatment we're receiving and the number of drinks he's had since dinner raise red flags I'd be stupid to ignore.

Davey glances up from his phone beside me, likely texting Natalie and telling her what a shitshow this is shaping up to be.

Dinner had been my attempt to soften Jeremy up. He was apprehensive about going out with me, especially after the board meeting, but I was adamant that it was just a chance for us to catch up. Davey joining us to serve as a buffer didn't hurt, either.

The entire evening felt like a first date. I made reservations at a steakhouse we both enjoyed going to with our mother. We sat at a preferred table, and the service was immaculate. The drinks were flowing, and I kept things light. Family memories, harmless jokes—anything to get him to relax—but he never got there. When I tried to redirect the conversation to something of substance, he would rebuff me with a joke or excuse himself to the bathroom. By the time the check came, the only thing I'd accomplished was getting him moderately drunk.

Then suddenly he received a call from one of his weekend friends, and now we're in this club where he seems to know every face and drink order.

He's loosened his tie and unbuttoned the top of his shirt, though his hair is still perfectly groomed. For whatever reason, I can barely stomach it. Maybe some of it is jealousy. I've never had the luxury of being so unburdened. But it's more than that. Jeremy's always been different. Behind the polished charm, there's a hollowness I can't define.

It's not from lack of trying to understand him, either. My mom worked hard to ensure that my siblings and I had a solid bond, knowing how isolating this life could be. She was convinced that even if everything fell apart, the three of us would always have one another.

Natalie and I took that seriously. We've spent most of our lives trying to build that invisible bridge between us, but Jeremy made it damn near impossible. I can rely on my sister for nearly anything, but I can't say the same for him. It's like he's never truly been *with* us, even when he's physically here.

I'm one to talk. I've been called cold and ruthless more times than I can count, but Jeremy is on a level even I'm uncomfortable with. It's not just detachment; it's like he's missing something vital. And if I can see it, who else can?

"How much do you think he's had?" Davey mutters against the edge of his whiskey glass, masking his words.

"Too much," I reply as Jeremy tosses back another shot, his laugh loud and easy as he flirts with a new waitress in leather shorts and a matching bra with metal studs on the edges.

Davey leans back against the booth, head cocked slightly. "You're not going to get anything out of him tonight."

"Don't remind me," I sigh, dragging a hand through my hair. The waitress, who just finished whispering something against Jeremy's ear, slinks away from our booth and moves to the neighboring one.

My brother turns back to us, raising his glass with that same broad grin that doesn't quite reach his eyes. "You two look like you're at a funeral," he jokes. "Lighten up, will you?"

I force a small smile, lifting my glass in response. "Clubs haven't really ever been my thing."

"Then why come?"

I shrug, letting my gaze drift with feigned interest. We're tucked into one of a dozen oversized booths lining the back wall, each one perched a few feet above the main floor. An oversized walkway stretches in front of us, framed by a glass railing that offers an uninterrupted view of the chaos below.

The dance floor throbs with too many bodies. Strobe lights slice across the crowd in erratic bursts, turning sweat-slicked skin into flashes of silver and shadow.

My focus returns to Jeremy. "We can't let you have all the fun alone."

He rolls his eyes, but there's no real heat behind it. "I don't need a babysitter."

"You're right," I say, keeping my tone measured. "But I'm still your brother, and I like to know you're good."

For a moment, something flickers across Jeremy's face, but it's gone just as quickly, replaced by that easy grin. The knot in my stomach twists tighter.

Davey speaks just loud enough for me to hear. "You're going to push too hard."

Not hard enough.

I lean forward. "So, how's everything going with the projects you and Dad have been working on?"

Jeremy stiffens before he masks it with a shrug. "What's there to talk about?"

"You tell me." I shrug. "It seems like you two have been spending a lot of time together."

Jeremy sets his glass down harder than necessary. "We have." The sharpness in the statement is unmistakable. "Why?"

"Curiosity." I don't take the bait. "He didn't mention your proposal before the meeting, so I was just wondering what else you two have been discussing."

Jeremy leans back, and his eyes narrow. "Why does it matter?" he asks.

"Like I said, I'm curious." I meet his stare evenly. "You've been working closely, and I want to know how it's going. What you've been focusing on."

"What I've been focusing on," he echoes, unsure.

"I want to understand what you're passionate about."

For a second, he just stares, processing the words. Then, something shifts. His apprehension molts into anger faster than I can blink; muscles coiling under his skin as if he's braced for an attack.

He scoffs, shaking his head. "I get it."

I exhale. *Shit.* "Jeremy—"

"Worried I'm going to embarrass you again with another idea in the future?" he snaps.

I shake my head. "I had to be objective. It's how I'd be for any member's proposal."

Jeremy snorts. "Yeah, well, none of those people are your brother."

Damn it. I have to salvage this. "You have a strong way of selling an idea. Your enthusiasm, the way you framed it—that takes skill." I pause. "I think you'd be great in sales."

He lets out a bitter laugh. "Jesus Christ, there it is." Lifting his hand to his jaw, he rubs at the tense muscles. "You're trying to push me into something else because you think I'm too stupid for operations."

"That's not true."

"Yes, it is." He says through gritted teeth. "Dad said you wouldn't get the vision."

The words press against the center of my chest. There's been no question that William has been pitting us against one another for months, but to hear it confirmed out loud is something else entirely.

I force myself to stay still. "What else does he say?"

Jeremy settles back into his seat, a smug expression settling on his lips. "That we'd make a great team."

We.

And he isn't referring to the two of us.

I nod once, carefully schooling my expression. "I'm going to grab another drink," I say, standing abruptly. The table has service, but I need to step away before I do something I can't take back. "You want the same?"

Jeremy waves a hand dismissively. "Do whatever you want, Silas. You always do."

Though I can feel Davey's eyes on me, I don't look toward him. I slide out of the booth without a word and make my way down to the VIP bar at the base of the stairs. It's marginally quieter here, tucked slightly away from the main floor, but not by much. I'm not sure if the vibrating running through me is the music or my own furious pulse at this point.

After a few minutes, the bartender meets my gaze and I order another round, my fingers drumming against the bar top in restless frustration.

I can't fucking believe him.

Either of them.

What am I supposed to do with any of this? Jeremy has never wanted to hear anything I have to say. We've been in some kind of one-sided competition our whole lives, and he'll only think I'm trying to sabotage him. It's definitely what my father has convinced him of, anyway, because apparently *they're* a team now.

And I've become the enemy.

"Silas Wells," a familiar voice says, warm and teasing. "As I live and breathe."

I jolt just as Alice Lancaster saddles up beside me, her glass of something-on-the-rocks in hand, gaze bright with amusement.

"Alice," I say with a practiced smile. "Didn't expect to see you here."

"Likewise," she replies, her tone laced with playful curiosity. "You don't exactly scream 'club regular.'"

"I'm not," I admit, nodding behind me. "Jeremy's idea."

"Ah," she says knowingly, her eyes flicking toward the booths. "Forever the responsible older brother."

"Hopefully, not for long. I think I'm going to hire out the job soon," I quip. Her laugh comes easily, just as her free hand rests on my bicep. She leans in, fingers tensing on my shirt sleeve.

"You always take on more than you should," she replies with a dazzling smile. "It's one of the things I like about you."

The compliment settles uncomfortably over me, but not as much as her touch. I turn back toward the bar, and her hand falls away. "Alice," I start, "I owe you an apology for not calling after our last date."

I was so disoriented from the whole argument at Natalie's that I dropped her off at her home without much explanation.

"I figured you had your reasons." There's a pause. "Did everything work out with... whatever that was?"

"It did." I glance at the bartender, who's preparing my drinks alongside several others. "I think it's only fair to let you know I won't be calling in the future."

Alice's smile falters before she nods slowly. "It's her, isn't it?" she asks. "The pretty brunette at your sister's house?"

"Yes." The word is out before I even think about it.

Elena and I agreed to take this one day at a time, to figure out what we could be if I didn't let my anger dictate everything. And in the process, I've started getting to know her the same way she seems to already know me. Scarlett was intelligent, stubborn, independent, and impossible not to want, but I barely scratched the surface. Elena is all of those things, but amplified. Every time I think I've figured her out, she proves me wrong, and what surprises me most is how much I want her to.

But wanting her and trusting her aren't always the same thing. There are some days when I can't let go of everything she's done and I force space between us to quiet the voices screaming in my head to end this before the same thing happens again. I see how much that affects her, and I hate it. It's the reason I haven't made any definitive decisions about us. Yet my answer comes too fast, like claiming her is instinct.

The realization unsettles me.

Alice exhales, a wistful smile tugging at the corners of her lips. "I thought so."

Her candor catches me off guard. "That obvious?" I ask, my voice softer than I intended.

"Yes," she says with a faint laugh. "Don't worry, your secret is safe with me. I just hope she's worth all the trouble."

The idea of anyone dismissing Elena without knowing her stirs something defensive in me. "She is." Another contradiction I should probably unpack.

Alice nods again, her shoulders relaxing. "Then I'm happy for you, Silas," she says and raises her glass. "Thanks for being honest. It's more than most would do."

"Thank you," I echo, meaning it. She takes a sip of her near-empty drink just as the bartender places three glasses on the counter in front of me. I hand him several bills and decline the change.

"I need to get back to my friends before they wonder if I've been kidnapped," Alice jokes. "See you around?"

"See you," I reply, offering a small smile before collecting my drinks and heading up the stairs without looking back.

When I return to the table, Davey is alone. I don't bother asking where Jeremy went. Instead, I slide one of the glasses of Macallan toward my brother-in-law and down the other as I sink back into the booth. The burn hits hard and sharp in my throat before flaring to my nose. I suck in a breath through my teeth, waiting for the sting to settle.

Now, what the hell do I do about my dad and brother?

CHAPTER 29

Elena

A wildfire blazes through my veins as I approach Silas's office. The door, now seemingly never locked, slams against the wall as I storm inside. Silas's head snaps up from his laptop. My chest heaves. There's a beat of silence. Someone clears their throat on the other end of his video call.

I don't care.

Not that I left Jeff and Natalie in the basement, startled when I abruptly ended my session fifteen minutes early. Not that Silas could be speaking with someone extremely important. Nothing matters except the headline that popped up on my home screen when I took a water break.

Wells Heir Spotted Again with Jewelry Mogul Alice Lancaster

The insufferable gossip article would have been easy to ignore if not for the photos that tinted my vision red. Picture after picture showed Silas and Alice at the bar. One had him smiling at her with an easy, charming grin. Another showed her tilting her glass toward him in a subtle toast. What pushed me over the edge was the shot of her leaning into him, hand curled around his bicep, laughing like they're sharing some private joke.

Funnily enough, this interaction didn't make it into any part of our conversation when he got home at two in the morning.

"Beth, I think I have an emergency," Silas says, eyes locked on me. "I'll give you a call this afternoon if I have any notes, but overall, this looks great. Good work."

He doesn't wait for a response. Just closes the laptop and sets it on the far edge of his desk. Then, taking his sweet time, he leans back in his chair and turns to face me head-on.

Those curious, coffee eyes scan me from top to toe. "What's wrong?"

My fingers curl tighter around my phone. I can't seem to form a coherent thought. Words are beyond me. This feeling is a living, breathing thing under my skin, demanding to be acknowledged. The onslaught of fury burns so brightly that it makes my eyes water.

I've never allowed myself to feel it, especially not with Silas. I didn't have the right to claim to him before, no matter how badly I wanted to.

But it's different now.

I inhale deeply, roll my shoulders back, and fix a smile on my face that doesn't quite mask the storm raging beneath.

"Remind me again," I start, placing my phone on the corner of his desk with more force than necessary. The sharp *thud* draws his eyes to it before they flick back up to mine. "How was last night?"

Confusion passes across his face, but it's gone quickly, replaced by that infuriatingly calm expression. His gaze sweeps over my disheveled braid. Wild frizz escapes from it, and the unmistakable flush of anger burns on my skin.

"Uneventful," he says, far too measured.

My pulse pounds in my ears. *Motherfucker.*

I close the distance between us and lower myself onto him, bracketing his hips with my knees. My rash guard and biker shorts are damp with residual sweat, ruining his slacks and collared shirt. He blinks rapidly, but his hands remain on the arms of his chair.

I lean in slowly, so close that our chests brush, my lips barely grazing his in a featherlight touch while threading my fingers into the base of his soft curls. His breath hitches, but he still waits.

"How was Alice?" I hiss, voice sharp as a blade.

Silas stiffens for just a moment before relaxing beneath me. Then he dares to let out a low chuckle.

A fucking *chuckle*.

"She was at the club with some friends," he explains. "We ended up at the bar at the same time."

He moves to touch my waist, but my hands snap to his forearms, slamming them down against the armrests. The impact echoes through the study.

His teasing demeanor shifts just enough to send a pulse of electricity through the air. "Careful, Lena."

I ignore the warning, my heart hammering as I press closer. "She really seemed to be enjoying herself," I say, biting off each word. "My favorite photo was the one where she's holding onto your arm."

There's a long moment of contemplation, his tongue running over his top teeth. Beneath my grip, his muscles flex, testing the restraint, but he doesn't push. We both know he could move me in an instant.

"You, of all people, know better than to read into gossip magazine photos," Silas provokes, though his voice is smooth as silk. Just as the final word leaves his lips, he's leaning forward to close the gap between our mouths. I retreat a fraction of an inch. His smile deepens.

He thinks this is a game.

My insides churn as I reach for the knot of his tie, toying with the fabric between my fingers. Then, wrapping the tail around my palm once, then twice, I tug him forward with slow, deliberate precision.

Our noses brush, his breath warm against my lips. A low vibration rumbles deep in his chest. I can't tell if it's a growl or a hum of approval, but it sends a rush of heat down my spine anyway.

"I understand to the outside world, I don't exist," I whisper, my voice eerily calm. "But in this house, I *do*."

His muscles contract beneath me.

"You chose to hold on to me, Silas Wells." Our chests are flush now, my frustration shaking his body almost as much as it's shaking mine. "And we agreed on monogamy."

For a moment, he stays still, as if waiting for me to break first, but I would rather chew on rocks than give him that much right now.

When I don't relent, his once-compliant hands begin to move. They skim over the sides of my thighs. As they round to the curve of my ass, his grip tightens enough to drag a soft gasp from my lips. His knowing smile grows as the restraint continues to unravel.

"You're a goddamn vision," he murmurs while giving me another teasing squeeze. "I should piss you off more often."

A pulse of irritation shoots through me. "This isn't a joke," I snap, though my voice wavers as I tug at the tie still wrapped around my wrist. "This is about respect and boundaries."

Silas lifts an eyebrow, his hands resuming their deliberate exploration. One hand slides up my back, slipping beneath the hem of my rash guard, fingers splaying across my bare skin. His calloused palm presses firmly against my spine.

"Boundaries," he repeats, tasting the word. "What are your boundaries, Lena?"

A shiver rolls through me, involuntary and damning.

"Boundaries," I repeat, trying to focus. "For starters, no more letting other women get comfortable enough to touch you."

His lips twitch slightly, but he doesn't interrupt. The hand on my back moves higher, his thumb tracing a lazy path along my spine and under my sports bra.

"Go on." His voice is so composed that it only makes the feral glint in his eyes more pronounced.

I grit my teeth. "No more lingering conversations with women, especially ones you've slept with," I continue as he leans in, lips brushing the hollow of my ear.

"Anything else, princess?" he asks, his other hand slipping down to my waist, his thumb beginning to trace slow, maddening circles against my hip. "I want to make sure I'm *very* clear on your expectations."

I arch into him without thinking. The tie slips from my wrist as my hands flatten against his chest. My head lolls, granting him access I hadn't intended to give.

"That covers it. No touching. No lingering conversations. And you make it clear you're taken by... someone," I answer, stumbling on the last word. "That's all of it."

As I finish my demands, his lips descend on me, tongue tracing the column of my throat in one devastating sweep. A shudder rips through me.

"Feel better now?" he murmurs against my skin, biting down in the junction of my shoulder and neck just hard enough to make me inhale sharply. "Because I do."

"Asshole," I manage, but there's no real resistance.

A low chuckle vibrates through him as he presses a lingering kiss to my collarbone before raising his head. Those capable, practiced hands find the waistband of my shorts.

"I could get used to this," he muses.

My breath catches as his fingers slip beneath the fabric, the contrast of his cool touch against my burning skin making every nerve in my body snap to attention.

"Get used to what?" I ask, though the words sound more like a pant than a question.

"You." His lips curve into a half-smile against my jaw, fingers ghosting along the edge of my underwear. "Barging in here like you own the place."

Heat licks up my skin, spreading to the apples of my cheeks, but not just from his touch.

How can he be so unbothered?

Sometimes, it seems Silas doesn't truly understand the impact he has on people and what they might do to hold his attention.

"How would you feel if it were the other way around?" My voice is quieter than before.

Silas pulls back just enough to meet my eyes. The warmth that was there just seconds ago hardens.

Suddenly, he's swiveling to face his desk and, with too much ease, lifts me off his lap and onto it. The mixture of the cool wood and the growing distance between our bodies leaves me feeling exposed.

There's a brief pause while he exhales through his nose, though his hands come to rest on my knees. "I don't have to imagine it because I saw it when you were on that date."

Oh.

The memories I pushed into the recesses of my mind come barreling to the front. Harrison's hands on me, his tongue in my mouth. The way I sat there and let it happen, played my role, because that's what I was supposed to do.

I don't realize my eyes have dropped to the space between us, my mind sinking into the dark waters of that night, until Silas is suddenly standing over me, forcing my chin up with his fingers.

"I wanted to break every bone in his hands," he says with no hesitation. "One by one."

A slow, traitorous warmth blooms low in my stomach. I shouldn't like the way that sounds, but I do.

The pad of Silas's thumb strokes slowly across my skin, back and forth, before stopping in the small space between my lip and chin. He holds me there, refusing to let me slip away from his gaze like I used to. Even though every instinct screams to retreat, I force my eyes to stay on his.

My thoughts spill out before I can second-guess them. "That's how I feel," I murmur. "Seeing her touch you, looking at you like that. It made me want to—" I swallow hard. "I can't even blame her. Of course, she'd try."

The stumbling confession strips me of whatever confidence I had left. I try to glance down, but Silas's grip tightens. He leans in, spreading my knees wider to accommodate his frame and closing the space between us like it belongs to him. His thumb drifts upward, pushing into the soft give of my bottom lip, then just slightly inward, pressing against the top of my bottom teeth. Heat pools low in my stomach.

Almost on instinct, I close my mouth around his finger, teeth catching his skin just enough to hold him still. His nostrils flare. "Alice did try to flirt with me."

I hum in acknowledgment, letting my tongue swirl around the digit. Each stroke makes his eyes darken. "I told her I was seeing someone," he continues, "the second she touched me."

His free hand moves between us, expertly sliding down the front of my shorts. His palm presses hard against my center with just enough pressure to steal the air from my lungs. A soft, broken exhale escapes me, releasing his thumb from my mouth.

Silas's head dips down, palm still pressed firmly between us. "She guessed it was you and was immediately respectful of it."

The knot in my chest loosens, but it doesn't disappear entirely. "Why didn't you tell me that last night?" My voice sharpens again, despite the way my limbs already tremble under his hands.

"I wanted to see what you would do," he admits with a diabolical smile. "And you didn't disappoint."

Fingers slip beneath my underwear and immediately find my clit, circling so perfectly, so excruciatingly slow that my hips jerk toward him. My whimper is muffled by his tongue as he invades my mouth in the same slow, teasing rhythm as his fingers.

Every calculated movement pulls me deeper under his spell, dissolving the sharp edges of my frustration. A hand slides into my hair to keep me from falling backward as I melt further into the desk.

"Are we going to keep fighting about Alice?" he breathes, pressing just a little harder, a little more insistent. "Or are you going to let me reward you?"

My lack of answer is all the invitation he needs. He works me purposefully, dragging out every ounce of pleasure with cruel precision. The slow burn that crawls up my spine is so hot that it's agonizing, but it's also so goddamn good I can't think straight.

His fingers pinch and circle, retreating just so, leaving me teetering on the edge. When the need becomes unbearable, my hips move on instinct, grinding against his hand, searching for friction. The look in his eyes is borderline feral as he lets me take what I need.

My scalp tingles where his hold bites deeper. "How am I supposed to even look at another woman," he growls, "when I have this?"

He drags his fingers lower, slipping inside of me and curling so quickly that the mind-melting sensation rips a strangled sound from my throat.

"When I can have *you* riding my hand?" Silas punctuates the words with a slow, deliberate thrust. "Moaning into my mouth? Falling apart for me just because I tell you to?"

My thighs quake as I gyrate. His grip tightens, forcing my chin up to meet his gaze—dark, molten, entirely in control.

"Let me have it," he orders.

I hiss out a curse, but Silas swallows it, molding his mouth to mine. His fingers don't slow until the white-hot ecstasy rips through every nerve in my body, pulsing deliciously with every erratic heartbeat.

My body bows into him, desperate to take everything he gives me. I ride his fingers, chasing every last spark of pleasure, dragging it out until my breath is nothing but wrecked gasps.

Silas doesn't stop. Even as I shake, his fingers keep working me. His mouth is everywhere: my jaw, the curve of my neck, the top of my shoulder. Lips and teeth creating a trail of reverence, mapping out each precious inch of skin with such intent that it feels like a brand.

Only when the tremors ease and my muscles slacken does he finally slow. Carefully, Silas withdraws his hand from my shorts and smooths the fabric back into place while his other arm keeps me upright. He adjusts his hold as he straightens, drawing me closer to the edge of the desk. Then, finally, his mouth claims mine again in a kiss that douses any remaining anger.

There's nothing like being the center of Silas's attention. Nothing compares to the high of being seen, wanted, and *devoured* by him.

When he pulls back, I see all the satisfaction of undoing me. It's carved into the sharp lines of his body, and impossible to miss in the bulge straining against his pants, pressing against my leg.

"That's my girl," he praises, lifting a hand to brush the strands of hair clinging to my cheek.

"Your *only* girl," I clarify without much muster. My head falls forward, pressing into the side of his neck where his pulse thumps wildly.

"Yes, Lena," he confirms, fingers curling to my nape while the hand that just shattered me drags up my thigh, slow and lazy, like he has nowhere else to be. "Only you."

Chapter 30

Silas

There's barely time for the timid knock at my office door to register in my mind before it swings open. My father strides in past Leslie, our gazes briefly meeting. Her eyes are wide and cheeks pink. She mouths an apology to me.

I wave her off with a subtle, reassuring nod. Rising from my chair, I button my suit jacket and plaster on a polite smile. "Dad," I greet him, my tone warm enough to pass as genuine.

Leslie's eyes flick between us as I approach, clearly debating whether to leave me alone with him. She's only a few years older than me, but as a mother of two and a longtime witness to my clashes with my father, those maternal instincts tend to kick in. In the almost decade she's been my secretary, she never breathed a critical word about him until about a year ago.

William and I thought we were alone on the floor that evening and in the middle of a loud, vicious argument in my office when we noticed a faint movement through the glass wall near Leslie's desk. She was sitting there, trying to disappear into her chair while working on her computer.

Only after my father left did Leslie come in, apologizing. She stayed late to finish some paperwork. I told her there was nothing to forgive, thanked her for her hard work, and wished her a nice evening. As she turned to leave the doorway, she paused and spoke so softly that I almost missed it.

"A parent should never speak to their child that way."

The funny part about it is, I don't even remember the insults my father hurled at me now .

Leslie's concerned gaze stirs the dormant ache for my own mother, growing where the comfort used to be. William brushes past me, his focus already on my desk as his fingers trail over the back of my chair.

"Run along," he mutters absently, lowering himself into it with all the grace of a king settling onto his throne.

My jaw tightens as Leslie steps out silently, shutting the door behind her. William leans back, his hands on the armrests, surveying the room.

I step away, positioning myself near the window and leaning against the credenza with my arms loosely crossed.

"Can I get you something?" I ask, keeping my tone neutral. "Coffee? Water?"

"Cut the act, Silas. I'm not here for pleasantries," he begins, crossing one leg over the other. "I've given you enough time to collect yourself since our last conversation," he says. "I'd like to discuss how you acted during the board meeting."

"What about it?"

William exhales. "You let Jeremy flounder," he answers. "What were you thinking, shutting down his proposal in front of the board like that?"

"That it wasn't a good proposal?"

His expression hardens. "It wasn't ready. You had the opportunity to shape it and make it viable, but instead, you left him twisting in the wind."

A clipped laugh escapes me.

"That's rich coming from you." I slowly cross the office, hands coming together behind my back. "Do you remember the topic of the first proposal I brought to the board?"

When he doesn't respond, I continue, "A strategic expansion into sustainable manufacturing by partnering with a new firm and integrating greener production practices."

William scoffs at the reminder. "It was a terrible idea."

I smirk. "You and the board made sure I knew. Tore it apart, said I didn't get margins and that 'sustainability' was a buzzword."

My father's eyes narrow, but he doesn't speak. I walk the length of the room. "The next time I wanted to present an idea, I looked at it from every perspective possible before bringing it forward." I turn to face him fully. "Why would Jeremy be an exception to that?"

William doesn't hesitate. "Because we both know Jeremy can use all the help he can get. You made him look like a fool in front of the people he was trying to impress."

Not criticism, not guidance. *Help.* Because my brother can't possibly do it himself. We need to hold his hand through it so he *and* my father don't look bad.

I release a fraction of my growing irritation in a long breath.

"He made a fool of himself long before I spoke. Even if the idea were solid, he thought that a half-assed speech was going to be enough to convince a room of experts of an operational overhaul. You know this. And instead of guiding him, you're here to reprimand me for doing my job."

William's eyes darken. "It's what we do for family," he says through his teeth.

"Is that right?" I meet his gaze. "Where's this mindset when I make proposals? Or when Natalie showed an interest in human resources?"

Nat was interested in far more than that, but it was the one thing she thought our father might entertain. It was never exactly clear what disqualified her, but he never gave her ideas the time of day, no matter who vouched for them. Eventually, she grew tired of trying and gave up, which is a damn shame because *she's* the one who would make a great COO.

209

Though the ice in his gaze remains, William dismisses the questions with the same annoyance he might a bug. "Clearly, you're too emotional to have a productive conversation about this," he says. "But maybe you can hold it together long enough to discuss our audits."

I rub my eyes under my glasses, the headache already blooming. "What about them?" I ask.

"Almost all have been completed besides IT," he says, "I want to know why."

I shrug. "From the updates I've received from Davey, there's a lot to work through."

"What *exactly* is there to work through?"

I keep my expression neutral. "I'm relying on Davey to tell me that. He's the expert." Brenden has been unusually quiet this past week. I'll have to have Davey keep a close eye on him.

My father shakes his head, running a hand through his peppered hair. "A waste of time and money," he mutters.

I fix my cufflinks. "I want to follow standard procedures. They should be wrapping up soon," I say, but haven't a clue when Davey and Elena's friends will be done decrypting those files. "Then we can hash out the details of the transition."

My father rolls his eyes, looking briefly up at the ceiling. "You and those damn details."

The details we need to make this successful and seamless for everyone. Why would he care, at the end of the day, when it will only reflect poorly on me and my leadership?

My tongue runs over my teeth as I lean on a cigar chair. "I'd be happy to refine those details on my own, if that doesn't interest you."

Disbelief flashes across his face. "So I can be blocked out completely by the end of this? I don't think so."

The accusation hits me hard enough that it takes a moment for my thoughts to catch up with the rest of me.

"Is that what you think I'm trying to do?"

I've kept him involved at every step, even in areas I didn't have to, and somehow, he believes I'm trying to cut him out?

He ignores my question, resting his elbows on the desk, steepling his fingers as his eyes bore into mine.

"If I'd known this was the kind of leadership you'd bring to the table..." He trails off, letting the thought hang for a moment before continuing, "The secrecy around the audits. The reckless personal choices. And now, leaving your brother out to dry?" He shakes his head, disappointment bleeding into every word. "I trusted you to be a team player, but now I'm starting to wonder if I made the wrong choice."

I blink, head whirling, but that's the most I'm willing to show.

"Well, just like Jeremy's nomination, you can try to reverse the executive transition if you think I'm wrong for the job."

His lips press into a thin line. "Do you think I won't?" he asks.

My chest burns. Slow and deep at first, then hotter, brighter, sharper with every second he holds my gaze.

He thinks he can threaten me with the one thing I've been groomed for since I could walk the halls of this building? The title he drilled into me like gospel? The job he swore he was proud to hand over at the beginning of the year, when we signed the papers and the board stamped their approval?

Something inside of me threatens to crack open.

For years, I swallowed my pride, kept my head down, made compromises to become the man he said he wanted me to be, and now he's pretending he can take it all back with a single sentence.

Over my dead fucking body.

"I think you can try," I reply, keeping my voice deceptively even. "If you really believe you can convince them otherwise, by all means."

The muscles in his jaw flex. He stands, smoothing his suit jacket as he steps around the desk.

"You're cocky, Silas," he sighs, "and that confidence will be your undoing."

I don't flinch. "Or it'll be the reason this company thrives."

The silence between us is so thick I could swim in it.

"You've made your position clear." *My position on what, exactly?* "We'll see how long you can hold it."

He exits without another word, leaving my office door open. Through the glass, he strides down the hall, and only when he's finally out of sight do I exhale.

It takes me a minute to pick myself off of the cigar chair, flexing my aching fingers from the fist I hadn't realized I was holding them in. Just as I move back towards my desk, Leslie approaches, her expression cautious.

"Is everything okay?" she asks.

I force a small smile, though it feels tight and unnatural. "It's fine," I say. "Thank you."

Leslie nods, clearly unconvinced. She closes the door behind her, and I sink into the chair William vacated, my hands gripping the armrests, wondering how the hell we got here.

CHAPTER 31

Elena

"Please don't take this the wrong way because I always love when you visit," Natalie starts, her gaze fixed on me from atop the small step ladder just inside the guest bathroom. "But why did you want to come over so badly today?"

The piece of wallpaper she's been battling for over ten minutes peels away from the top of the wall, draping over her head. The groan she releases sounds more demonic than human. I press my lips together, trying to suppress a laugh, but a snort escapes me anyway.

Natalie shoots me a glare as she pins it back into place, her tongue peeking out between her teeth in concentration. With one hand, she reaches for the scraper on the step near her chest to smooth out the bubbles. I smile at her from the floor and lean my head back against the wall.

I'd already offered to help her several times in the past two hours. She's attempting to correct her disaster DIY project from the spring when we were both confined to our homes. Each time, she's declined.

"Well?" she prompts.

My eyes wander, taking in the neatly pressed linens and the tidiness that makes it feel more like a hotel room than the place where I'd scattered my clothes just over a month ago.

Even as I try to distract myself from answering, Natalie waits.

"Silas needed space," I finally admit.

It was one of our bad days. I've told Natalie enough about them that she doesn't need more details. Not that I want to particularly relive them, anyway.

I could tell how the day was going to go the moment my eyes met his in the bathroom mirror this morning. Silas was fresh from his post-work-out shower, a towel wrapped around his waist. The resentment was etched in every line of his frown, the crease between his eyebrows, and his gaze hardened the moment he realized I had entered the room. The shame that flooded me was enough to fill the free-standing bathtub behind him and drown in it.

I must be a glutton for punishment because I still tested the waters, brushing my fingers lightly against his bare back as I passed to my side of the vanity. He recoiled just enough to confirm what I already knew. So, I withdrew, too embarrassed to ask if I did something in particular or if it was just the sight of me this time.

Instead of asking questions and hurting my own feelings more than they already were, I gave him the space he clearly needed and went back into the bedroom. Only when he was dressed and retreated to his study did I get ready for my day and try to be as small as possible.

Silas stayed locked away all morning. I didn't even dare to walk past his door, let alone try to speak with him. With Davey occupied at the office and no tasks for me, I was left to stew in my own thoughts.

After cooking myself breakfast alongside Kendall and a few hours of mindless television, the vastness of the mansion and the unbearable silence became too much. So, when I texted Natalie and learned she was wallpapering, I seized the opportunity and asked Lloyd for a ride to her townhome on his way to take over for Paul at the satellite office.

I left a note for Silas on the window seat of the music room, where I spent a lot of my free time now. I didn't want to insert myself into his thoughts with a text when he obviously wanted to avoid me. Leaving the note in the place he'd look for me felt like the best compromise.

"Ah," Natalie muses, lips pursing as she considers her next words. "It feels like it's been a longer stretch this time, at least?"

I give her a thin smile. She isn't wrong. Every bad day seems to be spaced further apart now. It's progress, although it's no less painful each time it happens. It's starting to feel worse, actually.

"How's the holiday party planning coming?" I ask, eager to pivot the conversation anywhere else.

Natalie is in the early stages of booking the venue for Wells—which feels crazy to be thinking about in September—but she tells me it's completely normal.

Even though her gaze narrows, she details the places she's toured, particularly an industrial event space closer to the suburbs, which is ideal since most staff don't live in the city. We brainstorm potential activities to focus the evening less on the free alcohol, though it's always the main attraction.

While discussing how she might go about a partnership with a car service or rideshare company, my phone buzzes. I pull it out to see Cillian's name flashing on the screen.

"Hi Cillian," I say, answering.

"Where are you?" The sharpness of his tone makes me pull the phone away from my ear.

"I'm at Natalie's," I reply, glancing up at her. Her brow furrows. "Why?"

Cillian exhales loudly. "Jesus," he mutters. It sounds like I'm on speakerphone and he's typing. "How did you get there?"

"I asked Lloyd to drop me off when he was leaving for the office," I respond slowly. Natalie steps down from the ladder, eyes trained on me.

"Silas is going to call you. Please answer him," Cillian says, then hangs up without waiting for a response.

Before Natalie can get out a single question, my phone vibrates again. I don't even bother to look at the screen before sliding it open.

"Si," I say immediately and pick myself off the floor, "is everything—"

"You can't do that, Elena."

My pulse spikes at the pure venom dripping from his words. Suddenly, I'm not in Natalie's guest bedroom; I'm back in that cold holding cell, tied to a chair with coarse rope digging into my wrists.

The edges of my vision blur, and I blink the darkness away.

"What can't I do?" I ask, my voice steadier than I feel.

"You can't just leave like that," Silas hisses.

My ears ring in the silence.

I glance toward Natalie, and with a sympathetic nod, she wordlessly excuses herself, rounding the bed and closing the bedroom door behind her. The quiet only seems to make the ringing louder, and the heat buried in the center of my chest starts to expand outward like a tea kettle ready to boil over.

My inhale is shaky. "I left you a note in the music room."

Silas scoffs, and there's a rustle, maybe him running a hand through his hair. "Another note? Really?" he mutters, almost to himself.

The heat is doused by an icy cold as the meaning of his words hits me.

I squeeze my eyes shut and sink onto the edge of the bed. The mattress gives under my weight, grounding me just enough to remind me which way is up and which way is down.

Silas's next words come out fast, "I went to look for you and you weren't anywhere. Not in the bedroom, or the kitchen, or the attic. Not even in that goddamn guest room."

His heavy breathing is the only sound between us for several heartbeats. My free arm curls around my middle, but it brings no comfort.

"I'm sorry," I whisper. "I didn't want to text you when you needed space." Guilt washes over me as I continue, "I forgot to tell Lloyd that you didn't know where I was going. That's my fault."

Another pause. "Did you think I'd be angry if you texted me?"

I shrug, even though he can't see me. "I don't know," I admit.

Silas swears softly.

"Elena, no matter what's happening, I don't want you disappearing like that." His voice strains, and I can almost picture his grimace. "I didn't even make it to the music room before I called Cillian because I thought you wouldn't answer my call."

It's hard not to imagine his panic growing as he failed to find me in every room he checked, wearing the same expression he had in the kitchen the night I left last time.

I clench my hand into a fist, my fingernails digging into my palm to distract from the aching in my chest.

How did I mess this up so badly?

I whisper another apology, but he's quick to interject. "Please stop apologizing. This—you shouldn't feel like you can't text me." The line goes silent for a long moment before Silas breaks it, his voice gentler. "Can I come pick you up?"

My mouth opens to answer, but nothing comes out.

Is that even a good idea? Once the relief settles, will he go back to hating me for the rest of the day? I'm not sure I can handle that at the moment. The idea of being left alone in that house when I have nowhere else to go feels like its own form of punishment.

He brings me back with the softest request, "To talk about it in person. Please."

A sad smile curves to my lips at his defeated plea.

"Okay."

Silas exhales. "Thank you," he whispers. "I'm sorry. It's not an excuse, but I'm still trying to figure this out."

I bite the inside of my cheek. "I know, it's okay."

"It's not okay. You've done nothing wrong."

A small, pitiful laugh bubbles up from my throat before I answer, "I've done plenty wrong."

He sighs. "I mean, when I get like this, I..." he trails off, letting out a frustrated huff while searching for the right words. "I don't want to be like this."

I wince.

It's impossible to wrap my brain around the idea that I've been un-raveling the discipline of a man whose emotions are so tightly reined in that they might as well be engineered, thread by thread.

Or the fact that he still wants to forgive me for everything I've done.

"How about we just focus on today?" I suggest, running my fingernail along the seam of one of the subtle florals stitched on the comforter. "Let's work on that and see how it goes."

"I can do that," he agrees. "Let's fix today."

My mouth turns up into a more genuine smile. "Okay."

"Hang tight. I'll be there in fifteen."

"See you soon." I don't wait for his response before hanging up.

My lock screen illuminates as I tilt my phone, displaying the photo I took in the attic last week. There's a blurred movie in the background, my bare legs tangled with Silas's sweatpant-clad ones on the couch. The soft lighting makes everything in the image seem muted and warm.

It's the most courage I've had to take any photos of him or us together. My cheeks were so hot when I took my phone out to snap the picture, and Silas barely tried to hide his smug smirk as he watched.

His composure only seemed to break the next morning when he realized I had set it as my wallpaper. In seconds, his eyes turned molten as they flicked back and forth from me to the phone.

"We're done talking," I call out, turning my head just enough to see Natalie crack open the door with a sheepish look on her face.

She opens it wider, but leans against the doorframe instead of enter-ing, her fingers still on the handle. "You okay?" She scans my face from top to bottom.

I shrug. "I think so. He's coming to pick me up so we can talk."

Natalie's jaw works as she considers my answer, arms crossing over her chest. "If there was anything remotely normal about this relationship, I'd be telling you to run for the hills because this hot-and-cold treatment is very unhealthy."

The space between my eyes starts to ache, and I rub it, nodding.

She picks herself off the door and rounds the bed, patting my knee as she returns to her ladder. "He's going to figure it out," Natalie continues, trying to convince herself of it as much as she is me. "By the end of all of this, it's going to be worth it."

I bob my head again at her words.

She's right and wrong.

If this were any other relationship, I'd walk away, but it's not. It's Silas. And no matter the outcome, there hasn't been a moment it hasn't felt worth it. Because, somehow, every time things fall apart, we find a way to drag each other back to the surface. And what's left of us is so consuming that it almost feels clean, like all the damage burned off on the way up.

And nothing compares to the days we both believe we want this.

So, I wait for the sound of his footsteps down the hall, ready to unapologetically pull me away from his sister, because after knowing what that high feels like, I'd rather it incinerate me than let it go.

CHAPTER 32

Silas

Davey leads me down a hallway, our footsteps echoing against the polished concrete to another metal door. He punches in a final code into a keypad next to the handle, and the heavy door cracks open.

The hum of the servers fills the air, machines sitting neatly in even rows across one side of the room. On the other side, a few cubicle-style desks are clustered alongside a conference table. The setup mimics what we had back at the warehouse—Andrew Mallory, one of my father's old friends, pulled out all the stops to make sure of it when he leased him the space.

Paul is stationed at a cubicle, his eyes flicking from his laptop screen to the three men who are technically our hostages.

They are all at the conference table, deeply engrossed in their work. Unfortunately, I am already acquainted with Luis, but Ben and Corey are just names I associated with voices until now.

One is medium height, with a forgettable blend of brown hair and an equally average build. The other sits slightly slouched, his features a stark contrast with sandy blond hair, which is a bit too long. These are the two men who managed to infiltrate the secured system we've spent millions of dollars to construct and maintain.

Their normalcy is almost alarming.

Scattered coffee cups, takeout boxes, and energy cans ring the table's edge, pushed aside repeatedly to make space for laptops and screens.

All eyes flick towards us, but it's Luis's gaze that locks onto mine. He looks nothing like the last time we met, bloodied and tied to a chair. The fading bruises and scabs are the only things that remain.

Pity.

I don't like or trust the fucker. He might have helped Elena disappear when she needed it most, but he also spent years working for Peter. Elena was young and inexperienced when she first started, and then she was blackmailed into staying. Luis, however, is a grown man. Maybe a few years older than me, and he knew exactly who Peter was. He had the autonomy to walk away. The fact that he didn't says everything I need to know about him.

We haven't heard a peep about Peter since Davey's source in California tracked him down just long enough for us to think we had something before he disappeared again. Looking at Luis is a reminder that Peter's still out there somewhere, and that just pisses me off more.

My only consolation is that Luis despises me. Not just for what I did to him, but for having Elena.

I've been about as subtle as a bulldozer on our daily calls about where she's living. Petty, maybe, but I'm not about to let him think he has a chance with her. Not that she's ever seemed to look at him that way, but I won't risk it. He's so obviously hung up on her that I wouldn't put it past him to try something if he could see her in person. Hell, it's most of the reason I won't tell her where they're temporarily living.

What's even sweeter is that Elena has been keeping her distance. No requests to see him or conversations beyond what's necessary about the servers. She's polite, even warm at times, but always professional. And every text Luis has sent asking to talk has been ignored. I never asked her to do any of it, but she's been passing this unintentional test with flying fucking colors.

And I hope that Luis knowing where she's been staying and why she's been avoiding him is torture. Wondering if she's with me. If I'm touching her. If she's giving me everything he wants. I pray that it eats him alive to think of us together. Imagining what she sounds like when she comes, like she did this morning with her hair fanned out across my pillow—one leg pinned high and tight against my chest, muscles flexing under my grip as I angled her just right, tits bouncing with every thrust while I scraped kisses and teeth up her calf.

Davey's voice cuts through my vivid memory. "The program is working, but we have to keep refining it as we go," he starts, leading me further into the room. My gaze wanders to the servers. "The deeper we get, the more unfamiliar encryption I see."

My unease grows. This mystery team had access to our most secure files, including cutting-edge research, patient details, and comprehensive financial records. And all for what, exactly? So William can keep the rest of us completely in the dark?

Once at the table's edge, I introduce myself to Ben and Corey with a nod, Ben being the brunette and Corey being the blonde. I skip the handshakes, which neither of them seems to expect or want. This is purely transactional, and none of us will pretend otherwise.

I turn to Luis. "You're looking much better than the last time I saw you," I remark. From my side, Davey releases a barely audible sigh.

Luis's jaw tightens before biting back, "Tell Cillian to go fuck himself."

I flash a grin, all teeth. "I'll be sure to do that, though he was just following orders. He's a *really* great listener."

Luis's tanned skin turns red, all the way to the tips of his ears. That reaction alone is the dopamine hit of a lifetime.

Just as Davey tries to cut in, my phone buzzes against my thigh. Elias's name flashes across the screen. I don't look at Luis again. "Any privacy down here?" I ask Davey, and he gestures to a side door.

The storage room he pointed to is small and cluttered with server tools. I flick on the light, shut the door, and hope the signal holds.

I answer, "Elias."

"Silas," he replies, sounding a bit worn. "How are the audits going?"

"So far, so good," I fib, sliding a hand into my pocket.

"That's great,"

There's a brief pause before I push for a lighter note, "Did you call because you miss the sound of my voice?" Normally, this would draw a laugh from him, but today, silence follows.

Elias exhales heavily. "Have you talked to Jeremy recently?"

I frown, staring at the floor. We haven't spoken since that night at the club before he ditched Davey and me for his friends.

Dread starts to trickle in.

"He came to my office yesterday, asking for a mentorship," Elias says without waiting for me to answer. "I asked him why he didn't ask you, and he was quick to say you're too distracted to help him."

Heat rises under my skin, but I keep my voice steady. "Did he now?"

The rustle on the other end of the line tells me Elias is nodding. "Your personal life is none of my business, but he mentioned your ex being back in town and how it's affecting your focus."

It takes all of my self-control not to bark out an incredulous laugh.

This is how my father thinks he will regain control. Because let's be honest, that's who formulated this idea. Who else could have told Jeremy that Elena is here?

I can picture Elias sitting uncomfortably behind his desk, being forced to listen to all the ways Jeremy regurgitated that Elena is a gold digger—her date at the Gilded Sear, the time she spent living with me in the spring, how she ran away.

My jaw flexes, though I try to relax the muscles there. "Do you agree that my mind and dedication have been elsewhere?"

"No, that's why I called." My shoulders deflate a fraction with relief. "But Jeremy seemed very adamant about discussing it. You know I sympathize with his situation, but I joined the board because of the vision *you* sold me on. So, I wanted to check in."

Though I see Elias first and foremost as a trusted associate, we've also become friends. I was the one who sought him out for the board after we were introduced at a charity event. His more progressive business stances aligned with mine and offered balance to a room that was mostly handpicked by my father. Both William and Jeremy knew this, and they still tried to plant seeds of doubt in the one board member most loyal to me, aside from Natalie.

There are two potential outcomes he's hoping for in this smear campaign: I cave to the COO nomination, or he's going to attempt a vote reversal on the CEO transition.

My own fucking father.

"Well, since my personal life seems to be on the table," I start with a lightness I don't feel, "Scarlett is back in Chicago. We're keeping things quiet, but my father has some unfounded concerns about her." The more half-truths I find myself saying, the easier it is to understand how Elena was able to fool me for as long as she did. "Davey's looked into her extensively. She checks out."

Elias responds, almost relieved. "Good. I liked Scarlett when we met. She seemed like she could handle you."

I almost forgot that I introduced them at the one gala Elena and I attended together. Elias's approval eases some of my tension, but just barely.

"She understands my work and where my priorities lie." Looking around the small storage room, I search for the right combination of words. "I think Jeremy is hurt over the last board meeting and has gotten himself stuck in the middle of this thing with my father and me."

Elias scoffs a little. "Yeah, well, they're lucky that the conversation ended when it did. I thought Everett was going to blow a fucking gasket when Jeremy suggested we'd figure out the financials as we went."

I manage the smallest chuckle. "I don't think any of us were prepared for how that conversation went, maybe besides my father."

Another small pause. "We were all surprised by William's response, even Randall. It's not like your dad to throw caution to the wind on anything, let alone an operational change that large."

My eyebrows lift. *The board is gossiping across party lines.*

"I appreciate you letting me know all of this," I say, breezing past his last comment. And I mean it. My father's mistake was sending my brother instead of handling it himself. Jeremy is great at misleading people from a distance, but he doesn't have an ounce of real finesse in his whole body, especially when it comes to swaying someone as intelligent and level-headed as Elias.

"Of course. I want to see you succeed. But I can't imagine that I'm the only person he's approached." Elias voices the concerns that have already seeped into the corners of my thoughts.

If William's desperate enough to come after my allies, there's no telling what he's feeding the rest. Beyond the board, if word gets out that Scarlett is back in town, it could reach ears I don't want it to—like Peter's.

"Looks like I have a lot of calls to make," I muse, forcing a joking edge to my tone.

"Let me know if you need anything in the meantime," he concludes as he shuffles papers on the other end of the line.

My tongue glides over the front of my teeth. "Thanks, E," I reply, and end the call.

As I slide the phone back into my pocket, silence closes in, the heat claws beneath my skin. I brace myself against the cool metal of a utility rack and focus on my breathing. If I step out now and Luis so much as glances my way, I might just hurl him into the servers.

Each time I think William has hit rock bottom, he grabs a shovel and digs deeper. I've witnessed this behavior from the sidelines more times than I can count, but being on the receiving end of it is a wholly different story.

The disagreements and arguments over the years were par for the course. Not everyone will align with my vision, and I accept that. But what's happening now beyond anything he's ever said or done before. This is a direct attack on the future I've been meticulously groomed for. The essence of my career at Wells.

All being orchestrated by the man who made sure I ended up here.

As these thoughts fuse, something simmers low in my gut. It's acidic. Corrosive. Eating away at my insides and demanding more.

Hatred.

The word enters my brain before I can stop it. And it's aimed at one of the people I never thought I'd feel it toward, in this lifetime or any other.

CHAPTER 33

Elena

S ilas stands beside me on the small front porch of an old craftsman house, the glow from the porch light casting a warm halo around us. Gripping the handles of the tinfoil-covered casserole dish a little too tightly, I glance up at him.

"Thank you," I say, breaking the silence, "for coming with me."

His response is a small smile, eyes meeting mine through the reflection on his glasses. He reaches for the dish again for the third time since we left the car and walked under the streetlights to the front steps. I angle it away, narrowing my eyes at him. Silas sighs and presses the doorbell instead before placing a hand on my lower back.

A bicycle hides against the far wall, and three different-sized potted mums crowd one edge of the door. The neighboring homes, which stand only a few feet apart, are also alight with lamps and evening routines.

"There's nothing to thank me for," Silas finally replies, his fingers sneaking under the edge of my jacket, warm against my shirt.

Before I can respond, the door swings open, flooding us with light. Jeff stands there, casual in jeans and a black t-shirt. He smiles and reaches for the casserole without hesitation. I let him take it.

"Hey guys, come in."

We walk directly into the living room, and the familiarity is almost eerie, though they've rearranged some of the furniture. The longer, brick-colored couch now sits under the window on the far wall, and the smaller, leather one is closer to the door. They both face the kitty-cornered television.

I'd spent many afternoons in the prone position on that smaller couch, propped up against pillows while Jeff flipped through the channels. He'd always stop on some nature documentary and tell me about his upbringing while it played in the background.

His parents were good but poor, though the "good" didn't stop him from falling into the wrong crowd. More than a few of those run-ins ended in bloody noses. The corners of his lips twitched when he asked me if that reminded me of anyone I knew. I rolled my eyes so hard I'm not sure how they didn't get stuck.

He grew up a few blocks from here, and this house had been slowly falling apart for years until it was finally condemned when he was a young adult. Somehow, he got it in his head he'd buy it and fix it up one day. All of it was a fantasy, of course, but he liked to daydream about it. It wasn't until he started dating Lauren after meeting at martial arts class that he realized it was possible.

To no one's surprise, she helped him get his act together, especially when she told him she couldn't marry someone content to coast through life, taking whatever side jobs he could find.

After that, Jeff had his eye on the prize. Within a year, he somehow talked an investor to helping him get the gym up and running. Right before the third year, he had paid back the loan and was ring shopping. By year five, they were married, and this house was in their names. They renovated it for two years and have lived here ever since.

A small fire crackles in the fireplace, an ambiance Jeff didn't stop talking about missing in the summer months. It's no surprise that he'd take advantage of the first truly cool night of the season.

The antique coffee table is laid out with cheese and crackers. Jeff nods towards the couches as he heads towards the hallway on the far side of the staircase. "I'll be back in a second. Toss your coats over the banister," he says, then pauses. "Your text said four-twenty for twenty minutes, right?"

Silas chuckles when Jeff departs without an answer and helps me out of my coat. I thank him with a smile and hang our coats as instructed.

On the other side of the room, Lauren emerges from the cased opening that leads into the dining area, her blonde hair pulled up in a messy bun. She wipes her hands against a dish towel that hangs lazily on the shoulder of her light blue sweater, and my heart stops beating.

"I thought we stopped taking in strays," she calls toward the kitchen, eyes wrinkling on the corners as she tries to contain a smirk.

Just the sound of her voice squeezes my heart so hard that it burns. My laughter is mixed with tears of relief as I rush to her. She wraps around me in a cocoon, and the remaining pieces of myself I'd been trying to force back into place finally settle.

"My girl," she hums against the side of my head, arms crossed around my shoulders. Her signature floral perfume overwhelms me, and the tears build once again. "Let me get a better look at you."

She pulls back just enough to hold me at arm's length, her free hand sweeping the hair at my neck to see the scar we discussed at length. I'd told her how worried I was that it wouldn't fade and had to be convinced multiple times that it would if I treated it properly. Lauren was right, of course. It's just a small scar now.

"You look so good." Her glassy eyes mirror mine as we grin stupidly at one another. "But I'm pissed it took you this long to visit," she chides.

"You've always been welcome to join us for training," Jeff butts in, returning to the room with two glasses of amber liquid and handing one to Silas. Lauren rolls her eyes at her husband.

"Because *that's* how I want to spend time with Elena," she retorts, tossing the green dish towel in her hand over her shoulder. Almost as if she forgot he was in the room, her eyes shift over to Silas standing in front of one of the couches, a hand in the front pocket of his fitted slacks.

Without hesitation, he sets his glass on a coaster placed on the coffee table and moves toward us. Lauren raises her eyebrows, hands falling from my shoulders.

"So," she starts, giving him a once-over, "this is the guy."

The corner of Silas's mouth twitches. "The guy?"

My cheeks heat. "Lauren," I mutter, but she's not interested in my pleas.

"She spent three weeks recovering from second-degree burns in this house, only worried about some guy she wouldn't tell us about." Her arms fold across her chest as she appraises him anew. "Unless I'm confusing you with someone else."

When I stayed here in June, I was determined not to tell Lauren or Jeff anything beyond my real name. I didn't want to risk involving them more than they already were, but I should have known Lauren would hear the tail ends of my sleepless nights and the phone calls I'd take with Lu as I cried over the life I lost.

My face burns even hotter as Silas nods, acknowledging Lauren's words with a quiet glance my way, though I can't bring myself to meet his eyes. He extends his hand to Lauren.

"Thank you for taking care of Elena when I couldn't."

The words are woven with so much sincerity that it sucks all the humor from the room.

Lauren looks at his hand and back up at him, her eyes softening on the edges as she takes it. "I'd do it again in a heartbeat."

A beep from the kitchen breaks the brief silence, and Lauren calls Jeff to come help her. He sets down his glass and follows her without a word, leaving us to obey Lauren's instructions to sit down. As she turns to leave, she promises to bring me a glass of wine.

Desperate for any type of escape, I move toward the coffee table, but Silas catches my elbow, drawing me back to his chest.

With a teasing smile, he whispers, "The guy, huh?"

I bite the inside of my mouth and roll my eyes. "I didn't realize Lauren was such a narc."

A laugh bursts out of Silas, the sound bright in the quiet room. "I'm glad you had someone to look after you," he says earnestly. "And I'm glad it was them." He pauses, eyes searching mine. "They live close to the warehouses."

My throat tightens.

I also hadn't realized how close Jeff lived to the warehouses until I decided I was going to ask him to hold onto my belongings the night I left. Almost exactly two and a half miles away. I convinced myself that the distance was a sign that my plan would work. I could grab my things and disappear without looking back.

I nod. There's another small pause before Silas speaks again, "Did you walk the whole way here?"

Unease prickles over every inch of my skin. It's not something we talk about much, and it's certainly not something I want to relive. I rehashed every detail of my conversation with Peter that night, but very little about what happened immediately after it.

The details are blurred and distant, but somehow, the phantom pain is as sharp as ever. "I don't remember most of it, so it wasn't so bad," I murmur. Though his response is just a quiet release of breath, I know he doesn't like that answer.

He kisses my temple, lips lingering for a long moment before guiding me down to the couch next to him. We settle into the cushions and allow his remaining questions to die on his tongue.

Not that we get the chance to say much else because Lauren and Jeff reenter the room, Jeff announcing that food will be ready in thirty minutes. Lauren hands me a glass of white wine, and they settle into the opposite couch.

Silas shifts the focus with practiced ease as he reaches for his abandoned drink. "So, Lauren, what's it like leading the cardiac nurses at Insight?"

My friend's face lights up. Jeff smiles, and his free hand falls against her back. The constellation of tattoos near his wrist moves side to side as he encourages her to speak. She doesn't need much convincing, though, and quickly starts in on her job.

It only feels like a few moments have passed when the oven timer dings.

"All jokes aside, he seems really great," Lauren murmurs as she scrubs at the stubborn burnt bits at the bottom of my casserole dish.

My lips curl as I dry the stainless steel pan she handed me, wipe away the last beads of water, and set it on the drying mat.

Bumping my hip against hers playfully, I reply, "I warned you he's annoyingly charming."

Lauren and I have been texting since Jeff started training with me again. Explaining to her who Silas is and the very broad strokes of our relationship was a journey. I told Jeff very little about why I suddenly had a bodyguard following me around when we trained previously, and he knew better than to ask questions. Forget the fact that neither of them read the local gossip magazines that printed the few photos of me and Silas together before everything fell apart.

To say she became adamant to meet him is an understatement, and only this past week did her schedule finally align with Silas's to make dinner possible.

She blows out a breath, sending her wispy bangs fluttering before they settle back on her forehead. "It also should be illegal to be that attractive," she quips, rinsing her soapy fingers under the tap and inspecting the dish for any missed spots before handing it to me. "No wonder he's sunk his teeth into you."

With a huff of a laugh, I take the ceramic dish before she turns off the water and reaches for another towel to dry off. "I'm a willing participant."

"Kinky," Lauren counters with a wink, turning to lean against the edge of the sink and watch me. "But hey, the feeling is mutual, so I approve."

I pause, and my hesitation draws a snort from her. "Don't be shy with me. I have two working eyes and have been watching him watch *you* all night," she continues.

A burst of cheers erupts from the television, accompanied by groans from Silas and Jeff, who had been discussing the end of the Cubs' season intermittently throughout dinner. We both glance toward the noise, though the living room isn't visible from where we stand.

"I did some pretty unforgivable things to him," I confess, setting my dish gently on the counter. Lauren hums, reaching for the half-empty wine bottle to top off our glasses.

"We've all done things we regret," she says, seemingly forgetting when I showed up at their front steps, how we ignored news of nearby fires, and that I refused to tell them much of anything.

She hands me my glass, and I narrow my eyes slightly. She shrugs, "I might not know all the details of what happened, but I have an idea. You learned from it, and you came back, right?"

"I didn't come back willingly," I say softly, lips on the edge of my glass.

Lauren waves me off. "Well, you're here now, and it looks like whatever you're doing is working."

I gaze into my wine, swirling it.

Sometimes it seems that way, but on those bad days, part of me still wants to mold myself into whoever Silas desires so that he can't reject the parts of me I hadn't let him see before. It can be unbearable, especially knowing *exactly* how I feel about him.

But I forced my way into his life, studying every shadow, with and without his permission. Maybe I fell so quickly because, no matter how many sides of him I saw, I kept getting pulled back into his orbit. Nothing I learned pushed me away. If anything, it only reinforced the gravity.

He deserves the time to decide if he feels the same.

My smile is tentative. Lauren's studying me, her wine glass casually dangling from her fingertips. "Hopefully that's true."

"It is," she asserts. When I don't offer any rebuttal, her attention drifts down to my thighs. "How are the scars? Are you keeping up with the regimen I gave you?"

I chuckle at the contrast of her clinical tone. "I have, and I'm still seeing some small improvements. A lot of them have faded."

Her gaze lingers on my legs, then she nods approvingly. "If you ever want laser treatments, just let me know. I have a few friends who work at great med spas."

I nod, contemplating. "Maybe, but I think I'm starting to like them," I reply, taking another sip of wine. Lauren's expression softens.

Movement near the doorway catches both of our attention before Silas pauses at the threshold, his eyes fixed on me in the dimly lit room.

"Don't tell me you're coming in here to rush my girl time," Lauren says over the top of her glass. His amusement with her hasn't faded this evening, evident in the growing smirk on his face.

I wasn't sure how tonight would go. Jeff has only recently become more comfortable with Silas, and Lauren is less predictable. Not only did we experience some intense, accelerated bonding during the weeks I spent recovering here, but she's also not one to hold back or censor her thoughts, no matter who's at the receiving end.

Still, Silas seems as entertained by her bluntness as he is by mine. "I wanted to make sure you weren't still cleaning," he explains. Earlier, Lauren insisted he join Jeff to watch the game, admitting it was to give us privacy only once he was out of earshot.

"All set, big guy." Lauren pats his chest as she brushes past him, heading back to the living room with her wine glass in hand.

Silas watches her leave, then his eyes return to mine, sparkling with mischief. "I like her," he declares, closing the small distance between us.

I lean back against the counter. "She likes you too."

The familiar curl that often tumbles over his forehead falls into place as he tilts his chin down, closing in until our chests nearly touch. His expression is so unguarded that it stuns me.

Is this what Lauren meant? Because when it's just us, I see it too. I feel it. It presses in with him. This quiet, undeniable force that makes it hard to breathe.

One of his hands settles on the counter, while the other moves to caress the side of my hair, gently drawing my face closer to his until his mouth is on mine. Any rational thought melts away.

My hands find his sides, fingers curling into the fabric of his sweater. The scent of the bourbon Jeff had offered him lingers on his breath—smoky, spicy, and inviting. My tongue traces his lips for a deeper taste, and he inhales sharply through his nose, fingers tensing in my hair.

He pulls me back by the strands just enough to show me the heat in his eyes. "Tease," he murmurs, and I let out a laugh.

"We can go whenever you're ready," I whisper, batting my eyelashes. His smile deepens.

"If Lauren wouldn't berate me, I'd say right now," he replies, leaning into me so that I can feel every line of his frame against mine. Despite the hard granite pressing into my back, I can't find it in me to care. "Thirty minutes," he decides with a quick nod.

"Thirty minutes," I agree quietly.

Silas leans down for one last chaste kiss, retreating only before I can tempt him further. He holds me there, his gaze intense as he studies my face.

"For what it's worth," he says, licking his bottom lip where I had, the faint sheen making it glisten, "I also like the scars."

My eyes widen. Almost as quickly as he spoke, he turns on his heel, picks my wine glass off the counter, and leads me back to where Lauren and Jeff are settled on the couch, eyes glued to the game.

If they notice the flush on my face that doesn't seem to fade as we sit, they don't mention it.

CHAPTER 34

Elena

It's been seven weeks since Ben, Corey, and Luis started working on the servers while I've been watching from the sidelines. I'd hoped that after a few weeks, Silas would send me with Davey to the satellite office, but that never happened. They've been worried about someone recognizing me, especially with Brenden still lurking. The last thing they want is for that information to get back to William, especially after Silas banned Jeremy from returning until the audit was complete.

Davey crafted several solid excuses for why this particular audit is taking longer than the others, but that hasn't lessened William's irritation. I've overheard enough late-night calls to Silas to know he's furious with the delays.

Still, I've done what I can to help from a distance. Mostly, I offer counsel over phone calls and help Davey patch up the corporate cloud by retracing the steps I took in the spring. We thought the server files would unlock everything about Sierra Blanca. Instead, they've felt like dead ends, again and again.

Silas's frustration continues to grow sharper, despite our efforts. Sometimes it feels like he's starting to doubt whether this will lead us anywhere, but there are too many vague threads for it to simply be a coincidence.

Even with all my certainty, I can't bring myself to tell him what I think more than I already have. His feelings toward me still fluctuate enough to remind me how fragile this all is, and I feel like I'm one contradicting comment away from pushing him too far.

If I'm too much of myself, he might finally decide he's done.

These thoughts plague my head while we work silently in his study. Silas is at his desk while I sit on the couch, reviewing some of the information Ben decrypted and sent over this morning regarding some offshore accounts. The afternoon sun pours through the windows, bathing the room in warm light.

Silas's phone starts to vibrate on the edge of his desk. He looks at the screen, slides open the call, and places it on speaker.

"Yes?"

"I'm at the satellite office," Davey begins, skipping any greeting. "I need Elena to make sure your laptop is secure before I email you."

Unease immediately curls in my chest and down to my stomach.

Silas's expression gives nothing away, but his movements are rigid as he stands from his seat in a silent invitation. I set my laptop down, my feet suddenly heavier than before. Once settled in his chair, I pull the laptop towards me and try to will away the slight tremble in my fingers.

"Corey figured out a way to automate the decryption process that bypasses the security triggers embedded in the files." Davey's voice sounds strangled. Silas's eyebrows furrow.

"Instead of unlocking each layer one at a time like we have been, he was able to make every decrypted key feed directly into the next layer," I murmur, though my mind is racing through the usual checklist. VPN, endpoint security, and firewalls.

Everything seems to move in slow motion.

"So you're making progress?" Silas asks.

"More in the past few hours than we have in a month," Davey confirms, but there's no satisfaction in his statement. "You need to see what we've found so far."

My fingers fumble on the keyboard. Silas doesn't bother to ask anymore questions—Davey clearly wants him to see what he's seeing.

Only when I've thoroughly reviewed all his settings and completed a full antivirus scan do I finally step back, giving Silas the space to take over, but he doesn't sit. Instead, he shoves the chair aside and leans over the desk, bracing his fingers curling to the edge.

"She's done," he mutters.

I hesitate before settling my hand gently on his shoulder blade, my thumb tracing slow circles over the fabric of his shirt.

"Silas. This... this is worse than I ever imagined," Davey says.

A chill shoots through me, my hand stilling as Silas stiffens. I've never heard Davey sound so broken.

The laptop pings. Silas doesn't hesitate as he clicks through his applications to open the email, bulk-downloading the documents. Multiple files flood the screen. He doesn't pause to read any until every last one is in front of him.

I finally let my gaze drop to scan the topmost document. My stomach knots as my eyes land on the title.

Cognitive Stability and Compliance: Phase III Trials of Experimental Antipsychotics

Blinking at the words, I try to process what they mean. Silas clicks faster, the force of his finger harder with every tap of the mousepad. He's moving too quickly to absorb it all, but he doesn't stop.

The muscles beneath my hand coil tighter and tighter. I want to ask him what he's seeing, but I'm at a loss for words.

As if sensing it, Davey clears his throat. "Your father—he—" His words falter, choking on themselves. "He's been conducting illegal medical trials on vulnerable populations."

The air leaves my lungs in a rush, and my hand drops from Silas's back.

"Since the late nineties, Silas," Davey breathes, almost like he can't believe the words himself. "The Deming facility is where it started. He moved the operation to Sierra Blanca right after Shaw left."

Davey swallows so hard that we hear it through the speaker. "Shaw's digital footprint is all over these files, too."

Silas is frozen.

"There are still thousands of files to go through," Davey admits. "But this—there's no way around this. Experiments on the incarcerated. The undocumented." His voice cracks. "The impoverished."

My pulse thunders in my ears, drowning out everything.

I've uncovered all kinds of things over the years. Some of it was outright deranged. Violent coups disguised as business acquisitions, money laundering schemes so intricate they took months to untangle. At other times, it was something as mundane as a tax evasion scandal.

It was always hard to imagine what was actually in these files. Some days, my mind drifted to something out of a dystopian film—some horrifying, larger-than-life government conspiracy. Other times, I thought smaller. William hiding payments to an illegitimate child, maybe. Some quiet, shameful secret buried in redacted documents and offshore accounts.

Silas is gripping the edge of the desk like it's the only thing keeping him upright. Even that might not be enough. His knuckles are white, the tendons in his hands straining. Under his glasses, his eyes shine, locked on the last document he clicked on. I don't even bother looking at it. I don't need to.

I've seen Silas in so many states in the short time I've known him. I've seen him burn with anger so consuming it feels like standing too close to a wildfire. I've seen him controlled, shutting down every emotion until nothing but logic remained. I've seen him vulnerable, in the quiet moments where his guard slips and lets me see the parts of himself he hides. But I've never seen him like this.

Because nothing has ever been this impossible to process.

My mind whirls.

How did William get them to comply? Was it force, or a false promise? How long were they held at Sierra Blanca, forced to endure whatever his sham of a research team pumped into their bodies? What happened when the medicines made them sick?

What happened when they died?

Did they have families waiting for them? Were those families told the truth? Or were they left to wonder, to grieve someone who disappeared into the system, never knowing what happened?

Did they get the funerals they deserved? Or were they discarded and erased as if they never even existed?

The questions keep coming, and this time, we have no answers.

There's no strategy, no power move, no clever manipulation that will undo decades of atrocities. This isn't a broken deal, or an honest misstep. Nothing Silas can salvage, bend to his will, or force into something manageable.

This is beyond me.

Beyond him.

Beyond everything.

CHAPTER 35

Silas

"What the fuck," Lloyd breathes, slumping on the leather sofa and fingers threading through his dark curls.

My throat is raw from speaking, legs stiff from standing behind my desk with Cillian, Lloyd, and Steven on the other side. Davey and Paul are on speakerphone, with Davey on his way here. Paul stayed behind at the satellite office with Corey, Ben, and Luis.

My desk chair, where Elena sat an hour ago after collapsing into it, is empty. She slipped out quietly when the others walked in, murmuring that she'd be downstairs if needed. I didn't fully grasp her departure until it was too late.

Cillian's expression is stone-cold. Steven rubs his face wearily next to Lloyd, who shakes his head at the ceiling. I've outlined everything we've learned, barely controlling the turmoil raging within me. William did it all rig

William did it all right under my nose, releasing a type of evil into the world that I never thought anyone could be capable of. And I contributed to it, whether I knew it or not.

All of my father's erratic and nonsensical power moves in the past six months have come into stunning clarity. Of course, he wanted Jeremy as COO. How else can he keep pulling his strings if he doesn't have one of his loyal dogs sitting at the helm?

But he chose Jeremy, who wouldn't be able to handle even the every-day tasks of a COO, let alone juggle those and some giant, demonic operation like this in secret.

I can't tell if it's William's age catching up to him or if he's just so goddamn desperate he'd latch onto anything with a pulse. Maybe it's both. Either way, it only shows how out of his depth he is now that I've dismantled every plan he had to manipulate me.

Everything I've worked for, every effort to help or improve the company, feels meaningless against this.

"Did you have any idea this was happening?" Cillian asks. The barely contained fury in his eyes might upset someone else in my position. As the first member I recruited—an ex-Seal recommended by a mutual friend—Cill is only more honorable than he is loyal. It's the reason I hired him and why he leads this team.

"If I had known, I would have stopped it myself," I answer.

He eyes me. I'm not sure what he's looking for, but after what feels like an eternity, he nods once. That small gesture causes both Steven and Lloyd to relax slightly in their seats.

Davey's voice cuts through the quiet. "Ben is cross-referencing Red-well Group and North Hollow Ventures on both the cloud and servers," he says, referencing the companies we bought the Deming facility from six years ago.

I remember thinking how remarkable it was that my father acquired such an incredible property while dealing with Shaw's departure. The board loved the space, and we signed the paperwork in a matter of weeks. Major news outlets covered the development, praising William for bringing more jobs to a remote area of New Mexico with so few career opportunities.

How were we all so blind?

My brother-in-law thinks we're going to find that one or both busi-nesses have always been a part of our portfolio and buried in our com-pany structure. I want nothing more than for him to be wrong, but it fits. My father is a selfish prick who would never risk *just* himself. If he's going to be caught, he's taking down everyone with him.

If that proves to be true, he likely used the same process for Sierra Blanca.

"Who else do we think knows?" Steven asks.

"Shaw, though we don't think his involvement extends past Deming," Paul answers, shuffling paperwork on the other end of the phone. "Maybe a few others. Besides that, hiring external contractors would be the only way he's kept it quiet for so long."

My mind spins.

Brenden definitely knows. Jeremy is still a wild card. I can see my father waiting until Jeremy's in a position of power first before bringing him completely into the fold.

Could Randall Harrington know? He clung to his board seat after retiring as CLO, always loyal to my father. His legal advice would be indispensable for the mess William created.

Was this their way of keeping tabs on things?

Davey adds, "The money funding the facility is likely in offshore accounts. I'm not going to have the details until I can sift through all of this, but that's the clearest picture we have right now."

The pain in my chest leaves room for nothing else, and I squeeze my eyes shut.

Visions of desperate people, drawn to these shell companies for hope, flash behind my eyelids. I blink.

Getting lost in that won't help anyone or anything.

"We're going to fix this," I assure them, catching each of their gazes. "But we can't go public with it."

The room tenses at my words, but I press on, "Going public would trigger thousands of lawsuits and bleed Wells dry. We wouldn't be able to compensate the victims properly, and we'd have to lay off thousands of people. We need to maintain enough control to rectify what we can and minimize the damage."

Paul's voice crackles through the speaker. "That's a bit too convenient for your family."

"Agreed," Steven cuts in. "William gets away with all of this while we clean up his mess quietly?"

A burst of fiery heat courses through me. "Absolutely not," I snap, fixing him with a glare. It's only when I see the concern in his eyes that I find the strength to roll my shoulders, reining in my fury. "I'd never ask or want you to trust me blindly. You'll have the power to act as whistleblowers and hold us all accountable. William will be held responsible for his actions, one way or another."

Davey adds, "I understand how this sounds, but I don't think we'll be able to provide compensation to the victims any other way."

Lloyd and Steven share glances, but Cillian nods, eyes darting back and forth as he turns over the words. "How soon do we move on Sierra Blanca?" he asks.

"As soon as possible. I want two of you to observe the operations discreetly. We won't engage yet, just gather information," I instruct.

All three nod in agreement. "We'll book the flights as soon as we wrap up here," Lloyd confirms.

Davey clears his throat. "This information does not leave this room. Cillian, I'll be leaving you to debrief Cora so Silas and I can speak to Natalie privately when they arrive at the house in an hour."

We list our next steps for the coming weeks. The elephant in the room—William—remains. The team expects me to lead that, but I'm unsure where to start.

How do you dismantle a man who's spent decades wielding influence?

When we conclude, Cillian, Steve, and Lloyd head back down to the basement. Davey and I stay on the phone for a few more minutes before I hang up, knowing he'll be here shortly.

Instead of jumping into the files Davey sent over, I find myself wandering to the first floor through the back staircase, something in the center of my chest pulling me forward.

My footsteps slow as I approach the music room. There's a quiet pride in finding her exactly where I expect, nestled in the window seat against the far wall with her eyes closed. The early evening sunlight bathes her in a soft halo, accentuating the auburn highlights in her shoulder-length waves. Her legs stretch out across, head tilted back.

The sunlight not only plays in her hair but also casts a gentle glow across the column of her creamy throat, revealing a burn scar that peeks out from under her t-shirt and up the side of her neck.

I step further into the room, and her eyes flutter open, the brown of her irises lit by the sunlight, as they meet mine.

"Hey," Elena murmurs and pulls her legs in, crossing them to sit up straighter. I take the seat next to her. "How did it go?"

I ignore her question. "Why did you leave?"

Her eyes drift away as her fingers find a loose thread on her jeans. She tugs at it gently, not quite meeting my gaze. "I felt like I was overstepping," she finally says. "I left so you could discuss what you needed to without having to worry about... me."

Shifting to face her directly, I carefully choose my next question. "Why would I be worried?"

Elena's eyes narrow with a knowing look. "I thought that making the decision for you was easiest, and if you wanted me to stay, you would have said so." She bites the inside of her cheek. "I respect your choice."

There's a flicker of pain in her expression, but she buries it so quickly I don't know if I'd be fast enough to follow it.

She's right. I could have asked her to stay or texted her to come back, but I didn't.

Suddenly, my throat feels tight.

Covering her hand with mine, I halt her nervous picking. My thumb brushes over the soft skin, and when she doesn't pull away immediately, I lean closer. The golden flecks in her eyes dance nervously as our noses touch before I press my lips softly against hers.

Elena stiffens. I feel her hesitation all the way to the marrow in my bones and rips through me as my heart pumps harder. The woman who has eagerly received my affection for over a month is gone, and what's left is the woman I was trying desperately to accept me last spring.

I pull back just enough to look at her. The uncertainty is now rolling off her in waves. My grip tightens on her hand. "I'm not thinking straight," I admit. "I should've asked you to stay. I'm sorry."

The smile she forces is strained, but she holds it. "You don't need to be sorry for how you feel, Si."

It's not how I feel.

I open my mouth to tell her just that, but she's faster than I am to change the subject. "Tell me how I can help you."

It's like swimming through sludge just to catch a single coherent thought, and I have to blink to keep the world upright.

She's wrong. So painfully wrong. But how can I initiate that conversation right now? Where do we even start? What about everything else that's falling apart?

My body seems to know what to do more than my brain, because I'm moving without thought. The hand holding hers slides to the base of her neck, drawing her back to me. The warmth from her lips, soft and heated by the sun, feels so damn good.

Elena's hands remain in her lap, her crossed legs tightening between our chests, keeping me at arm's length. The anger is quick to light, flooding my body from the tips of my ears all the way down to my toes.

She said she'd be here as long as I'd have her, but I can feel her preparing to rebuild the walls she said were gone, brick and mortar at the ready.

My hand moves to her jaw, applying just enough pressure where the joint meets to coax her mouth open. Her lips part, but there's still hesitation in the way her breath catches. I press forward anyway, sweeping my tongue against hers in a slow, claiming stroke. She barely reacts, and it nearly guts me.

She isn't allowed to pull away.

Not now.

Rising to a knee, my free hand lands on the wall behind her head, leaning more weight onto her. She lets me feed on her light, but takes little in return.

How can I accept *this* when I know her fire burns just as hot as mine if she allows it to be seen and felt?

Under the pads of my fingers, the muscles in her jaw begin to relax like a slow unraveling of cords. Her mouth yields a little more, and it's only when her shoulders relax that the panic loosens.

My fingers shift along her jaw, trail down her throat, and I feel her pulse still racing. Her hand wraps around my wrist—tight and trembling. Still not quite pulling me closer, but it's enough.

We break for air, but I maintain my hold on her so her face stays angled up at me. "We're not done talking about this," I assert. "But I need your help. Natalie will be here soon, and I want you with me."

Her smile, though still small, feels less forced. Right now, that will have to suffice because I have to break this news to my sister, and I don't know where to start.

Elena pulls back to stand, yanking me out of my thoughts. My hand falls from her neck, but her hold on my wrist hasn't faltered. She pulls me to my feet with her before sliding her fingers down to lock with mine. Without a word, she leads us to the door and down the dark hallway to the back staircase.

I'd give anything not to be the one to shatter my sister's world, but if I have to be the one to do it, at least this time, Elena will be there.

Chapter 36

Elena

No matter how many times I've begged Silas to slow down in the three days, he hasn't. Not logic, not compassion, not even my usual attitude, which typically earns at least a flicker of irritation or amusement. Besides the fleeting moments he seeks comfort—a searing kiss that ends as abruptly as it begins, or pulling my body to his late at night—he's been swallowed whole by some darkness, and I don't know how to lure him out.

Watching him unravel is its own form of torture, especially knowing the hand I had in it. Peter might have sent me here, but my involvement is what broke the illusion Silas lived under, and I can't stop thinking about whether he's realizing the same thing.

Natalie learning what was on the servers hasn't helped. We spent hours in that study after she arrived with Cora. I held her hand while Silas and Davey explained to her what they found, let her go when she lashed out at us in denial, and was a sounding board for every intrusive thought that came with the overwhelming grief. By the time we finished talking and crying, the only thing remaining in her was rage.

It seems to fuel Silas. Between that and the steady stream of horrific files Corey, Ben, and Luis have decrypted, I feel like I'm standing in the eye of the storm, bracing for the tail end of it.

In a desperate attempt to escape the mansion and the past few days, we're at Natalie and Danny's, sitting at their dining table. Silas is focused entirely on the glass of whiskey in front of him, his fingers circling its rim in slow, idle patterns.

Dinner has come and gone, the empty plates cleared away, leaving an untouched cheesecake as the lone centerpiece. The silence stretching between us is broken only by the occasional clink of a glass or the subtle scrape of a chair shifting against the floor.

It's unbearable, waiting for this quiet collapse. Silas isn't the life of the party on his best days, but at least in those moments, he *has* life. I want to shake him, but instead, I have to wait for the moment when the last of his sanity snaps.

"We need to do something," Natalie finally says, of her words drawing our attention like a magnet. Her bloodshot eyes lock on her brother. Davey, who had already moved closer to her during dinner, shifts nearer.

Silas leans back in his chair. When he finally speaks, his voice sounds borrowed. "What would you like to do, Nat?"

"He needs to answer for what he's done. I don't care how, but he has to face it." She exhales sharply, her arms tightening across her chest. "And if he won't, then he's too much of a threat to be left unchecked."

Silas's hand stills on the glass as he stares at her. "Are you saying you want to—"

"I'm not saying I *want* to do anything," she interrupts, "I'm talking about what we *need* to do."

The air leaves the room.

Davey's lips press into a thin line. "That feels like a big leap," he admits quietly.

Natalie's eyes shoot toward him. "You know my father as well as I do. You see what he's doing. There are no leaps left to make. We have to talk through every possible outcome, because he might not give us a choice."

I search Silas's profile for some kind of reaction. His jaw works, and the flicker of something dark in his eyes makes my stomach twist.

"You'd do that to your own father?" Silas asks.

Natalie turns back to her brother. "He stopped being my father the moment he decided human lives were expendable." Her palms flatten on the table, one landing on her abandoned napkin. It crumples under her fingers as they contract. "He made his choice."

Silas's shoulders visibly coil, but he doesn't argue. There's something about the way he examines her that confirms the fear I didn't dare voice.

"You've thought about this," I whisper.

Silas shifts his soulless eyes to me and it takes everything in me not to shrink away. He stares for a beat too long before looking at Natalie again. Davey's face drains of color.

"He could refuse to atone."

Natalie straightens in her chair. "Then we do what needs to be done." Her voice drops, but the words maintain their bite.

Silas rests his elbows on the edge of the table, hands clasped tightly in front of him. "You're asking me to make that choice."

"No," she says, quieter now. "I'm asking you to help me see Dad for what he is and decide if he's worth saving at all."

The sag in Silas's shoulders is almost imperceivable, but he nods.

Davey's gaze darts back and forth between his wife and brother-in-law before landing on me. The panic in his green irises has to be a reflection of what's in mine, but I'm just as frozen as he is.

"We'll give him the chance to answer for this." Silas agrees. "But if he refuses..."

Natalie nods, her gaze softening just slightly as she reaches across the table and places her hand on his. "We'll do it together."

No.

Her anger burns so brightly, so fiercely, and I can't deny that I understand it. I feel it too. William deserves to pay for what he's done, for the lives he's destroyed, for the people he's treated like disposable assets. But even if they stop William and do what's necessary, they'll have to live with the guilt for the rest of their lives.

I open my mouth to speak, but Silas's waiting glare chokes the words in my throat.

There is no arguing with him on this, and anyone who tries to deter him will become an enemy—even me.

My jaw clamps shut, fingers twisting in my lap to keep them from shaking. The untouched cheesecake in the center blurs as my eyes sting with unshed tears.

William should pay. He deserves to face every consequence, but not in a way that destroys Silas and Natalie along with him.

———

The mansion's hallways are unnervingly quiet as Silas and I walk down the second-floor corridor. Dinner at Natalie and Davey's left my nerves frayed, and Silas's silence feels colder than usual.

Silas stops so abruptly that I keep walking before I realize he's no longer beside me. I turn back to find him standing in front of his study door. His hand hovers over the biometric keypad, fingers twitching slightly. The pale blue glow of the keypad casts faint shadows across his face, accentuating the tension carved into his features. His finger presses against the scanner.

"Silas," I call softly, just as the keypad emits a low beep.

The small green light blinks on the pad, and the door clicks faintly, easing open just enough to tempt him further. Instead of stepping through, his hand stays on the keypad, like the act of unlocking it has taken something from him.

"Silas," I say again, firmer this time. His head turns slightly, just enough for me to catch the turmoil swirling in his eyes.

"Go," he murmurs, voice devoid of warmth. "I'll join you later."

I step closer, reaching out to gently touch his arm. His gaze drops to the contact, and for a second, I think he might pull away. "Come to bed with me," I whisper.

His jaw tightens. "I have too much to do." The words sound like gravel scraping against stone.

"You can do it tomorrow," I counter, taking another step closer. "Just come to bed. Please." My hand trails down his arm. "You need sleep, Silas. You need to let yourself breathe."

Tension radiates off him in waves, but I still lean in, brushing the corner of his mouth with a featherlight kiss. "Come with me," I repeat.

For a brief moment, I see him—the Silas who isn't consumed by rage and guilt and duty. His hand lifts to my waist in a hesitant touch before he nods. It's small, but it's enough.

I reach around him to pull the study door closed and then thread my fingers through his, leading him toward the bedroom. His feet are heavy against the polished wood floor. I glance back at him as we walk. Whatever glimpse of him I'd seen a moment ago has been buried again.

In the bedroom, Silas crosses to the closet while I head to the dresser, both of us gathering pajamas. The quiet synchronicity of sharing this space still takes me by surprise. It feels intimate in a way that nothing else does.

I follow him into the bathroom, where the glow of the vanity lights softens the sharpness of his profile. As I set my pajamas on the counter, we slip into a silent rhythm. After brushing my teeth and washing my face, I reach for my hairbrush, running it through my hair, but my attention is on Silas through the mirror. He rinses his mouth of toothpaste, though his shoulders remain tight.

All I can see is the exhaustion in his eyes, the weight pulling at the corners of his mouth. He grips the edge of the sink, knuckles white against the marble.

"What?" Silas demands, those cold eyes meeting mine in the reflection. "You've been staring at me like you have something to say. So say it."

I freeze. "I..." The words get lost somewhere between my brain and my mouth.

He despises it when I hold back, but if I don't, how will he not hate *me*?

"Well?" he presses, his voice harsher now.

I take a breath, lowering the brush to the counter. "I'm worried about you," I say quietly.

He scoffs, turning away from the mirror. "I'm fine," he mutters as he moves toward the towels hanging next to the bathtub, busying himself by unfolding one he doesn't need.

"You're not fine," I counter, turning to face him. "And I understand why. But this—" My hand gestures vaguely toward him, "—isn't sustainable."

He tosses the towel onto the edge of the tub. "What do you want from me?"

"I just want you to let yourself feel it," I answer. "This isn't just another problem to fix, Silas. It's your family. Your *father*."

His bitter chuckle cuts through me. "That's not the problem. The problem is that while I'm trying to figure out how to handle all of this, you're judging everything I do. The way you looked at me during dinner proves it."

My breath catches. "I think Natalie's suggestion tonight was impulsive," I say truthfully. "And dangerous."

Silas's laugh sharpens. "Suddenly, you've found a moral compass. Tell me, Elena, when did that happen? Before or after you fucked me over?" he spits.

I flinch. Even as the ache in my chest spreads, my eyes stay fixed on his. "I'm not saying I'm perfect." Each pulse of my heart feels poisonous. "God knows I'm not, but aren't my concerns at least worth considering?"

"What's there to consider? He's a monster. People are dying because of him. You want me to sit back and do nothing?"

"That's not what I'm saying," I respond, running a hand through my hair. "I just—I don't want you to carry guilt for the rest of your life. You and Natalie both. This will change you."

"What do you know about carrying guilt, Elena?" He throws the words at me like he's been waiting to use them.

I steady my breath and close my eyes, willing my body to absorb the pain. *This isn't really about me.*

"I made reprehensible choices." When I open my eyes, my vision grows hazy around the edges. "When you first brought me back here, you told me you were going to make sure I was really dead this time. I told you I didn't want you to be the one to do it." His pacing halts abruptly, and I press the words past the lump in my throat. "I still don't want that for you now."

Silas turns toward me fully, his eyes pools of spilled oil ready to ignite. "How can you say that?" he demands. "Knowing what he's done?"

"We're on the same team," I plead. "Your father needs to face the consequences for his actions." My voice drops as I take a tentative step closer. "But I'm not worried about him. I'm worried about you."

Shaking his head, Silas backs away, his fingers curling into fists at his sides. "Stop trying to make this about me."

"It *is* about you!" I counter, my frustration boiling over. "You'll have to live with it, Silas. And I know you think you can handle it now, but what happens if you can't?"

His voice drops to a dangerous growl. "You think this is some new part of me? Some reaction to what my father's done?" Just as quickly as he created distance between us, he closes it, towering over me. "This—" he gestures sharply to himself, to the fire raging behind his eyes, "—this has always been here."

"Silas—"

"No," he cuts in, looking at me with a sharp, predatory focus. "I think you're smart enough to realize you weren't the first person I've put in those holding rooms." His lips curl into a self-loathing smile. "I enjoy this part of it, and he'd be no exception."

The words drip with both shame and defiance, daring me to flinch, to create space. But I don't, even as my pulse races and my heart pounds against my ribs.

I swallow hard. "I know those parts of you exist, Silas," I admit. "But they're not who you are as a whole. You're more than what *this* is."

His mock amusement only worsens at this as he shakes his head. "You can't compartmentalize me to separate the pieces you're comfortable with and ignore the rest. It's all or nothing, Elena." He takes a significant step back, arm sweeping toward the door in a cold, deliberate motion. "And if you can't handle that, there's the door."

For a moment, I stand there, taking in his challenge. To leave and let this fire consume him. And maybe, for a fleeting second, I consider it. Maybe I should save myself and find peace somewhere far away.

But I won't.

No matter how much he wants me to be, I'm not scared of him. His capacity for both destruction and devotion has always spoken to something in me in a way I can't explain. It's part of why we're so good together when we let ourselves be.

And I know what this is. I've seen this before—I've *done* this before. I pushed Silas away when I knew I had to leave in June, and now he's doing it to me. But there's nowhere for him to hide, and even if there were, I'd go scorched earth to find him just as he found me.

I take a step closer, then another, until I'm standing directly in front of him. "Don't you dare push me away, Silas Wells," I demand, quiet but resolute.

His eyes narrow into slits. Tentatively, I reach out a hand, my fingers brushing lightly against his chest. "I'm not leaving." I glare up at him. "Fuck you for trying to make me."

I don't give him a chance to respond before rising onto my toes and kissing him. At first, he doesn't move, and I think maybe I've pushed him too far.

Then he breaks.

Fingers curl into the soft skin at my waist, hauling my body closer to his until there's nowhere left to go. His tongue presses against the seam of my lips, and when I comply, he kisses me like he's trying to rip my soul from my body. There's nothing gentle in it. Nothing tender.

It's a battle of wills, and neither of us will concede.

Slowly, the hardness in his shoulder starts to soften. When he feels malleable and relaxed against my hands, I pull back, inhaling. "You're going to take me to bed," I whisper a little breathlessly, gripping the front of his shirt. "And then, tomorrow, we're figuring out a new plan, because I'm not letting this destroy you. Do you hear me?"

The black abyss I've become accustomed to in his eyes over the past three days recedes just enough to reveal the chocolatey brown beneath. Thawing into something—if not entirely warm—at least a bit more human.

His lips twitch. "You think you can handle me right now, Lena?" Hearing that nickname hits me like a balm.

I don't flinch. "I've always handled you."

His hand slides up to the back of my neck, his fingers tangling in my hair as he tilts my head. "Good," he murmurs, kissing me again, slower this time. He walks me backward toward the bedroom without breaking contact, and for the first time in three days, I feel like I've pulled him back from the edge.

If only for tonight.

CHAPTER 37

Elena

The basement lights cast a harsh glow over the grappling mats and mirrored walls, reflecting our movements as Jeff and I spar. Every hit I land on the pads is harder than usual. Jeff picks up on the intensity of my strikes, but he says nothing. Instead, he adjusts his stance, absorbing my blows without pushing back too much.

The clatter of footsteps announces Natalie's arrival, though she doesn't even glance in our direction. A small smile creeps to Jeff's mouth before he speaks, "Nice of you to grace us with your presence."

Without missing a beat, Natalie throws back, "God forbid anything take precedence over training."

Jeff's eyebrows raise before looking back at me. I give him a single, subtle headshake.

Natalie and I haven't seen each other since Silas called a meeting with Davey, Cillian, her, and me. They all thought we were there to agree on the details of the plan he and Natalie had already put in motion. No one expected me to take control of the conversation.

I tried to stay rational, laying out my concerns about how involved Silas and Natalie planned to be if William didn't comply. Davey looked like I'd handed him an escape hatch, his shoulders sagging with relief. Even Cillian nodded quietly in agreement. Silas sat with his fingers threaded through mine, giving me the space to share my thoughts. I thought I'd gotten through to them until I made eye contact with Natalie.

My sweet, thoughtful friend looked at me with such contempt that she might as well have slapped me across the mouth.

The conversation didn't get much better after that. No matter which way I tried to explain it to her, she was stuck on the idea that I thought *she* couldn't handle it. I had told her so many times over that the concern was for both of them, that a decision like this could damage anyone beyond repair, but she didn't want to hear it.

By the end, Natalie realized she was outnumbered and secluded herself in the corner of Silas's study while we discussed logistics. She didn't even stick around for the phone call from Steven and Lloyd, who had been in Sierra Blanca for several days, to give us an update on their surveillance. When she left without a word, with Davey following behind her.

That was three days ago, and I've been giving Natalie the space she clearly wants, even if it hurts like hell to have her so angry with me after just gaining some of her trust back.

Jeff acknowledges my silent plea, and we resume our training. Instead of the gym buzzing with our usual chatter and jokes, the only sound that echoes is our quick breaths and the slight squeak of Natalie's shoes as she starts her warm-up. Her movements are already more refined than when she began working with Jeff weeks ago.

When it feels like I'm about to set a good rhythm with my hits, I can see Jeff's focus slip. His eyes flick back and forth between Natalie and me, trying to gauge whatever is going on between us.

"This is weird, you know? Both of you acting off won't lead to a good session." Even distracted, he catches my next strike with infuriating ease. "If you guys can leave it off the mat, great, but it doesn't seem like you're going to."

The urge to drive the edge of my foot down onto his is so sudden and sharp that I have to physically restrain myself from doing it.

That nosey son of a bitch can't help himself.

Natalie is quick to respond. "Why don't you ask your precious protégé what's going on then?"

My heart sinks a little, but I keep my focus on the pads. Under my breath, I mutter, "Can't you ever just keep your mouth shut?"

I know Jeff's heart is in the right place, but his timing can be so catastrophically bad that it's like he does it on purpose.

"Yeah, Jeff. Poor little Natalie can't handle confrontation," Natalie's snips, her voice dripping with sarcasm.

Jeff's eyes widen before releasing a low whistle, a sound that fills the gym and fades just as fast.

I turn to face Natalie as she stretches her hamstrings on the floor. "Jeff has already done enough for me, and he doesn't need to be wrapped up in anything else we have going on," I tell her, trying to keep my voice even. Jeff shoots me an annoyed look as he wipes the beading sweat from the side of his shaved head with the back of his forearm.

Natalie rises to her full height, her eyes flashing dangerously. "*We* are in this mess because of *you*," she clarifies, and though the lines on the corner of her mouth tell me she wants to take the statement back, she doesn't.

Her echo the same doubts and self-blame that have been screaming in my own head. I wince.

Jeff moves to step between us, but I stop him with a gloved hand on his arm. "It's alright," I say quietly, forcing a calm I don't feel.

When I look back at Natalie, she's coiled like a spring. The raw edge of anger in her posture is visible, all the way down to the set of her jaw.

"I don't want to fight with you, Nat," I whisper, shaking my head.

"Why? Is it another thing I can't handle?" she seethes.

"You're capable of handling just as much as the rest of us."

"What is that supposed to mean?" Her voice is all broken edges.

"That you're incredibly strong," I start, loosening the gloves. "But we all have limits."

She wants to unleash her frustration, to fight it out, but I'm not going to be the one to give it to her—she's too important for that.

I soften my stance, shaking off the gloves onto the floor before letting a slow breath. "Nat, I love you in a way I never thought I could again after losing Drew."

She blinks in surprise, but I press on. "I never want you or Silas to experience that type of pain with someone you care about. I wouldn't wish it on anyone." My voice thickens. "I had to say something before it was too late."

She shakes her head. "It's not the same. You had nothing to do with her—"

"But didn't I?" I cut her off, my head tilting to the side. "I'm the reason she is gone. It's something I have to live with for the rest of my life, even if I wasn't the one holding the knife."

Jeff sucks in a breath behind me, but my gaze remains on my friend.

"I don't want this for you," I say.

Natalie's shoulders slump just a fraction. "That's not your decision to make."

I nod. "You're right. You can do whatever you want, but that won't stop me from telling you what scares me. I don't disagree with the consequences," I continue, glancing briefly at Jeff. "But the way we get there matters. This will change who you are."

Natalie blinks rapidly, her defenses waning as tears threaten to spill. "It has already changed me," she admits, her voice cracking slightly.

I nod again. "I know, and I'm sorry," I pause. "Davey seems worried about this, too. Have you asked him how he feels?"

Natalie's expression shifts, shoulders falling more as she turns away to hide her face from the shame. She doesn't have to respond for me to know the answer.

I close the distance between us before carefully wrapping my arms around her. She tenses as I whisper close to her ear, "No one thinks you're weak."

Her breath hitches, body trembling slightly against mine. "You don't have to agree with me. That's fine. But I'd rather be wrong and you hate me for a while than lose another friend."

Natalie stifles her tears, her arms hesitantly coming around to hug me back. She doesn't speak, but her grip tightens until I have all of her weight pressed into me. My chest seizes, wishing more than anything that I could take these heavy, immeasurable decisions away from her.

"I don't hate you," she breathes, squeezing me tighter.

Despite everything, I chuckle. "I'm glad."

Only when she takes back some of her weight do I start to pull back, her eyes red-rimmed and cheeks splotchy. My lips turn up in a small, reassuring smile, and, through unshed tears, she returns it.

Jeff clears his throat.

"Is the therapy session over? Can we get back to work now?" His tone is teasing, though when I turn back to him, there's only warmth behind his gaze.

We laugh, the sound echoing off the mirrored walls. I nod at Jeff, a small, grateful smile playing on my lips, then glance towards Natalie with a playful glint in my eye. "Why don't you take out some of that frustration out on Jeff?"

A wry twist appears on her lips as she retorts, "Oh, I plan to."

Jeff grins, bouncing lightly on the balls of his feet as he ditches the strike pads from his hands and tosses them onto the cement floor. "Let's see what you've got, champ," he taunts, inviting her to step onto the mat.

And she does.

CHAPTER 38

Silas

The Hawthorne Club is always quieter than I remember. My father brought me here for the first time when I was twenty-four years old. On the car ride to the members-only restaurant, he told me that it was time I saw what progress looked like behind closed doors.

That afternoon, we sat across from Luke Keeley, the CEO of a small biotech firm that had developed a promising anti-inflammatory drug. William wanted Wells to manufacture it, and Keeley didn't want to sell.

Keeley came prepared with charts and projections that explained the very logical reasons his company wants to retain production rights. He was willing to compromise with licensing tiers and potential shared oversight. My father listened and nodded at all the right moments.

Then, William leaned back and swirled the whiskey in his glass. He placated Keeley, but didn't fail to mention how much of a shame it was that he had heard rumors of their grant discrepancies. Just a few vague concerns he'd "come across" prior to this meeting.

My father laid out the facts, one after another, of the research grant that ultimately funded luxury lab equipment and a recruitment event in Bermuda. Keeley's composure slipped with each statement until the man looked as though he were on the verge of being sick. The man scurried out of the private dining room before dessert, and William couldn't wipe the smile off his face.

The deal was finalized just weeks later. Wells received everything it asked for, and Keeley was appointed to the advisory board with a feature in the press release written by our public relations team.

I asked my father if he really thought stiff-arming a small company like this was the right move. He didn't hesitate to tell me that Wells had the capacity, distribution channels, and relationships to get the drug out to people faster. Smaller companies could only take an idea like this so far before it died in committee, and we could get it through the red tape while keeping it out of competitors' hands.

He had the numbers to support it. Months of research conducted by our internal teams confirmed that this was a great move for Wells. William was convinced that the benefits outweighed the risks, and I believed him.

The Hawthorne Club became the place where I'd sit beside my father and watch him dismantle companies. Its strict privacy policies made it all so much easier. We acquired many promising products this way—drugs, devices, patents—you name it. We had the resources they needed to do what they couldn't. I told myself these facts made it right. We were the good guys, weeding out the bad businesses without letting their best ideas go to waste.

How did I ever believe we were the good guys?

I pass through the unmarked side entrance, nodding at the concierge who doesn't bother to ask for my name. The corridor is dimly lit, with lined with polished wood panels that gleam under the soft light and ornate-looking carpeting that muffled our footsteps.

A staff member in a sharp black suit waits at the end of the hall, hands clasped behind their back. They nod as I approach and gesture to the door.

Room 8.

They press their thumb to the hidden scanner beside the door, and it unlocks. I step inside, and the door closes behind me with the same soft precision.

Two of the private dining room's walls are lined with dark wood shelves and meaningless leather-bound books, while the far wall holds large privacy windows that face the backside of a community garden. There's a single discreet service door in the corner, which is only ever unlocked when prompted by the guest. In the center of the room is a large rectangular table covered in a bright white tablecloth and a chandelier overhead that drips with glass.

My father sits at the head of the table facing the door. Natalie is to his left, her posture impossibly straight. When our eyes meet, she gives me a small glimpse of the anger she's kept locked away since arriving thirty minutes ago.

William's fork is halfway to his mouth when he finally looks up. His expression hardens before he sets his utensil down, and it clinks against the fine china.

"Interrupting a private lunch, Silas? That's beneath you," he says, dabbing the corners of his mouth with the linen napkin in his lap.

I pull out the chair across from Natalie, then fold into the seat and unbutton my jacket.

"I invited him," Natalie responds. Her gaze doesn't waver from our father. "We need to clear the air."

William blinks, his surprise fleeting before it's replaced by something far too smug. He leans back in his chair.

"Ah," he says, a smile spreading across his face. "A family intervention." He chuckles softly, as though the idea is amusing. "Let me guess; you two want to mend fences before January? Natalie, I didn't realize you had such a diplomatic streak."

Of course, he can't imagine Natalie could be anything but a mediator. I remain silent, letting him dig his own grave.

"You're right, Dad," she says smoothly. "I wanted to talk about the family and how we move forward from here."

I want to wipe that self-satisfied grin off his face with my bare hands. "I'm glad to hear that." His voice drips with false sincerity. "This friction between Silas and me is unnecessary. I've been saying that for months. I think we can start focusing on—"

William's words falter as his gaze follows Natalie's movement. She reaches down to the briefcase hidden under her chair, sets it on the table, and clicks it open. Inside, there's a thick stack of documents in various folders. With bold hands, she pulls them from the case and lets them land on the open area of the table closest to our father with a dull *slap*.

He frowns. "What's this?"

"This," Natalie says, her voice losing its familial edge, "is the truth."

She slides the top folder closer to him. He picks it up, his frown deepening as he scans the first page. First comes the shock—a slight widening of his eyes, a twitch in his jaw—but it's gone in an instant, replaced by the rage I've come to expect. He glances at the next pages, his agitation growing with every turn.

"What is this?" he repeats, fingers curling to the paper.

Natalie opens another folder in the stack and taps her perfectly manicured nail on a line of text near the top. "Davey found some interesting reading materials while conducting the server audit," she answers. "Apparently, they're a treasure trove of secrets."

His knuckles whiten and, just as quickly as the anger rises, it disappears. Smothered under his usual cold, calculated exterior.

"And let me guess," he says finally, "you're going to save the day by confronting me over lunch? How noble."

Natalie leans back in her chair and crosses her arms over her chest. "I'm here to tell you that it's over. You're done."

William's lips curl into a humorless smile. "This isn't a game, Natalie. You're out of your depth."

The inside of my cheek is raw from holding back.

Natalie needs this. He's walked over her, all with claims of protecting her. She maintained our family bond for Mom and Davey, but whatever remnants of love she's forced herself to feel for him are withering by the second.

"You've been out of your depth for years," she counters, pointing to the papers still in his clutches. "You think you can brush this under the rug? This—" she gestures to the stack of documents between them, "—this isn't just a mistake. This is unforgivable."

William's smile falters. "Unforgivable," he repeats. "Do you have any idea what you're talking about? Or are you just parroting whatever Silas has told you?"

My hands curl into fists. Natalie shakes her head, leaning forward now.

"No," she says firmly. "This isn't about Silas. This is about *you*. You've jeopardized the company and ruined our family name. For what?" She slaps her hand down on the stack of papers between them.

His face contorts, the paper still in his hands crumpling under his curling fingers.

"You have no idea what it takes to build something like this," he snaps, tossing the documents next to his half-eaten grilled chicken. "Do you think this company runs on goodwill and wishful thinking? That our advancements come from playing by the rules? Some of our greatest achievements are because of those trials."

The laugh Natalie huff's out is strangled. "You're actually defending this."

"You can't make an omelet without breaking a few eggs." William's eyes flash with something between anger and conviction. "That's the reality of this business. Of this world. The treatments we've developed outweigh the cost."

My sister's lips pull into a tight line. She extracts two more thick files and lays them on the table, open. Her fingers graze the pages before she angles it toward him.

"This," she says, her voice clipped, "is a trial conducted on undocumented workers for an Alzheimer's drug." She flips to a page marked with a neon sticky tab, pointing to a section of text. "Seizures. Psychosis. Permanent neurological damage. Paralysis."

William's gaze barely flickers over the page. "There are always risks in the pursuit of progress."

She opens the second file with a sharp motion, flipping to another section marked in bold. "And this one? Cancer drug testing on incarcerated women. A 42-year-old woman who had already survived breast cancer volunteered for your trial, likely because it was her only option for better medical care." Her voice grows tighter, colder. "She developed severe organ failure and was denied treatment because, according to the report, her condition was a 'necessary endpoint.'" She blinks the sheen away from her eyes as quickly as it settles.

Our father leans back in his chair and exhales as though he's bored with this line of questioning. "Every failure gets us closer to the right answer," he reasons.

Natalie looks as though she's physically holding herself back. "Those are not failures. Those are *people*. People who felt they had no choice and no way to advocate for themselves when they were either forced or coerced into what they thought were legitimate pharmaceutical trials with zero compensation."

William shrugs, the gesture so casual it makes my stomach churn. "You're letting emotion cloud your judgment," he says with maddening calm. "These people have laid the foundation for some of the greatest advancements this company has ever seen. Advancements that you and Silas have benefited from."

The room falls silent, and while I can see the confusion still swirling in my sister's eyes, I've never seen William more clearly.

It doesn't matter what information we show him or how his decisions have harmed thousands. All he sees is progress and his stupid fucking legacy. When Natalie presents our offer, he's going to say no.

Nausea churns.

This is where it comes from. The part of me that revels in control, that thrives in the darker, uglier corners of this world.

Is this what I'll eventually become?

Natalie's voice snaps me out of my thoughts, and I'm not sure how long I've been lost in my own head. It sounds like they've been talking in circles, her calm unraveling with every response he gives.

Finally, she cuts off his latest comment about the trials' benefits. "How do you not feel anything about this?" she demands. "How do you not feel a goddamn thing?"

His expression is almost amused. "Because, my beautiful daughter," he says, his voice condescending, "this isn't about feelings. I knew at a very young age you had too big a heart for this line of work. It turns out I was right."

Disgust floods her face, her hands gripping the edge of the tablecloth like she might rip it apart.

William looks between us, the faintest flicker of impatience in his expression, but mostly, he seems entirely unbothered. He picks up his fork, as if he's about to resume eating.

I can't hold back anymore.

"How was Martin involved in all of this?" My words are low and sharp.

Our father pauses, brows knitting. "Martin?" he echoes, feigning surprise. "Why does that matter?"

"Did you really think that if we'd found these files, we also wouldn't have seen he was helping you?"

William sighs, setting his fork down again with exaggerated care. "Martin handled logistics, and things I couldn't be bothered with."

Natalie inhales sharply. The weight of her stare on my profile could crumble buildings.

"And when he left," I ask, running a hand over my chin. "You, what? Pinky promised to keep it a secret and hired someone else to do it?"

He rolls his eyes. "I didn't need to convince him of anything. He was just as complicit as I was, so we called it a draw. Although, all that involving him did was make it difficult to get rid of him when he started to overstep his bounds."

Overstep his bounds.

My spine goes rigid at his choice of words. "Overstep how?"

William scoffs at the memory. "He started to think he could get away with anything. He became arrogant. Sloppy."

"In what way?" I press, my voice sharp enough to cut through his practiced indifference.

He waves his hand dismissively as he reaches for his iced tea. His gaze flicks to Natalie for the briefest of moments over the top of his glass, and I see it. The slight shift in his expression.

I want to look at Natalie to see if she caught it too, but I can't. My pulse quickening. "Overstep how?" I repeat.

He knows exactly what I'm asking, and for the first time, there's something uneasy in the way he adjusts his posture. "He took liberties where he shouldn't have."

My stomach plummets. Natalie doesn't move, doesn't breathe. My fingers curl into fists against the table, the rage simmering just beneath my skin. "Liberties," I echo, my voice cold, flat. "Like the ones he took with your daughter?"

William doesn't break eye contact with me, though there's a slight flutter in his jaw muscle. "What he did was abhorrent," he counters like a practiced politician. "And in the end, it gave me the excuse I needed to cut ties. It worked out for everyone involved."

The room tilts.

He knew. He knew about my altercation with Martin when I caught him cornering Natalie in the hallway at that goddamn summer party. I thought I'd kept the scene contained, smoothed over by the party's chaos and the fact that Martin limped off without saying a word. I should've known better. Of course, William knew. He always knows.

And he did nothing.

He let it slide because it worked in his favor. Martin was a useful pawn, and Natalie's safety was just another thing he was willing to gamble with to keep his empire intact.

Natalie's chair scrapes loudly against the floor as she stands. She doesn't say anything, doesn't even look at William. Instead, she turns to me, her expression carefully blank except for the fury burning in her eyes.

She gives me a single, sharp nod. Then, with a grace that feels almost haunting, she walks toward the door. William watches her go, nothing more than a look of annoyance on the edges of his features.

And that's all it takes. The last thread snaps.

Whatever part of me still hoped there was some humanity left in him, some shred of decency, disintegrates into nothing.

William looks at me, raising an eyebrow as if he expects me to follow Natalie's lead as the door closes and automatically locks behind her.

Slowly, I reach into the inner pocket of my suit jacket until I touch the orange bottle, the hard surface cool against my skin. I pull it free and place it on the table between us. The sharp sound of plastic meeting polished wood cuts through the oppressive quiet like a gunshot.

William's eyes flick down to the bottle. For a split second, there's uncertainty there, but it's gone as quickly as it came.

Elena's warnings echo, but she can't understand. Looking at William now, I know: this moment is mine.

And I'm going to savor it.

I lean forward, resting my forearms on the table, fingers loosely interlocked. "Here's what's going to happen."

His gaze snaps up to meet mine, his lips curling into a faint smirk. "Oh, I'm dying to hear this," he says.

My mouth twitches.

"Here's how this is going to go," I reiterate quietly. "Cillian and several of my team members are stationed just outside this door. When I call him in, you're going to hand him your phone. Then, he's going to escort you back to your home."

His brow creases. "And why, exactly, would I do that?" he asks, his voice laced with forced disinterest.

I continue as if he hadn't spoken. "He is going to drive you home because you started developing a nasty migraine during lunch and want to rest. Once you're inside, you'll have two options."

He leans forward despite himself, unable to hide his curiosity—or perhaps his unease.

"The first option," I say, holding up my index finger, "is that you accidentally take too many of your beta blockers, thinking it was your migraine prescription." I nod to the pill bottle on the table holding the heart medication he's been taking for a few years now. "You'll pass peacefully in your own home, and the world will mourn you as a martyr."

His shoulders stiffen, though his smirk remains in place. "And the second option?" he asks.

"The second option," I answer, staring him dead in the eye, "is that we will drag you home and Cillian forces you to take them. You'll still die, but there will be no martyrdom. I will spend the rest of my life burning everything you've built to the ground. The Wells name, the company, every ounce of respectability you've cultivated. I will destroy it all."

The force behind my words seems to surprise him. He tries to mask it with a scoff, leaning back in his chair. "Do you think for a second I believe you'd go that far?"

A dark laugh escapes me, sharp and hollow. "That's where you're wrong." Poison laces every syllable. "I've never been more disappointed to be a Wells or willing to torch it all."

The insult burrows under his skin, and suddenly, he pushes back from the table, chair screeching. The mask of composure finally cracks. "How dare you threaten me—"

"Sit. The. Fuck. Down."

My voice doesn't rise, it sinks.

The sound fills the room and vibrates off the walls. My eyes remain locked on his. There's no son in me now. Just the man he built doesn't know has dragged secrets out of stronger men with only this voice.

My father's eyes widen, his fury momentarily eclipsed by something I've never seen before: hesitation. And then, slowly, he lowers himself back into his chair, though his glare never falters.

Power surges through me like an electric current. For the first time in my life, I hold all the cards. And it feels good.

"You have no remorse for what you've done and no plans to change. This ends now, one way or another."

The same brown eyes that I stare at in the mirror every day glow with hatred. "I'm not the only one who has access to that information." His voice is steady, but I catch the slight hitch in his breath. "If anything happens to me, they'll release it."

I smirk. "Liar."

Uncertainty flashes across his face.

"I already combed through your personal servers," I say with a flick of my hand. "You *really* should have invested in better security measures for those, like I told you years ago."

His nostrils flare.

"But there's nothing on them, which I assume was intentional," I continue. "This company is the only thing you've ever truly cared about. You used it as a shield because if you burn, everyone burns. That's always been your safety net."

My father opens his mouth to speak, but I cut him off.

"You never trusted anyone else with that kind of power. That's why Shaw never blackmailed you. You made sure there was no one who could destroy your stupid legacy but you."

His eyes widen a fraction, and the muscle in his jaw flutters once before it locks back into place.

I examine my nail beds before speaking. "Now that we have that all cleared up—"

William's palm slams against the table, rattling the glassware. "What gives you the right to play God, Silas?" he spits, face turning a new shade of red as each second passes. "You condemn me, and yet here you are, deciding life and death. What makes you any different?"

"If you can't see the difference," I say with a shrug, "then there truly is no helping you."

His body vibrates. "You think this will work?" he sputters, clinging to anything he can. "Someone will realize what you did. The timing is too coincidental. You think no one will question it?"

"Why would I kill you? It's not as if any of your attempts to turn the board against me were successful. It would be insane for me to do something so horrific when I just have to wait until January."

The corners of his mouth skew into a disgusted frown.

"But you're right," I agree, bobbing my head. "It would be hard to hide something like this if I weren't prepared for it."

William's face pales.

There's nothing but pure amusement in my words now. "You were just telling me a few weeks ago that my ego would be my downfall, but I'm not the one who missed what has been planned right under his nose."

His breathing quickens.

"You didn't think twice about Natalie picking you up from the office and leaving your own security behind because you'd be with your daughter and her team. You assumed, as always, you were untouchable."

The fingers splayed on the table curl into a fist.

"That's why we chose this restaurant," I continue, gesturing lightly to the room around us. "No cameras. No documented reservations. Nothing to connect this meeting to anything or anyone.

"When Cillian takes you home, I'll return home to finish my workday. Leslie already has your team busy with some minor tasks that will delay them from checking in with you." My lips curl up. "Natalie has already informed several people that you cut your lunch short because you weren't feeling well. A headache, wasn't it? And how nice of Cillian to offer you a ride since he was in the area."

His eyes dart from my face to the doors.

"Meanwhile," I add, my tone lightening, almost conversational, "my team has infiltrated your home security systems. Your staff is already receiving messages, directly from your account, instructing them to leave early so you can rest. The house will be empty. Just you, Cillian, and Cora. And what a pity that your home security systems have been malfunctioning on and off for the past week, so the footage will be sadly corrupted after capturing Cillian's SUV leaving the property."

Reaching across the table, I begin to collect the paperwork Natalie left behind, tapping the edges against the table to line them up neatly. "You see, *Dad*, I've thought of everything. By the end of today, you'll be dead, and the world will be better for it."

With almost too much care, I place the papers down in front of me. "You're lucky Mom isn't here to see this." My voice doesn't even sound like my own. "What you've done would have killed her all over again."

For a moment, the only sound is his panting. Then there's a quiet knock at the door. It opens, and Cillian and Cora step inside. The restaurant staff member slips out as quickly as they let the pair in, leaving the room sealed once more.

I rise slowly, buttoning the front of my suit jacket. Cora comes to the edge of the table, brushing past my father to collect the documents he was holding earlier.

For the first time, he looks small. Powerless.

Leaning in close, I drop my voice low enough that only he can hear. "You always told me to be ruthless. To never leave anything to chance. So really, *this* is your legacy. Congratulations."

His lips part, but no sound escapes.

For the first and last time in my life, the great William Wells was left speechless.

Straightening, I turn on my heel and walk toward the door. I don't look back. I don't need to. The soft *click* of the door closing behind me is enough.

Chapter 39

Elena

I t's 9:42, and I'm sitting on the edge of the bed, staring at the television mounted on the wall. The headline scrolls across the bottom of the screen in bold, bright letters, illuminating the dimly lit room.

As the hours slipped by after their scheduled lunch with no word, a small, desperate hope crept in. Maybe William felt the weight of his actions and his children's disgust. Maybe he wanted to fix things and that's why no one called. Maybe Silas and Natalie didn't have to cross that line.

The message I'm staring at shatters any of those naive fantasies.

CEO AND PHILANTHROPIST WILLIAM WELLS FOUND DEAD IN HOME FROM APPARENT HEART ATTACK

The news anchor's mouth moves, but her words are drowned out by the ringing in my ears. The prepared family statement appears next, featuring an older photo of Silas, Natalie, and Jeremy alongside their father on a red carpet somewhere. The words are kind and polished and tell me exactly which option William took.

My phone lies beside me, its screen dark and still.

The pressure in my chest is unbearable. My fingers twist the edge of the comforter, and the fabric bunches between them.

Where is he? Did he go to William's mansion? Is he at the coroner's office? Should I call him? Should I go to him?

There's a faint shuffle of footsteps in the hallway. My head snaps toward the door just as Silas steps into view.

His gaze is fixed on the television, where the news plays a montage of William's public life. Charity events, corporate galas, ribbon-cutting ceremonies. It pauses the longest on what might be the last family portrait they ever took.

In the photo, Silas's mother sits in the center, her health already fading. William stands behind her, his hands resting on her shoulders. Silas and Natalie flank their mother with polite smiles on their younger faces. Teenage Jeremy stands slightly off to the side, as though he doesn't quite know how to fit into the frame.

I fumble for the remote. The screen goes black, but it does nothing to hide the shadows under Silas's eyes. The tie around his neck hangs loose, his dress shirt wrinkled, and the suit jacket he left wearing this morning is nowhere to be seen.

I stand and take a hesitant step towards him. "Silas," I say, my voice barely above a whisper.

The muscles in his jaw are set so tightly that his cheeks appear frail and hollow. Slowly, he turns. A pair of blank eyes meet mine, the whites are tinted an irritated shade of red.

"What do you need?" I repeat the question he once asked after I was assaulted, hoping it might offer him even a fraction of the comfort it gave me.

Silas blinks.

"I don't know."

Every cell in my body aches at how unsure he sounds.

I take another cautious step toward him. "Then let me help you figure it out," I offer.

The tension in his shoulders eases slightly. I close the remaining distance and wrap my arms around his neck.

Rising on my toes, I press my cheek against his. "I'm sorry he couldn't see what he was losing," I whisper, my voice steady despite the way the rest of me shakes.

His movements are hesitant, but he takes little time to slide his hands around the back of my waist. Against my ribcage, I can feel the pulse of his rapidly beating heart, and he lets his head drop to my shoulder in a defeated slump.

"I fucking hate him," he says, his lips trembling against my collarbone. Heat prickles under my skin. What I wouldn't give to have William in front of me so I could kill him myself.

My fingers slide into his hair, thumb moving back and forth in comforting strokes. "I know," I murmur, pressing a kiss to his temple. "I know."

The world outside fades out just enough for me to whisper the reassurances he needs.

"You did the right thing."

"He didn't want to change."

"He would have hurt more people."

"We can fix this now."

"I'm sorry."

Only when his arms relax around my middle do I pull back enough to hold him at arm's length. "A shower might help," I suggest softly. "Let me get it ready for you."

His expression is still distant, but after a pause, he nods. I lead him to the bathroom, flipping on the dimmest lights as I go until everything is soft and golden.

Releasing his hand to turn on the water, I test the temperature with my fingers. When I turn back, Silas is standing in the center of the room, his eyes tracking my every movement.

Stepping toward him, I reach for his glasses first, gently sliding them off his face and folding them with care. I place them on the edge of the sink. The gesture always feels strangely intimate to me, and tonight, it feels even more so.

I move to his tie next, carefully loosening it and sliding it over his head. The silk slips through my fingers. Then I'm onto the buttons of his shirt, undoing them one by one. When it hangs open, I slide it down his shoulders and let it fall to the floor. I unbuckle his belt and tug his pants down. He steps out of them to stand in just his boxer briefs.

Crouching down to slide his briefs off, I tap the side of one leg. He lifts it, then the other, before they're on the floor, too. Rising to my full height, I meet his gaze again. The way he's watching me is like he's waiting for me to tell him what to do next.

With a hand on his chest, I stand on my toes to press a tender kiss to his mouth. "Go ahead," I whisper against him, nodding toward the warm cascade of water. "I'll be right behind you."

He exhales a shaky breath that feels like a small victory and steps past the glass door and into the shower. The muscles in his back seize as the water hits him before melting with the droplets that run down his skin.

Quickly shedding my own clothes, I let my hair fall loose from its ponytail and follow him. The steam wraps around my limbs, easing the tension in my own muscles. Silas stands with his back to me, the water tracing the hard lines of his body.

Taking a small step forward, I place a hand on his back. When he doesn't react, I slowly wrap my arms around him from behind, resting my palms flat against his chest and stomach. The side of my face presses lightly against the wet skin between his shoulder blades.

He stiffens beneath my touch, locking up as though he's bracing for something. For a moment, I wonder if I've gone too far, but I don't loosen my hold. I press closer, letting the warmth of the water and him surround me.

Our relationship has always been a force of nature that burned hotter than it ever soothed. Though he doesn't believe it, it's always been Silas leading us through those fires, forging ahead while I've done everything I can just to keep pace. How do you offer comfort to someone who's never waited for anyone? Who's carved his own path through every storm?

I just want to meet him where he is. To know I see it. I see *him*.

"Let me in." My voice is barely audible over the steady hum of the water. I press a kiss to his shoulder, letting the words linger there. "Please."

I feel his inhale stutter against my palms. Instead of pushing for an answer, I let my hands glide over his chest comfortingly.

Finally, he breaks the silence. "I don't regret it."

I nod against him, my fingers tracing soothing patterns against his skin. "That's understandable."

"He knew—" Silas sucks in a sharp breath, "—he knew about Martin assaulting Natalie."

The confession ripples through me.

I take a slow breath, forcing out the rage that threatens to rise. "That fucking asshole," I say. It's all I can manage.

Silas's hands curl into fists at his sides, the muscles in his forearms straining. Then, suddenly, he pulls away. The rejection stings. My arms drop to my sides as he turns to face me, his jaw clenched so tightly it looks like it might shatter.

Finally, he exhales. "The second I realized he would never change..." He trails off, his eyes distant, focused on some invisible point beyond me. "Every good emotion I ever felt toward him just flipped off. Like a switch."

My throat tightens.

"I enjoyed the rest of it," he continues, his voice dipping lower. "Watching him come to terms with the fact that there was no way out. No deal he could make. Nothing to save him." He pauses, his gaze snapping back to mine. "I *loved* it."

The bitterness of his confession is so palpable, I can taste it. "But I'm worried about other things now," he whispers.

I tilt my head slightly, my heart pounding. "What other things?" I ask.

His gaze drops to the floor. This time, he doesn't pull away when I step closer.

"What this means for me." The emotion begins unraveling in his eyes. "What if I end up just like him?"

Silas's voice cracks on the last word, and it steals my breath because he believes it. Sees it in his future like it's written in stone. Even after everything. All of the sacrifices he's made and the good he's done. The way he cares so deeply about people, his family, and me. Hell, he should *already* be just like William. And yet, he's standing here after making an impossible decision today because it's what was necessary and right.

Without hesitation, I reach up and cup his face in my hands, my thumbs brushing gently over the stubble on his cheekbones. "You're not him." The anger is almost as strong as my conviction. "You're nothing like him."

Silas tries to look away, but I hold him there. "You're good, Silas," I whisper. "You're good because of how much you love Natalie and Davey. Because no matter how hard it is to get along with Jeremy, you don't want him hurt."

His chest rises and falls unevenly beneath my own. I don't stop. "You know what William did is wrong, and you want to fix it. And, despite everything I've done to hurt you, you're trying to forgive me."

Tears prick my eyes, but I blink them away, threading my fingers through his wet hair. "You're good, Silas," I repeat. "And if there ever comes a time when you're not, I'll tell you. I'll help you."

Only when his hand settles on my waist and he begins to lean into me do I angle his face towards mine and kiss him. It's a soft, quiet question, and he answers. Silas's hands explore my body with more care than urgency, like he's reacquainting himself with every inch of skin. Water flows over our shoulders and between our chests, a steady rhythm that seems to slow everything down around us.

He guides us backward, my back meeting the cool tile of the shower wall. One hand lands on my hip to keep me in place while the other slides upward, fingers grazing my ribs. His thumb brushes over my nipple with just enough pressure for me to suck in a breath.

My head tips back on instinct, a quiet sigh slipping free as his mouth moves down the length of my jaw and the curve of my neck. He rolls my nipple between his fingers, and the stubble along his chin scratches lightly against my skin. I whimper. The sound makes the hand at my side tighten to the point of pain, but I lean further into it.

The steam swirls, thick and slow, just as he cups my breast more fully, palm splaying across my skin with a kind of worship that makes my stomach flip.

Without a word, Silas lifts my leg with his free hand, hooking it around his hip. His body presses into mine, and for a moment, he doesn't do anything except look at me. Lust and pain war in his expression—fierce, conflicted, impossible to separate. It's all there, and I can't tell which one is winning.

God, I hope I'm not the cause of that pain. That he's not thinking about my part in all of this. Not while he's touching me like I'm the only thing that's ever made sense.

The length of his cock strokes between my legs. A moan escapes the back of my throat when he pulls back just enough for the head to graze against my clit before sliding down again. My fingers tighten on his shoulders, and I can feel the way his muscles contract beneath my palms.

Then he's lining up and pushing forward, filling me completely. My breath stutters as I adjust to the bite of pain. Every inch, every pulse, every bit of weight he presses into me is like he's trying to fuse us together. A calloused palm glides up my lifted thigh while the other finds the back of my neck, angling my face so he's the only thing I see.

I can't help but take inventory of the freckles spilling across his nose and cheeks. The slight pink tint of his skin. The water dripping from the curls that have flattened against his forehead. Then I meet his unrelenting stare.

Only when I hold his gaze does he finally start to move. His thrusts are measured in a way that feels like both punishment and reward. Each one drags against every nerve ending, stoking something deep and molten that spreads through my core, inch by inch.

He wants me to come undone slowly, by his design.

My hands roam over his chest, fingers tracing the lines of his muscles, nails leaving faint crescents in his skin. Our tongues tangle as if we have all the time in the world. When I lick the roof of his mouth, the sound he makes sends another wave of fresh heat pulsing through me.

Silas pulls back just enough to breathe against my lips. "I love you."

Those three words wash over me both like the gentlest lap of water and a tsunami barreling across a shoreline.

I've dreamt about the way he hissed them at me in his kitchen all those months ago. I held onto that fragile tether and anchored my own will to it, because even though it was directed at a person who doesn't exist—for a few precious moments—I felt like the center of his world.

And this time, he's saying them to *me*. Not Scarlett.

Me.

All the fear and doubts fall away, if only for now, because this was worth every second of the ache that came before it.

I don't give myself the space to hesitate as I whisper back, "I've never loved anything like I love you."

His eyes widen just a fraction, the dark brown seeming to glow so bright that they burn before settling to the color of charcoal. The rhythm of his thrusts slow even further, each stroke drawing out the friction, dangling me over the edge without letting me fall.

My blood is boiling. Every nerve alive. Then he shifts just slightly, angling his hips until he hits that spot inside me that sends a white-hot shockwave through my entire body. My legs tremble. My fingers dig down the hard lines of his traps as a cry tears from my throat.

"There it is," he murmurs against my ear in the perfect combination of possession and tenderness. "That's it. Let me hear you."

The sounds that escape me are uninhibited, echoing. He groans against my neck, his pace quickening just enough to fray the control he's been holding onto so tightly.

"Come for me." His voice shakes with restraint. "I want to feel it."

His command undoes me. With one more deep, punishing pump, I'm consumed in a wave of pleasure so intense it feels like I'm splitting in two. I writhe, hips grinding against him to siphon every millisecond of the high, desperate to feel it all.

Silas curses my name in a ragged breath before he follows me over the edge. His body tenses, pressing me harder into the wall, filling me with every last drop.

I heave, each rise and fall grazing our slick chests. Silas eases back just enough to look at me, eyes searching. Then, he brushes a damp strand of hair from my face, thumb delicately dancing over the top of my cheekbone.

"Thank you," he murmurs so sincerely that it steals whatever words I might've had.

Then he kisses me again, pulling a quiet sigh from somewhere deep inside me. Only when he lets me up for air do I manage to pull together a coherent thought.

"Anytime," I whisper, and I mean it.

For him, it will always be anytime.

CHAPTER 40

Davey

My fingers rake through my hair, digging into my scalp as I wait for the elevator to make its descent. Getting here was a goddamn nightmare. I stupidly assumed that I'd have no issues leaving at five in the morning, but the paparazzi were peaking over our back fence before I even walked the short distance from our townhome to the carriage house.

A pack of vultures was camped just outside the garage doors as they opened. The flashes were going off before I even took my car out of park. Steven stood guard at the back just to make sure none of them tried to sneak in behind me.

They were disappointed to find it was just me behind the wheel, but not too disappointed to put their cameras down. One of them had the brilliant idea to step directly into my path as I pulled into the alley, daring me to commit vehicular manslaughter before sunrise.

The last time we had cameras outside our door like this was in the weeks leading up to our wedding. Thank God I had the foresight to ask Cora and Steven to come to the townhouse before we parted ways last night. If they hadn't shown up just as I was putting on my jacket, I wouldn't have felt comfortable leaving Natalie to sleep alone. William's death has put a microscope on everyone. From what I've heard, Jeremy is dealing with the same swarm.

Don't these people have lives?

We'd been discussing the idea of Natalie and me investing in our own team. It first came up in the spring, but we shelved it when we assumed Elena was behind the threats being made against my wife. Since then, we've relied on Silas's crew as we always have. They've been generous, and I've come to see them as extended family, but they're at their limit. Between whatever Peter Lynch might be up to and this latest surge in media attention, the cracks are starting to show.

My body sways when the elevator jerks to a stop. The biometric scanner blinks awake beside the door, waiting for my passcode and thumbprint. I give it both. It flashes green, then the doors slide open with their usual groan.

The hallway is mostly empty, aside from a few folding chairs stacked against one blank wall. Down at the far end, a closed door muffles a sharp voice. I don't slow down to listen. Instead, I turn to the unmarked door just a few feet to my right, twist the handle, and push it open.

It's not a big office, but it's enough. A handful of chairs, a coffee machine, a mini-fridge, and a tower of monitors stacked along one wall. Only three screens are lit. Silas and Elena are perched at the edge of their seats as they watch Brenden Mercer's head snap back when Cillian's fist connects square with his nose. Blood pours down his face from multiple angles.

Neither acknowledges me. Their eyes stay glued to the man who might hold some or none of the answers we've been looking for.

I grab a chair near the door and drag it beside Elena before settling into it. "How long have they been at it?"

"Hour and a half, give or take," Silas says, leaning back.

"When did you get here?"

Elena shrugs, her gaze fixed on the screen. "About an hour ago."

"You arrived just in time. I think Cillian is done playing around," Silas admits, nodding towards our friend's face on the screen, each line around his mouth etched with frustration.

Though we're confident that no one has immediate access to the files William hid on the servers, we're still not entirely sure who might've known about the facilities just by proximity.

Last night, I asked Natalie if she wanted to come with me this morning. I knew Elena would be with Silas. It wasn't that I wanted her to witness this, but she has just as much right as the rest of us. Regardless, she turned me down. For all the fire she had in her just days ago, it vanished the moment she walked away from that final lunch with William. I don't blame her.

He knew about what Shaw did to her, and he did *nothing*.

I've never wanted to kill a dead man more in my life. Drag him out of the morgue just to put a bullet between his eyes. Since that lunch two days ago, Natalie's gone quiet. I hate it, but if that's what she needs to process it, she can take all the time she wants. I've got nothing but time when it comes to her.

A flicker of movement catches my eye. Brenden's purple-ringed eyes dart wildly from one captor to the other as Lloyd steps behind him. Blood still pours from his nose, thick and steady, down to the front of his shirt's collar. Thin, red lines streak down his forearms.

Lloyd's always had a preference for scalpels. They're efficient. Maybe there's something else he likes about them, but I've never asked.

Brenden Mercer is in his early forties and spent almost fifteen years at William's side. Officially, he's been called everything from senior advisor to executive liaison. Truth be told, he's a glorified PA. William strung him along with title changes and raises, but his role stayed the same. Still, he's the most likely to know something about Deming and Sierra Blanca, or maybe just enough to point us toward someone who does.

Still, I have to give credit where credit is due; I didn't expect him to hold out for more than a few minutes, let alone over an hour.

Lloyd grips Brenden's thinning hair and yanks his head back, exposing his neck. Cillian saunters closer, a slim blade twirling expertly between his fingers. His dirty-blonde hair is slicked back, as if he's dressed for the occasion.

"Come on, Bren," Cillian says. "Just give us something to work with here."

Brenden stutters out the most pathetic sob. "I–I d–don't know anything!"

Cillian exhales, long and slow. Tired. Disappointed.

Wrong answer.

In a blink, Cill buries the knife into Brenden's thigh. His scream slices through the speakers and bounces off the walls. Elena jolts, her eyes going wide. Silas's hand lands on her knee with a reassuring squeeze.

"You don't have to watch this," he offers, though the words are nearly lost under all the shrieking. The top of Brenden's tan pants is already soaking through, red flowing around the knife. A stain of piss forms around his groin. I grimace, watching Lloyd's boots take the brunt of both.

When Elena doesn't answer, I peek over at her. Her eyes stay locked on the screen, but her hand now circles Silas's wrist, thumb gliding over his skin in silent reassurance.

"It's a shame," Cillian says, drawing me back to the show. "I always liked you. We were all upset when we saw your name on the Sierra Blanca and Deming server files," he lies easily, twisting the handle.

Brenden howls. The blood trails over top and under the fabric, down to where his thighs meet the chair. Cillian's always careful to miss major arteries, but this one might be cutting it close.

"I–I shouldn't be!" Brenden croaks, his voice breaking through a mess of tears, snot, and blood. "I barely knew about them! Wi–William handled those! H–he didn't t–trust me."

Bingo.

"He trusted you enough to tell you they existed," Cillian counters, looming over him. "And to have you keep tabs on Davey while he audited the servers. I'd say that makes you one of his more trusted confidants."

He presses his palm into the knife's hilt, driving it deeper into Brenden's thigh. With a wail, Brenden tries to lurch forward to stop him, but Lloyd and the rope binding his body hold him still.

"You're really willing to die protecting a dead man?" Lloyd asks, incredulous. "William would've thrown you to the wolves like he was doing to his own son. All he ever cared about was keeping you useful."

Cillian hums in agreement and finally lifts his hand from the blade. Brenden exhales shakily, relief loosening a fraction of tension in his shoulders, but he's still tightly coiled.

"Things would just be easier if you complied," Cillian says, taking a small step back. "It doesn't have to be so... painful."

Though Cill does nothing in particular, panic splits across Brenden's face like a fault line finally giving way.

"I knew about them," he gasps. "I knew what was h–happening, but I wasn't involved. I swear to G–god, I wasn't part of it!"

Lloyd leans over the top of Brenden's head, grip tightening in his hair. "Then who was?"

"William!" Brenden nearly shouts. "He handled e–everything himself after Shaw. Said he c–couldn't trust anyone."

Cillian tilts his head. "Why?"

Brenden swallows hard. "I d–don't know. When Shaw resigned, he said that segregation was safer. F–fewer eyes on each part."

"Who managed logistics?" Lloyd asks, arms crossed now. "Transportation? Procurement?"

"William. He worked with m–many teams," Brenden admits, his breathing hitching. "But in Deming, Shaw ha-handled it. He had his own resources to find the k–kind of patients they needed for the research."

Cillian's voice sharpens. "What kind of resources?"

"I don't know," Brenden insists, voice cracking when Cillian moves toward the knife again. "I don't *know*. Whoever it was, t–they could create fake identities, forge d–documents, clean up leaks. If someone tried to go public, they disappeared. If a patient started talking, they were relocated or h–handled."

"So a fixer."

Brenden nods frantically. "Exactly. That's what it w–was."

Next to me, Elena goes eerily still.

In the glow of the monitors, her free hand trembles. She lifts it to her mouth, covering it. Her eyes are glassy, disbelief flooding every inch of her face as something clicks together in her brain.

"Lena," Silas says, voice sharp. He takes her hand, lacing their fingers together. "Talk to me. What is it?"

With unsettling calm, Elena reaches forward and presses a button on the keyboard in front of us. The red light on the microphone flashes on. Across the screen, Cillian lifts his head at the unexpected cue, the earbud he's wearing now visible.

Then Elena speaks. Her voice is low but clear. Stronger than it has any right to be, given the way she's shaking.

"Ask him if he knows Peter Lynch."

I go rigid. So does Silas.

On the monitor, Cillian gives the barest nod before turning his attention back to Brenden, arms folding across his chest.

"Have you ever heard of someone named Peter Lynch?"

Even before Brenden answers, I see it. That flicker of recognition in his swollen, bloodied eyes.

"Yes," he breathes.

CHAPTER 41

Elena

The hour after Brenden's confession passes in a way I can't quantify. Time stretches and folds over itself until I don't know how long I've been sitting in that office. The only way I held onto reality was to glance at the clock on my phone every so often just to be sure.

Cillian and Lloyd kept questioning Brenden, even as he bled. His reaction to Peter's name had been instant, but he didn't *know* Peter. He'd just heard the name passed between William and Martin, and it faded out around the same time Martin left Wells.

As for other people who might know about Deming or Sierra Blanca, he was just as useless. He didn't believe Jeremy knew, but he couldn't say for certain. Anyone else Cillian asked about was met with equally unsure responses.

It doesn't matter how little or much Brenden could actually tell us. I already know one person who was involved, and I feel like an idiot for not realizing it sooner.

Peter is nothing if not meticulous. The only thing that ever rivaled it was his ruthlessness. However, the moment he sent me to Chicago, all of that discipline vanished. At the time, I thought the client was putting pressure on him to deliver results, but I should have known that Peter doesn't answer to anyone.

Does he want to use the information or destroy it? And why is it so important?

I'm pulled from the spiral of questions by the pressure of Silas's hand resting lightly against my lower back. Wordlessly, he guides me through the short corridor that leads to the executive parking garage. It sits just one level below the ground floor.

Once they realized Brenden didn't have anything else to give, they ended the conversation, and it was time to head home. Silas didn't share what they would do with him, but truthfully, I never planned on asking, either.

There are only a few cars parked in the garage at this early hour. One of Silas's SUVs sits tucked into a far corner, occupying his personal space. The blacked-out windows reflect the low overhead lighting as he leads me to the passenger side. He's barely said a word since Brenden's confession, and neither have I.

I always knew we'd have to deal with Peter eventually, but never considered how definitive it would feel. I can only guess what's taken him so long to come back to Chicago to finish the job himself, but it doesn't change the fact that he *will* come back. And soon.

A few months ago, I thought it was over. I really believed I was free from the man who held my leash for over a decade. I was learning to breathe without waiting for his voice in my ear. Now, every breath feels borrowed again.

A shiver rolls through me, starting at the base of my neck and creeping all the way down before curling into my gut.

Silently, Silas opens my car door and offers his hand. I take it and glance up at him, but his eyes are on my feet, focused on making sure I'm safely inside before he closes the door behind me.

I sit back and inhale. The interior smells like leather cleaner and something faintly citrus. It's dark, save for the glow of the oversized smart screen embedded on the dash. Everything in here is sleek and custom. Reinforced glass, bullet-resistant paneling, a full communications override system. It might as well be a tank.

Silas climbs in and starts the ignition, but doesn't shift into gear. He just sits there, hands gripping the steering wheel. His jaw flexes. Still no words.

I get it. I only stopped shaking ten minutes ago.

The concrete wall in front of us is faintly lit by the SUV's headlights. Folding my hands over my chest, I try to contain the growing panic.

How the hell are we supposed to prepare for anything when we're chasing ghosts?

Silas reaches over, his palm warm as it settles gently against the side of my face. I turn and lean into the touch, catching the way his head is tipped back against the headrest, neck taut. I offer a small, sad smile.

His fingers are calloused but featherlight where they rest against my cheek as he studies me, eyes skimming over every flicker of thought I can't seem to hide from my expression.

I study him back.

The exhaustion sits heavy in his eyes, but everything else is still perfectly composed. His stubble is trimmed, and his curls fall into place as they always do. If I say it enough times, I could almost convince myself that we're normal.

Silas's voice cuts through the quiet like a thread snapping. "Do you have a permit to carry?"

I blink. "What?"

His hand falls from my face, but he doesn't look away. "A concealed carry permit. Do you have one?"

My heart kicks against my ribs, hard.

"No," I say too quickly. "I don't."

It was always a passing thought on the job, usually right after something reminded me just how vulnerable I really was. I was never in one place long enough to make it happen, and even if I had been, Peter would've seen it as a threat and the consequences for that...

Silas shifts, fingers curling around the latch for the center console and lifting the lid. For a second, my brain catalogs the usual contents. Sanitizer wipes, napkins, several pens, a bottle of hand lotion, but then

I see it. It blends into the black interior, mounted cleanly to the inside wall closest to him with a lock and biometric scanner.

A handgun.

Suddenly, the air in the cab feels thinner.

"Do you always have that with you?" I ask a little breathlessly.

"When I can," he says. "It doesn't exactly send the right message if someone sees me concealed carrying. That's why I have the team." He shrugs, like that should be the end of it. Then he adds, quieter, "Still, I'd rather be prepared. Especially when I'm alone."

My gaze drifts from the gun back up to his face. He's already watching me.

After a moment, he closes the console. Slowly, tentatively, he reaches for my forearm. His fingers wrap around it, thumb brushing back and forth.

"I want you to learn how to shoot," he admits.

Maybe it's the lack of sleep, what we just learned, the violence I witnessed, or my nerves getting the better of me—maybe all four—but a laugh bubbles up so hard that it burns the sides of my throat.

There's no way I just heard him correctly.

One corner of his mouth lifts, just barely, though the seriousness never leaves his eyes. Then, the hold on my arm tightens. I suck in a sharp breath as he pulls me halfway over the center console. His breath is warm against my face.

The tension in his body coils around both of us. "I'm worried," he says, voice fraying around the edges. "About what happens next."

Our noses brush as he ducks his head. "What we just learned..." His jaw tenses. "It changes nothing and everything. We're still going to find him."

Silas's fingers move to my wrist, cradling it, thumb pressing lightly over the veins.

"But I'm more worried about what he's going to do when he finds out about *you*." He swallows hard. "I don't want you to ever feel helpless."

I shake my head. "I don't. Not with you, not when—"

"There are going to be times I'm not there." Silas cuts me off, voice hardening. "And if something happens to you... If you're not safe—" He leans in the final inch, forehead touching mine.

My lungs constrict painfully as he pulls back enough to lock eyes with me.

His voice stays steady, low. "I'm going to show you where all the gun safes are hidden in the house," he says, picking up a strand of my hair and running it between the pads of his fingers. "And add your prints to the scanners."

I don't look away.

"I'll teach you how to handle a gun properly. How to shoot. How to clean it. Everything." He pauses, just long enough for the weight of it to settle between us. "If you ever decide to get a permit to carry, I'll help with that, too." Then, softer, he asks, "Will you do that for me? Please?"

He tenses. I feel it in the hand still resting against my wrist, in the breath he doesn't take.

The word *no* sits at the edge of my tongue, but it doesn't fully surface.

We don't know what Peter's going to do. Once he finds out I'm alive and here, he won't stop. He'll burn the whole place down if that's what it costs, including everyone and everything I care about. And like *fucking hell* am I going to let that happen.

The lump in my throat feels impossible to swallow. "Okay."

CHAPTER 42

Silas

I sit on a chair in my formal living room, fingers tapping an impatient rhythm against the dark mahogany armrest. Jeremy and Natalie occupy the couch across from me. Jeremy's sunk deep into the cushions, while Natalie stares off at the wall, lost in thought.

The grandfather clock in the corner ticks so loudly. We're all waiting for William's lawyer to show up, as well as Davey, who is supposed to be on his way after attending a few in-person meetings.

Technically, we're on bereavement for another three days, excluding the services next Tuesday, but the world doesn't stop when someone dies. Even for the great William Wells.

Elena stepped out of the room just before my siblings arrived. She shot down my protests, saying her presence would only add tension with Jeremy here, especially because he had such a poor reaction to learning her real identity during a phone call yesterday.

It was only a matter of time before he found out, and I assumed that it was better to tell him myself, but all he could focus on was being the last to know. He started to go off on a tangent about how our father was right about her before I cut him off with a single warning. He hung up on me only seconds later.

She's probably right, but it doesn't change the fact that the buzzing under my skin hasn't stopped since she left.

The last anyone knew, William's substantial assets, including his Wells shares, were to be split equally among the three of us. But with the way the last few months have gone, there's always the possibility that my father revisited the family trust to divide his assets in a new way as a final "fuck you" after I refused to bend to his every desire.

My only hope is that he was arrogant and believed he had ample time to change it, or was waiting for Jeremy to become COO before committing to anything.

Natalie catches my eye, her lips pressed into a thin line.

That singular look seemed to be enough for Jeremy to notice. "Why the fuck don't either of you care?" he asks, head jerking as he moves back and forth to look at both of us.

The rims of his eyes are red, whether from lack of sleep or shed tears, I can't tell. His shirt is wrinkled and untucked, hair disheveled as if he's been running his hands through it all night. For all the ways that my brother seems to lack emotion, he isn't lacking it here. Next to him, Natalie and I might as well be from a different universe.

Natalie's quick to respond. "We all handle things differently. I wasn't close to Dad like you were."

"But he's our *father*," Jeremy shoots back, looking at me expectantly. Sitting up in my seat, I run a hand down the length of my face.

"I'm trying to focus on what's in front of me, and right now, that's a corporation that lost its CEO." My words are as tired as I am of pretending to give a damn about William anymore.

Jeremy scoffs. "That's all you ever care about, isn't it?"

"The thing Dad cared about most? Yes," I correct, jaw clenched. Defending the bastard feels like poison on my tongue. "People are relying on us to be rational and level-headed. I'm compartmentalizing."

Jeremy's voice drops as he speaks through his teeth, "Don't talk to *me* about what was important to Dad."

The blood in my veins boils, but I reel in the anger from seeping out into my words. "You're right. You and Dad were thick as thieves these past few months." My neutral tone seems to temper Jeremy's anger. "I've been meaning to ask you. Did he tell you why it took so long for us to audit the servers?"

Jeremy stiffens. Natalie turns slightly towards him to also take in the pinch in his eyebrows. Instead of waiting for an answer, I lie.

"Dad had an outside team encrypt the servers without our knowledge," I say, leaning back in my seat, tracking every change in his expression. "It took Davey a while, but what he's found shows evidence of tax evasion. If this information gets out, it would severely damage our reputation and the board would question all of our involvement."

My words only make the crease in his forehead deepen. "We're correcting it so it's no longer an issue, but did he tell you about what else he might be hiding? If you know anything we should get ahead of, now's the time to speak up."

My brother's eyes narrow.

"You've got to be fucking kidding me." His posture hardens from top to bottom, first his facial features and then every muscle down to his feet, which are now firmly planted on the ground, as if he's getting ready to lunge.

"He has to ask, Jer," Natalie answers softly, uncrossing and recrossing her legs.

Jeremy whips his head to our sister. "You already knew about this."

He knows well enough that Davey wouldn't keep that type of information from his own wife. However, it does nothing to dull his anger. "So, this was the plan all along? Wait until we're alone so you both can gang up on me?"

"No one is doing that," she sighs, reaching over to place her hand on his forearm. Jeremy tracks her movement, lips pursed with disgust. The skin on my neck burns. Still, Natalie continues, "We need to make sure that we're all on the same page and share information with one another."

He huffs out a bitter laugh. "Oh, please. You both–"

Rising abruptly, I tower over my younger brother, who suddenly seems much smaller, slumped against the couch cushions. I'm aware of Natalie's glare to reel it in, but I ignore it.

"You're lucky I'm asking you directly after some of the shit you pulled," I seethe so low it's barely audible. Jeremy's eyes widen. I have no idea if it's fear or guilt that holds him hostage, but he stays quiet. "Sneaking around to board members with Dad, trying to make them doubt my abilities." Jeremy shrinks under my gaze.

I lean in, eyes not straying from his. "I'll ask you one more time, and you better consider your answer carefully." My voice drops. "Is there anything you want to tell us?"

Jeremy's face flushes a deep red before he crosses his arms.

Almost reluctantly, he mutters, "He never told me what was on the servers. He just asked me to go with Brenden to the satellite office and report back on what Davey was finding." He pauses before continuing, almost to himself, "I guess that makes sense now."

Natalie and I exchange a look. Jeremy's always been a terrible liar. Incompetence can be masked, but Jeremy never mastered that art outside of superficial interactions.

My eyes flick back to my brother and then to my sister again before I nod once. Natalie silently agrees. Jeremy has likely been in the dark as much as the rest of us have.

Something eases in my chest knowing that my brother won't have to be another person I need to deal with. But it doesn't change the fact that I don't trust him, and probably never will.

The sound of footsteps on tile breaks the silence that had settled over the three of us. All at once, we look through the cased openings as Davey comes into view with my father's lawyer and an old family friend, Jonathan Hale, in tow.

My siblings and I adopt our well-practiced facades. Sad smiles are exchanged, and we move in for brief, consoling hugs with Mr. Hale. The veneer of solidarity, whenever outsiders are present, is a dance we learned early in life.

Though Jeremy maintains a slight distance, Natalie greets Davey. Not wanting to delay this any longer, I gesture for everyone to take a seat, with

Mr. Hale positioning himself on the couch to utilize the coffee table for his briefcase.

"Let's discuss the next steps," he suggests gently, pulling out his documents. As if flipping a switch, we set aside our grievances for the moment, our expressions schooled into those of attentive children.

I take the lead, gesturing for Mr. Hale to begin. "Please, go ahead."

Mr. Hale has been hunched over the coffee table, which has served as his temporary desk for almost an hour, going over many of the finer details of how the trust works, including how we can contest it if we so choose. However, he made it clear that this option was an uphill battle.

His paperwork is organized into neat stacks across the polished surface, documents meticulously ordered. As he flips through each section, his wire-rimmed glasses slide down the front of his nose.

"Per the terms of the primary family trust, Mr. Wells's outside investments are to be divided equally among his three children. This includes any commercial real estate assets not already held in corporate structures. Detailed contact information for his financial advisors has been provided to assist in the transfer process," he announces.

We each nod in quiet acknowledgment before he moves on.

"In addition," he says, flipping to the next page, "a lump sum of two million dollars will be granted through the Wells Charitable Trust to the Harper Foundation for Ovarian Cancer Research. Mr. Wells noted this was an organization he and his wife, Caroline, supported during her treatment, with the hope that this gift will bring further awareness and access to early detection resources."

Hale and Jeremy's expressions soften, and I almost roll my eyes.

Even when my mother was alive, there was little my father would *actually* sacrifice for her. Every decision was calculated. This one probably hit a tax bracket and a PR sweet spot simultaneously.

Still, if this helps someone else's mother catch it early, then maybe that counts for something.

"To his surviving sister, Mr. Wells allocated his extensive collection of paintings," Hale continues, tone returning to neutral. "Though Georgia was invited to join us, she was unable to attend. We'll ensure she receives all relevant documentation regarding the transfer and management of the collection."

Natalie stiffens at this. Those paintings are probably the only items she actually cared about. In typical William fashion, he'd never paid attention to what mattered to her.

Davey places a comforting hand on her back, and she leans into him slightly, a faint, sad smile flickering across her lips.

Hale shifts again. "The primary residence, along with its contents, was moved into a residential property trust last year. Ownership and all decision-making authority regarding the house and its belongings are assigned to Jeremy Wells. William's personal properties in Cape Elizabeth, Mustique, and Portofino are to be split equally among the three children, with trustees managing the sales or distributions."

There's a beat of silence where no one says a thing. I stare ahead, but the room blurs slightly at the edges.

The house where our mother raised us.

Where she died.

I'd always assumed there'd come a day when William might finally let me keep some of the things that still made her feel real. The mahogany writing desk in her hobby room. The fine china she picked out in Italy the year she was pregnant with me. The painting of her in the formal sitting room I used to get lost in every time I visited.

Now it's all Jeremy's, and he gets to decide who keeps what. *If* he decides to share anything at all.

Mr. Hale clears his throat as he begins reading from William's written statement. "It is my hope that Jeremy will use this home either to establish his life and continue our family legacy or, should he choose, sell the property to fund his own passions and pursuits. This provision reflects my belief in his potential to forge his own path, with the necessary resources to support his endeavors."

What an eloquent way to tell us all that Jeremy needs the additional financial cushion. Though I can hear the underlying insult, my brother doesn't seem to notice it. His eyes brighten, and my stomach sinks.

"Lastly, William's thirty-six percent share in Wells Corporation—" Mr. Hale begins.

My jaw clenches so hard it aches, and it's barely enough to distract from the way my heart pounds violently against my ribcage.

"—was placed in a family business trust six years ago and, per the trustee appointment, will be divided equally among his three children."

I don't exhale so much as collapse. Natalie's shoulders drop just as Davey releases a long, quiet breath, like he was holding his, too.

My eyes squeeze shut, fingers pinching the bridge of my nose under my glasses. Thank God.

Maybe we'll actually claw our way out of this.

Then I open my eyes.

Jeremy's mouth is tight, his stare hardening on the document still in Hale's hand. It's the face of a man who was promised more than he was given.

My relief is eclipsed by a new wave of unease.

When every items has been laid out before us, Mr. Hale reiterates a shorter version of the speech he had given us when we began. Jeremy's expression gives nothing away, but he's smart enough to know that contesting the trust is a shot in the dark at best.

Hale hands each sibling a folder filled with documents pertaining to our new inheritances. "I must say, I truly was sad to hear of William's passing," Mr. Hale remarks quietly. "He was a good friend, and I will miss him greatly."

"We're going to miss him, too." My words are practiced and polite. "Can I offer you some coffee or lunch before you go?"

Mr. Hale declines with a courteous shake of his head, packing up his briefcase. "Thank you, but I must be off. You have my contact information if you need help with anything. Take care of yourselves and each other." With a few final handshakes, he makes his exit.

Natalie and Davey have yet to rise from their seats, both fingering through the folder in their hands as they quietly discuss the next steps they need to take.

Jeremy wastes no time following Mr. Hale out after collecting his things. He's almost at the door when I call after him, "You don't need to rush off, Jer."

He barely pauses, his response slightly cold as he glances over his shoulder. "I've got a house to sort out."

His wording tells me it won't be long before he sells it. I just hope he won't throw everything away when he does.

Only a few breaths after the door shuts, Cillian appears from around the corner with Elena a step behind.

"How'd it go?" Cillian asks. Glancing down at the folder in my left hand, I nod, feeling a rare flicker of hope.

"We maintain control of Wells. And with Natalie's increased shares, we'll have more leverage with the board," I explain.

It's impossible to miss the way Elena's shoulders relax behind Cillian. She remains by the cased opening, and I extend my hand to her. She hesitates, but eventually steps forward. When she's within reach, I pull her to my side.

"It's business as usual for now," I say, looking around at each of them. "Natalie is going to make some calls to gauge if pushing for an emergency board meeting is in the cards. We'll ask Everett to call the meeting if we have the votes, and once that's settled, Sierra Blanca becomes our main priority."

"We were able to send out discreet memos to severely limit operations at the facility for the time being," Cillian adds, glancing at his phone. "They've halted all trials and have been instructed to provide thorough care to all patients to pause their medications and maintain their health while they wait for further instructions."

"So, now what? We wait?" Elena asks, eyebrows knitting together in concern as she looks up at me, searching for answers.

My lips press into a thin line, wishing I had more to offer.

"Unfortunately, yes. Now, we wait."

CHAPTER 43

Elena

I stand in front of the mirror, staring at my reflection. My fingers brush over the fabric of my dress again, smoothing invisible creases.

It's flawless. The high neckline grazes my throat, and the short sleeves balance the form-fitting bodice, before the skirt flares out into graceful folds that skim the mid-calf. My hair is swept into a low bun with a few soft pieces framing my face. It's classic, appropriate, and exactly what the day demands.

Every detail feels like a final, deliberate touch, to the point that the reflection doesn't feel like me—which, I suppose, is the point.

The house is quiet with Silas in his study down the hallway. I can picture him with his phone pressed to his ear, speaking in that steady, commanding tone of his. He's been on calls almost constantly, and it sounds like the emergency board meeting will happen by the end of next week, if not sooner. In days, Silas will be stepping up as CEO.

I glance back at the mirror, biting my lip. *Is this enough? Do I look the part?* Today isn't about me, but I can't shake the weight of what standing beside him means.

A pang of uncertainty coils in my chest, and I try to push it down.

It's one thing to think about what the press will say when the story breaks; it's another to think about the people I spent months cozying up to as Scarlett Page finding out.

How are they going to react when they realize she wasn't real?

Silas and Davey came up with a carefully crafted story to soften the fallout, which they'll leak to the press in an hour. The official story is that I was a private cybersecurity advisor who used pseudonyms, like Scarlett Page, while consulting on high-profile cases. Silas had hired me under that alias to handle some of his personal security concerns, and over time, our relationship evolved. When my contract was complete, I left, but I have since stepped back from consulting to re-enter the public eye under my real name, so that we can be together.

The whole thing frames me as successful but private. To really sell it, Davey spent several days building a digital trail, just enough to look convincing. Luckily, if the story were true, my digital footprint would have been limited, anyway.

I smooth over my dress again.

"Beautiful," Silas's voice caresses me from behind.

I turn to find him leaning against the doorframe. His black suit is perfectly tailored, white shirt crisp, and black tie immaculately knotted. The morning light catches on his glasses, and his neatly trimmed curls frame his face.

"Is this okay?" I ask, gesturing to my outfit. My voice comes out softer than I'd like.

He gives me a pointed look while crossing the room. "More than okay," he says, cupping my face in his hands gently. "You look perfect. Thank you for coming with me."

I nod, my throat too tight to speak. He lingers a moment longer, thumbs brushing softly across my cheeks before he straightens to adjust his tie as if preparing for battle.

Those words should fill me, but they don't. Not after our conversation a few days ago, which left me feeling hollow despite my telling myself I understood.

It replays in my mind on loop. Silas and Davey had called me into the study to talk. Davey spoke first, asking if I'd feel comfortable attending the funeral services with Silas. For a fleeting moment, I was thrilled.

They'd thought of me. Considered how I might feel. Silas wanted me there by his side, in public. But the illusion shattered only seconds later.

"This might be the fastest way to draw Peter out of hiding," Silas's added with a clinical tone. *"He's likely following the story, and if he sees you're still alive and back with me, he'll want to do something about it. The sooner he does, the sooner we can put all of this behind us."*

All of the progress I felt we had made, and the concern he had for my safety just days ago, vanished like a puff of smoke.

Silas's reasoning is logical and practical. His team will be there, and the services are for invited guests. It's the perfect, controlled environment to make the most impact. But his words only made it harder to decipher whether he wanted me there for me or because I make good bait.

"Of course." I manage a small smile.

His returning smile is tender, and for a moment, it feels real, but it fades as the corners of his mouth tighten and his eyes harden around the edges like frozen dirt. Before I can ask what's wrong, he leans in, brushing his lips against mine with a care that doesn't disturb my lipstick.

When he pulls back, only a fraction of the warmth has returned to his gaze. "There's someone here to see you."

"Someone?"

He exhales softly, his jaw flexing before he answers. "Luis."

It takes me a moment to process the words. "He's here?!"

Ben and Corey have been gone for several days. They were cleared to leave thanks to Corey's automation. Davey debriefed me on their departures and the deal they had reached to keep quiet about what they were involved in. Given their line of work, I can't imagine it took much convincing to agree to stay out of one another's business. I'd assumed Silas had sent Luis on his way, too.

"It's the safest time to get him back to Colorado," Silas explains with too much control. "The services will keep eyes elsewhere." He pauses, studying me for a beat. "He requested to see you before he left."

"Oh," I murmur, caught between surprise and something else I can't quite name.

"It seems," Silas says, his tone quieter, "Luis has *quite* the soft spot for you."

I blink and then shrug. "We've been through a lot. He's a good friend."

Those dark eyes narrow just slightly, but he says nothing else.

I can't read into his reaction. Jealousy is fickle. It doesn't necessarily mean Silas has decided to keep me forever or even long-term. It may just be a fleeting feeling, nothing more.

"He's waiting downstairs," he says, stepping back and gesturing toward the door. I grab the black peacoat and small handbag draped on the edge of the bed before following him out.

Silas holds my hand down the hallway and the main staircase. The only sound is the soft click of my heels until we reach the bottom. I glance up at him, but he's already looking toward the formal living room.

Through the cased openings, Luis sits on one of the couches. He looks well, better than I'd expected, and the tight knot I'd been carrying for him begins to loosen. Silas and Davey promised to get him back to Colorado safely, but I still worried.

He's alive. Intact. And if there are scars from his time in those holding rooms, I can't see them.

I limited my contact with Luis after Silas brought me here. Silas never stopped me from contacting him, but I didn't need to hear the words to know how he feels about the friendship. Silas asked me to choose him, and this was one way I needed to, even if it hurt like hell to do it to one of the only true friends I'd ever known.

Luis's face lights up, his smile wide and warm. Like he's been waiting for this. For me.

I smile back. Before I can take a step, Silas gently tilts my chin up, forcing me to meet his eyes. The polite smile he wears for society is firmly in place, but I see the tension underneath.

"I'll be in the other room while you two talk," he says, slipping the bag and coat from my hands like they're his responsibility. "You won't need these."

I nod, swallowing the questions that rise to my lips. As he steps back and turns toward the adjacent room, I take a breath, pushing down the flicker of unease he's left behind.

Luis stands as I step into the formal living room. Before I can say anything, he wraps me in a tight hug and I hug him back just as hard, mumbling into his shoulder, "I'm so sorry, Lu."

He pulls back, meeting my gaze. "It's not your fault."

I huff a soft laugh, shaking my head. "You've always been a terrible liar."

His hands resting lightly on my arms as he surveys my appearance. After a moment, I gesture to the couch and he nods. I settle beside him, taking his hand in mine the way old friends do. It feels familiar in a way that doesn't need words.

"How are you?" I ask, my voice soft. "How did everything go?"

Luis sighs, his shoulders sinking slightly as he glances down at our hands. "The first week... I don't want to get into it." There's a shadow in his voice. "But after that, it was fine. Honestly, it felt like working for Peter again. Just with a nicer apartment."

I roll my eyes, nudging his shoulder lightly with mine. He smiles faintly, though his eyes remain shadowed. Silence stretches between us.

"You look like you're doing well," he says, though there's a subtle question woven into his words.

I nod, but it feels half-hearted. Am I doing well? I'm not sure I'd even know how to answer. I'm simply in limbo, waiting to see where I fit in Silas's life.

My hesitation must show, because Luis's brows knit together in concern. "Are you okay?" he leans in, voice quieter now. "Do you feel safe here?"

"I'm more than fine, really." I glance down at our hands, exhaling. "I'm here until he tells me to leave," I say simply, though the statement makes my chest tighten.

Luis frowns, but he doesn't push. Instead, he squeezes my hand, and I shift the conversation before the heaviness can linger too long.

"Thank you for everything," I say, meeting his gaze. "And please thank Ben and Corey again for me, too."

He nods, his expression softening. "They'll appreciate that," he says, but then his features turn thoughtful, more serious. "What's the plan with Peter?" he asks.

I hesitate. "I'm not entirely sure yet," I admit. "Silas and Davey are working on it, but I'll let you know if I can."

Luis studies me closely before eventually leaning back against the couch with a small nod. "Fair enough," he says, though his expression says otherwise.

There's a brief pause, and his hand twitches lightly in mine before he exhales. "Elena, I want you to know you always have a room at my hous—"

"Luis," Silas's voice cuts through the room. "I hate to interrupt, but we need to be on our way."

Luis's fingers contract as he glances toward Silas in the doorway, who is now wearing a coat. There's a short moment when I think Luis might not listen, but he suddenly stands, pulling me with him. Before I can blink, he is wrapping me in a hug that lasts seconds longer than it probably should.

I pat his back a bit awkwardly. "Let me know when you're home and settled," I tell my friend, pulling back.

The look in his eyes can't be described as anything other than unsatisfied. "I will," he promises.

Behind us, Silas clears his throat. Luis releases me, though his hand lingers briefly on my arm before stepping away. When I turn, Silas is already there, a hand settling firmly on the small of my back as he gives me my bag before draping the coat over the tops of my shoulders.

Silas guides me toward the front door, Luis trailing behind us. When we reach the entryway, I spot Cora, her hands clasped neatly in front of her. Silas acknowledges her with a smile before turning back to Luis.

"Cora will be taking you to your next destination," Silas says, his tone polite but curt. "She'll ensure you get home undetected and safe."

Luis nods toward Cora, though his eyes flick back to me once more, lingering. Silas pulls me a fraction closer to him, and whatever Luis was about to say stays unsaid.

"Take care, Elena," he says finally, his voice softer now.

"You too," I reply, matching his tone.

Cora gestures for Luis to follow her toward the garage entrance, and he does, the steps slow and reluctant. When they round the corner and are out of sight, Silas leads me to the front door.

The black town car waits just beyond the gate, sleek and gleaming in the October sun. The clear blue skies feel almost too nice for the occasion. Silas opens the back door for me with practiced ease. I slide into the cool leather seat and wait for Silas to circle the car to the opposite side. Cillian is looking at me in the rearview mirror.

"Good morning, Elena," he says with a faint trace of warmth.

"Hi Cill," I reply. Things between us have softened a little since I started working out with Jeff in the basement.

Silas gets into the car a moment later, but instead of settling near the door, he keeps moving until his thigh presses fully against mine. His hand lands on my leg, the palm firm against the fabric of my dress.

I raise an eyebrow at him, tilting my head slightly. "Are you alright?" I ask.

He leans in, his grip on my thigh tightening before his mouth claims mine. There's no hesitation. Only heat and something sharper as he presses into me. The small breath I manage to suck in is all the permission he needs to evade my mouth, tongue and teeth claiming me. For a second, I remember Cillian is in the front seat. It's too bold, too intimate—but the thought barely forms before it disintegrates. The weight of Silas and the way he moves against me drowns out everything else.

By the time he finally pulls back, my heart is thundering. I force my expression into something close to neutral, even though my pulse betrays me.

A streak of dark red stains Silas's mouth. I let out a breathy laugh. With a trembling hand, I brush my thumb across his lips to clean them off. He lets me, the hardness in his eyes softening with every swipe of my finger.

When I finish, his smirk curves into a real smile. "You'll need to fix your own."

I roll my eyes, muttering under my breath as I dig through my bag for my compact and lipstick tube. Silas shifts his attention to the front and gives Cillian a nod.

"Let's get this over with," he says on a tired exhale.

"Yes, sir," Cillian replies smoothly, the engine humming to life as the car pulls away from the house.

His taste lingers on my tingling lips, and I focus on fixing my lipstick instead of dwelling on it. Silas's neutrality returns, and he says nothing more. Whatever he feels, whatever that kiss was meant to convey, I know better than to ask.

CHAPTER 44

Silas

I f there was one thing my father excelled at, it was being prepared for *almost* anything. After my mother passed, he pre-planned his own services and paid for them in full, down to the smallest detail. It was entirely self-serving, of course, but now I can almost imagine him rolling over in his grave, knowing how much easier he's made it for Natalie and me to put on a performance for the rest of the world.

The services are being held at Holy Name Cathedral because God forbid he do anything understated. The cathedral's towering spires, intricate stonework, and gilded accents fit perfectly with the larger-than-life image he always cultivated. Even so, there's barely enough room for all who came. By the time we arrive with most of my team in tow—purposefully just before the start of the service to avoid lingering conversations I have no patience for—most of the seats are already taken by colleagues, extended family, and old friends.

Leaving Cillian at the guarded door, I lead Elena down the long center aisle toward the front row where Jeremy, Natalie, and Davey are already seated. With a firm hand, I guide Elena to lead us into the pew. Jeremy stands and offers us a small nod, averting his gaze. I clap him on the shoulder and give a small squeeze, anyway. Davey and Natalie also stand, both offering brief hugs before we make our way to the empty spots next to them.

My father's older sister, Georgia, is directly behind us, along with her husband, Philip. I lean over the back of the pew to greet them and introduce Elena. We don't see them often. Gatherings with the Wells side of the family were never exactly warm, but Georgia had a decent relationship with my father. They had another sister who passed away young, and with both my grandparents gone, they'd grown closer as they aged. Still, I don't know much about this woman, even while tears shine in her eyes as she claims how unfair it is for a good man to be taken so young. All I can manage is a pained smile before turning with Elena to sit.

Religion has never been a cornerstone of our family life. I suppose I'm technically Catholic, though we didn't practice beyond Confirmation and the occasional Easter service. Still, I can't deny the beauty of Catholic architecture. The cathedral is breathtaking, especially in the late morning light. Rays of sun stream through the stained-glass windows, casting bursts of color across the polished stone floors. The arches of the ceiling seem to stretch endlessly upward, allowing every murmur in the crowd around us to echo.

One beam of light falls directly in front of Elena's seat. It catches her profile when she leans forward, the soft glow accentuating the curve of her cheekbone and golden streaks in her eyes.

"Do you need anything?" she whispers over my lap to Natalie.

My sister shakes her head, her lips pressing into a faint, thankful smile. Natalie reaches across me to pat Elena's arm. "I'm fine, thank you," she answers. Then she leans back, her attention shifting to Davey, who murmurs something in her ear.

We don't get another moment to speak before the priest emerges from a side door and approaches the altar. The room quiets immediately, save for the faint shuffling of feet and the rustling of hymnals as the congregation settles. I try to focus on what he's saying and the cadence of his voice as he begins the service, but the words blur together.

For most of the service, my gaze is pinned just above the priest's head, fixing my focus somewhere between the intricate carvings and the

313

towering crucifix behind it. Being in a church feels like using a muscle I haven't flexed in years. I still know when to make the sign of the cross, when to mumble the correct responses, when to stand or kneel, even if I don't think about what any of it means anymore. It's automatic, like driving when you're too tired to remember how you got from point A to point B.

What keeps me tethered to the present, though, is Elena. She doesn't move to follow any of the cues. She sits beside me, attentive and respectful, but not a single word leaves her lips. The hand she might have used to sign the cross stays firmly clasped in mine and only lets go when I move to kneel or stand. The moment I'm back in the seat, she's reaching for me without looking, her thumb brushes lightly over my knuckles.

The corner of my mouth twitches at the irony of someone with the last name Cross not having any ties to religion. Maybe it's not all religion, just this one. I've never asked if she believes in anything, and the thought amuses me more than I care to admit.

The priest's words blend into a monotone hum that feels endless. None of the siblings or Georgia chose to speak, all citing that it's too emotional and we couldn't possibly give a speech worthy of our father. Those stories are only half-true. Jeremy's always been a shit public speaker. As for Natalie and me, I don't think either of us can stomach more of this charade than we absolutely have to.

And thank whatever divine power out there that my father insisted his casket only be present at the burial site. At least I'm spared the task of carrying his dead weight out of here.

Just a few hours.

That's what I keep telling myself. A few hours of holding back the eye rolls, of nodding politely while people wax poetic about a man they barely knew. Then I can take Elena home. Maybe I'll take her out for a nightcap. Not because I particularly care to drink, but because I want an excuse to keep looking at her in this dress.

My eyes trail over to her lap, the fabric hugging her legs as she sits so perfectly still beside me. My gaze moves to the way the bodice cinches at her waist, emphasizing every graceful line of her. The high neckline is supposed to make the dress modest, even sweet, but nothing ever looks modest on Elena.

Luis also noticed this earlier, taking in the dress as Elena approached him to say goodbye. His gaze lingered too long. I'd been sitting in the adjacent room, listening to their conversation, pretending not to care, when she said that one quiet comment that cracked open something I wasn't ready to face.

"I'm here until he tells me to leave."

I've barely let myself think that far ahead. Hell, I'm still working on letting go of the anger. Most days, it feels like I'm making progress, but then there are moments where I still want to blame her for everything, even though I know she's not at fault. Peter forced her into this, and my father has no one to blame for his evils but himself; yet, knowing that doesn't stop the thoughts from existing. Right now, I can't promise that I won't always feel this way. Even though she wronged me, Elena doesn't deserve to spend her life dealing with that.

And then Luis, without a moment's hesitation, interjected to tell her she was always welcome to stay with him. I couldn't believe my ears. She dragged him into this mess, and yet there he was, acting as though none of that mattered.

It wasn't just the audacity of Luis propositioning Elena in my own home that enraged me; it was the fact that he could offer her so readily what I couldn't. The thought of him trying to take her and give her something I wasn't ready to made my hands itch to strangle him.

Now, sitting beside her, I can't shake how she made Luis pause. She could walk into a room wearing a paper bag and still be the most stunning woman there, but this dress feels like it was made to torment me. It hints just enough without giving everything away, leaving me to fill in the blanks. And I can't stop. My mind wanders, remembering what's under the fabric, the curve of her back, the line of her neck. Every movement she makes is deliberate, poised, and yet so effortlessly sensual.

It's maddening.

Without thinking, I lean closer, my lips brushing the sensitive spot just below her ear. She smells of coconut body wash and her subtle vanilla perfume. The faintest hitch in her breath betrays her, and she glances at me from the corner of her eye.

That soft, almost inaudible puff of air she takes in makes my cock twitch, and I smile against her skin, lowering my voice so only she can hear.

"Ever had sex on an altar before?"

Her response is immediate; fingers squeeze mine, warning me to behave, though the small smile tugging at the corner of her lips says otherwise. That expression sends my mind spiraling.

She's so composed, so beautiful, and all I can think about is ruining her. Messing up that carefully pinned hair, wrinkling that perfect dress, leaving marks on her skin that she'd have to explain later.

My thoughts grow darker, more vivid, until the burn of lust low in my stomach is the only thing I can concentrate on.

Lost in those fantasies, I almost miss Communion. I'm jerked back to reality when Natalie tugs my forearm, her expression making it clear she knows I might skip it. She wouldn't have been wrong, but appearances matter today, so I rise and follow her lead.

The rest of the service feels like it drags on for another eternity. Finally, the priest begins explaining how the funeral procession will work, asking attendees to remain seated until the immediate family has exited first. I've never been more thankful to fall into that category.

The second it's our turn, I'm on my feet, pulling Elena up with me. She threads her fingers through mine without hesitation.

She stays half a step behind as I walk us as efficiently as possible past the rows of curious eyes. They watch and whisper about my father, about me, about Elena, who they still know as Scarlett, until they watch the news this evening. I move faster to outrun their gossip.

By the time we make it to the entry doors, the early October breeze feels like salvation. I take a deep breath. The weight in my chest eases slightly, even with the cameras aimed at us from the sidewalk and the hired security keeping them at bay. I glance over my shoulder at Elena.

"There's still time," I say, the corner of my mouth tugging into a grin. "Altar's empty now if you've changed your mind."

Elena rolls her eyes at me, the faintest blush coloring her cheeks as she shakes her head. "You're an idiot," she mutters, though her lips curl into a delicious, subtle smirk.

———

The burial service is quicker than the church service, yet it somehow feels longer. Our security team has set up a tight perimeter, but I still catch sight of photographers and a cameraman from the local news stations lurking at the edges of the cemetery, their cameras trained on Natalie, Jeremy, and me. And on Elena.

It bothers me to position her in plain view as part of a strategy, but Davey and I agreed it's the best move. The sooner we deal with Peter, the sooner we can start setting everything right without interruptions. His embarrassment might make him sloppy, and we use that to our advantage.

If we can finally kill the bastard, then all the inevitable headaches that come with doing so will be worth it, for my family and Elena. She'll be truly free of him for the first time in over ten years. No more constantly looking over her shoulder.

No more fear.

The thought brings relief, but it also stirs something uncomfortable deep in my chest.

She said she's here for as long as I allow her to be, but will that still be true when there's nothing holding her back from walking away and starting over to live virtually any life she wants?

Would she escape across the world? Go back to Luis? Settle down somewhere new and try to find someone to build the rest of her life with?

The idea twists in my gut, nauseating and sharp. I force myself to look ahead, focusing on the priest's words as dirt is ceremoniously tossed over the grave.

Without thinking, I lift Elena's hand to my mouth, pressing a soft kiss to the back of it. My lips linger for a moment, warm against her cool fingers. In my peripheral, she glances at me with a faint, closed-mouth smile. I lower her hand to my lap, cupping it between both of mine for the rest of the service.

When they begin lowering my father's casket into the ground, I can't look away. The process is painfully slow, and the urge to jump on top of the box to shove it down with my own two hands flashes through my mind more than once.

This part of the service was intentionally kept small, as per my father's request, with mostly his closest friends, family members, and long-time associates in attendance. There are only a few dozen of us compared to the few hundred at the church an hour and a half ago.

We stand from our seats, and I brace myself for the inevitable parade of condolences.

"Well, I have to admit, it was a hell of a turnout at the church. Your father would've been proud."

My spine stiffens. Martin Shaw stands a few feet away, though his name wasn't on this guest list.

Jaw tight, I look towards my team. *How the hell did he get past them?*

My father's ex-business partner looks like hell. His suit, though expensive, is wrinkled, and his tie is slightly crooked. His face is pale with shadows under his eyes that make him look like he hasn't slept in weeks. And yet, for all his disheveled appearance, his posture is straight and his expression smug.

It takes everything I have to swallow the fury rising in my throat and bury it deep. There are eyes on us. Not just people I know, but those damn news cameras on the edge of the trees.

Without a word, Natalie and Davey turn their backs and head toward other guests.

"Martin," I say, keeping my tone even as I look him over. "You're looking... well."

He smiles faintly, unfazed by the jab. "And you're looking every bit the heir apparent," he responds. "Not an easy day, I'm sure."

His gaze shifts to Elena, his stare far too appreciative. "Scarlett."

"Martin," she replies coolly, and doesn't correct him about her name.

Martin's smile doesn't falter, though his eyes narrow slightly as he looks between the two of us. "I just wanted to offer my condolences personally," he says, turning back to me. "William was a force of nature. Tough, brilliant, and endlessly determined."

He continues, tone almost conversational, "He built something incredible. A legacy most people could only dream of. Big shoes to fill, Silas. I'm sure you'll do your best to live up to them."

The anger threatens to surge again, but something else drifts in like fog, curling around the edges of it. It doesn't consume as much as it soothes, whispering low and certain: *Don't worry, we'll get him soon.*

My head tilts almost of its own accord. A smile pulls at my mouth, just enough to let the venom peek through.

"Yes, he did. And it's tragic, isn't it?" I lower my voice, watching his expression. "What happened to my father. It's the kind of thing that could happen to anyone, no matter how *brilliant* they are."

Martin's eyes widen a fraction before settling into the cool, indifferent gaze that my father taught him so well.

"Well," he huffs, cheeks reddening just slightly, "I have bigger concerns than the ghosts of old men."

"I wouldn't be so sure about that."

My answer only makes his face flush more. A retort is on the tip of his tongue, but it never comes to pass. His expression hardens just as he dips his head in our direction. "Take care, Silas. Scarlett."

Martin turns on his heel without waiting for a response and walks toward Jeremy, who is standing alongside some of our mother's cousins.

Jeremy's face lights up as he approaches, and they embrace. Several yards away, Davey's eyes meet mine, and I give him a subtle nod. He immediately pulls out his phone to text the team.

"Si?" Elena's voice pulls me back, soft and questioning. "You okay?"

I'll be okay when this day is done.

I exhale slowly, the tension in my chest easing slightly. "Yeah, I'm ready to go," I sigh before adding, "Though, I'm still game for that altar."

Elena snorts, rolling her eyes. "You're *still* an idiot."

Chapter 45

Elena

The hostess leads Silas and me through the chic interior of the upscale Italian restaurant and out onto the patio. It's a strangely warm October evening. The sun is at just the right angle to let the overhead bistro lights and discreet patio heaters take over. Everything is bathed in a warm, inviting glow.

It was impossible not to notice how the staff seemed to have been waiting for us, expectant smiles on their faces as Silas guided me inside. Ten seconds barely passed before they led us wordlessly to a table he undoubtedly selected when he made the reservation.

We are slightly removed from the cluster of other tables in a corner, but still in full view of the restaurant's interior through the expansive windows. Just on the walk outside, we'd encountered several familiar faces, and even more of Silas's peers seem to be scattered on the patio with us.

Their eyes feel like needles in the side of my head, and my body grows hotter with each heartbeat.

Silas pulls out my chair, and I sit, carefully adjusting the blazer resting on my shoulders so it doesn't slip off. The weight of it feels almost protective against the hushed whispers rumbling across the dining area. After months of blending in this spring, I suddenly feel starkly out of place. But that's exactly why we're here, isn't it?

Since the funeral, and despite the media spinning our story into some fairytale romance, the people in Silas's circles have been anything but welcoming.

Natalie has been keeping tabs on the reaction, and they feel betrayed. Most are suspicious of me, and I suppose I don't blame them. Silas saw this coming, though. He insisted that hiding away now won't do us any good. If we act normal, they'll get over their shock quicker, and we'll be old news by the time the next scandal pops up.

We didn't get the response we were hoping for from Peter, either. Davey's sources have no updates on his reaction to my resurrection or whether he has set any new plans in motion. They believe that this might help provoke Peter, especially if he still has ears in Chicago.

Two birds, one stone, and all.

So this evening's plan was born. A time and day of the week that was picked for peak visibility. Cillian, Lloyd, and Cora are just beyond the lattice patio walls in one of the SUVs. Silas's belly band holster, carrying his preferred Glock 43, is perfectly concealed under his clothes.

Once I'm settled in my seat, Silas pulls out the chair on the opposite side, but he doesn't sit. He begins to rearrange the table, sliding his chair directly next to mine before moving the dinnerware in front of it. I watch him curiously as he maneuvers the furniture and places his jacket over the back of his now adjacent seat, revealing a black sweater with the sleeves folded up his forearms, before sitting.

Without missing a beat, Silas reaches under me and pulls the leg of my chair. The seat scrapes against the pavers, drawing even more attention from the guests around us. Beneath the table, his hand finds the top calf of my crossed legs, lifting the fabric of my wide-leg trousers just enough to rest his hand on the bare skin of my calf.

My eyebrows shoot up in surprise. Silas, however, doesn't bat an eye.

He picks up the wine menu, holding it out between us with his free hand. "Do you have any preference on the wine?" he asks, flipping it over. "I was thinking of getting a bottle of Barolo. It's a good year for it." The way his thumb caresses back and forth under the table tells me his thoughts are on a *very* different subject.

My mouth is too dry.

I reach for the pre-filled crystal water goblet at my place setting. Though Silas doesn't turn his head, I can feel his gaze pressing on me over the top of his glasses as I take a long sip. I clear my throat and manage to murmur, "That sounds good."

Silas nods once before setting the wine menu down, all the while, his thumb continues its slow strokes.

As if on cue, a waiter approaches us. "Mr. Wells, welcome back," he says with a genuine smile.

"Jacob, it's good to see you. How have you been?" Silas replies.

It shouldn't surprise me that Silas remembered this waiter's name, but seeing him act so painfully human still throws me for a loop.

Jacob, probably in his early twenties, brightens. "I'm hanging in there. Just counting the days till I'm out of Fluid Dynamics. It's a killer this semester."

Silas chuckles. "I can imagine. Hang in there, you're halfway through," he encourages before turning slightly to look at me, "This is my girlfriend, Elena."

His words carry across the patio with a weight I'm unprepared for. I have to clamp down on my outward shock, and my ears burn. Jacob turns his smile towards me with a nod. "Nice to meet you, Elena."

Recovering quickly, I return the gesture. "It's nice to meet you, too."

Silas asks for the bottle of wine he mentioned previously. Jacob promises to return with it in a moment. As he walks away, I release a long, quiet breath in an attempt to settle the flutter of nerves in my stomach.

"Hey."

I jump at the closeness of Silas's voice. His fingers pause on my leg, prompting me to turn my face back toward his. "What's wrong?"

My next inhale catches in my lungs while I search for the right words. "This is a little overwhelming."

He offers me a small, understanding smile. "You're doing great."

Not long after, Jacob returns carrying the bottle of Barolo. He presents it to Silas with practiced ease. Silas nods, and Jacob proceeds to open it, carefully pouring the red liquid into a decanter.

Jacob expertly fills two glasses, presenting one to Silas for approval. After a contemplative sip, Silas gives another appreciative nod. As Jacob sets down a glass in front of me, Silas leans closer. His proximity under Jacob's watchful eyes causes a warm flush to spread across my cheeks.

"Are you okay with me ordering the carpaccio?" he murmurs, and I barely manage a nod before he orders.

Jacob bows his head in acknowledgment and heads back into the restaurant. Silas lifts his glass towards me, a soft smile playing on his lips. We clink them together in a quiet toast.

He shifts closer again, breath warm against my ear, "You look so goddamn beautiful."

My heart swells and deflates just as quickly. For a moment, I forgot that this isn't just a date. It's another maneuver in the endless game I've been forced to play for years.

I'm not sure there will ever be a time when there isn't some small part of me that wonders if he will miss this if life ever becomes normal. Will I lose all my appeal when we're just two people existing together? When all the adrenaline and drama fades, will he still treat me this way in public, even if it's not to purposefully flaunt our relationship?

Despite the delicious wine and Silas's warm eyes on me, bitterness lingers at the back of my throat.

Feeling a little desperate to break the spell he has me under, I ask softly, "Laying it on a little thick, aren't we?"

Silas finishes his own sip with a new sharpness in his gaze.

"What does that mean?"

Under his questioning stare, I want to take the impulsive words back. My neck heats as I shrug, averting my eyes back to the table. Silas, however, tenses his hand on my calf. Knowing he isn't going to let the comment slide, I reluctantly look back up at him.

His eyes search my face. "I miss that smart mouth of yours quite a bit," he admits, "I'd like to hear it now."

I drum my nails on the tabletop, biting the inside of my lip. *Why can't I just enjoy this for what it is?*

Feeling defeated, I answer, "You don't need to do all of this."

Confusion washes over his face. "All of what?"

My eyes dart around the patio. Most people have returned to their own meals, though several still stare. Filled with a shameful awareness, I elaborate quietly, "I appreciate your attention, but just being here together has done what you wanted it to. Your plan worked."

The intensity of his gaze is unsettling. He leans back in his seat, the hand on my leg falling away. I struggle not to let the loss of his warmth show on my face.

He doesn't take his eyes off me as he lifts his crystal water glass to his lips and says, somewhat bewildered, "You think I'm doing this for show."

Before I can muster a response, Jacob arrives with our appetizer. The practiced smiles return like second nature, and we assure Jacob that we'll need a few more minutes with the menu. He nods understandingly and leaves us once again.

The sun dips further below the buildings around us, casting shadows that I hope mask our strained expressions. I touch Silas's inked forearm with a tentative smile.

"It's okay," I whisper. "I know what this dinner was meant to do, but this type of public affection," I pause to clear the nerves from my throat, "makes it hard for me to keep my expectations in check."

Silas looks down at the hand resting on his arm and then back up at me. The silence stretches, and I'm suddenly desperate to salvage the evening I just ruined.

"I–I made things weird. I'm sorry. Just forget I said anything."

He doesn't respond, so I serve the carpaccio. My hands shake, utensils clattering as I transfer thin meat slices onto his plate.

When I'm about to retreat into the quiet task of arranging my own serving, Silas's fingers encircle my wrist, stopping me. I close my eyes, taking a deep breath before setting down my utensils. His gaze is all fire, and I want to shrink away.

"Do I treat you poorly in private?" he asks under his breath.

There's a sudden pinch in my chest. "No."

"Am I more affectionate with you in front of others than when we're alone?"

I swallow. "No."

"Do you not want to be seen in public with me?"

My head is shaking before the word leaves my mouth, "No."

"Did I make tonight feel like a job?"

My teeth tear into the side of my cheek. "Yes," I breathe.

Silas's expression softens. Those dark brown eyes flick across my features while the gears turn in his head.

Gently, he lifts my hand to his lips, pressing a kiss to my wrist before holding my palm against his cheek. Each scrape of skin sends a tingle down my arm.

"I've been looking forward to this," he confesses. "Doing something normal with you and not having to hide it."

Heat explodes from my stomach and flows to the ends of my fingers and toes.

Silas exhales a soft sigh. "I'm sorry if that got lost in translation," he continues, "I haven't done a single thing tonight that I didn't want to do."

The warmth radiating from his hand and face seep into me, settling deep beneath my skin in a way that blurs where I end and he begins.

I search his face for doubt. Even as curious eyes glance our way across the patio, his focus stays fixed on me. He waits, patient and quiet, like he has nothing but time for me to believe him.

And I do.

The feeling of relief is almost physical as I sink more comfortably into my seat. The corners of my lips curl up, and the moment Silas sees it, he answers with his own grin. He lowers my hand and uses it to pull me over the armrest of my chair, lips finding mine in a slow, tender kiss that turns my insides molten.

Against me, he murmurs, "Can we start over and just have a nice dinner together?"

I nod, and he kisses me again before releasing my arm and straightening. "You better figure out what to order," he says, switching his plate of carpaccio with my empty one and picking up his abandoned menu. "If we don't order soon, Jacob's going to start to wonder if we know how to read."

Laughing softly, I scan the specials. Silas's hand returns to my calf. Suddenly, all those curious eyes I've avoided since we arrived cease to exist.

CHAPTER 46

Silas

I excuse myself from the boardroom on the far end of the executive floor, the remnants of too much small talk and too many handshakes clinging to me like a second skin. I waited until a few others left before making a polite exit.

The silence of the hallway is almost deafening. My footsteps are muted by the carpet, a stark contrast to the chaos in my head.

Silas Wells, CEO of Wells Corporation.

The echo of the vote lingers in my ears, even in the quiet leading back to my office. It was the final move in a series of calculated days.

Technically, I had enough support going into the emergency meeting to force the vote. Natalie, Everett, Amy, Miriam, and Elias all confirmed their support early. Thirty-six percent was three higher than what was necessary, but barely scraping by would've reeked of desperation. I needed more confidence. So, I spent the past week peeling off one board member at a time from my father's camp.

Mark came around quickly. Stability speaks louder than sentiment when you're holding other people's money. Venessa took more work. As a pharmaceutical executive, she's pragmatic but cautious, not fond of being rushed. I made it clear she wasn't taking a gamble, and she finally accepted that it was me stepping into the future a few months early.

Randall and Jeremy held the line, of course. Loyalists to the end. I expected as much, but forty-one percent stood with me, and that's enough to quiet any whispered doubts.

The formalities moved quickly after that. Once the vote was in and I was called back into the boardroom to announce the decision, the legal team entered, and we proceeded to the paperwork and signatures. It had already been drafted back in January when the original succession plan was signed. All they had to do was move up the timeline.

There had been a brief discussion about a future celebration, and I deflected, suggesting that maybe we could consider something in the new year. They assumed it was out of respect for my father, and I'll let them think that.

Right now, there's too much to be done to fix all of his mistakes, and I can't be bogged down with something so trivial.

As I approach Leslie's desk, I'm already talking. "Can you hold all of my calls and visitors?" I ask, knowing the flurry of reactions that the company memo will soon ignite. "Public Relations and Marketing are going to handle the media, but I don't want to be disturbed for the rest of the day. Just tell anyone who reaches out that I'm in virtual meetings."

Leslie snorts, her gaze slipping past me through the glass wall to where Elena stands at the windows overlooking Lake Michigan, bathed in the afternoon sun. Cillian dropped her off not long ago.

With a quick, knowing smirk, Leslie teases, "I'll be sure to do that."

I smile. "Thanks, Les," I reply and turn towards the door.

"Oh yeah," Leslie says, snapping her fingers. I look over my shoulder. "I almost forgot—congratulations." She winks and swivels toward one of her filing cabinets.

My fingers are already moving to lock the door before I even fully step inside the room, the other hand hitting the privacy switch next to it. The glass separating my office from the rest of the executive floor immediately frosts over.

Elena is walking toward the small bar cart tucked away in the corner when I turn around. On top of it, an ice bucket cradles a bottle of champagne, and two of the flutes that usually hang from a glass rack on a lower shelf have been cleaned and placed neatly next to the bucket.

My lips curl up into a devious smile. "What's the occasion?"

Elena smirks and shrugs, ignoring my question as she takes off the champagne cage. Her wavy hair sits perfectly against her shoulders, and her freshly manicured nails glisten in the light. She looks every bit the part of a CEO's significant other—not that it matters. Even if she showed up here in her shorts and rash guard, I'd take her any way she was willing to give herself to me.

With a hand towel, she twists the cork open, managing to keep the *pop* almost silent before pouring the golden liquid. It fizzes softly as she fills each flute.

After setting the bottle back in the ice, Elena picks up the glasses and extends one to me. I take it just as she tilts her glass to tap the edge of mine. The sound is a soft, satisfying ring.

She takes a step closer, her free hand slipping under the edge of my suit jacket. Her palm is warm against the fabric of my shirt. "Congratulations, Mr. Wells," she whispers with a small smile. "No one deserves this more than you."

A lump forms in my throat, making it impossible to form words. So, instead of stumbling over them, I follow her lead and tilt the glass to my lips, eyes never leaving hers.

Unlike her cautious sip, I down the entire glass in one go, the bubbles sharp against my nose and throat. As I move around her to place the empty flute on the bar cart to free up my hands, Elena chuckles, light and knowingly.

She sidesteps out of my reach, almost as if she anticipated my next move. I watch while she creates distance between us, and can't help but follow. My fingers move to unbutton my jacket, shrug it off, and lay it across one of the cigar chairs I pass.

Her hips sway as she walks, accentuated by the business casual dress she's wearing. It's forest green—the color she knows I like most on her.

Hell, it might just be my favorite color of all time.

Elena skims a fingernail down the length of my sparsely adorned desk, her expression thoughtful. "I've only been in here that one time you brought me to wait for Dr. Carrow," she notes, her voice carrying a trace of disbelief. "It feels like it was another lifetime."

I've pictured her here more times than I care to admit. To the point that it feels like she comes to work with me every day. In the shower of the adjoining bathroom, on the couch where she rested, right here on the edge of this desk, against the windows...

"I suppose you're right," I respond, my voice a bit gruff. "It *is* a bit strange, given everything."

Turning, Elena leans against the desk, the champagne flute dangling from her fingertips. I take no time to pin her there, using my knee to make space between her thighs. The move forces her to sit back fully to accommodate me. The amused expression she wears turns a shade wicked as she lifts the flute back to her mouth.

The moment the liquid touches her lips, my index finger is at the bottom of the glass, gently tipping it upward. Her eyes narrow from over the edge, and my grin widens.

I push the glass slightly too far as she reaches the end, just enough that a dribble of champagne escapes from the corner of her mouth, trailing down to bead enticingly under her chin.

Only once the flute is empty and she sets it down do I reach for that streak of champagne, dragging my thumb up to the corner of her lips before bringing it to my mouth, salivating at the tartness and her.

Elena's pupils dilate. My heartbeat is pounding in my ears so loudly I can barely hear anything else.

I carefully slide the champagne glass further from her side and then, with a bit more force than intended, thread my fingers through her hair. The angle I tilt her head allows me to see all of her, prompting the most beautifully genuine smile to grace her full lips.

Elena rubs the silk material of my tie between her fingers. "I'm so proud of you," she breathes, blinking away the small sheen that coats those honey eyes. Every muscle in my body contracts before I pounce.

My mouth crashes to hers so hard that my glasses dig into the bridge of my nose, but I don't care. Elena uses her hold on my tie to pull me down just as hard as I am pressing. I invade her mouth, stealing any breath she might have.

But it's not enough.

Her hands wander to my abdomen, fingers tracing the contours until they reach the front of my belt. She shimmies to the edge of the desk and begins to undo the buckle, sending waves of pure fire down my spine, the heat pooling right beneath her hands.

I pull back just enough to whisper raggedly against her mouth, "Will you be quiet for me?"

Biting the edge of her lip, Elena nods and whispers back, her breath hot against my skin, "Only if you can do the same for me."

With my body nearly vibrating, I barely register that Elena has also unbuttoned my pants, slipping her hand under my boxer briefs to free my cock from the already strained fabric and firmly wrapping her fingers around my length

I let out a groan, definitely too loud. Elena quickly hushes me, "Ah, ah. Quiet, remember?"

She begins her expert ministrations between our stomachs. Sparks zip through me; one hand shoots out to steady myself on the desk, the other digs into the flesh of her thigh. I lean into her, head dropping near her shoulder, hips pumping as she squeezes and pulls just the way I like. Her vanilla perfume invades my senses, caressing me like her hands.

I can barely catch my breath when Elena's teeth graze my earlobe, her voice dropping. "Do you want me here or against the windows?" she asks, speaking my fantasies into existence. Her thumb swirls around my tip, spreading the bead of precum across the head before working my shaft once more. "Or maybe you want me on my knees under the desk?"

The image of her submitting to me so prettily ricochets through my mind like a bullet.

Jesus fuck. This won't last more than ten more seconds if she keeps going.

I grab her wrist and pull. Her exhale is sharp as I turn and press her chest flat against the desk, the sound filling the room with an audible *whoosh*.

My hands find the edge of her skirt, hiking it over her hips to reveal the panties hugging her perfect ass. Scars disappear and reappear around the edges of the fabric. I nudge her heels apart with my foot, and she shifts obediently, granting me the space I need.

I admire the view and squeeze the base of my cock.

Pressing my chest to her back, my fingers slide between her legs and over the soaked material that hides what I want. I have to stifle another groan. "All this for me?"

A soft whimper escapes her lips in our silence as I apply just a hint of pressure. *She's such a good listener like this. Always willing to take whatever I give her.*

My thumbs hook into the sides of the panties, yanking them down her legs until they reach her knees. Only then do I use the tip of my shoe to press them down to her ankles and fit my cock to the seam of her ass. A tremor racks her body.

I pull back just enough to line myself up, savoring the wet heat that greets my tip. With a firm hand, I guide myself home in one long stroke. Her cheek falls to the cool surface of the desk, fogging up the shiny wood as she tries to contain her initial moan.

Fucking stunning.

My rhythm is sudden and punishing, needing to feel her grip and slide around me like I need my next breath. Elena's body glides up and down the desk before she plants her hands firmly on the opposite edge, bracing herself and pressing back into my strokes. The champagne glass chimes faintly, vibrating with the movements.

When I pull her back and impale her fully on my cock, her mouth opens in a silent scream. I curse, stars dancing behind my eyelids, trying to think of anything to stop myself from emptying into her too soon. My fingers dig into her flesh as I touch every part of her. But even as I grab her ass, her hips, her thighs—whatever I can reach—I'm not sure I'll ever be fully satisfied unless I'm living under her skin like a parasite.

Hooking a hand under Elena's ribs, I pull her up until her back is flush against my chest. She obeys, allowing me to take whatever I need. One of her arms loops around the back of my neck to draw me down until our mouths meet over her shoulder.

My hands greedily roam up and down her sides, kneading her breasts through the thin fabric of her dress and bra. Each little gasp Elena lets escape only fuels me further.

I raise a hand to her throat, my middle finger and thumb clamping just below where her jaw hinges so she can't even think about looking away. "Eyes, Lena," I demand on a hiss. "I want to watch you."

She inhales shakily, her breath mingling with mine, and that small, vulnerable noise completely shatters any pretense of restraint I have left as I roll my hips and drive up, plunging in and out.

"You're always so good for me." The words come out in a harsh whisper. Her neck bobs against my palm when she swallows. "Do you feel how well you take me? It's perfect." Her eyes are locked on mine, mouth slightly agape, spellbound. The fingers near my neck curl into the base of my hair. Goosebumps erupt just as the tingle sets down my spine and into my balls. "Fuck—you're perfect."

Elena fights to keep her eyes open, those beautiful cheeks flushed with the effort of holding back her sounds as her walls clench around me like a vice, hurling me over the edge with her. My vision goes white as she shudders, milking my cock with each convulsion of pleasure.

I release her jaw and chase the tail end of our highs, fingers finding her clit through her dress to lure every last drop of it out of both of us before eventually stilling inside her.

My forehead topples forward to rest against her neck, and I struggle to catch my breath. Her chest heaves. Neither of us moves. We just stay there, tangled and silent and sated.

This is the only celebration I wanted.

While my heartbeat has finally started to slow, the throb of her pulse is still so pronounced that it brushes against my lips with each delicious beat. I can't help but lazily descend on the vein, drawing the tender skin into my mouth, teeth grazing the surface before gently sinking in.

Elena's head lolls, granting me unrestricted access to the expanse of her throat. My arms slide up her body, tracing lines across her chest and stomach, pulling her even tighter to me.

She laughs softly as I work up to the sensitive space just below her ear, leaning harder into me with each bite and kiss. The sound of her breathy giggle and the scent of her skin overwhelm me just as my thoughts converge into a moment of intense clarity.

I'm keeping Elena Cross.

The calm that washes over me is visceral and fast, seeping into me until it settles in the center of my chest.

The remaining fragments of resentment I've been worried about suddenly seem so small. Insignificant, even. They barely matter when nothing outweighs the way *this* feels.

I'm going to take it, even though I don't deserve it. Not after everything I ignored and rationalized. For all of the ways I made excuses for my father's decisions, thinking it was for the greater good. Elena saw my father for who he was, what he did, what I allowed, and she's still here, wrapped around me like I'm worth something.

She's flawed. No question. Complicated, guarded, but wholly good. It's in everything she does, even when she's not trying. I shouldn't be allowed that kind of good, but I'm a selfish bastard, and if the way to keep her here is to let her believe I'm worth the risk, then so be it. I'll manipulate her commitment to winning me back if I have to. Anything to stop her from realizing that she's better off without me.

"Christ, I love you," I murmur, nose skimming the red mark I just left behind.

It's only the third time I've said it out loud to her. The first was raw and frantic, thrown out like a lifeline the night she left. The second came just the other week, whispered as she held me together, still laced with unease even as it slipped free. But this time, it feels right. No fear. No desperation.

Just truth.

The breath Elena releases sounds like it came from the depths of her soul. She turns her head, a hand sliding from my nape to the side of my chin to lift my gaze to hers. The way she looks at me is like—God, is that the way I look at her?

Her fingers slide gently up and down my stubble. "Careful," she answers, scanning my expression from top to bottom. "Saying things like that will get my hopes up."

My heart begins to pound again, but there's no hesitation in my movements as I place my mouth against her ear.

"Let me be very clear about what I mean." My voice is deathly quiet, so she has to listen to every single word. "There is no place on this earth, no dark corner or safe haven where you can ever hide from me again." Elena's entire body stiffens. "I'll drag you back here by your hair, kicking and screaming if I have to. This is it. There is nothing else."

A tremor wracks her body. I pull back to find tears shining in her eyes. She arches an eyebrow, the corner of her mouth kicking up as she only says one word in return.

"Promise?"

Chapter 47

Elena

"Davey and Paul just finished up a call with Silas and are headed to bed," Natalie announces, not looking up from her phone as she types away next to me. The tinted windows darken the interior, early morning light struggling to penetrate the glass.

My eyebrows shoot up. I'd assumed Silas had been in the gym when we left, but it turns out he was in his study.

It's been just over a week since the emergency board meeting. Only yesterday did they manage to get someone on a plane to Sierra Blanca. The delay was frustrating. They had to strategize to avoid drawing unnecessary attention and couldn't risk scaring off the team at the facility.

Despite his eagerness, Silas couldn't attend the meeting with the contacts we'd extracted from the server files. Leaving town for an undisclosed location, especially at such a critical moment, was out of the question. Plus, the press was more intrigued than ever by our relationship and were following him like bloodhounds.

As soon as they received the green light, Davey and Paul booked flights to El Paso. They had an entire day of meetings, and we've barely heard from them since yesterday morning. Depending on how the conversations went with the team at the facility, Silas and Davey needed to devise a plan to discreetly wind down the operations and then decide what to do with the building.

The slow pace grates on me, and I've not been shy about expressing it. Silas keeps explaining why rushing could worsen things or make them unfixable, but understanding the strategy doesn't ease the knowledge that people are suffering this very moment and will continue to until it's completely shut down.

Cillian hums in acknowledgement from the driver's seat. "Good. I'll call Silas while you're working out and fill you both in on the way home." He flicks on the turn signal and checks the rearview mirror before taking a left onto a side street.

Natalie yawns, briefly glancing at another message before locking her phone. The streets are quiet, but that will change soon as the morning rush begins.

"Jeff's lucky I like him," she mutters, stifling another yawn. "This is an insane time to be awake, let alone working out."

Jeff is having maintenance done in his gym's bathrooms. He didn't want to stray far while the work is underway, so he asked to shift our training sessions to an ungodly hour so he could supervise the plumbers. We didn't realize he meant at the crack of dawn when we initially agreed. By the time he told us, it was too late to back out. Neither of us was interested in his relentless teasing if we changed our minds. Cillian felt comfortable with our security since we'd be the only ones in the gym. That's why we've stuck with it this week. Luckily, today is our last session before we go back to our normal routine.

I can't help but chuckle as we approach the main road, Ironworks looming up ahead. "Usually, your brother has already worked out and headed to the office by now."

"He's also a psychopath," she shoots back, as if that explains everything. I press my lips together, holding back another smile.

As we pull up to the gym, Jeff is already there, unlocking the front door. With so little traffic, he hears us approach, looking over his shoulder with a broad smile. He waits patiently as Cillian pulls into a street spot right in front of the door; one of the only perks of being up so early.

Cillian fumbles with some messages on his phone, so Natalie and I hop out without him to greet Jeff. Despite our grumbles about the ungodly hour and morning chill, Jeff greets us cheerfully, proclaiming, "Beautiful morning, yeah?" Natalie blinks at him, adjusting the gym bag on her shoulder in mild annoyance.

"Reel it in, sunshine," I answer with an eye roll.

Jeff smirks. "I almost forgot how much of a peach you are in the morning," he taunts.

"Can't wait to show you how much of a peach I am on the mat," I retort, my lips curving into a small smile.

The car door slams behind us as Cillian finally gets out and rounds the front of the vehicle. The quiet is briefly pierced by other distant sounds—a car or two stirring in the streets. Just as Natalie opens her mouth, presumably to try and wiggle out of her cardio as she does every session, Cillian's voice slices through the air.

I turn to him, but he's looking down the road behind me. His body tenses as if ready to sprint when a sudden force yanks my arm, and suddenly I don't know which way is up.

A loud buzzing sound in my ears almost drowns out the several sharp pops, and I'm slammed to the ground by an unseen weight. On instinct, my forearms fly up to my face just as the air is ripped from my lungs. I heave, chest burning and arms stinging. The pressure on my back is so intense I can't tell if the weight is preventing me from sucking in a breath or the wind had been permanently knocked out of me.

Then, as quickly as it came, the pressure lifts. With a gasp, I roll onto my back. My ears ring. The building edges and the clear sky spin in my vision. I squeeze my eyes shut and then open them again to look for Natalie.

She's less than a foot away, on her stomach. Her breathing is ragged, eyes wide with confusion and fear. There's a smear of red across her cheek and on the cement below her face.

I reach for her, placing my hand on her forearm and squeezing. Everything seems to move in slow motion for several heartbeats while I try to figure out what happened, but then her gaze shifts past my face, eyes widening in a fresh wave of panic.

When I turn my head, reality snaps back. Cillian is kneeling over Jeff, who lies face down, his head turned away. The sting of the cold air fills my lungs as I suck in another breath and scramble to my knees. Blood coats Cillian's hands, and the metallic smell of iron hits me with full force.

Cillian's voice cuts through the shock, panic growing in his eyes. "Get in the car! We need to move him and get out of the open. Now!"

The back of Jeff's sweatshirt is riddled with holes, blood soaking through the fabric.

I'm already crawling toward him, a string of whimpers leaving my lips as I reach Jeff's face. The relief I feel when I see his bright blue eyes open only lasts a second before he gasps under the weight of his injuries and Cillian's desperate attempts to stem the bleeding.

My fingers find his face, the warmth of it seeping into my palms as I force him to look at me. His eyes are glassy and unfocused. My hands shake, heart seizing in my chest as tremors rack my body.

Cillian screams Natalie's name. She's instantly on her feet, springing into action in a way I can't focus on, because Jeff's eyes are already fluttering shut.

"Jeff," I whisper, pressing my fingers into his skin to hold his attention. I don't get a chance to see his reaction because Cillian is grabbing my arm, pulling me up with enough force that it snaps my head back to him.

"Elena! Focus!"

I shake my head once.

Cillian rattles off instructions to me. We're going to lift Jeff into the backseat to lie flat on his stomach. "You have to apply pressure to the wounds," he tells me urgently. "Focus on the one near his chest. Can you do that?"

I nod, swallowing hard to muster the semblance of control I need.

With Natalie's help, we hoist Jeff's limp body. He moans—a sound that tears at my heart. The arm wrapped around his back is warm and wet, and blood trickles a path under us, webbing out over the sidewalk.

Cillian's focus shifts between us and the empty roads with a predatory focus.

I'm not even sure how we manage it, but we get Jeff into the SUV. I climb in behind him, bracketing my knees around his hips for the best leverage to apply pressure. Cillian slams the doors shut, and within seconds, he's in the driver's seat with Natalie next to him, peeling out of our spot and back onto the streets.

I press my hands firmly against Jeff's back, concentrating on the wound near his chest and trying to cover the others, but two are near his lower back, and the other is in his shoulder. Each bump in the road sends a new ripple of fear through me, but I hold steady.

Natalie reaches back to help as she frantically gives Cillian GPS directions to the nearest hospital. Despite the clear roads, we're still fifteen minutes away from the nearest ER.

Cillian curses and slams his hand against the steering wheel, leaving streaks of blood, before hitting the accelerator harder.

Tears blur my vision. Jeff's face contorts with pain against the cold leather of the seat. His eyes open only when jolted by Cillian's frantic maneuvers through the streets. My hands, warm and sticky, press down desperately. I close my eyes and suddenly Drew is behind my eyelids—her pale face, her already cool blood between my fingers, my own screams echoing in our empty living room.

I blink. The boundaries of reality and my nightmares blur so much that I can't even see straight. The SUV's tires screech as Cillian takes another sharp turn. Jeff groans. It's the only thing that anchors me back to the present.

"Why would you do that?" I hiss, voice trembling. "How could you be so fucking stupid?" The anger spills out, cracking on the last word.

Somehow, this makes Jeff laugh. It's a gurgled, harsh sound that's more of a choke. "I told you... I always got you," he manages to say between strained wheezes.

Something inside me begs to break. Jeff has been there, right from the day I walked into his gym. He accepted me as Scarlett. As Elena. As whoever I needed to be at any moment. There were never any pretenses. He took me in, hid me, healed me. He is family. My *only* family.

And his life is literally slipping through my fingers.

I shift closer to his face. "You better not fucking die," I rasp. "We said no more hero stunts. That included you."

He responds with a weak smile, teeth stained red.

No, no, no.

The tears well up again, but I fight them. Crying now won't help. Jeff doesn't need to see it, either.

I swallow the lump in my throat and force my breathing to steady, even if I can't find the words to reassure him with much of anything.

"Lauren'll... never date again," Jeff suddenly mumbles, each breath getting wetter and wetter. "You need to find... a nice guy to change... her mind. No one... better looking than me... though, okay?"

"Shut up," I snap just as soon as he finishes the last word. "You're going to tell your wife that yourself, so she can kick your ass for saying it." His laughter, weak and pained, follows my outburst, and more blood trickles from the corner of his mouth.

Then, softer, gentler, he says, "I'm proud of you... you know." His words cut through me, tearing open the well of emotions I've kept dammed up for five years.

I can't do this again.

I can't survive this twice.

The next several minutes are spent with Natalie dangling over the center console, her hands pressed on the wounds near my legs that I can't reach. We both take turns telling Jeff to open his eyes, but each time, there's more silence, and his jokes lose all their muster.

Cillian cut down some of our time, but we're still four minutes out when Jeff speaks again, voice cracking, "Don't take me to... Insight. I don't... want her... see me like this."

Lauren's hospital. Dread douses me. The certainty in his strained words tells me nothing I do will help.

Nothing at all.

I abandon my pressure on his wounds as Natalie crawls to replace my hands, and I drop into the cramped foot space near his head. There's no stopping the sob that rips through my throat when our eyes meet.

"You aren't allowed to go. You need to stay." I place a blood-stained hand on his shaved head, his skin far too cold and slick with sweat. "What about Lauren? What am I supposed to tell her?"

Jeff slowly reaches for my forearm, giving it a weak, reassuring squeeze. "It's okay," he soothes, his eyes watery, lips coated with a thin sheen of blood as they shiver. "Elena... it's going to... okay."

Tears stream down my cheeks, and I lean my forehead against the side of his. "It's not." My voice breaks. "Please, J. Don't."

"Tell Laur... love her," he wheezes, eyes squeezing shut as he tries to find the breath to finish his thought. "You too... kid."

Three heartbeats barely pass before his eyelids relax and his tattooed hand grows slack, slipping from my forearm and off the side of the seat.

I whimper more pleas, pulling it back into mine, but his fingers and wrist limp. My tears run down his temple, mixing with the smear of blood I left on his scalp.

Underneath my wet lashes, I can see the contours of his face. If I say it enough, I could convince myself he's sleeping. I found him many times on the recliner in his guest room, sitting with me in recovery, taking a nap in the sun that streamed through the windows. All I have to do is throw a pillow on his lap, and he'll jump up from his spot to tell me he's been awake the whole time.

It's only when I pull back enough to look at his frame, already pale, coated in blood, and so still, that the illusion shatters.

And suddenly, the world stops spinning.

CHAPTER 48

Silas

T he bedroom door closes behind me, echoing in the quiet. For a
moment, I stand just inside the threshold, allowing my eyes to
adjust to the dim light filtering through the drawn curtains.

Elena is facing away from the door, the outline of her body visible
under the covers, curled into a tight ball. Her back rises and falls with
each shallow breath. It's hard to tell if she's asleep or not, especially when
she's been so still.

Steam from the chicken pot pie I holding tickles the edges of my nose,
fresh from the oven. I asked Kendall to make it for dinner, but it was
ready early, and Elena liked it so much the last time we ate it. It's another
Hail Mary. She's barely taken anything besides water in the past three
days, and even that's been a struggle.

Just as I'm about to take a step towards her, my phone vibrates in my
pocket. A curse forms in my head as Everett's name flashes on the screen
before I send him to voicemail.

I've been working from the lounge chair next to the fireplace and
taking calls in my study, but always returning to her side immediately
after. Everyone has been accommodating, especially after the local news
identified who was involved in the shooting, but life hasn't stopped
moving.

There's so much to do, but I just—I can't leave her like this.

Shoving the phone back into my pocket, I quietly approach the bed, placing the bowl on the side table before lifting the covers and sliding in as gently as possible. I slip one arm under her pillow and the other across her stomach, pulling her back against me.

She doesn't tense in sleepy confusion or acknowledge my presence. I hold her anyway, pressing a kiss to her dirty hair. I haven't been able to convince her to shower since the afternoon we got home from the hospital, when she spent over forty minutes rubbing her skin raw, silent tears streaming down her face as she did it.

Thinking about her in that state makes the ever-present nausea churn in my gut. The moment I saw her slumped in that emergency room chair beside my sister and Cillian, surrounded by police officers, will haunt every nightmare until my last breath.

She was still covered in blood, her expression so tight she barely looked like herself. Her arms were crossed over her chest as she spoke, and though streaks of old tears stained her cheeks, she looked hardened.

When our eyes met over the shoulders of the people questioning her, she blinked, like she didn't know what was real and what wasn't. Then the hardness cracked, and every barrier she'd spent years building to protect herself after Drew splintered in an instant. The sob that tore out of her when her chest crashed into mine took a piece of my soul with it.

After more than a decade of pushing forward to survive, Elena Cross finally let herself fall apart, and I'd never felt so goddamn helpless.

I barely even had time to ask what happened when Lauren plowed through the emergency room doors, her eyes frantically searching the room for her husband. When she finally caught sight of us and realized who was missing, she just knew.

Lauren collapsed to the floor in a heap. Though there was nothing but fear in Elena's eyes, she ran to her, apologies pouring out as she sank to the floor in front of her friend, wrapped her arms around her, and wept.

The hours blurred after that. We stayed with Lauren, and Cillian eventually took Natalie back to my place so she could get clean and rest after Cora and Lloyd arrived. It wasn't until Lauren's parents and Jeff's mother showed up that I started to pull Elena back.

She resisted, of course, but I could see what she couldn't. Lauren was starting to absorb it all, and Elena's shock had worn off. Her growing panic wasn't helping. If anything, it was making it harder for Lauren to breathe.

Still, I didn't have to push her. Lauren hugged her first. "I'm okay," she said softly, even as her voice cracked. "Go home, rest. We'll talk later."

Elena nodded, but her apology tumbled out anyway, sharp and full of guilt. "I'm so sorry, Lauren. I'm so sorry—"

Lauren hushed her before I could. "It's not your fault," she said. And somehow, she meant it. Still comforting Elena even as the weight of what had happened settled into her own bones.

I didn't give Elena a chance to spiral again. I guided her out through the automatic doors, toward my SUV, and took her home.

I've been in contact with Lauren's parents, who have been staying with her. Lauren has postponed the services for now. She can barely make it through an hour at a time, let alone plan and host a memorial for the person she thought she was going to grow old with.

It took a little convincing, but they agreed for me to have a service drop off several meals a day, along with any other resources they might need. Grief counselors, house cleaners, funeral services when she feels ready—whatever it is, it's theirs. My offers have no timeline or limit. All the resources in the world can't undo the damage done, but I have to try.

Elena's stomach moves beneath my hand, her breathing a gentle, needed reminder that she's still here. Alive, just like Natalie.

Because of Jeff.

I haven't been able to shake the images from the CCTV footage. It happened so fast. Even Cillian barely had time to react to the tinted SUV that sped past, its back window sliding down to reveal the muzzle of a gun. Jeff's quick dive to shield Elena and Natalie before the chaotic scramble that followed.

We received the autopsy results yesterday morning. Jeff was shot four times: in the aorta, pelvis, shoulder, and liver. They were simply too far from the hospital to stop the bleeding in time. It's a cruel, clinical summary of someone who did something so selfless.

I'd started warming up to Jeff when he started coming to the house, but I liked him more after meeting Lauren. He watched her with adoration and pride, a softness in his eyes that I only saw muted versions of when he interacted with Elena. It was no wonder he was one of Elena's favorite people.

He was good. Loyal. Brave.

Jeff probably never realized it, but all his cumulative actions since he met Elena had done the impossible: he bought us time. He trained her to keep her safe and gave her a place to heal and hide from me until enough of my rage had burned off to keep her alive.

Jeff's the reason we're here right now. I owe him everything. And now, that debt is Lauren's, because she has to figure out how to survive without him.

Elena breaks the quiet, startling me. "Have you figured out who did it yet?" she asks, voice hoarse.

Davey was back in Chicago within twelve hours of Jeff's death. We sent our private plane to bring him back while Paul stayed behind to monitor the facility, which remains in a state of limbo but stable.

He has also been handling his work and our investigation from home, keeping an eye on Natalie, who seems to be coping slightly better than Elena. We have been working relentlessly to track down the SUV, but it's all led to dead ends. Not to mention the police's involvement has only complicated things.

Apart from the footage captured on Jeff's cameras, all other surrounding surveillance videos have been wiped from any available systems we've been able to identify within a two-mile radius of the gym, which are already sparse in that area of the city to begin with. The SUV was stolen and the car was ditched not far from the shooting, leaving us no trail to follow.

Each problem has been an infuriating echo of the issues we faced when searching for the man who held Elena at gunpoint and the subsequent ransacking of her apartment in the spring.

The team is certain these are Peter's methods—meticulous, brutal, erasing every trace aside from the one camera they wanted us to see. Even with everyone agreeing, I can't bring myself to tell Elena. She already knows the answer, but admitting it out loud will only confirm her worst fear. She is already haunted by guilt for things she couldn't control. I can't be the one to tell her Peter killed another person she loves. I just can't do that to her.

Gently, I roll Elena to face me. A sliver of relief cuts through me at the sight of her red-rimmed eyes. Dried tears stain her cheeks and her lips are chapped, but she's lucid.

"We don't have anything concrete," I tell her, which is the truth. We don't have definitive proof it was Peter. I don't give her a chance to respond or press for more details. Instead, I draw her close, brushing my lips to her forehead and lingering there.

She remains motionless, and a deep ache spreads through me, wishing she'd place a hand on my side, my chest—anywhere.

I speak softly, letting the words flow directly onto her skin, "You need to eat something."

The silence that follows feels as heavy as the darkness surrounding us until she murmurs back, "I'm not hungry."

"I know," I say, running a hand up her side. "Kendall made chicken pot pie." My voice softens. "Try to have a little, for me. Please." The words are almost desperate.

I don't rush to get the bowl yet, choosing instead to savor this brief moment of clarity, though her lack of refusal lifts some of the weight off my chest.

She lets me hold her for longer than she has in days, but it's only a few minutes before she begins to tremble. Her whole frame shakes with the effort of keeping the sobs contained. All of my limbs tighten, as if I can absorb the pain and carry it for her.

"I love you," I breathe, my voice low and fervent. "So damn much. I'm so sorry." It feels like the only thing I can say, and it still isn't enough.

Elena exhales raggedly, and then she leans into me, her arms wrapping tightly around my middle. The pressure momentarily steals my breath. *She's hugging me back.*

Her sobs continue: relentless, raw, and broken. I whisper every comfort I can think of into her ear, my hand tracing soothing paths up and down her back. And we ride out the worst of it, her fingers digging into my sides while she convulses in agony for far too long.

It feels like hours, but eventually—thankfully—Elena's sobs begin to diminish into painful whimpers. She buries her face into the crook of my neck, her breath still uneven.

I'm poised for a brief reprieve, but instead, her voice shatters it. "I'm going to kill him," she rasps, each word a serrated edge against my skin. "With my bare fucking hands." Her body locks up in fury. "He's going to beg for me to by the end of it."

Her honest, brutal words stir something in me. The parts I've spent the past few weeks trying to rebury. I'd forced them deep beneath the surface, desperate to put as much distance as possible between those instincts and the man I'm trying to be, despite how easily they once defined my father.

But her voice calls them back like a summons.

They stretch under my skin, retesting their limits. It burns from the inside out. Not with heat, but a blaze of pure ice, pumping through every inch of vein until it's unbearable. This time, I don't force it down this time. I let it settle. I let it live. Because if this is what she needs, I'll give it to her.

I'll be the monster. I'll do it gladly.

Grasping her chin, I tilt her head back to meet my gaze, her angry tears still streaming. I wait, thumb gently wiping her cheeks, until her eyes are clear enough to truly see me.

"When we find him," I start, smoothing the top of her hair, "you call the shots. Whatever you want to do to him, however long it takes, it's yours. There are no rules, no limits, and absolutely no fucking mercy."

Chapter 49

Elena

No one knows how many times a soul can shatter before it's beyond repair. In my mind, three always felt like a solid number.

The first time it happens, it knocks the wind out of you. Somehow, you manage to stand, gather the shards, and try to fit them back into place, slicing open your fingers and palms as you do. By the time you're done, it's not quite the same, but it's close. You convince yourself that with time, the edges will smooth over, and it'll morph into something nearly like it was before.

The second time, you're a bit more prepared and manage to breathe through it. The pieces are smaller now, more delicate. They break as you handle them, tiny slivers embedding in your skin, impossible to remove. Stepping back, you have to squint a little to make it look almost like it did before it first broke. Maybe, you think, time will help again.

The third is different. What's left isn't even pieces; it's just grains of sand. With the slightest breeze, they scatter. Entire sections are missing now, gaps that you can never fill, and even the small piles you manage to gather are just one strong gust away from disappearing, too. By this point, you're so exhausted that you let fate take over, waiting for the rest to blow away until there's nothing left.

And yet, I'm still here, despite having sprinted past what I was sure had to be the limit.

Even so, the pain leaves no room for anything else. I can hardly remember feeling anything but this. My heart barely beats through it.

It doesn't help that every time I close my eyes, Jeff is there.

In every dream and every nightmare.

Sometimes it's the last moments in the SUV, me leaning over him, hands soaked in his blood, begging him to stay. Others, we're back at Ironworks in our old routine. Once, Peter was with me, standing over Jeff's grave with that smug look on his face, telling me that he's going to take everything and there's nothing I can do to stop him.

The one that hurts the most is when Lauren makes an appearance, clutching Jeff's lifeless body and asking me, "*How could you do this to us?*"

I haven't spoken to Lauren since the hospital, nor have I tried. I wouldn't even know what to say. The idea feels cruel. She likely doesn't want to hear from me, and she shouldn't have to. If anything, she should stay as far away from me as possible. Everyone should. No matter how I try to change, I only ever seem to destroy other people's lives while I somehow survive.

I thought I was doing it right this time.

But I knew better deep down, didn't I? I could have told Silas to send Jeff away and shut down the whole idea of training before it started. That's what any good person would do.

I was just so excited to see him.

The man who gave me a place to go. Who sheltered me, protected me, who had my back. And he did. Right up until his very last breath.

Agony cuts through me as images of Jeff and Drew blur behind my eyelids. They only asked to be let in, and now they're both gone.

Because of me.

Silas's voice startles me out of my thoughts. "Lena." He's behind me, but I don't turn to face him. "What are you doing?"

It's a fair question, especially considering it's the first time in two weeks that I'm out of bed for more than just a shower. Eating has been a different story, but beggars can't be choosers. I can't seem to keep anything down, anyway.

He's also probably wondering why I'm standing in the middle of the guest bedroom I stayed in as Scarlett and haven't set foot in since I came back as myself. It's almost eerily unchanged. The bed is crisply made, and the chairs in front of the fireplace where I once spent my days exploiting his kindness are meticulously arranged. It's the perfect preservation of the place where I ruined everything.

I've never wanted to incinerate anything so much in my life.

Silas's hand slides across my lower back, a silent announcement of his presence as he steps beside me before it falls away. We stand side by side, his eyes flicking from me to the rest of the space.

Eventually, he pushes up his glasses and says, "I hate this room."

His words pull my gaze to his profile, watching him scan the walls and furniture, likely recalling all the ways I hurt him here. Used him. Manipulated him. Poisoned everything I touched.

Though I have no right to agree because I caused it, the words slip out anyway. "Me too."

Silas stuffs his hands into his pockets and walks forward, his head tilting as he surveys each familiar corner before finally turning to face me. He went into the office this morning to attend some meetings, as he had several times this week, only to return home before lunch. Though he's dressed in one of his perfectly tailored dark gray suits, it hangs a bit more loosely than it used to.

He studies me intently, his gaze lingering on my still-damp hair. There's a softening in his tired eyes as he speaks, "It's good to see you up."

The sincerity in his voice echoes painfully through me. I'm acutely aware of how much I've complicated his life, especially with everything else he's trying to balance.

Last night, when he thought I was asleep, he whispered his hopes into the darkness. He held my back against his chest and wished for me to get better, begged me to show him that I'm still here. The effort it took to keep my breathing even and stifle the sobs threatening to break free nearly crushed me.

353

Listening to him like that, I could finally feel the toll this is taking on him under all my grief. I've been granted too many chances to live to keep wasting them like this. So instead of sleeping, I laid there collecting every scrap of strength I could find to get my shit together. For him, for Drew, for Jeff. For everyone who has given me chance after chance to make things right.

My smile is thin as I cross my arms over my chest, biting the inside of my cheek. "I... I'm starting to feel a little better."

"That's good," he replies, though we both know I'm lying.

Silas watches me, assessing from top to toe. When he seems to gather himself, he takes a hesitant step forward, pausing to gauge my reaction. I remain still, and step by cautious step, he closes the distance between us until he stands just a breath away.

I tilt my head back to meet his eyes just as he pulls his hands from his pockets. There's a moment's uncertainty before he reaches out, his touch landing gently on my bicep. His thumb begins to trace small, soothing circles. The warmth seeps through me, stirring something that's been dormant for weeks.

The tension in my arms eases, the crossed barrier at my chest unfurling. Silas takes a deep breath, relief flooding his features. This gives him the courage to raise that same hand to my neck, caressing the sensitive skin.

His voice is so soft it almost blends into the air. "Can I kiss you?"

When's the last time we kissed?

I blink, unable to wrap my mind around the idea, and nod solidly. Silas's shoulders sag as though he'd been holding his breath. Slowly, he frames my face before closing the gap between us.

His lips meet mine with a tenderness that undoes me—slow, reverent, savoring. I feel his fingers tighten slightly, like he's holding himself back from trying to fuse every part of us together. My palm finds its way to his chest, pressing against the rapid beat of his heart. The simple touch draws a shaky exhale from him, his breath mingling with mine, stealing the air from my lungs.

God, I miss him. The feel of him, the taste, his voice. Everything about us that's electric and good. The relief pours out from him, like he's trying to flood some of my darkness with his light.

I've spent so many years surviving on my own that crawling back into myself was the only instinct. But he's here, right in front of me, alive and real. I almost lost this for a second time.

Jeff gave this to me.

Every cell in my body aches under that ugly truth.

Silas pulls back, and I open my eyes to find him gazing at me with a gentle smile. He whispers, "Hi."

My lips curl up slightly. "Hi," I whisper back, my voice a feather.

He holds me there, and I find myself lost in the details of his face. The sharp cut of his jaw, the well-groomed beard, and the faint freckles that dust his nose and cheeks. His glasses slightly magnify his eyes, my favorite feature—dark and swirling with warmth, like pools of melted chocolate.

I press myself up on my toes, my lips finding his again. This time there's more weight behind it, more need. I lean fully and melt into the solid feel of him.

A low, guttural sound escapes him as he wraps his arms around me, drawing me closer. His body vibrates with unmistakable restraint and love. I feel it in the way his hands settle in my hair and on my back, in every gentle tug. The way he selflessly molds his body to mine to shoulder some of the burden I caused. Taking care of me the way he has been for weeks. Quietly. Unfailingly.

When I let people care for me, it all falls apart. When I feel safe, I lose more than I can bear. Peter will have to pry Silas from my cold, dead hands before I let him take this, too.

Silas takes what he needs. What he *deserves.* Only when he slows do I sink back onto my heels, breath shaky, lips tingling. He doesn't let me get far, our noses brushing.

There's no more hiding behind others. No more hesitating. And it starts with the reason I came into this room in the first place.

I let the words slip out before I can reconsider them. "Can we turn this room into my office?"

Silas stiffens at my question. I feel it in the subtle shift of his hands, the quiet tension that coils through his frame.

Swallowing my fear, I press on. "I want to help close down the facility in Sierra Blanca and find Peter." It all comes rushing out of me faster than I mean for it to, and I have to inhale sharply, forcing myself to slow down. "We both hate this room, so let's change it."

This is a gamble. He could say no. I'll accept that, but I wouldn't be able to live with myself if I didn't at least ask because we don't have to let this space just exist. It could be a place where I start to make things right.

Silas studies me for a long moment. I can almost feel him weighing every word I've just spoken, testing them for cracks. The silence stretches until it starts to feel like its own kind of punishment, broken only by the steady rhythm of our breathing.

Then, finally, he nods. Slowly, almost reluctantly, like his heart is still trying to catch up with his decision. His hands grip my waist and hair a little tighter.

"Okay," he says, voice low but resolute. "But there will be parameters." His throat bobs. "You share everything you learn with me and the team. There's no going rogue. If I ever find you trying to handle something on your own, so help me—" Silas pauses to suck in a breath. "We do this as a team, Elena. Start to finish."

"Together," I agree, locking eyes with him. "Until the very end."

What's Next?

Briana is working on several writing projects, including the third and final novel in the Veiled Truths Trilogy.

Want to receive updates? Sign up for her newsletter!

authorbrianasullivan.com

Special Thanks

To Danny: I can't let your ego get too big with multiple book dedications, can I? All jokes aside, I love you. Thank you for helping me edit this novel and selling the shit out of *Half-Truths* at trivia. You show me every single day what true love is, and though I don't always deserve it, it never goes unappreciated or unnoticed. You are my favorite person, and did I mention that I love you?

To Jeff: My truck-driving father-in-law, who might be the biggest fan I've ever had. You'll know why I'm saying this once your wife reads the book, but I'm so sorry. Trust me, I didn't want to do it, either. I hope this makes up for it! Thank you for supporting me, giving me plenty of laughs, and always keeping your "book burning" gasoline tank on the front porch.

To my friends: The love and support I've been shown since *Half-Truths* was released have been one of the most insane experiences of my life. You will never know how much it means to me. Thank you so, so much.

To those I once shared hallways and offices with: The sheer number of you is hard to grasp. Having support from people I barely knew or I've lost touch with moved me in ways I still can't quite put into words. It's been the most humbling, wonderful experience. Thank you.

To the strangers who took a chance on my novels: Hi! I'm so happy to meet you! Thank you for trusting me with your time, curiosity, and a sliver of space on your bookshelf (or Kindle). You are incredible, and I'm so grateful to you.

www.ingramcontent.com/pod-product-compliance
Lightning Source LLC
Chambersburg PA
CBHW021956130726
47903CB00014B/1483